EX
LIBRIS

Romance Treasury

THE ROMANCE TREASURY ASSOCIATION

NEW YORK · TORONTO · LONDON

These stories were originally published as follows:

THE BAHAMIAN PIRATE
Copyright © 1976 by Jane Corrie
First published by Mills & Boon Limited in 1976

MASTER OF BEN ROSS
Copyright © 1977 by Lucy Gillen
First published by Mills & Boon Limited in 1977

FLORENTINE SPRING
Copyright © 1977 by Charlotte Lamb
First published by Mills & Boon Limited in 1977

ROMANCE TREASURY is published by
The Romance Treasury Association, Stratford, Ontario, Canada.

Editorial Board: A.W. Boon, Judith Burgess, Ruth Palmour,
Alice E. Johnson and Ilene Burgess.

Dust Jacket Art by William Biddle
Story Illustrations by William Biddle
Book Design by Charles Kadin
Printed and bound by R.R. Donnelley & Sons Co.

ISBN 0-373-04078-4

CONTENTS

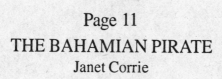

THE BAHAMIAN PIRATE

The Bahamian Pirate

Jane Corrie

What harm could it possibly do to make an old lady's dream come true? Serena's tender heart would not let her refuse to act as Mrs. Tonetti's granddaughter.

It wasn't as if she were in any hurry to face the question of marriage to Roger Alton. A few more days on lovely Blue Island in the Bahamas was just what she needed.

The first act of Mrs. Tonetti's little charade passed without a hitch, but Jordan Kerr and his disgusting suspicions caused the second act to take a dramatic turn! Jordan was as dominating and masterful as his pirating forebears. How could Serena be attracted to a man who seemed to hate her?

CHAPTER ONE

SERENA blinked and stared at the woman by her side, then half shook her head as if to clear the fog that had suddenly descended on her senses.

"Pretend to be your granddaughter?" she said blankly. "I couldn't possibly! I mean, I know nothing about you. Have you lost touch with your family? If so, perhaps I could make some inquiries for you?" She broke off, still partially recovering from the slightly unusual request from her companion.

Giving the woman another swift side glance, Serena surmised that she was not as old as she had thought at first, but so frail-looking, as if a puff of wind might blow her away. The woman was well wrapped up in a mink coat that Serena knew the price of, as her mother possessed one. Whoever the woman was, she was a lady of means. Serena rather wished she could pass the episode off as an odd whim on the elderly lady's part, but there was a pleading in the faded blue eyes that ruled out this wish. She was not an eccentric, and she was in deadly earnest.

Serena's lovely violet blue eyes met the blue ones

squarely. The look of compassion in hers reached through to the older woman. "Look, I'd like to help you, but I don't see how I can. I'm only on holiday here. In fact, I should have left for New York yesterday," she explained patiently.

"Couldn't you possibly stay a day or two longer?" pleaded the woman. "It means so much to me. Oh, dear," she exclaimed, "I'm explaining this so very badly. You must think I'm mad. Well, to tell the truth I must have been at the time. I really don't know what possessed me, but Clarissa Simpson would keep on and on about how wonderful her granddaughter was, and wasn't it a shame I had no one, so you see it really wasn't surprising I did such a stupid thing." She looked at Serena with her head on one side, reminding Serena of an expectant sparrow.

Having a somewhat scatty mother had its advantages at times, Serena thought. She was perfectly able to follow the reasoning. "So you made a granddaughter up," she said.

Her companion nodded eagerly. "You do understand! I knew you would! When I saw you sitting here all alone, you looked—forgive me, dear, for my bluntness—but you looked as if you were trying to come to some decision. As if you needed to be alone to think something over." She gave Serena a sweet smile. "I think I would have stopped and spoken to you anyway, but it was the colour of your hair that made me decide to put this outrageous suggestion to you. Not only that, but when you turned and answered me and I saw those lovely eyes of yours, it—it was as if you had come just to help me." She patted Serena's hand. "You're very lovely, my dear," she said gently. "But I'm sure you've been told that many times." The woman looked away quickly and gazed out to the bay below them, but not before Serena caught the glisten of tears in her eyes.

"You see," she went on, "you're going to find this hard to believe, but you're just as I described my granddaughter. Long blue-black hair, violet eyes. Oh, even more perfect than I'd conjured up to put that woman's nose out of joint. Her granddaughter's fair, you know, with a sort of film star glamour. Keeps all the bachelors on the island on their toes, had it all her own way since she came back from finishing school." She sighed. "Personally, I can't stand the girl, and to think that Jordan . . ." She went off in a kind of reverie and stared out to sea.

Serena was beginning to feel she was losing out; she had done perfectly well up to now, but it was time a few points were clarified. "Hadn't we better introduce ourselves?" she asked gently.

"Isn't that just like me!" exclaimed her companion. "I'm so sorry, dear, I'm so used to everybody knowing everybody else it never occurred to me. I'm Mrs Tonetti. My husband was Italian, I came here a year ago after losing him."

Serena solemnly held out her hand. "Serena Belmont," she said.

"Serena," breathed Mrs Tonetti. "What a lovely name, and suits you perfectly."

Serena smiled. She hadn't been feeling so serene a little while ago when Mrs Tonetti arrived. It was odd how perceptive she had been, Serena thought. Thinking things over was just what she had been doing; having managed to persuade her mother to go on to New York and leave her to snatch a few days of peace away from Roger's dominating presence, Serena was determined to make the most of her brief spell of freedom. She was safe for a week at least; Roger was attending a conference important enough to warrant a daily attendance. As for trying to come to some decision, Mrs Tonetti had been perfectly right in that, too.

It was now two years since her father died, and being an only child, Serena had been coddled and watched over by her adoring father. She still missed him dreadfully; only he had known how to handle her affectionate but irresponsible mother.

As her father had been a successful financier, money had been plentiful, but his sudden death had coincided with the collapse of some shares he had invested heavily in, and the loss, coupled with death duties, had brought a drastic change to Serena and her mother's way of life.

They could have managed, providing Mrs Belmont had faced up to the facts of life, but Marion Belmont never gave a thought to the morrow. Money was meant to be spent, and spend it she did.

Roger Alton, banker, and friend of Serena's father, had stepped into the breach and taken their affairs into his own hands; not without an ulterior motive. He made no secret of the fact that he wanted to marry Serena. Roger, in his early thirties and a successful man, was a force to be reckoned with. Serena quite liked him, but she did not love him, and had made this fact quite clear to him; but her refusal to contemplate marrying him had not deterred Roger in the least. As yet, there were no rivals to worry about, and he was sure it was just a question of time.

Until three days ago, when they were due to join Roger at his invitation in New York, and from there go on to cruise through the Bahamas, Serena had been content to take life as it came. She was tired of trying to instil some measure of economy into her spendthrift mother, and had decided to look around for some form of employment, to stave off the inevitable crunch when it came. That in itself had been a problem; Serena had no experience to fall back on, or indeed training for any specific work. In the past she had filled her days, or to be more precise, her mother had filled them with various social occasions, such as helping to organise a charity ball, or garden party. This was about the full sum of Serena's past experience and hardly qualified her for obtaining the type of work commanding a high salary, which if they were to survive, was badly needed.

This problem however, was slight compared to the one her mother presented her with the day before they were due to fly out to New York. Serena closed her eyes; how could her mother have been so foolish? In her mind's eye Serena recalled the scene

of her walking round their London flat in that
dreamy gossamer dress and asking Serena whether
she liked it or not. The dress must have cost a small
fortune, and it was not as if her mother really needed
the dress; her wardrobe, like Serena's, was well
stocked from the days of plenty.

On Serena's horrified exclamation on the cost of
the dress, Mrs Belmont airily told her daughter she
was not to worry, as the dress had been placed on
Roger's account. Serena could only stare at her
mother and when she was capable of speech she told
her she must either take the dress back or recom-
pense Roger for it straight away. Mrs Belmont had
opened her blue eyes innocently and said she
couldn't see what all the fuss was about. Roger had
given her carte blanche to get whatever she wanted
for the holiday.

With a sinking feeling in her stomach, Serena demanded to know how many other things had been
bought and found it was worse than she had imagined. Her mother had taken Roger at his word and
practically bought an entire wardrobe. Gazing bewilderedly at Serena's white face, Mrs Belmont explained that she had only bought what she needed
for the holiday, and Roger wouldn't quibble about
the price anyway, he was practically family, wasn't
he?

On Serena's tight-lipped assertion that she wasn't
going to marry Roger, her mother had shrugged her
elegant shoulders and said soothingly, "Nonsense,
of course you will, you're quite fond of him really."

Serena began to see the writing on the wall; slowly but surely she was being drawn into a well-laid trap. It was obvious; Roger knew full well her mother's weakness and had deliberately encouraged her. He'd been extremely clever; he would never mention that account, he was too much of a gentleman for that—no, he'd known Serena would eventually find out about it, for he knew how strict a watch she had to keep on her mother's spending and soon the pressure would become more than Serena could withstand. Instinctively Serena knew this was only the start; she had been allowed as much rope as he had been prepared to give her, the lasso was now being tightened around her. Her lips straightened; it appeared she had underestimated Roger's determination to marry her. She ought to have known better; men of his calibre did not accept defeat.

Now, after a few days on this beautiful island in the Bahamas, Serena was no nearer a solution to her problems and couldn't see how she could extricate herself from the subtle bonds that were being woven about her. Feeling a light touch on her arm, she was brought back from her musings.

"You are worried, aren't you, dear?" murmured Mrs Tonetti. "Forget my stupid suggestion. It was selfish of me to ask it of you. I don't suppose talking over your problem would help, would it? I'm not trying to pry, but I know it sometimes helps. I've often wished in the past I had someone to confide in."

Serena glanced down at the frail woman by her side. Not only perceptive, but very sweet as well, she thought. She smiled at her, for those few words had helped her to come to one decision at least; she would help Mrs Tonetti if it were at all possible. She would stay the whole week, that would give her three more days on the island. She presumed all she had to do was make an appearance, be introduced as the granddaughter and fade out of the picture.

It could, of course, be tricky; Serena hadn't much experience of duplicity and was not sure she could carry it off, but was game to try. "I could stay a few days longer," she said suddenly. "But I must be on the New York flight on Saturday, or Mother will worry."

It took a minute or so for Mrs Tonetti to fall in, then she gave Serena a searching look and gasped, "You mean you'll do it? Pretend to be my grand-daughter, I mean?" Impulsively she caught Serena's hand. "Oh, my dear," she said, dabbing at her eyes. "I'll never be able to thank you enough." Her eyes sparkled as she added, "Just wait until Clarissa Simpson sets eyes on you!"

"It might not work, you know," warned Serena. "I've never done this sort of thing before. Suppose they ask me something and I say the wrong thing? It would be awful if it went wrong, have you thought of that?"

Mrs Tonetti refused to be discouraged. "I firmly believe in fate, my dear. Why should I suddenly come across you when I'd been so worried about the Centenary celebrations?"

"Centenary celebrations?" echoed Serena.

"That's what it's all about," replied Mrs Tonetti. "If I hadn't been so naughty as to fabricate a story about a granddaughter, I wouldn't be in this mess. Never lie, Serena: it just doesn't pay, even though you're sorely tempted—and if Clarissa Simpson wasn't the devil's weapon, I don't know who was! One lie, told in absolute frustration, can completely snowball as this one did. She won't let me forget it. Always mentions my granddaughter and how I must miss her, and wasn't it strange she never came to see me." She sighed. "I even had an old friend in England post out letters now and again to keep the deception up. In this part of the world, you know, there's not much goes on that isn't noticed."

Serena tried to compose herself, but the ironies of the situation were too much for her and she broke out into a deep chuckle. Mrs Tonetti gave her a surprised look. "Sorry," smiled Serena, "but having just agreed to become your accomplice I find the advice a little untimely!"

Mrs Tonetti tried to look stern but failed, and gave a little chuckle herself. "Well, perhaps what I should have said was take a lesson from what happened to me," she said.

"You were telling me about the Centenary celebrations," Serena reminded her.

"Oh, yes," answered Mrs Tonetti. "It's quite a big occasion, you know. In fact, quite a lot of visitors will turn up for it. We have one or two occasions during the year, but this one is special. The whole island has a holiday, they'll even re-enact the landing all those years ago of the pirates who took the island by storm. Jordan's ancestors, you know."

"Er . . . Jordan?" queried Serena, once again beginning to feel lost.

"Jordan Kerr, dear, the owner of the island. You'll meet him, of course. Such a sweet man, he'll be very pleased to meet you, he's asked after you often, purely for kindness' sake, I assure you. I hated deceiving him, you know, he's been so thoughtful and kind to me since I came here to live, but he's like that, takes everyone's welfare on his shoulders, and he's such a busy man too." She gave Serena a bright-eyed look. "Not everyone can settle here, you know. He vets them first." She gave a slight shiver and gathered her coat around her.

"Ought you to be out now that it's getting chilly?" Serena asked.

"Not really, I know. The doctor did warn me . . ." Mrs Tonetti broke off suddenly. "Well, you know what it is when you get old. They always want to coddle you, but it would be rather foolish to catch a chill just when life starts getting exciting."

Serena was not feeling quite so happy about the situation. Quite a lot of people, it seemed, had heard about the mythical granddaughter. This Jordan Kerr, for instance: well, it depended what sort of a man he was. If he really was as kind as Mrs Tonetti said he was, it might perhaps be wise to let him in on the deception, for if things went wrong Mrs Tonetti could depend on him to smooth things over. She put this to her companion.

"My dear, I couldn't possibly! You don't understand. I couldn't bear it if he knew I was such a . . . wicked liar!"

She spoke with such vehemence and got so upset about it, Serena did not press the point. In any case, Mrs Tonetti seemed anxious to drop the subject.

"Where are you staying?" she asked Serena quickly.

"The Royal," Serena replied.

"A wise choice," Mrs Tonetti remarked. "Not that the other two are bad, but the Royal is considered the best. However, I do not intend to put you to the expense of spending two more days there, their rates are not all that cheap. We'll collect your luggage, and you must come and stay with me, it would look odd if you didn't."

Having agreed to help, Serena had now burnt her boats. Mrs Tonetti was right, it would look odd if she continued to reside at the hotel. She was glad she had spent the last two days avoiding contact with other residents; spending her time taking long solitary walks among the hills framing the old harbour, Serena had wanted no distractions, for she had a lot on her mind.

As they slowly descended the slight incline down to the hotel grounds, it occurred to Serena that it was a pity she had not inherited her mother's penchant for bizarre situations. Had she been thus approached she would have been in the seventh heaven and plunged into the role with uninhibited enthusiasm—what was more, she would carry it off to perfection. Mrs Belmont did not believe in half-measures!

As they neared the hotel, Serena was grateful they did not have much further to go. Her companion seemed to tire easily, and she wondered how they were going to get to wherever it was that Mrs Tonetti lived. Serena could not possibly carry her three cases, and Mrs Tonetti obviously could not help. She knew there was a shortage of taxis on the island as she had had to wait at the small air terminal for one on her arrival, and she had heard tourists at the hotel complaining about the shortage. Serena remarked on this to Mrs Tonetti.

"We're only a small island, you know, dear," answered Mrs Tonetti. "I don't think there's more than half a dozen all told, and at this time of day they'd be pretty busy with fares wanting to visit the night clubs. Even so, residents are given precedence."

When they arrived at the hotel Mrs Tonetti proved her case, as within ten minutes of Serena packing, a private car stood waiting outside the hotel.

Serena's cases were carried out of the hotel and put in the boot of the car by a tall West Indian wearing the uniform of the hotel, and as they got in the car, Mrs Tonetti met Serena's raised brows with a smile. "Residents, dear—as I told you, we're very well looked after. Straight home, Charles," she ordered as the man settled himself behind the wheel.

Mrs Tonetti's residence lay beyond the island's small township. Serena could not see much once they had left the twinkling lights of the main street behind. The journey took only ten minutes or so. The lights were on in the porch of the sprawling chalet-type dwelling they drew up in front of. Charles, as Mrs Tonetti had addressed him, carried the cases into the hall and with a grin that spread from ear to ear, wished them goodnight before returning to the hotel.

"Molly?" called Mrs Tonetti as she led the way through the hall. "Come and see who I've got with me." In an undertone she murmured to Serena, "My housekeeper."

A few seconds later a stout Negress in a sedate green overall waddled towards them, her white teeth gleaming in a welcoming smile that seemed to come so naturally to these natives of the islands.

"Serena, meet Molly. My absolute treasure, cook, housekeeper, and general dogsbody, eh, Molly?" said Mrs Tonetti, smiling encouragingly at her. "This, Molly, is Serena, my granddaughter. How's that for a surprise?"

Molly's welcoming smile broadened, she held out a large brown hand and took Serena's in hers. "Sure am pleased you come, missy. Now Missus okay, eh?" She beamed at her employer.

Mrs Tonetti nodded slowly, her smile a little tremulous this time. For a second Serena felt a brush of sadness in that smile, then as quickly as she had become aware of it, it had gone. Mrs Tonetti moved into a room leading off the hall, drawing Serena with her. "I'm sure Serena would like a pot of tea while we wait for dinner," she called to Molly before she settled Serena into a comfortable cane-backed chair.

Once seated herself, she let out a sigh of pure relief and Serena noted how tired she was, and again wondered how old she was. Her beautifully waved white hair framed her delicate almost ivory features. High cheekbones, now with the skin stretched tightly over them, gave a hint of the beauty she must once have been. The blue eyes, now faded, would in her youth, have been devastating. Serena sighed inwardly; it must be terrible to be completely alone, she thought.

Mrs Tonetti rested her head back on her chair and gave Serena a sweet smile. "Now we can talk," she said conspiratorially.

"Ought you to have given Molly my real name?" queried Serena. "What name did you give your granddaughter?"

"Oh, don't worry about that," answered Mrs Tonetti quickly. "It's Lisa, as a matter of fact, but I thought it might complicate things if you had to remember to answer to the name. You see, my dear, I've not only manufactured a relation, but a career for her as well. It was the only thing I could think of to give you some excuse for not coming to see me." She gave Serena another of her delightful smiles accompanied by a half apologetic look. "It's rather a glamorous career, too."

Serena blinked and hoped it wasn't anything in the film line, for if she were asked any questions about the movie world she would be stumped for a start.

"You're a model, dear," explained Mrs Tonetti. "Not as yet top class, but with a little luck and hard work, you should make the top grade."

"Thank you," answered Serena solemnly, her eyes brimming with mischief. "I shall endeavour to do my best."

Her companion chuckled. "So convenient, isn't it? Your name is so perfect for the role. Your height, too!" She studied Serena with her head on one side. "Not only that, but your clothes, my dear. If you don't mind my saying so, you do rather look as if you have already made the grade. That's a Balmain suit unless I'm very much mistaken."

Serena nodded, and was about to ask whether she had mentioned where she was supposed to be working, when the door opened after a soft tap and Molly appeared with a tray of tea things. When she left, Serena asked her question.

"Oh, London, dear. At least you're stationed there. You do travel back and forth on the Continent for the fashion shows."

As she accepted a cup of tea, Serena thought there should be no difficulty there. She knew at least four fashion houses in London, and one in Paris. It would be easy to mention one of them and she had the added good fortune to be quite friendly with one top flight model. So far, so good—there was just one little problem. "Are my parents alive?" she asked, smiling inwardly at the thought of her mother's indignant reaction to the question had she been privileged to hear it.

Sipping her tea slowly, Mrs Tonetti swallowed and shook her head. "No, dear. There's only you and I, so don't worry about that side of things, it was all explained away."

"What am I to call you? I'm afraid I don't remember my own grandparents," Serena said.

Mrs Tonetti appeared to give this question some thought. "I never did like being called 'Gran', I think I would prefer 'Nan'—what do you think?"

Serena heartily agreed; she had no inclination towards the name Gran. Somehow it would seem impertinent. "When is the Centenary?" she asked.

"Thursday," replied Mrs Tonetti, a note of satisfaction in her voice. "There's a Centenary Eve Ball at Jordan's home tomorrow evening," she gave Serena a hesitant glance. "I'd rather like to take you there. I think it would be a good place for you to make your first appearance. Not the sort of place where an inquisition can be held, if you see what I mean. There'll be introductions, of course, and you'll obviously be asked to dance," she broke off chuckling. "In fact, my dear, I shall be very surprised if you aren't stampeded—-and that," she said a little maliciously, "will keep you out of Clarissa Simpson's prying eyes. She'll be so frustrated! I just can't wait to present you to her."

"What exactly happens on Thursday?" queried Serena.

"Well, as I've said, they do this landing thing, all dressed up as pirates. I don't know whether Jordan will take part on the day itself, or not. They had a rehearsal the other day, and you should have been here, my dear, it was wonderful—Jordan dressed as his forebears, with a scarf around his forehead and in the dress of the day. He was the image of a portrait in his library of the first Jordan Kerr who took the island all those years ago." She gave a sigh. "You know, those must have been exciting times, sometimes I rather wish I'd been part of them."

Serena shivered, not because of any change of temperature in the room, which was pleasantly warm, but she quite suddenly had a vision of a bunch of marauding pirates wading ashore, knives in their mouths and cutlasses swinging. Heaven help anyone who got in their way! She, for one, was thankful those days were over.

"And then," went on Mrs Tonetti, "we have a carnival parade through the town and that takes most of the morning. In the afternoon, there's canoe racing and a barbecue on the shore. Later, another dance at Jordan's place. It's a very hectic time, and of course, I shall keep you with me the whole time, so you won't have to worry about saying the wrong thing. You did say you had to leave on Saturday, didn't you, dear?"

Serena nodded. "Don't you think it would be a better idea if I were to take off on Friday instead of Saturday?" she asked.

Mrs Tonetti looked woebegone. "Oh, do stay another day, dear. You won't have to meet anyone, I shall say you're going on Saturday and that I intend to have you to myself for that one day. Not even

Clarissa Simpson can argue with that!" She gave
Serena a hopeful look. "I do so enjoy having company. I really don't get much these days, I have a stupid complaint that prevents me doing too much in
the social line. Don't look so alarmed, my dear," she
added hastily, "what else can you expect at my age?
Will you stay until you really have to go?"

Serena would have liked to have gone on Friday,
but she had no defence against those pleading blue
eyes. Smiling wryly, she gave in. "Saturday, then,"
she said.

CHAPTER TWO

AFTER a delicious meal of chicken cooked in a rich wine and garnished with button mushrooms, tiny shallots and herb sauce, followed by a fresh cream gateau, Serena and her hostess relaxed in the spacious beautifully furnished lounge.

Declining the offer of a liqueur, Serena protested, "Really, I've had ample. I hate to think what would happen to my figure should I stay here for long. Do you always have such mouthwatering dishes?"

Mrs Tonetti smiled. "No, my dear, Molly never gets the chance to show off with just me. I usually exist on some kind of light diet. I expect you noticed the tiny portion she allotted me, as a sort of a treat, you know. I'm afraid I haven't much of an appetite these days. You'd never believe some of the dishes she puts before me were some form of fish or chicken, she's a genius at disguise; not only that, they taste delicious as well."

Silence fell between them while they sipped their coffee. Serena's thoughts were busy with her forthcoming events; would it all be as easy as her extraordinary but beguiling companion thought it would be? She could well understand the loneliness and

frustration that had made Mrs Tonetti invent a relation. Going back to her childhood days, Serena
could remember how often she was tempted to do
the same thing at her boarding school, but her inven-
tion would have been a brother or sister. How often
had she listened to her friends and their tales of the
doings of their family; of Patsy Johnson's irresponsible brothers and the tangles they got into.

As an only child, Serena had felt left out of things.
She sighed; yes, she could see the old lady's point of
view. This Clarissa Simpson must be an insufferable
person to have driven a lonely, harmless woman to
such lengths of deception. Thinking back to their
previous conversation, Serena remembered something that had puzzled her; what had Mrs Tonetti
said about not liking being called "Gran"? Almost,
mused Serena, as if she had once been addressed as
such. Had the fantasy taken such a hold of her that
in her mind the granddaughter really did exist?

A wave of compassion touched her, and Serena
was determined to do all she could to help Mrs Tonetti. For a short space of time it would take her
mind off her own troubles. Time enough to face up
to them when she joined her mother and Roger in
New York on Saturday.

Glancing across at Mrs Tonetti, Serena found her
making an effort to keep awake, but her lids were
gradually drooping; she must have missed her afternoon siesta, Serena thought.

"Would you like to go to bed?" Serena asked her
gently. "I've some unpacking to do and would welcome an early night myself."

Mrs Tonetti made another effort to rouse herself. "I shouldn't be surprised if Molly hasn't already unpacked for you, dear," she murmured drowsily. "But I must agree it's time I rested, especially if I mean to do a little socialising in the next few days." She smiled at Serena. "So if you'll excuse me, I shall go to bed."

On reaching the door, she turned and gave Serena another smile. "Molly would have put you in the best guest room; she'll take you there when you're ready." She hesitated for a second, then added softly, "You can't imagine how grateful I am to you, my dear. We'll have a nice long chat in the morning."

While Serena waited for Molly to collect the coffee tray she glanced through some magazines lying on a side table. They were mostly American, similar to the more exclusive journals printed in England. There were articles on the doings of the high society, gossip columns, and the usual speculation on who would eventually marry whom. Serena's eye caught a paragraph that mentioned a name she had heard recently—Jordan Kerr. Her brows rose as she read the news snip.

"Jordan Kerr, wealthy owner of Blue Island in the Bahamas (incidentally, reported in our last issue as one of the six most eligible bachelors in the world!), was spotted lunching with the delectable Miss Myrna Simpson at Kilroy's on Friday. Will another diehard soon bite the dust?"

No photograph accompanied the news item, and Serena was a little disappointed, for she would have liked to have seen what Jordan Kerr looked like. She was also a little surprised to find the man Mrs Tonetti talked of in such warm tones coming under the category of one of the world's most eligible bachelors; not that that automatically made him a playboy, but it somehow did not gell with the description Mrs Tonetti had given of him. A little smile played round Serena's mouth as she thought of Mrs Tonetti's reaction to that paragraph. Myrna Simpson, she mused, would be Clarissa Simpson's granddaughter, the one who kept all the bachelors on their toes.

A short while later Molly appeared. "Missus said you'd like to go to your room, Miss Serena," she said shyly.

Serena smiled at her. "Yes, please, Molly, if you would show me the room you've put me in."

The room Molly took her to could have been no other than the best guest room, as Mrs Tonetti had surmised it would be, and was certainly extra special. It was purely feminine; the main colour theme was peach and a delicate pastel blue. Peach linen on the bed and a beautiful embroidered bedspread of peach and blue blossoms echoed the delicate hues of the pastel walls and the blue velvet curtaining. There was an ornate dressing table with gold-framed mirrors and an exquisite brush set, the backs of which were decorated with paintings of peach blossom on a blue background; Serena did not have to examine them to know they were antique and highly valuable.

Serena's gaze slid round the room, at the thick carpet, a darker blue than the curtains, the chairs with dainty spindled legs, another collector's item, and a gorgeous full-length mirror framed in an alcove next to the inbuilt wardrobe that ran the length of the room. The bedside lamp next caught her attention, and she moved to the cabinet beside the bed to have a closer look at it, and caught her breath. It was enchanting; a nymph with delicately sculptured limbs held a torch above her head in what could only be described as a triumphant pose. Serena was not sure, but rather suspected the metal was just what it appeared to be, gold. She wondered whether Mrs Tonetti had any idea she was living in a collector's paradise. It was just as well, Serena thought, that Jordan Kerr vetted all newcomers to the island, for had Mrs Tonetti elected to live elsewhere, her life would have been one long fight against the intrusion of collectors or their agents.

Undressing, Serena smiled as she noted that Molly had even gone to the extent of laying out her nightdress and negligée. She was certainly receiving V.I.P. treatment!

After her bath, Serena returned to her bedroom and stood before the dressing table wondering where Molly could have put her toilet case. Having apparently packed hers away, it was obvious she expected Serena to use the beautiful set laid out on the dressing table, but Serena felt this would be an encroachment and looked for her own, eventually finding the case in the top drawer of the dressing table. As she took it out, a photograph caught her eye and she looked closer at it.

It was of a girl standing against a background of rocks. Whoever had taken the photograph had not been an expert; the girl was shading her eyes against the glare of the sun and her features were partly in shadow. She was tall, with long dark hair, and judging by the style of the dress she wore, the snap was probably taken about five years ago. Serena could well remember wearing a similar style when she was eighteen.

There was a name scrawled at the bottom of the snap, and Serena bent closer to read it and frowned when she made out the name "Lisa". Closing the drawer, she sat for a few minutes staring at her reflection in the mirror, then started brushing her hair. Was that where Mrs Tonetti had got the name from? Was she a daughter of a friend? Serena recalled her words about not liking being called Gran, then she shrugged. Mrs Tonetti could have got that snap from anywhere, sent perhaps from England; the background rather suggested England than a sub-tropical island in the Bahamas. She would have to have something to show folk in order to prove the existence of the fabricated granddaughter.

Having seen the photograph Serena could now understand why she had caught Mrs Tonetti's attention. The girl in the photograph might well have been herself; there was a curious likeness there, and they were about the same height. The fact that the features were obscured was a point in Mrs Tonetti's favour, and Serena half-smiled; no wonder she had thought Serena the answer to her problem!

A tiny frown creased her forehead. Mrs Tonetti must have often regretted the mad impulse that had placed her in this position. Serena wasn't sure she was helping things either; to appear, then disappear, would surely complicate matters further. She gave this some thought, then brightened. She could send her a letter now and then, in fact, she decided, smiling at her reflection, she would adopt Mrs Tonetti as her official grandmother! She couldn't think of a nicer person to fill the role! On these thoughts Serena climbed into bed and was soon fast asleep.

MRS TONETTI WAS NOT AN EARLY RISER, and Serena breakfasted alone on the patio at the back of the chalet. She was quite content to laze in the warm sunshine and gaze at the panorama spread out before her. The gardens front and back were quite large, but beautifully kept, from what Serena could see of them. She decided to ask permission later to explore them.

Her eyes dwelt on the splashes of colour; pinks, blues, bright reds and brilliant whites all proclaimed a gardener's paradise. She heard the calls of birds and the strident screech of the brightly coloured parakeets as they flew by intent on their search for food. As the perfume of the flowers floated towards her, Serena took a deep breath. How heavenly, she thought, to be able to call a place like this your own. Her worries seemed to recede in this peaceful setting. It was as well she was leaving on Saturday, she thought, for she had a feeling that a longer stay would make it impossible for her to leave. She sighed wearily. It was no use indulging in wishful thinking; she had to face the future. There was her mother to consider.

"You're back to your problems, aren't you, Serena?"

Serena gave a small start and turned to give a rueful smile to Mrs Tonetti.

"Are you sure you wouldn't like to talk about them? I'd like to help, if I can. If you'd let me, that is . . ." Mrs Tonetti ended a little hesitantly, not wanting to intrude on Serena's private life unless given permission.

"I don't see why I should burden you with my problems," Serena said gently. "To be honest, I'm not sure there is an answer, apart from one I'm trying to avoid."

Not quite knowing how it happened, she found herself telling the whole story. In a way it was a relief to talk about it. There was no one else she could confide in. All her friends were friends of her mother and Roger, and if asked would say she was foolish to turn Roger down. Jean Woodson, for instance, who adored Roger and would marry him tomorrow were she but given the chance, would think Serena mad for even considering refusing him.

Mrs Tonetti listened attentively, only interrupting once to ask how old Roger was, and was silent for a while after Serena had finished explaining the position.

"Well, one thing is certain, dear," she said gently. "You're not to even consider marriage unless you love the man. As for your mother, I know it sounds callous, but isn't it about time she learnt to stand on her own two feet? The more you shield her from her own stupidity the longer she'll take to realise her responsibilities. You can't be expected to go on protecting her from the realities of life."

Serena sighed. "Oh, I know you're right, but if you only knew Mother! She hasn't ever had to fend for herself. She'd be game to try, you know, but she wouldn't have a clue. Father managed everything—and he did rather spoil her. He spoilt me, too, come to that." There were tears in her eyes as she said this and it took a second or two to compose herself before going on, "I feel awful about it, but I can't help hoping she could meet someone like him again. I know it's what he'd want, too. She isn't short of admirers, she's still quite lovely, and there's a good possibility that she might meet someone on this cruise Roger's got lined up. I do know he's asked several of his New York business acquaintances to join us. He's pretty astute, you know, and I wouldn't mind betting he's already lined up a few presentable types who might fit the bill."

Serena looked away and concentrated her gaze on a lovely purple blossom entwined on a trellis running the length of the low patio wall. "I was so grateful to him," she went on tonelessly. "But when I found out what he was up to, encouraging Mother to splash out like that, I was furious with him—still am, as a matter of fact. He knows how much I hate being in debt to anyone," she sighed. "He's often told me I'm too independent, but someone in the family has to watch points if we're to keep our heads above water."

"And your mother is in New York now, is she?" Mrs Tonetti asked.

Serena nodded. "Yes, I told her to go on ahead. She's all right on her own, we've several friends there and they'll look after her until I join her on Saturday. Roger will be free by then, too. The cruise starts the following Monday—that reminds me, I ought to cable her and tell her I won't be joining her until the weekend. She was expecting me tomorrow."

"Do so right away, then," urged Mrs Tonetti. "Use the phone."

After Serena had made the call she rejoined her hostess on the patio, remarking cheerfully, "You're right, it is a small island! Whoever took the cable was consumed with curiosity about me. She knew where I was speaking from and short of actually asking me who I was and why I was here, she tried everything else in the book! I didn't give my surname, just signed the cable Serena."

Mrs Tonetti chuckled and all but clapped her hands. "That would have been Beryl Johnson, I'm sure. By this evening it will have got round the whole island that I have a visitor named Serena. I wonder if they'll guess who you are?"

"Oh, dear, does that mean you'll have floods of visitors tomorrow?" Serena queried worriedly.

Mrs Tonetti chuckled again. "No, dear, it's the ball tomorrow evening, remember? They'll know better than to expect me to entertain if I intend to go, and I shall let it be known that I will be present."

"Oh, I see," said Serena, not really seeing at all. Nevertheless, she was slightly relieved, wanting to put off the actual moment of duplicity as long as possible.

"I've been thinking," Mrs Tonetti remarked consideringly. "When you were sending off the cable, it occurred to me that your best course would be to invent another young man. This Roger of yours would have to give up the pursuit if you found someone else, wouldn't he? You could even make that your excuse for not joining them until Saturday," she added brightly.

Serena found herself chuckling. "You're incorrigible," she scolded gently. "Soon I'll be as bad as you are." Then she looked serious and slowly shook her head. "It wouldn't work, I'm afraid. You don't know Roger. I'd not only have to present the mythical young man but show him an engagement ring to boot! The only reason I've been left in peace for a few days is because he doesn't know which island I'm staying on. When Mother gets that cable I expect to hear from him directly. If it weren't for the conference he'd be here on the next plane."

Mrs Tonetti looked somewhat despondent, then brightened. "Well, there's time enough yet, dear. We've several nice young men on the island and you just might meet the right one at the ball. I'm a firm believer in fate, as I believe I did tell you, and I'm sure it wasn't just chance that you picked this island to try and find a solution to your problems."

Serena wished she could echo this sentiment, but was rather of the opinion that it had been sheer chance she had chosen the island—that, and the plain simple fact that she had liked the name of the island, for blue was her favourite colour, and she really didn't think fate had much to do with it at all.

MRS TONETTI RETIRED AFTER LUNCH, leaving Serena free to explore the gardens, kept in such immaculate order by Thomas, Molly's brother. She told Serena, "He comes every day for a few hours, and he should be around somewhere, so do ask him anything you want to know. He's immensely proud of his work and rightly so."

As she strolled through the grounds Serena looked back at the chalet, admiring the way the building sat on its elevated position overlooking one of the many small bays that surrounded this island paradise. It was quite a large establishment and she did wonder why Mrs Tonetti had chosen it. A cottage or a smaller bungalow would have been ample for her wants, she thought, particularly as she had decided to retire there.

The gardens sloped gently down a terraced incline and Serena found Thomas, or to be more precise, Thomas found her admiring some huge purple convolvulus. The blooms were at least three inches in diameter and absolutely begged for attention. Serena was able to recognise a lot of the flowers and the variety surprised her. With delight she spotted species of honeysuckle, its sweet perfume drifted towards her as she stood admiring a mass of brilliant orange nasturtiums thinking with wonder of their English counterparts that seemed to be almost dull in comparison, a poor relation indeed to these exotic blooms. Such was the case of each species she recognised, the flowers larger, the colour intensified to an almost translucent beauty.

One plant evaded her and she asked Thomas its name. It had large fleshy leaves and pendulous flowers of a green and purple colour and grew in profusion, appearing every now and again in between the riot of flowers and seemed to act as a foil for their brilliance. "What is that plant, Thomas?" she asked.

Thomas, unlike his sister, was tall and thin, and a little shy, but eager to be helpful. He gave Serena a grin that showed white even teeth. "Don't rightly know, missy, but we call them Poppers."

Serena frowned. "What an odd name," she commented. "Must be an abbreviation of the botanical name."

Thomas grinned again and picked up his spade. "See, missy," he said, and selected a large bud of the plant on the point of opening, and to Serena's surprise gave it a sharp tap with the spade. The next moment there was a loud crack sounding like a mild explosion in the sultry stillness of the garden.

"Good gracious!" commented Serena. "It ought to be called 'crackers'!"

Thomas accompanied her on the rest of the tour of the gardens. The rear garden was, if anything, more beautifully laid out than the front. Terraces with frangipani-entwined arches covered the walks. Here shrubs were more in evidence, all in full flower and forming partitions from one section of the garden to another.

It was at the end of the grounds that they came across the part of the garden that Serena fell in love with. The lawns had been replaced by a small paved courtyard, and a roselike flower grew in profusion on trellises surrounding the area. In the middle of the courtyard stood a lovely statue of a nymph holding an urn on one graceful shoulder. Serena stood entranced. There was peace in this corner of the garden and she sensed it was somehow special. The layout inevitably reminded her of Italian gardens and their love of courtyards and neatness combined with beauty. She felt she knew now why Mrs Tonetti had chosen this particular place to retire to. She sighed; it made her feel a little sad, for it was obvious that the old lady loved her husband very much.

Her thoughts were communicated to Thomas. "Mr Tonetti, he came here often," he said, and indicated a small covered archway with seating accommodation for two. "Now, only Missus come."

Serena looked at Thomas in surprise. "Did you know Mr Tonetti, Thomas?"

Thomas nodded. "He and Missus come every year

for holiday. Always have this place. Boss said keep it
for Mrs Tonetti.''

She frowned. Boss? Did he mean Mr Tonetti?

Thomas's next words answered her unspoken
question. "Plenty like to get this place. Mrs Simpson
always on at Boss, wants to buy it, but Boss likes
Mrs Tonetti, he won't sell.''

Things were getting a little clearer to Serena now.
No wonder Mrs Tonetti didn't like Mrs Simpson,
and vice versa! Mrs Simpson was obviously put out
because this boss, whoever he was, preferred to have
Mrs Tonetti as a paying guest rather than receive
hard cash at what Serena surmised would be a fabulous figure. Properties in this part of the world could
rise to almost astronomical heights.

CHAPTER THREE

WEDNESDAY evening and Serena's debut as Mrs Tonetti's granddaughter came all too soon for her. She had enjoyed two days of idyllic peace and cosy chats with her charming hostess, to whom Serena was growing very attached.

Now the time had come for her to fulfill her promise, and as she dressed for the ball she found herself wondering how she had ever let herself be talked into the masquerade in the first place. It was too late now to back out and she would have hated herself for trying, but she couldn't help wishing Mrs Tonetti would decide to call the whole thing off.

Upbraiding herself for her cowardice, Serena gave her attention to the dress she would wear and eventually chose the deceptively simple velvet one of midnight blue with long full sleeves buttoning at the wrists. The dress clung to her slender figure and the neck not too low, dipped into a sedate V which emphasised the creamy whiteness of her neck. Her only ornament was a long gold filigree chain necklet of flowers and leaves entwined. This had been her father's gift on her twenty-first birthday and was her favourite piece of jewellery.

Before joining Mrs Tonetti, Serena gave herself one last critical inspection; her glance passed down the dress to the gold sandals on her feet, she then stood back from the mirror to get a glimpse of the overall effect and frowned as an odd sensation swept over her. She didn't feel at all real and her reflection solemnly staring back at her accentuated this feeling. She had left her hair long and parted in the middle, and it fell in a dark cloud on her shoulders to frame her pale features. Her eyes looked enormous and she wondered whether she ought to have chosen a slightly darker eye-shadow instead of the greenish-blue one that appeared to highlight her eyes so much. She wasn't sure whether it was the dress that gave her such a wraithlike appearance, almost, she mused, as if she had stepped out of medieval times, making her feel there should have been a knight in attendance somewhere.

She grimaced at her reflection. Bizarre situations brought bizarre thoughts, didn't they? and shrugged impatiently, she was just being fanciful. Taking a deep breath she collected her stole and evening bag. It was all in keeping with her role; models were supposed to stand out in a crowd. These thoughts brought her no comfort, and as she walked towards the lounge to join Mrs Tonetti, the first pangs of nervousness assailed her and her fingers gripped her evening bag more firmly. She must remember to give Mrs Simpson a wide berth. From all she had heard of that lady she was the most formidable obstacle she was likely to meet.

Mrs Tonetti sat quietly awaiting her and did not at first see Serena as she entered the room. Serena saw she was lost in thought and a hope that she might be considering changing her mind about going through with the deception sprang into life. Her plain black silk dress, relieved only by a single string of pearls, drew added attention to her fragility and Serena was on the point of asking her whether it might not be a good idea to forgo the ball, when Mrs Tonetti became aware of her presence and gave a gasp of delight. "Oh, my dear," she said softly. "Paris— Pierre, it couldn't be anyone else!"

Serena's brows rose. For an old lady she certainly knew about fashion! She nodded. "Yes, but how . . ." she began.

Mrs Tonetti smiled. "We lived in Paris for a while not long after we were married," she explained. "Pierre was a special friend of ours, he was only just beginning in those days, but I'd know his creations anywhere. You know," she added wistfully, "I only wish he could see you in that gown. He must have had you in mind when he created it."

The sound of a car drawing up in front of the house put an end to the conversation, and to any hope Serena was secretly nursing about a cancellation. Mrs Tonetti picked up her wrap and Serena placed it over her shoulders for her. "Thank you, my dear," she smiled, and sniffed appreciatively. "I'm a little behind with the perfumes," she said with twinkling eyes. "But I like it, whatever it is. Now, are you ready for the fray?" she asked brightly as they moved towards the door.

Serena's stomach started churning again, but she put a brave face on it and managed to smile back at her. "I only hope I don't let you down," she replied, trying to sound airy about it.

Mrs Tonetti patted her arm. "Of course you won't, and if anything does go wrong, and I really don't see how it could, it will be entirely my own fault. I ought to have known better." She gave Serena a wicked look and added conspiratorially, "Isn't it exciting? I wouldn't have missed it for worlds!"

As they left the chalet Serena couldn't help wishing once again that she had more of her mother's character in her, not to mention courage!

The car waiting to convey them to their destination was an opulent Rolls, and not an early model either, in fact the very latest on the market, Serena suspected, but surely a little unusual to be used as a taxi service she thought.

"Jordan's, dear," Mrs Tonetti supplied in answer to Serena's unspoken query. "So kind of him, isn't it?"

A thin wiry man detached himself from the driving seat and walked towards them.

"Good evening, Jake," greeted Mrs Tonetti. "This is my granddaughter, Serena." She turned to Serena. "Jake is Jordan's jack-of-all-trades, almost as useful as my Molly, eh, Jake?"

Serena caught the flash of white teeth at this gentle raillery, but could see little else of the man as he stood in the shadows. He spoke in a soft singsong voice and she hazarded a guess that he was probably Polynesian. "Pleased to meet you, Miss Serena."

During the short ride, Mrs Tonetti inquired solicitously after Jake's wife and family, and all, it appeared, were doing well. During this exchange Serena was able to follow her own thoughts, and she thought of Jordan Kerr. The more she heard about him, the more she warmed to the man. He must be extremely busy, but he found time to see to the welfare of an old lady—not that Mrs Tonetti was just any old lady, she was a sweetie, but nevertheless not many in his position would bother. Suddenly she was sure that if anything did go wrong with the proposed scheme she had only to tell the truth and he would see that Mrs Tonetti received no backlash. On these thoughts Serena's fears slipped away from her. She could now go on to join her mother and Roger in New York with the comforting knowledge that all would be well. As the car swept down a long bordered drive and drew up in front of an imposing mansion, she found herself actually looking forward to the evening's entertainment.

The strains of dance music drifted towards them as they mounted the stone steps to the entrance of the house. Serena looked about her with interest. Two stone pillars supported the ground entrance porch and lighting from the open windows limelighted the bordering flowering shrubs flanking the entrance. Bougainvillaea in brilliant colours crept round the stone verandah and two stone nymphs holding urns of yet more exotic blossoms stood either side of the great studded doors of the house, now thrown open to welcome guests. For a moment Serena stood inhaling the perfume-laden air, then noting the fact that they were alone with no other guests either arriving or in the immediate vicinity, she asked, "Are we very late?"

Taking her arm and leading her into the house, Mrs Tonetti replied, "A little late, yes, dear."

A young West Indian girl in a brightly coloured sarong drifted towards them one slender arm extended to take their stoles. "Ah, May," greeted Mrs Tonetti smilingly. "We shall be going early, dear, so leave them somewhere handy, won't you?"

The special smile the girl gave in answer proved once again to Serena that Mrs Tonetti was not only respected but well liked by the islanders.

Giving Serena a mischievous look, Mrs Tonetti murmured, "Now for it! Don't worry about our being the last to arrive, Jordan knows I tire easily. We'll only stay an hour or so, just so everybody sees you." She gave Serena an apologetic look. "Of course, my dear, if you're enjoying yourself we'll stay longer."

As they walked down a long richly carpeted corridor, Serena hastily replied, "I shall be quite ready to leave whenever you are. I'll be on tenterhooks in case I say the wrong thing," adding tentatively. "I rather feel it might be better if I acted dumb, you know."

Mrs Tonetti looked slightly alarmed at this pronouncement, and Serena grinned. "Perhaps what I should have said was quiet, not talkative, I mean."

The increasing volume of music told Serena they
were almost at their destination, and they were. The
double doors of the large room opened on to a gal-
axy of colour. All the colours of the rainbow seemed
to be represented by the gowns worn by the women,
their displayed jewellery flashing as they were pi-
rouetted round the dance floor by their no less re-
splendently dressed partners.

As she entered the room Serena felt slightly bemused. The ballroom was magnificent and dated
back several centuries, although one would never
have realised this by its present décor. The walls
were hung with rich tapestry depicting scenes of
what Serena presumed to be the island's history.
One huge exquisite chandelier hung from the centre
of the ceiling, its glittering light throwing out sparks
that scintillated over a deep purple, intricately
moulded ceiling, giving it a fascinating pattern no
decorator could hope to emulate.

Although many of the guests were dancing to the
strains of a waltz played by a small orchestra seated
on a dais at the end of the vast room, Serena could
feel the curiosity their entrance had aroused, and
was sure Mrs Tonetti was just as aware of it as she
was, for she laid a comforting hand on Serena's arm
and led her down the room.

The carefree attitude Serena had talked herself
into in the car on the way to the ball deserted her,
and the pangs of nervousness returned with interest.
Her throat felt dry and she was absolutely certain
she would ruin the whole plan within minutes of her

entry. She couldn't understand why they all seemed to be staring at her. She swallowed hastily and chided herself for her heightened sensitivity. The trouble was she had a guilty conscience and was dramatising the whole thing, and if she didn't pull herself together soon she really would spoil everything. After giving herself a good talking to, she was almost composed by the time they reached a small knot of people and the first introductions began.

Mrs Tonetti was greeted with much enthusiasm, and remarks were made such as how nice it was to see her at a social function. After solicitous inquiries about her health had been exhausted, Serena was introduced. She shook hands with them and before a general topic of conversation could be introduced, found herself whisked away by Mrs Tonetti and on to the next group.

The initial skirmish over, Serena began to relax. She had to hand it to Mrs Tonetti, whose timing proved masterly, and who she rather suspected was having the time of her life if the wicked twinkle in her eyes as she met them on their way to join yet another small batch of folk was anything to go by!

Serena didn't know when she first became aware of the scrutiny, but as she was led from group to group and small talk developed, a definite sense of being watched gradually bored into her consciousness. At first she thought she had imagined it, there were so many curious stares in her direction, but the feeling persisted so strongly she found herself glancing across the room if only to satisfy herself that her

nerves were playing tricks on her, and found herself
meeting the gaze of a tall man with reddish-gold
hair, and she hastily looked away again. So she
hadn't imagined it. With an effort she pulled her
thoughts away from the man who was subjecting her
to that microscopic examination and tried to concentrate on the conversation around her. She found this
harder than she had thought, for a feeling of unease
had crept into her senses and even though she smiled
and answered a question posed by a frankly admiring young man on whether she would grant him the
first dance when all the introductions were over, she
was still very much aware of the stranger across the
room.

It did occur to her that the man might have met
her in London at one of her mother's charity balls,
and if this were so, she only hoped he did not know
her mother, because if he did the whole thing would
go up in smoke. She bit her lip and wished she could
have a few minutes alone with Mrs Tonetti and warn
her of this possibility.

However, Serena was given no opportunity of
communicating her fears as they had now begun the
round of introductions on the other side of the room.
Serena was just receiving a compliment from a
portly man with a strong American accent when she
heard Mrs Tonetti exclaim, "Jordan dear, do come
and meet Serena."

Serena turned smilingly towards the newcomer
and almost gasped when she found herself meeting
the gaze of the man whose earlier attention had so

discomfited her. His voice was deep and well-modulated and as far as looks went he was quite the handsomest man she had ever met, but Serena took particular note of the fact that his smile did not reach his eyes. They were rather striking eyes of a grey-green colour, more green than grey, she decided, and about as cold as an arctic winter.

As her hand was lost in the large strong one offered, she felt a stab of disappointment. She had been so sure she would like Jordan Kerr, but she didn't. She knew she had no right to judge him on first acquaintance and reminded herself he had been very good to Mrs Tonetti and that was really all that mattered, so when he requested the dance that was just starting Serena did not hesitate in accepting, although she knew she had promised the first dance to someone else, but she felt under the circumstances the young man in question would understand, for Jordan Kerr was, after all, her host.

When they began to dance, Serena found his hold tentative, yet not so. After the first few steps she felt as if there were a brick wall between them. His clasp on her hand was light and she received the distinct impression he would have preferred to have kept his distance.

She was a little perplexed by this treatment. As an exceptionally attractive woman, she found his attitude intriguing, to say the least. She stole a quick look at him under her lashes and saw that his features were stiff; he was plainly not enjoying the dance. For one brief second she wondered if he were shy, then instantly dismissed the thought. He was too self-assured to have such a charge levelled at him. Was it reserve? she wondered. Was he so intent on preserving his bachelor status? She almost grinned at this thought. He was so good-looking, and by all accounts wealthy, he had probably been driven to adopt such tactics. Women, she mused, would find him a definite challenge. She remembered the gossip snip she had read about him and wondered if Myrna Simpson had managed to get under his armour. One thing she did know about him, he was no playboy. A man's man, if ever she saw one.

Serena was so immersed in her thoughts that she actually jumped when he suddenly asked, "Did you get tired of Beroni, or was it mutual?"

She was so surprised that she missed a step and almost cannoned into him, but an expert side step of his prevented the collision. Serena wondered whether she had heard aright and felt like shaking her head. Who on earth was Beroni? She cast about in her mind for some connection of the name with the fashion world, but failed. Her heart sank. It was all very well for Mrs Tonetti, she thought miserably. It appeared this was something she had not clued her up on. Deciding to play safe, she answered airily, "Oh, it was mutual," and hoped she had plumped for the right answer.

Judging by the way he retreated back into his ivory tower again, Serena presumed he was satisfied. She almost sighed with relief—that had been a close thing; she must somehow have a private word with Mrs Tonetti and find out what he had been talking about before she really put her foot in it.

When the dance ended, Serena knew relief, for Jordan Kerr's sake as well as her own. Neither of them had enjoyed the duty dance, for that was what it had obviously been. With studious politeness he escorted her back to Mrs Tonetti and excused himself shortly afterwards.

From then on the evening flew by for her. There was no opportunity of a quiet word with Mrs Tonetti, for as she had predicted, Serena found herself inundated with dancing partners. Returning after a succession of dances, Serena found her in the company of an elderly woman, and one glance at the expression on Mrs Tonetti's face told Serena the woman's name. Mrs Simpson was introduced, and it was not long before Serena found herself in complete agreement with Mrs Tonetti's point of view. The woman was dictatorial, inquisitive and, Serena suspected, the worst kind of snob.

Her small black eyes darted over Serena's dress and Serena knew she was mentally pricing it. Her voice was high-pitched and grating. "Myrna's here somewhere, you know. We ought to have been here earlier, but the flight was delayed. Myrna insists on doing her shopping in New York. We nearly didn't make the ball." She peered over at the dancers. "Oh, there she is!" There was a note of satisfaction in her voice. "Jordan's making up for lost time, I see."

Serena glanced to where Mrs Simpson was looking and received a slight shock. Jordan Kerr was dancing with a fair girl—fair in every sense of the word. Mrs Tonetti had not really done her justice, Serena thought as she watched them dancing. They made a delightful pair—the girl so slight and utterly feminine, and the tall, broad-shouldered man.

It was the man who held Serena's attention, and she found it hard to believe that it was the same man who had partnered her earlier, no longer withdrawn and haughty, but now smiling down at the girl in his arms. Had she been closer, Serena was sure that his eyes would be laughing too. She felt a twinge of anger against Jordan Kerr—so he was interested in Miss Simpson; the gossip columns had been right, but it hardly excused the frigid welcome he had extended to her.

Serena's thoughts were interrupted by Mrs Tonetti's abrupt, "He's already danced with Serena. The poor child hasn't had a moment to herself, but I knew how it would be," she added a little maliciously.

"Jordan," Mrs Simpson determinedly pointed out, "practically pounced on Myrna as soon as we arrived."

"But he's such a sweet man, isn't he?" purred Mrs Tonetti in swift reply. "Hates anyone to be left out."

Somewhere, thought Serena, a bell ought to be rung for seconds out! She was very much afraid her champion was backing a loser if she hoped Serena would steal some of Myrna's thunder. She had not only left the haughty Jordan Kerr cold, but positively icy!

Fortunately supper was then announced, and whatever remark Mrs Simpson had been about to retaliate with was never uttered. With a look of pure disdain she went in search of a bosom friend of hers.

"She has two days' news to catch up on," Mrs Tonetti told Serena with twinkling eyes. "Poor Beryl Johnson's terrified of her, for she bullies her shamefully." She placed a hand on Serena's arm. "Shall we find some refreshment, dear? I must say I could do with a nice iced drink." She smiled as a young man who had partnered Serena earlier, now hovering hesitantly near them and obviously wanting to escort Serena to the buffet room. "Would you care to join us, Gerald?"

The request was received with a grateful smile and the offer of an arm to each lady. Serena would have preferred to take supper with Mrs Tonetti alone. If Jordan Kerr felt another duty dance was called for later in the evening, there were a few things Serena needed to know, such as who this mysterious Mr Beroni was!

A cold buffet was laid out in the supper room, and various dishes of enticing-looking food were arranged on a long table running the length of the room. Gorgeous floral displays filled spaces in between the dishes, turning an ordinary cold buffet into a work of art. Serena thought it was a pity to disturb it.

Even with such an array of tempting food, Serena

was not particularly hungry, but she allowed the said Gerald to place a few exotic-looking pastries on her plate. Mrs Tonetti did not partake, but an iced drink was secured for her.

There were individual tables and chairs scattered about the room so that the food could be consumed in some degree of comfort, and seeing Mrs Tonetti's lips thin after a look down the room, Serena followed her glance and saw Myrna Simpson sitting with Jordan Kerr and was certain Mrs Tonetti was disappointed that he had not joined them for supper.

Serena had a guilty feeling she had let Mrs Tonetti down, which was ridiculous; it was hardly her fault that Jordan Kerr's affections were bespoken, and, she thought a trifle wryly, hardly Myrna's fault that she had such an unlovable grandmother! However, when several other unattached young men found an excuse to join them, making a table for four do duty for six, Serena felt a little vindicated, and Mrs Tonetti was clearly pleased with the way things were going.

The talk was general and very gay. Probes were put out as to how long Serena was staying on the island, and there was a general lowering of spirits when they were told the date of her departure.

"Surely," asked a fair young man named Don, "you could stretch it a bit longer. What's New York got, that we haven't?" he appealed to Mrs Tonetti. "Couldn't you persuade her to stay on for a while?"

Mrs Tonetti gave a rueful smile. "I only wish she would. I'm going to try my best, anyway."

Serena looked up, startled at this reply. Mrs Tonetti knew very well she had to be on that Saturday flight.

Meeting her eyes, Mrs Tonetti smiled apologetically at her. "Forgive an old lady's selfishness, Serena. Of course you have to go." She patted her hand and turned to the disappointed admirers. "But she'll be back, you know. And next time she will stay longer, won't you, Serena?"

There was not much Serena could say to that, apart from agreeing, which she did. She only knew she wanted to come back, and very soon.

The deep voice coming from behind her did not startle her at all, for she had felt his presence long before he spoke.

"Now don't overdo it, Esme. Jake's standing by whenever you've had enough."

Mrs Tonetti smiled up at the man standing behind Serena. "Thank you, Jordan dear. To be honest I did think of leaving after supper. It's been a lovely evening, hasn't it, Serena?"

Serena echoed these sentiments, only too pleased that the evening had come to an end. Now there was only one more day to play out the role, and next time, she told herself, she would stick to her adopted grandmother's side like glue and avoid a repetition of further awkward questions.

Her relief was shortlived, for with some trepidation she heard Jordan Kerr smoothly suggest that she stayed on—it was a pity to deprive her of the rest of the evening's entertainment; he would see her safely back, etc.

Serena cast a look of desperation at Mrs Tonetti, who appeared to be wavering. "It's very kind of you," she answered hastily before Mrs Tonetti could speak. "I've only been here a day or so," she lied, "and travelling always tires me, I'm quite ready to leave when Nan does."

She was quite surprised the way the name "Nan" came so readily, as she had anticipated having trouble over it, and thanked her lucky stars she had been alert enough to use it. She had to crane her neck to look up at Jordan towering above her, and knew by the slightly altered mouth line that he was not pleased with this information. Well, it couldn't be helped, she thought, and there was nothing he could do about it. But she soon found she had misjudged him.

"Come now," he said a little silkily, and to her sensitive ears a little challengingly. "You don't expect me to believe that, do you? Surely you're used to travel?" He glanced back at Mrs Tonetti. "I appeal to you, Esme. I expect Serena is being extra thoughtful on your behalf, don't you?"

Mrs Tonetti got quite carried away, and Serena could see why; Mrs Simpson was standing a little way away and was taking more than a passing interest in the conversation. Basking in the light of success, Mrs Tonetti ignored the plain S.O.S. Serena's eyes were sending her. Jordan had shown an interest in Serena, and all else was forgotten.

However, Serena was not beaten yet. "I do assure you, I am tired," she insisted, fixing a look of "don't you dare leave me" on Mrs Tonetti.

"Nonsense, child!" Mrs Tonetti exclaimed. "Jordan is quite right. Why shouldn't you enjoy yourself? I shall go straight to bed when I get home, anyway. So you stay, my dear. I know I can rely on Jordan to see you safely back."

Serena was not even given the chance of a hasty few words with her before she left, as her wrap was immediately sent for, and Jake appeared saying that the car was waiting, leaving Serena feeling like a shipwrecked mariner cast ashore on a desert island.

CHAPTER FOUR

As soon as Mrs Tonetti was out of sight Gerald, determined to steal a march on his rivals, asked Serena to dance. His reign was short, for as soon as the dance was over an apprehensive Serena found Jordan Kerr waiting to claim the next one. With a smooth, "Excuse me, old chap," to Gerald, he whisked her on to the floor for a quickstep.

The impression she had received before was even more pronounced this time, and Serena wished she could define it. They were dancing, yes, but they might have been on opposite sides of the room. Partly to relieve her tension she attempted to make conversation. "I do appreciate your concern for my grandmother," she said quietly, and smiled up at him.

The smile was not returned; if anything, he seemed to freeze a degree lower. "Do you?" he answered coldly.

The answer completely nonplussed Serena, who decided to give up. She had tried, hadn't she? What an exceedingly odd man he was. Perhaps he had a thing about brunettes! Out of the corner of her eye she caught sight of Gerald hovering by the side of the dance floor and knew he was waiting for an opportunity to claim the next dance. The sight gave her some consolation; whatever effect she had on Jordan Kerr she was grateful it was not catching! The thought made her smile.

"Something amusing you?" asked Jordan Kerr haughtily.

Serena glanced up at him. Now she was angry and her eyes showed her feelings, but she answered airily enough, "Just a passing thought, Mr Kerr."

When the dance ended, Serena, meaning to show this autocratic man that she did not require any more attention from him, if it could be called that, murmured, "If you'll excuse me," and made a move to pass him.

As if she had not spoken, he asked abruptly, "Are you interested in past history?"

Serena stared at him. Now what? Was he making an effort to entertain her for Mrs Tonetti's sake? She wished she could state quite categorically that she was not a bit interested in history and end the uncomfortable interlude for both of them, but she knew she was under an obligation. She had promised to help Mrs Tonetti, although, she thought darkly, the said lady really didn't deserve any such consideration, not after deserting her like that, throwing her as it were into the lion's den. She corrected that last thought on noticing the way Jordan Kerr was watching her with those extraordinary eyes of his, now more green than grey. Panther's eyes, she thought, and almost shivered.

She was quite at a loss to understand why he should want to discuss such a subject, then she remembered the Centenary. He was probably very proud of his ancestors, and the fact that she had made a point of attending the celebrations would, from his point of view, mean she was interested. Besides, she mused, it would take his mind off other matters—such as this Mr Beroni, and any other tricky questions he might throw at her.

"Well, yes," she replied, managing to produce a bright smile at him. "I'm afraid I don't know a lot about the island's history. It's very kind of you..."

Before she had completed the sentence Serena found herself being guided out of the ballroom and down a long corridor, and it occurred to her that no matter what her answer had been she would still be taking this walk. She tried to quell the waves of apprehension flowing through her and told herself she was just being fanciful again. Really, she was just not cut out for this kind of masquerade.

When they reached the end of the corridor Jordan Kerr opened a door on his left and indicated that she should precede him into the room. Doing so, Serena found herself in a large room that was obviously a study. Her eyes rested on a handsome mahogany desk placed near a large bay window, then moved to the bookshelves that took up the whole of one wall. Her fears were now dispelled, for this would be where the books on the island's history were kept; the maps too, she thought, as her eye caught sight of an ancient-looking map framed and hung on the wall behind the desk.

Jordan Kerr closed the door behind him and selecting a chair picked it up and placed it in front of the desk. Sitting down behind the desk, he silently gestured Serena to the chair in front of him.

A variety of thoughts flashed through Serena's mind, most of them alarming. She looked at the cold handsome face of the man seated in front of her. This was no pleasant tête-à-tête, in fact it looked more in the nature of an inquisition!

Serena thought she had the answer—Mrs Tonetti had not fooled him for one moment—he knew she was an impostor! Did he think she was some kind of adventuress and meant to warn her off? She felt a kind of relief, for she would now have to tell him the whole story. She was sure Mrs Tonetti would understand and she was also sure Jordan Kerr would respect Mrs Tonetti's odd but very understandable duplicity.

Having worked it all out in her mind Serena relaxed and sat back in her chair, then looked up to meet those strange eyes closely watching her; she smiled at him and was a little disturbed to see no change of expression on his face. This was a new experience for Serena, for her smiles usually worked wonders.

"We shall dispense with the pleasantries, if you please," Jordan Kerr said in an intimidating voice. "Also with the fancy name you've bestowed upon yourself." He shot her a look of disdain. "I suppose you found it in one of the society magazines?"

Without giving Serena a chance to answer, he continued, "I shall address you by your real name. Under the circumstances, I hardly feel the name Serena is suitable." He leaned forward towards her, his long sensitive fingers spread out on the desk top. "So— Miss Tonetti, we meet at last!"

Serena did not like the look in his eyes as he said this and lowered hers to concentrate on those hands. Strong hands, she thought absently.

"I must say you're running true to form," his voice held disgust. "I rather expected you to turn up around now. I hope you note," he said silkily, "that I have not asked you why you're here. I know why. In fact, Miss Tonetti, there isn't much I don't know about you, so I'm afraid for once you're going to find those smiles of yours are wasted. How did you find out about your grandmother?" he suddenly shot out at her, and again giving Serena no chance to answer he carried on, "With someone like you there would be ways and means, wouldn't there? I see you've managed to ingratiate yourself with the right people. Running quite high, aren't you?"

His glance flicked over her dress and Serena knew he had correctly priced it. She was getting a little tired of this one-sided conversation and decided it was time she made some contribution, if only to get things straight. "There's something you ought to know," she said quickly. "My name really is Serena Belmont. I . . . ." She cast him a look of bewilderment. "I simply have no idea what you're talking about." She frowned, then added hesitantly, "Whatever it is, it appears to be of a personal nature concerning Mrs Tonetti, and I find myself in an embarrassing position." Her lovely eyes were wide as she met the enigmatic eyes of Jordan Kerr. She sighed. "I apologise for the deception, but I do assure you that Mrs Tonetti approached me a few days ago and asked me to—" Here she faltered. What could she say? That she had agreed to act out a figment of an old lady's imagination?—only it wasn't imagination, the granddaughter did exist—not only did she exist, but she had apparently made a formidable enemy of the man now seated opposite her.

Serena swallowed; no matter how mad it sounded she had to tell the truth. She began again. "When Mrs Tonetti asked me to pretend to be her granddaughter I had no idea that a granddaughter existed—In fact, I was led to believe that she was alone in the world. It seemed harmless at the time," she commented. "However, it appears to have backfired."

Jordan Kerr leaned back in his chair and studied her with hooded eyes. Serena had a nasty feeling he hadn't believed a word of her story, and she was right; his next words proved it.

"I understand you were leaving on Saturday," he said offhandedly, completely disregarding her explanation.

Serena wondered what he meant by "were". She met his gaze levelly. "I leave for New York on Saturday," she confirmed hoping the information would please him. There was no doubt that Miss Tonetti was not welcome on his island.

"I said, 'were', Miss Tonetti, and I meant exactly that," he said harshly.

Serena stared at him and meeting his haughty glance felt a stab of temper. Who did he think he was, anyway? She had told him the truth and he wasn't even going to give her the chance of proving her identity.

Her lovely eyes flashed shoots of violet blue as her temper rose. She wasn't going to take any more from this man. She stood up, her slim shoulders straight, and angrily brushed away a stray tendril of hair that clung to her cheek. "And I said I was leaving on Saturday," she said coldly. "Furthermore, I see no point in continuing with this conversation. I am not used to being called a liar," she added haughtily as she swung round towards the door. She did not wait for his answer and with her head held high walked to the door and attempted to open it, but it remained closed; it was locked!

She turned furiously to face the man calmly watching her. "Unlock this door at once! Do you hear?" she commanded. "Or I'll scream the place down!"

To Serena's further fury she saw him smile, and it wasn't a pleasant smile, nor was the look in his eyes. She felt the first pangs of fear. He was mad! He must be!

"I must congratulate you on a fine performance," he drawled. "By all means scream if you want to. The room is soundproofed—however, I don't advise you to try. I'm in no mood for hysterics and I don't think you'd care for the remedial treatment. Now stop this play-acting and come and sit down." He glanced at his hands now lightly drumming the desk top. "I realise all this must have come as a shock to you; you hardly expected anyone to know your past indiscretions, did you, let alone force you to make some amendment."

Serena's eyes opened yet wider. What had she walked into? And what exactly did he mean by "amendment"? She made herself remain calm, although she wanted to scream at him that she knew nothing and it was all a ghastly mistake.

"Sit down," he ordered. "This is going to be a long session. You leave when we come to an understanding, and not before. The sooner you realise you're no longer dealing with a frail, sick woman," again his voice held disgust, "your grandmother, no less," he thundered as his fist hit the desk top making Serena jump. "Did you ever give her one thought in those five years?" he ground out. "Did you know what you did when you stole those bonds?"

Serena went pale—she was shocked, and it shone out of her eyes.

Seeing her stunned reaction, Jordan Kerr nodded grimly. "Oh, yes, I know it all—every sordid little detail, and I only wish I'd known at the time; it would have been a different story if I had. You wouldn't have got far, even with Beroni's help." He shrugged. "As it was, I didn't hear about it until six months afterwards. Your grandfather tried to cover up for you. He was forced to sell everything he had to pay back those bonds."

Serena's shocked eyes watched his long slender
fingers curl into a ball and saw the knuckles whiten.
He was silent for a moment or so, then went on
harshly, "I don't suppose he would have told me
then, but he had to throw himself on my charity.
Two of those bonds had been mine and he couldn't
raise the money in time to redeem them." His jaw
hardened. "As if I cared a damn about the money!
Antonio was my friend; the money meant nothing to
me. I eventually got the story out of him, but by that
time he was a very sick man. Worry and the effort to
raise that amount at such short notice had taken its
toll."

Serena was numb; her legs felt weak; she had to sit
down now. All too clearly did she see what Jordan
Kerr was leading up to. She moved slowly towards
the chair and sat down wearily on it.

Giving her a contemptuous look, he continued.
"Not a pretty story, is it?" he sneered. "And I'm going to tell you something else, just to show you that
it's no use your pleading youth and ignorance; I took
it upon myself to bring you back—I wasn't too sure
that you weren't just a headstrong girl swayed by the
smooth wooing of Beroni; for that's what your
grandfather had convinced himself was the case. He
said that if he'd known of the association he would
have put a stop to it—but you were both very dis-
creet, weren't you? He only called when your grandparents were otherwise engaged." He stared at her,
his grey-green eyes blazing for a moment. "I suppose he found it hard to believe that an eighteen-

year-old girl was capable of robbing her own kith and kin, especially as they had given you a home when your parents died."

Apart from a sense of shock, Serena was horribly embarrassed; this was none of her business. She wished she could make him stop, but she knew she couldn't, and she felt sick.

The voice ground on, "But I found different, didn't I? Beroni was a babe in arms compared to you! After following your somewhat unsavoury trail from hotel to hotel, and finally the not so flash boarding houses, I couldn't stomach any more. I had meant to restore you," his voice grew harder, "back to the bosom of your family, as it were. It would have been some consolation to a broken man who I knew hadn't much time left. However, I came to the conclusion that they were better off without you. You were a tramp!"

Serena's startled eyes flew to his and his lips thinned as he met that look. "I make no apology. You might as well know where you stand right now. I know what you are; those wide-eyed looks are lost on me. Having met you at last, I do however now re-alise how you've managed to survive. With your looks you'd have no trouble in arousing sympathy from the male species. You weren't fussy, after all, were you? I found out you'd dropped Beroni soon after you'd landed in England. He'd served his purpose, hadn't he? And you probably felt you could do better for yourself."

He nodded towards her dress. "And you did,

didn't you? But you couldn't resist seeing whether there were any pickings left this end, could you? And that's where you made your first mistake. As I said, I'd been expecting you, although I found it hard to believe you'd have the gall to attempt a reconciliation with your grandmother. Seems I underestimated you—you had the gall, all right!"

Feeling as if she were in the middle of a nightmare, Serena said faintly, "Please stop. You're making a dreadful mistake. I'm not Lisa Tonetti—I know you don't believe me, but please speak to Mrs Tonetti, she'll tell you the truth when she knows what's happened."

His fist hit the desk again. "Do you want another death on your conscience?" he all but shouted at her. "And don't say you don't know what I'm talking about. You wouldn't have dared come back if she'd known what you'd done. You knew very well your grandfather would have kept quiet about it— he was very fond of you, wasn't he? He made some story up about a slump in stocks—and even if you weren't sure, those notices in the agony columns inserted in all leading papers for months after the death of your grandfather asking you to contact your grandmother would have given you the answer. Oh, yes, you gauged things just right, and I'm warning you, you breathe one word of our conversation to her and I'll have you arrested within hours. Some of those bonds were mine, remember? If you cause your grandmother one moment's further unhappiness, I shall take great pleasure in doing just that."

Serena's muddled senses tried to sort out the implication of these words, but failed utterly. She had had enough; she couldn't begin to make sense of anything—not now.

"So," he went on in that toneless voice, "you will stay. Do you understand? Your grandmother's living on borrowed time anyway. For what time she has left, you'll make her happy, do you hear? You'll be a sweet, considerate granddaughter until the end of her days. She deserves that much from you. You'll cancel that New York booking—or rather I'll cancel it. Don't try to leave or you'll be sorry. I've many business acquaintances in New York and in most other capitals, so your escape will be shortlived, I assure you. I'm a wealthy man and there are ways and means, as I'm sure you know, of getting information, and I'll not hesitate to use any method at my disposal to track you down."

CHAPTER FIVE

SERENA did not remember the journey back that night; she only knew she was grateful that Mrs Tonetti had gone to bed and she need not face her until the following morning, by which time she hoped she would have gained some measure of composure.

Thankfully closing her bedroom door after refusing Molly's kind offer of a hot drink, Serena leaned weakly against it for support. She still couldn't believe that that traumatic interview had actually taken place. "I'm dreaming it," she whispered in the silence of the empty room, and shook her head bewilderedly. It simply couldn't be true—any of it. Jordan Kerr looked sane, but he obviously was not. For some reason he had taken a dislike to her and had thought up some ridiculous story to frighten her with. Her lips straightened; she was not so easily frightened. Her palpitating heart told her otherwise and she swallowed hastily, then took a deep breath.

It was all very well trying to convince herself Jordan Kerr was mad when she knew very well he was not; he was horribly, coldly sane. Her brow creased; but if he was sane why had he made such outrageous accusations against someone he had admitted he had never met? Her fingers curled into a ball. A tramp, he'd called her. She bit her lip—no, not her; Lisa Tonetti.

With legs that felt like rubber she walked over to the dressing table and with fingers that shook took out the small snap she had found earlier that evening in the drawer. For a while she stared at it, then with an impatient shrug put it back again. It was just a photograph of a girl. It couldn't tell her anything apart from the fact that the girl could have been herself, but wasn't.

Sinking wearily into a chair, Serena was forced to admit to herself that she was in a predicament and the sooner she pulled herself together and brought some cold logic into the situation, the sooner a sensible answer would present itself. Her lips twisted wryly when she thought of how she had felt that very morning; how she had wanted to do just what Jordan Kerr had ordered her to do—stay on the island. She frowned; she had wanted an excuse to cut herself free from Roger's determined attentions, but not this way. Her frown deepened; in any other circumstances she would have entered into the spirit of the thing, but even if she had wanted to see it through, it wouldn't work; Roger would see to that.

Her eyes narrowed. Jordan Kerr didn't know about Roger. Serena almost smiled; she only hoped to be present when the confrontation took place. It would give her some consolation to see the autocratic Jordan Kerr stopped dead in his tracks. She tried to imagine him actually apologising to her, but failed to bring the scene to life. He would be more likely to give her a lecture on her stupidity of agreeing to pose as Lisa Tonetti.

The name brought back the ordeal she had recently gone through and with it an uncomfortable feeling that things weren't going to be that straightforward. For instance, she mused; just how ill was Mrs Tonetti? Serena recalled the short walk to the hotel and her breathlessness, and she had admitted that she had to rest a lot. At this point she remembered Jordan Kerr's remark, "She's living on borrowed time," and his harsh, "Do you want another death on your conscience?" Serena shivered as the truth hit her; heart trouble—it all fitted—in other words a shock could and probably would, kill Mrs Tonetti!

An extremely miserable and apprehensive Serena prepared for bed. Cold logic had only served to emphasize the explosive position she had unwittingly landed herself in. Somehow she had to find a solution to the problem and she devoutly hoped the morning's clear light would provide one.

SERENA AWOKE to the call of birds and lay for a moment or so listening to their shrill cries; she drowsily watched the patterns of sunlight filter through the sunblinds and play on the deep blue carpet, until Molly tapping on the door and entering with her usual cheery smile and her morning tea broke her spell of contentment.

As she sat up to accept the tea it was as much as

she could do to return the smile and try to match Molly's happy observations on the day's forthcoming events.

Listening to her gay chatter while she put her evening dress on a hanger and hung it in the wardrobe, Serena felt a pang of guilt. She ought to have done that herself and not left it to Molly to clear up after her, no matter how weary she had been. She apologised and said she had been rather tired.

Molly received the apology with some surprise, then grinned at Serena. "My pleasure, Miss Serena," she said shyly, adding as she left the room, "Missus happy now. Okay, now you come."

This gentle observation did nothing to lighten Serena's depression; if anything it only underlined her tenuous position.

While she dressed, Serena rehearsed in her mind what she would tell Mrs Tonetti when she inquired how the rest of the evening had gone. She would particularly want to know how much time Jordan Kerr had spent with her. Serena's fingers stilled in the act of zipping up her dress. How much was it safe to tell her? She was certain that their absence would not have gone unnoticed, particularly by Mrs Simpson, not to mention her granddaughter, Myrna. Her fingers went cold; supposing Jordan had told Myrna the whole miserable story? He would have to have given her some explanation for deserting her and devoting the rest of the evening to a complete stranger. And if Myrna knew... She closed her eyes; how long before Mrs Simpson got hold of the story? Serena swallowed: it didn't bear thinking about!

When she was ready she made her way to the patio, grateful that she would have at least another hour before her hostess put in an appearance. Perhaps by then the solution that had so far deserted her would come to mind.

On reaching the patio, however, she saw with dismay that Mrs Tonetti had risen early and was waiting to take breakfast with her. In spite of her feelings, Serena managed to answer her bright smile of welcome and sat down wondering how she was going to manage to swallow a cup of coffee, let alone partake of any food with her stomach feeling as if it had twisted itself into a knot.

After making solicitous inquiries as to how she had slept, and how she was sure Serena had enjoyed the rest of the evening, Mrs Tonetti lapsed into silence.

Serena was slightly astounded, and far from being grateful for her hostess's lack of interest in the past evening's events, found her preoccupied manner more worrying than the questions she had surmised she would be asked.

Even Serena's lack of appetite went unnoticed, and she was a little grateful for this; above all, she had to act naturally and normally her appetite was a healthy one.

Only after Molly had cleared the table and left a fresh pot of coffee for them did Mrs Tonetti attempt to raise herself out of her reverie long enough to inquire whether Serena would like another cup.

Serena shook her head and sat back watching Mrs

Tonetti; instinct told her to hold her tongue and not, as her by now ragged nerves were prompting her to do, cry out that it was all right, she knew the whole story and she wasn't to worry about it.

"If only," sighed Mrs Tonetti, "Lisa had been more like you!"

Serena held her breath and felt her pulse quicken. Now it was out! How much did Mrs Tonetti know? Had she guessed the truth? She met her sad eyes half-warily, desperately trying to keep the anxiety out of her own.

"I'm afraid I lied to you, dear," Mrs Tonetti said quietly. "You've been so sweet and understanding." She twitched her finely woven shawl closer to her as if she felt the cold, yet it was a warm morning. Straightening her back, she gave Serena a pleading look. "I want to tell you about her," she said firmly, "and ask you to forgive me—although," she said softly, "I'm sure you'll know I didn't really mean to deceive you." She hesitated. "It's only that if you'd known Lisa really did exist, you wouldn't have agreed to help me. You wouldn't have understood, you see, that there's no likelihood of her ever coming back."

A stab of apprehension flowed through Serena; she was now certain Mrs Tonetti knew the whole miserable story. "Please," she said quickly, "it doesn't matter, you know. Whatever it is, I'm sure it's very personal, and," she added a little desperately, "I am enjoying myself. I wanted an excuse to stay here, remember? and honestly I'm very grateful to you."

Mrs Tonetti continued to gaze at her with those sad eyes of hers and with a sinking heart Serena knew she had failed to divert her from the subject.

The old lady patted Serena's arm and smiled. "And I want you to go on enjoying yourself," she said gently. "However, I want to tell you about Lisa—you see, there hasn't been anyone I could talk to about her. It isn't easy, you know, explaining why your only grandchild doesn't come to see you."

She was silent for a moment or so and her gaze left Serena and centred on the panoramic view before them, but Serena knew she was not seeing the view. Miserably she knew that short of a sudden earthquake, there was nothing she could do to prevent Mrs Tonetti reliving the unhappy past.

"I'd better go back to the start," Mrs Tonetti began wearily. "That way you'll understand how things were. Antonio and I had only one child, a son." She broke off again as if assembling her thoughts and Serena longed to interrupt and tell her it didn't matter, she didn't want to know, but she couldn't; it would only upset Mrs Tonetti and might make things worse.

"I'm afraid Antonio and Michele hadn't a lot in common," she continued sadly. "In a way, I don't suppose I helped matters by spoiling Michele. I used to think Antonio was too hard on the boy and I tried to make up for it," she sighed. "Antonio always intended that Michele should follow him in the family business. He was an accountant, you know, and a very successful one, only—" she hesitated "—he made a bad investment just before we retired, and things weren't easy."

Inwardly Serena breathed a sigh of relief. She wasn't going to hear about Lisa's treachery. It looked as if Jordan Kerr had been right and she did not know the true facts.

"But this, of course, was a long time afterwards," went on Mrs Tonetti, sounding impatient with herself for her slight deviation. "As I said, Michele and his father were always at loggerheads, and after one particularly sharp disagreement Michele slammed out of the house." There was another tiny silence, then Mrs Tonetti swallowed quickly and continued, "We didn't hear from him until three years later. He told us he was married and wanted to patch things up; I was delighted, of course; I even had hopes of him agreeing to settle down and take his exams. He was only twenty-one, you know, and had passed his prelims before the flare-up with his father."

She fingered her shawl agitatedly and Serena wished she could hurry her through this painful period of her life.

"But it didn't work out," she said quietly. "He did come back and he brought his wife with him. It didn't help matters when we found the girl was well advanced in pregnancy." She smiled apologetically at Serena. "I do apologise, dear, but you must see how things were, or you wouldn't understand—you see, Antonio had a strict upbringing—good Italian families have, you know, and it was quite obvious that Michele had had to marry the girl." Her hand twitched her shawl again. "I don't think I'd ever seen Antonio so furious." She sighed. "Even then, I do believe things would have worked out if Michele had really wanted to settle down and join his father in the firm—or at least, have had a try at it—but all he wanted was money; and I must confess neither Antonio nor I cared much for the girl he had married. It soon became very obvious that they were not in love and the girl had married him in the expectation of a wealthy future. At that time, you see, we were quite well off.

"So we come to Lisa." She looked at Serena. "It's hard to believe that two girls could look so alike, yet be so very different—you're all I wanted her to be." She nodded gently. "You are like her in looks, Serena. I did tell the truth when I told you that, apart from your eyes. Lisa's were dark blue, not that lovely violet colour of yours." She sighed. "And she was harder than you are, even when she was seventeen I saw that. That was how old she was when we first saw her, you know. She just turned up and told us who she was. We didn't even know whether Michele's child had been a boy or girl, for after Antonio had given him the money he wanted, he told him there wouldn't be any more payments like that. Either he came back and joined the firm, or got himself a steady job of some kind—whichever it was, he'd have to earn the next amount." The hand clutching the shawl tightened, showing the almost transparent veins on her thin hands. "We never heard from him again," she swallowed. "Lisa told us her father had died when she was fifteen." Her voice had a weary bitterness in it. "Her mother apparently, didn't bother to inform us."

Serena interrupted quickly, hoping to get Mrs Tonetti's thoughts away from that memory. "And Lisa's mother?" she asked.

Mrs Tonetti nodded. "That's why Lisa came to find us. Her mother had told her that if anything happened to her, she was to come to us." Her eyes moistened. "I really thought that at last. . . ." she closed her eyes. "We did everything to make her happy, spoilt her shamelessly—you see, in our way we tried to make up for the past. There were faults on both sides, and there had been too much bitterness." Her smile was bitter-sweet. "Antonio spoilt her even more than I did," her voice faltered. "But it didn't work. I'm afraid she became infatuated with a married man." She made a small moue of distaste. "Not a very nice man, either."

Again there was a small silence and Serena hoped she had come to the end of her narrative, but there was more.

"Everything seemed to happen at once," Mrs Tonetti sighed. "Lisa running away with this man, then the bad news about our finances. Antonio wasn't a young man, and he ought to have retired a year before, but there was no one to carry on the firm, you see, and he was reluctant to sell the practice. He never really got over it, it wasn't only the financial worry. I think he blamed himself for not keeping a stricter eye on Lisa's activities; he'd grown extremely fond of her during that year she was with us."

Knowing the real cause of Mr Tonetti's unhappiness, Serena wondered how anyone could be callous enough to do what Lisa Tonetti had done.

The thin tired voice went on, "I tried to find her, you know, after Antonio's death. I advertised for months, not only in Italy, but in England too. All to no avail; in the end I was forced to come to the conclusion that we meant nothing to her. It's been five years, and I've not even had a postcard from her. If it hadn't been for a friend of ours who actually saw her in London three years ago, I might have wondered whether she'd met with some accident."

"Perhaps—" began Serena gently, meaning to point out that she had been mistaken for Lisa herself and that it hadn't been Lisa but someone else.

Mrs Tonetti forestalled her with a sad smile. "Oh, yes, dear, it was Lisa. Mrs Carstairs saw her quite plainly and actually called out to her, she was only across the street from her. She told me Lisa had looked up quickly to see who was calling her and then deliberately walked away in the opposite direction."

Serena was effectively silenced until another thought struck her. Surely, if Lisa Tonetti were as avaricious as Jordan Kerr had intimated, wouldn't she have tried to make a comeback when the money ran out? She didn't know how much was involved, a goodly amount if she had managed to survive for five years on it, she thought dryly, then she remembered something else. Jordan Kerr had said she had left Beroni as soon as they reached England. That meant whatever amount was involved would have to be split two ways. He had also said something about following her trail from the good class hotels to the not so good boarding houses, so unless Lisa was reserving her resources, it didn't make sense. She frowned, then asked suddenly, "Does Lisa know where you are now, do you think?"

Again she received that sad smile from Mrs Tonetti. "Yes, dear," she said gently. "It was often discussed that we would come here for our retirement years. We used to spend our vacations here every year, but when Lisa was with us we decided to go to Paris instead, she was so keen to go there, and there isn't really much in the way of entertainment for young people here, you know. Jordan doesn't cater for tourism, he doesn't encourage it nor discourage it, but if they come here in the hopes of 'living it up' then I'm afraid they're soon disappointed. There are no gambling casinos here, or cinemas. The only concession Jordan's made in that line is in nightclubs, and really they're more in the nature of a late-night restaurant, no floor shows, as it were."

Her question answered, Serena saw a chance to steer the conversation away from the unhappy past to the present, and she quickly asked about the Centenary. "It's more than a hundred years, of course, isn't it?" she queried. "Since the landing, I mean."

To her relief, her tactics worked. Mrs Tonetti frowned in concentration for a moment. "I think it's

the fourth, dear. I believe it took place in the sixteenth century." She glanced at her wrist watch.
"Good gracious, is that the time? Thank goodness
you reminded me. We must get ready at once. Jordan's sending a car to collect us and it will be here in
fifteen minutes."

Before she entered her bedroom, Mrs Tonetti reminded Serena to take a hat of some kind. "It gets
quite hot, and we shall be standing about on the
beach for quite a while."

CHAPTER SIX

SERENA changed into a turquoise linen trouser suit with a sleeveless tunic and lime green organdie long-sleeved blouse, that would let whatever breeze there was to be had filter through to her.

Her one and only hat was a wide-brimmed white straw she had bought specifically for the cruise. Unlike her mother, Serena did not care for hats and only wore them under protest, but she knew from past experience that unless she could produce one she would be prevailed upon to wear one of her mother's. To Mrs Belmont, hats were a vital part of her ensemble, and Serena had once heard her declare that she felt undressed without one! Of course, there were hats, and hats; her mother's always seemed to consist of a concoction of frippery dreamed up by a designer with surrealistic tendencies!

As she placed the hat on her head, Serena's thoughts went from her mother to Roger and his reaction to the news that she would not be joining them for the cruise. Meeting her reflection in the mirror she paled; he would be simply furious! Serena had an idea of what he had planned for the culmina-

tion of the cruise—an engagement ring on her
finger! She was also sure he had already bought the
ring, ready to slip it on her third finger when he had
worn her down.

Her even white teeth caught her bottom lip; she
couldn't see Roger leaving it at that. He would
come, she knew he would. It wouldn't be too difficult for him to find out where she was staying. In her
mind's eye she saw him arriving at the chalet demanding to know the reason why she had cancelled
the cruise. She sighed; even the enterprising Mrs Tonetti would be hard put to it to think up a plausible
excuse at such short notice. Of course, thought Serena, she could warn her, but that wouldn't get them
anywhere either. She could hardly see him condon-
ing her well-meaning, but as it had turned out, foolish duplicity. Neither could Serena see him agreeing
to respect the confidential news about Mrs Tonetti's
state of health, particularly when he heard about
Jordan Kerr!

Depression settled on her like a cloud; the meeting between Roger and Jordan Kerr which she had
envisaged with so much pleasure the previous evening now loomed on the horizon as Mrs Tonetti's
death knell—Serena shivered. There was nothing
for it but for her to leave on Saturday. Somehow she
must make Jordan Kerr see that. If he really wanted
to protect Mrs Tonetti he had to be made to see it.

The car drew up just as Serena joined Mrs Tonetti
in the lounge. Mrs Tonetti had also changed and
wore a heavy silk navy blue suit with matching straw

hat. Smiling at Serena, she commented, "You're going to enjoy this, Serena. Now come along, or we'll miss the landing."

Following her out of the chalet, Serena thought it all depended on whether she could make a certain individual see sense; if not, Mrs Tonetti's confident prediction would go sadly astray.

She was jerked out of her miserable musings by the awesome sight of a piratical-looking character waiting to convey them to the beach.

Mrs Tonetti chuckled and asked, "It is you, Jake, isn't it? I suppose if you're taking part in the landing we ought not to keep you waiting."

Jake grinned and opened the car doors for them. "Plenty of time, Mrs Tonetti," he assured her as he seated her in the front seat, then assisted Serena into the back.

Having only seen Jake in the half-light the previous evening, Serena was now able to take in his features. As she had guessed, he was Polynesian, with the warm honey-coloured skin of that race. Her eyes travelled from his smiling face to his apparel, firstly to the bandanna tied tightly round his forehead giving him a slightly villainish look, then moving on to his clothes. His open-throated white blouse-like shirt had full sleeves, and his black breeches were adorned with a brass studded belt. Black plimsoll-type shoes completed the outfit. With a slight start, Serena realised she was looking at what must be an almost identical copy of the clothes worn by the seafarers of old, and her gaze centred on the studded belt with its ominous small hooks at each end to hold no doubt the swinging cutlass and lethal dagger. In spite of the heat, she shivered. It was beyond her comprehension that those times should be recalled, let alone celebrated!

It was only a short ride to the beach and when they arrived, instead of following the track down to the beach itself, Jake swung the car on to the slightly elevated ground running parallel to the beach track. For a second, Serena wondered why as they seemed to be heading away from the main sightseeing area, then as they rounded a bend and joined several other cars pulled up a little in front of them, she saw the reason for the diverted course. The whole sweep of the beautiful bay was before them. Not very far below them lay the beach, now crowded to capacity with what Serena presumed to be the entire population of the island, but on catching sight of several people sporting expensive-looking cameras making their way determinedly to the front of the crowd, she amended that last thought to include tourists.

Alighting from the car, they made their way towards a row of seating, and Serena, holding Mrs Tonetti's arm to make certain her step was firm on the uneven ground, saw with a start of dismay that among the occupants already seated were Mrs Simpson and Myrna. All her earlier fears crowded in on her; she ought to have known they would be present, but she had somehow imagined a crowd of people among which it would be possible to keep one's distance. Serena had a horrible feeling that nothing—

but nothing—was going to go right for her, and she didn't know why she bothered. She might as well give in gracefully and accept whatever fate had been combining to throw at her.

To take her mind off these disturbing thoughts she concentrated on the two figures in front that had prompted her near-hysterical line of reasoning. Myrna, she noticed, also wore a trouser suit; its well-cut navy blue jacket emphasized her slim shoulders. A small flap at the back of the collar with white piping gave it definite naval undertones and the pert navy blue boater that rested on her fair head completed the illusion. Serena's thoughts went back to the previous evening and her brief introduction to her after that nerve-shattering interview in Jordan Kerr's study when they had met her on the way out of the study. She had come to find out what was keeping him so long. Serena had been in no state for polite conversation—not, she thought, that Myrna would have welcomed it. The hand held out after the introduction had been as cold as the look in her light blue eyes.

As they reached the seating Serena gave a thankful sigh that the seats on either side of the Simpsons had just been taken, and she prayed that Mrs Tonetti would choose the seats at the end of the line, thus forestalling any chance of further skirmishing on the two elderly ladies' part.

As if Serena had willed it, Mrs Tonetti did choose the end seating, and after the greetings from the other residents and a cool nod from both the Simpsons, they settled down to watch the proceedings.

Gazing out at the blue expanse of the bay, Serena sent up a little "thank you" for this first obstacle cleared. Her eyes, resting on a small clump of palms that seemed to form a natural barrier of shelter for the small bay, softened for a moment. It was so beautiful; white foam gently lapped the shore and was almost soporific in its action; Serena felt she wanted nothing more than to be allowed to stay there forever, listening to the sea's eternal lullaby.

Serena's moment of tranquillity was soon over as a sudden movement on her right caught her attention and she glanced across in time to see the tall form of Jordan Kerr effortlessly vault up the slight incline that separated them from the beach.

As she watched him stride towards them she was thankful he had not elected to join the landing party; the very sight of him put her nerves on edge, and she hated to think what effect he would have had on her dressed in pirate's costume. After that first quick glance in his direction, Serena looked straight ahead of her and tried to concentrate on the view that had previously held her attention, but she could still see the man who had forced her into her present predicament. She knew exactly what he wore; the way the blue blazer sat on his wide shoulders and the blue shirt that was open at the neck, even to the dove grey tapered slacks.

Bestowing a lazy bronzed smile on Mrs Tonetti, he asked as he joined them, "What do you think of the good news?"

Serena cast a wary look towards him, then looked

at Mrs Tonetti, who was frankly puzzled, her brows raised in query as she glanced from Serena back to Jordan again.

Feeling the quick warning look Jordan Kerr gave her, Serena's heart sank; he was taking no chances of her backing out.

"I've persuaded your granddaughter to lengthen her stay, haven't I, Serena?" he said smoothly, meeting Serena's smouldering eyes with a glint in his.

Very clever, thought Serena, only he wasn't going to get away with it. Refusing to meet his eyes, she murmured, "Well, let's say I'm considering it. Nothing," she said firmly but with a stab of regret as she watched the hope in Mrs Tonetti's eyes slowly fade away, "has been settled. And," she added brightly, "there'll be other times, won't there, Nan?" she appealed.

The strident voice of Mrs Simpson cut across whatever remark Jordan Kerr would have made in reply to Serena's defiant stand.

"Aren't we running a bit late, Jordan?" she demanded, unable to keep the irritation out of her voice at his preoccupation with Mrs Tonetti and her granddaughter.

His slight frown of displeasure showed that he had not liked the interruption, but he answered casually enough, giving Myrna a quick smile and brief salute in greeting as he said, "It's all under control."

Serena's hopes that he would now move on were quickly dashed as she saw him glance at his watch, then turn his attention back to her. "I'll see you later," he said softly but meaningfully, and favoured Mrs Tonetti with another charming smile. "It seems," he drawled, "that she needs a little more persuading. But I think we'll eventually convince her, don't you?"

Mrs Tonetti chuckled. "Jordan, that sounded a little like a threat! Stop teasing her. Of course I want her to stay, but there are other considerations, you know—her job, for instance."

His eyes rested momentarily on Serena before he replied laconically, "Ah, yes, her job, of course."

There was a deep gong-like sound and Jordan Kerr glanced again at his watch. "Time I was moving," he said casually, and with a brief salute went back the way he had come.

As she watched him stride away Serena knew she hadn't as yet won the game; all she had accomplished was a brief stay of execution. That "see you later", threat would take place at the ball that evening, she was sure. Her lips tightened; it couldn't come quick enough for her; the sooner he learnt you couldn't just push people around like that, the better! She had never thought she would be grateful for Roger's attention, not to mention protection. In fact, the more she thought about the coming interview, the more she found she was looking forward to it. She had been so shocked by Jordan Kerr's disclosures thrown at her as it were out of the blue, she had temporarily lost her senses. Now she had regained them and even that autocratic chunk of masculinity would be forced to see the sense of her argument.

She relaxed and smiled at Mrs Tonetti, who had been holding a conversation with a friend of hers who had just arrived, and was now able to give Serena her undivided attention.

"I must say," she commented with twinkling eyes, "Jordan seems to have taken an interest in you, Serena. Perhaps we won't have to look far for an excuse for you to stay after all."

Serena's brows went up, feigning surprise; if only Mrs Tonetti knew just how near the mark she was! Only for entirely different reasons from the ones Serena guessed she was hoping for. "Well, he does take your welfare to heart, doesn't he?" she replied airily, deliberately misconstruing the subtle hint.

Mrs Tonetti chuckled again, then said softly, "Yes, he does, but I've an idea there's a little more to it this time."

Serena was saved the necessity of thinking up a suitable rejoinder as a shout went up from the crowd on the beach. "There she blows!"

Her breath caught in her throat as she looked ahead of her—there, just appearing from the screen of palms, was a full-masted galleon. It moved slowly but majestically into the bay—an awesome, yet wonderful sight. Serena sat entranced; she felt as if the years had rolled back. This, then, was how the first Kerr had come to the island to claim it for himself and his descendants. She wondered how the inhabitants had felt when they sighted the great ship.

Her eyes fixed on the flag now plainly visible and a cold feeling played along her spine as she saw its markings. It was black with crossed swords worked in gold and somehow more daunting than the skull and crossbones motif.

The cold eyes and harsh voice of Jordan Kerr came unbidden to her as she watched the long boats being lowered slowly down the sides of the ship. Mrs Tonetti had said he was the image of the first Jordan Kerr, and Serena could well believe it! And not only in looks, she thought; this man would be just as ruthless in obtaining his objective, as she had good cause to know!

Making a mental effort to shrug off these thoughts, Serena asked Mrs Tonetti about the galleon. "Is it the original one?" she queried.

"Yes, dear. Of course, it's had to be renovated from time to time, timbers replaced and so on, but it's been faithfully reproduced each time. It's kept in the blue lagoon, beyond the palms over there. There are some natural caves that provide an ideal shelter for it. It's quite an attraction for the tourists on its own."

The first of the long boats was just heading into the beach, and Serena watched as its piratical occupants leapt out on to the shore uttering blood-curdling shouts and waving wicked-looking cutlasses. By the way the crowd scattered, accompanied by the shrieks from the ladies, one would almost think it was for real, Serena mused as she watched, then suddenly she stiffened. The leader of the first boat

ashore was none other than Jordan Kerr; there was
no mistaking his height and the way he carried himself. His hair touched by the rays of the sun was a
fiery red and as she watched him he suddenly lifted
his head and she felt as if he were looking straight at
her.

Trying to still her racing pulses, she told herself
she was imagining things again. Myrna was up there,
wasn't she?

The shouting on the beach had now turned to
laughter and squeals of mock terror, and Serena
turned her attention there and half-smiled when she
saw the reason. The pirates were capturing the girls
of their choice, slinging them over their shoulders
and making their way back to the boats. So that was
why Jordan Kerr had been looking up there—he
was warning Myrna!

When the awesome figure of the pirate captain
hove into view, Serena felt no qualms but only wondered whether Myrna would put up a mild struggle
or charmingly surrender.

As it turned out, Myrna had no choice, nor had
Serena! Her eyes opened to full capacity as he stood
before her and with a slight ironic bow said quite distinctly, "My prize, I think."

Before she could move Serena found herself flung
over his shoulder and being borne off back down the
incline to the beach. His hold was not gentle
either—he might have been carrying a sack of potatoes, she thought furiously as she struggled to free
herself. Her hat parted company from her as he

landed on the beach. "Put me down!" she hissed angrily. "I've lost my hat and it's the only one I've
got!"

It was as if he hadn't heard her, yet Serena was
sure he had. "Do you hear?" she demanded, making
another frantic attempt to dislodge herself from his
hold.

"I hear," he said in a clipped tone. "Someone will
collect your hat. That's the least of your worries
right now. You and I are going to have a little talk."

"So we talk," snapped Serena, vainly trying to
keep her hair out of her eyes, but held as she was
hanging over his shoulder it was no easy task. "For
your information, I'm not a yoga addict," she added
icily. "Put me down, will you?"

"And worry Mrs Tonetti?" he said sarcastically.
"Oh, no; this is the way it's got to be done. Take it
or leave it."

Making a grab at her shoulder bag which was
threatening to join the hat, she thought bitterly, as if
she had any choice!

Serena's uncomfortable journey was over when
they reached the boats and she was unceremoniously
dumped in the nearest one. As she sat trying to get
her breath back she looked up and met the amused
eyes of a vaguely familiar pirate and when he spoke
she placed him; it was Gerald. "Seems I wasn't quick
enough," he said in a low voice, glancing at Jordan
Kerr now busy organising the oarsmen for the return
journey to the ship.

Following his glance, Serena saw Myrna Simpson,

her pert straw still miraculously in position. Gerald, then, had "captured" Myrna, and from the sulky expression on her face, Serena presumed Myrna had not liked that one bit. As if she felt her gaze on her, Myrna looked straight at her and Serena almost held her breath. It was a look of pure dislike, and Serena was sure she knew the reason for Jordan Kerr's interest in her. He would, of course, have had to make her promise to keep the information to herself. Not an easy task, Serena thought, particularly when it made someone like Myrna take a back seat for probably the first time in her life.

At a sharp order from Jordan Kerr, Gerald was pulled into service, obeying the order with a wry grin at Serena.

As the boat slowly put out to sea, Serena, watching the oarsmen, found her eyes inescapably drawn to Jordan Kerr. He led the stroke and his powerful shoulders bent forward and backward with the dip of the oars. She noticed that unlike the rest of the men he wore a peacock blue bandanna, and although his dress was of the same period as Jake's and the rest of the men, that was as far as the resemblance went. His shirt was of fine linen with lace cuffs that fell in soft folds against the tan of those strong hands of his. Serena wondered if it could be the original worn by his predecessor, and was almost certain the sleeveless jerkin of black velvet with gold threaded stitching in intricate patterns was indeed as old as it looked.

She glanced up as they neared the ship, then

wished she hadn't as it loomed up in front of her like a gigantic whale. Surely they wouldn't be expected to scale that? But as they neared the side it became painfully obvious by the rope ladders hanging in wait that that was just what was expected of them. She glanced quickly at Myrna to find her watching Jordan with a possessive glint in her eye. She didn't, thought Serena, look a bit perturbed at the prospect of scaling what appeared to Serena as the side of a mountain! Her glance then fell on Myrna's shoes; sensible navy blue pumps. Myrna would know the drill, of course. Serena then looked at her own footwear, surveying the slim platform soles with dismay; there was nothing there to give her grip. Well, she didn't know what the point was in hauling the girls to the ship, and they would have to return the same way they came anyway, so she would stay right where she was, ready for the return journey.

Unfortunately for Serena, Jordan Kerr had his own ideas on what she would do and made no bones about it. He was the first on the rope ladder and indicated briefly that she should follow. Serena stared at him, then at the swaying ladder, and went pale. She was hopeless at heights; she gave a decisive shake of the head. "I'll wait for the return journey," she announced firmly.

"You'll only get wet if you fall," drawled Myrna behind her.

"My weight holds the ladder firm," said Jordan Kerr in the sort of voice that told Serena she was going up that ladder whether she liked it or not.

"I'm right behind you, Serena," Gerald offered encouragingly.

"I still think I'll stay," said Serena, making a last-ditch stand, and remembering her shoes held one foot slightly in the air. "I couldn't possibly get a grip in these, could I?" she appealed to Gerald, who she felt she could rely on to protect her interests.

Jordan Kerr's eyes narrowed and he gave her another ironic half bow. "You have been snatched by pirates, milady, and therefore have no choice."

About to argue the point, Serena for the second time that day found herself hauled up and over Jordan Kerr's shoulder. While marvelling at his strength for he had still kept one hand on the ladder, she rather felt things had gone far enough and kicked out in an attempt to dislodge his hold. She wasn't afraid of falling in the water; anything was preferable to this sort of treatment.

Myrna gave a derisive, "Really! I know we're supposed to be entertaining the visitors, but there's no need to overdo it. For goodness' sake, Jordan, if she's so scared, leave her. We'll not be staying long anyway."

Gerald heartily agreed with this sentiment. "It's the height, I expect, old boy. And she's not like the rest of the girls, they knew what was coming."

Neither need have spoken, for Jordan Kerr had started the ascent with a hold of iron against Serena's kicking legs and useless protests.

"I say," began Gerald indignantly, "aren't you carrying..."

"You look after your catch and I'll look after mine," Jordan Kerr interjected, adding smoothly, "All's fair in love and war."

Serena closed her eyes—and this was war, there was no doubt about it! Her face brushed the smooth velvet of his jacket and felt the slight roughness of the worked-in stitching. It was a lie, she thought hysterically, that first piratical character that took the island hadn't died at all! He was still here; just as ruthless as he had been all those years ago!

CHAPTER SEVEN

ONCE they were on deck Serena found herself put down with the same carelessness as she had been dumped in the boat. With an abrupt, "Follow me," Jordan Kerr went on ahead with Serena languidly following.

To ease her frustration at such treatment Serena worked out ways as to how she could make this ruthless character pay for her humiliation. An apology simply wouldn't be good enough, she thought. Not even if he went down on his knees! Almost tripping over a heavy rope, she decided she would sue him. He was a very rich man, wasn't he?—well, she wouldn't have to worry about her mother's expenditure in future; in fact she would encourage it! It would be Jordan Kerr's money they would be spending!

The uneven deck made her stumble suddenly and as her shoulder-bag swung open, scattering most of its contents on to the deck, she cast a look of fury at the tall form striding in front of her. As she stooped to pick them up, her fingers were just too late in reaching her passport. One large brown hand was there before her.

Giving Jordan Kerr a look of pure dislike, she held out her hand for her passport. "Thank you," she murmured coldly.

To her further fury he calmly ignored her outstretched hand and placed it in his jerkin pocket, then without a word walked on in front of her again.

Wanting to scream at him but knowing it wouldn't get her anywhere, Serena was forced to follow him. She almost stopped in her tracks as a thought hit her—her passport! Why, oh, why hadn't she thought of that before—you couldn't manufacture passports! Her name was on it—just let him argue that one away!

Precisely two minutes later that was exactly what he did do! Seated in what she presumed was the captain's quarters, Serena listened while her brainwave went up in smoke.

"I have to hand it to you," he drawled. "On anyone else, it might have worked. Unfortunately, I know a little too much about you. When I said I'd given up the search for you, it wasn't strictly true. I just passed the odious task on to a highly reputable detective agency. I know for a fact that you have two aliases, so why not a third? The sort of company you kept you'd know how to get your hand on a passport. That information is now paying off, isn't it?— but not to your advantage, I'm afraid."

Serena's glimpse into the wily ways of the underworld was something of a revelation to her. However, she felt she could have done without it at this particular time. She was now getting slightly desperate. "Look!" she began, forcing herself to remain calm, knowing it was imperative that she somehow got through to him. "Can't you see it would be better for me to go? I promise to write to Mrs Tonetti and keep in touch."

"You can't even call her Grandmother, can you?" he said harshly. "As for keeping in touch, I don't believe a word of it. Once back to the bright lights and you'll conveniently forget she exists." His eyes narrowed. "There's nothing for you to come back for, is there? There's nothing left for you to inherit, you really shouldn't have been quite so greedy before."

Serena's eyes flashed; she wanted to hit out at him, but knew he was having trouble keeping his hands off her and would dearly love an excuse to throttle her, so provoking him would not help. "All right!" she said bitterly. "I only wanted to explain the position—and believe it or not prevent Mrs Tonetti from . . ." she faltered a little on seeing the tigerish flash her constant use of the name produced, then went on firmly, knowing it was no use trying to convince him she wasn't Lisa Tonetti. "How will it look," she demanded, "when the man I'm practically engaged to charges in on the next plane? You won't be able to bully him, I can assure you; and Roger knows nothing about Mrs Tonetti," she paused, biting her lip. "For goodness' sake! Can't you see the result? How can I explain a grandmother he never knew existed—let alone explain that I've decided to stay with her? If you think Roger will leave it at that, you're very much mistaken. He won't rest until he knows the whole story, and that you're keeping me on the island by force. Just how are you going to explain that part of it to my—er—grandmother?"

Seeing the start he gave at her last question, Serena felt a surge of triumph. He couldn't argue against that—not if he wanted to protect Mrs Tonetti. She pressed on with her advantage. "Short of kidnapping Roger at the airport," she purred, "there's nothing you can do about it. Roger," she said sweetly, "will not take kindly to being pushed around. He also has business connections," she added airily, feeling as if a great weight had been lifted off her shoulders. "I'm quite sure he can match whatever influence you think you have in certain circles." She flashed him a smile of triumph. "So in the circumstances I think you'll agree it would be better if I went, don't you?"

Noticing the small muscle twitch at the side of Jordan Kerr's mouth, Serena felt like cheering. He was furious and she could feel the inward struggle he was having not to shake the daylights out of her. She had him cornered; not a position he was used to; she doubted whether such a thing had ever happened before to him. Her relief that it was all over made her magnanimous. "I meant what I said about keeping in touch with my—grandmother," she added kindly.

Completely ignoring her last remark, Jordan Kerr shot out, "Roger who?"

Serena almost grinned; he had chosen not to believe her again. A few inquiries would ascertain

Roger's existence and his standing in the business world, not to mention the fact that Serena Belmont was a person in her own right and not an alias.

"Roger Alton," she replied, her eyes squarely meeting the ice flecked ones carefully watching her.

His brows rose sardonically. "You do fly high, don't you?" he commented sarcastically. "I suppose the poor devil's well and truly hooked."

An indignant Serena felt a start of surprise that he had heard of Roger, and she chose to ignore his other comments. She would make an extra fuss of Roger, she thought, when she saw him on Saturday, and she even felt it possible to forgive his encouraging her mother. As for this domineering character . . . "I can't say it's been nice meeting you," she snapped as she got up to leave and held her hand out for her passport. "My passport, if you please."

"But I don't please," he said in a soft deadly voice. "You very nearly brought it off, didn't you? I'm going to take a leaf out of your book. You've had a change of heart, Miss Tonetti—we're engaged," he said, smiling unpleasantly at Serena's white face and wide eyes echoing the shock his words had produced.

He nodded grimly. "Yes, I would go that far to make you pay your debt to your grandmother. I'm not so easily discouraged as you'll soon find out. So your friend arrives breathing fire and brimstone—let him! There's not much he can do about it, is there? It's happening all the time, isn't it?" he said casually.

Somehow Serena found her voice. "You're mad!" she said huskily. "Roger will never believe a story like that." She shook her head as if to dispel the cotton wool feeling of unreality. "For goodness' sake," she said wearily, "if you haven't a better card to play than that, I should forget it—it won't work. Why not for once accept defeat? In spite of what you think I am not Lisa Tonetti and I do intend to leave on Saturday."

He leaned back in his chair and folding his arms across his powerful chest surveyed her through narrowed eyes. "Oh, but he will," he said silkily. "Especially when a few unpleasant facts come to light. I'm considered a good catch, you know, and can more than match him in the financial stakes."

Serena wondered whether it was her imagination or not, but the captain's quarters seemed to be getting smaller and the man sitting in front of her, larger. Her eyes flicked nervously towards him as he sat calmly watching her much as a cat watched a mouse it had trapped. She felt the cold feeling run down her spine and managed to suppress a shiver. He would enjoy watching her quake. With a mental effort she pulled herself together; that diabolical costume he wore hardly helped either, but she wasn't going to be intimidated by that.

"Why do you hate her so much?" she asked suddenly.

Jordan's face had a closed look about it as he answered coldly, "Hate? Oh, no; hate is an emotion, Miss Tonetti, and where you're concerned I have no emotions. A motive, yes; to make you pay for the misery you caused your grandparents." His eyes met hers inexorably. "So why don't you take your own advice and give in gracefully?" He grinned satanically. "I can well understand your refusal to acknowledge your name; it's a well known psychological fact that the mind rejects what it doesn't want to remember. I do realise how hard it must be for you particularly as it appears you've now turned—er—respectable." He gave her a glinting look. "Not only respectable," he went on smoothly, "but with a rosy future in front of you as the wife of a successful financier." He shook his head mockingly. "It couldn't have happened at a worse time, could it? Being found out, I mean. You have my deepest sympathy."

"Sympathy!" echoed Serena, almost choking over the word. "You don't know the meaning of the word!"

Unable to bear another minute in his presence, she got up quickly and turned towards the cabin door, but he was there before her, covering the distance between them in seconds. Serena could hardly credit that a man of his size could move so swiftly.

He held her arm in a painful grip. "Oh, no, you don't," he bit out. "Is this the way to behave with your beloved?" he jeered. "Remember, my sweet, it was love at first sight."

His eyes narrowed as he traced the delicate lines of her features. "A great pity," he murmured. "You look so innocent too. You really are one of the devil's angels, aren't you?"

Serena could feel the magnetism of the man who stood so close beside her. He was so tall he had to bend his head to avoid contact with the low oak rafters, bringing his face dangerously close to hers. Her eyes fell on the well-moulded lips and she wondered what his kiss was like, then blushed as she realised where these thoughts were leading her.

"So we can still blush, can we?" he said hatefully. "Or is it temper? Of course, it must be. You're way beyond the blushing stage, aren't you?"

Serena tried to break the compelling hold he had on her arm, but he only tightened his hold. She winced as the steel-like fingers bit into her arm. It appeared she had lost hands down, nothing she could say would convince Jordan Kerr he had made a mistake and yet she had to try. Roger was not a fool and not likely to be taken in by the ridiculous story of an engagement to someone she barely knew. She ignored his taunts and the temptation to slap that arrogant face; she was in enough trouble without asking for more. Managing to keep her voice calm, she said, "I still say you'll have to think again. An engagement after only two days is hardly feasible, is it?" She swallowed. "Roger mustn't come here," she added quickly. "You must see that."

This produced his grim smile again and his hand relaxed his hold on her arm. Serena quickly drew away from him. "Most perceptive of you," he sneered. "Only it's a little longer than two days, isn't it?" he went on silkily. "You arrived on Saturday, didn't you?" He acknowledged her start grimly.

"I've done a little checking, you see. Oh, you kept well away from the other guests, and it's not hard to guess why. There was no point in advertising your presence before you'd done a little research and found out if it was really worth your while to attempt a reconciliation. What had you in mind? A touch for the trousseau outlay? They had been very generous in the past, hadn't they?"

Serena's fingers clenched; she was finding it hard to believe that anyone could be as bad as Jordan Kerr was painting Lisa Tonetti. It appeared to be a fixation of his and his vehemence didn't really justify the cause. So he was protecting Mrs Tonetti because he was fond of her—or was there a little more to it? Serena was sure there was.

Jordan Kerr's smooth voice cut into her musings. "Going back to your Roger I find myself for once in agreement with you, for very different reasons, of course. Mine being the welfare of a very old friend; yours—self-preservation." His eyes narrowed. "You're very sure of him at the moment, aren't you? And I'm pretty certain you don't give a damn about the man himself; it's what he can give you that matters, isn't it?"

Serena flushed. He meant that she didn't love Roger, and she didn't, but she couldn't very well argue that one through.

Watching her reaction he nodded, grimly satisfied. "Very smart of you not to attempt to deny it. It seems you do give me credit for not being stupid enough to believe otherwise."

He was silent for a few seconds and Serena hoped that she had managed to persuade him to let her go. The door was so close, yet so far, she knew if she made a move towards it she would receive that painful hold again. He hadn't finished with her yet.

"I'll have the airport watched," he said abruptly. "If Alton comes, as I presume he will, we face him together."

"T—together...?" faltered Serena.

Jordan Kerr gave her a look of distaste. "Together," he confirmed. "We can hardly expect him to accept the story without your presence, can we?"

Serena felt as if she were in a fast-moving river and slowly going under. If Roger came, that would be that; she wasn't that good an actress and the whole charade would be exposed. She shook her head vehemently. "No!" she exclaimed. "It won't do."

Jordan Kerr studied her insolently. "It must," he sneered. "And don't work out any schemes for evading the issue, either. But then you're smart, aren't you? No doubt you've already worked out the penalty for failure. Not only will you lose the chance of a rich husband—if things work out for you, that is, but you'll find yourself on the wanted list. I shall immediately press charges against you. When it's over..." his face hardened and Serena knew he was referring to Mrs Tonetti's death, "you can patch things up with him always providing he hasn't found anyone else, he doesn't sound too fussy, at that. So you might consider you're getting off lightly when you stop to think about it. A few months of what you'll probably consider hard labour after the kind of life you've been leading, at the beck and call of your grandmother, and I'll be around often enough to see you keep to the bargain.

"Nothing more," he added disdainfully, "will be required of you, and don't start getting ideas of staying on and capitalizing on our association, will you? When the time comes I want you off my land. You'll be pushed on to the first plane to touch down. Alton's welcome to you."

CHAPTER EIGHT

FOR the rest of that day Jordan Kerr was Serena's constant companion. The only breathing space she was given came when she accompanied Mrs Tonetti back to the chalet to dress for the ball later that evening, and by that time the whole of the island must have been aware of Jordan Kerr's single-minded preference for Serena's company.

It was not easy for her to accept the role so unceremoniously thrown at her and on one or two occasions she was tersely directed to look as if she were enjoying herself, as he caustically pointed out in a low undertone, "There's no pot of gold on the end of this rainbow; but think of the penalty you'll incur if you fail."

Nor was it easy trying to meet Mrs Tonetti's twinkling eyes with an answering smile in hers, and it was taken for granted Serena would be staying longer than the original period. Apart from a knowing smile and an "I told you so" look, nothing was said.

Quite apart from the problem of Roger's appearance on the island, Serena had her mother to consider, and both as yet were unaware of the fact that she would not be on the Saturday flight. All chance of slipping away to catch the flight was now lost; Jordan Kerr held her passport and was not likely to give it back to her until his conditions were fulfilled.

To save her mother worry Serena cabled her hotel telling her she would not be arriving Saturday, adding "letter following". Not that the letter would ever be written; it wouldn't be necessary—not after Roger was acquainted with the news!

Serena's spirits were low as she selected the dress she would wear for the ball, and as she slipped the frothy white organdie gown on she recalled Jordan Kerr's scathing remarks on her being one of the devil's angels. Her soft mouth twisted as she met her reflection in the dressing table mirror. If she remembered rightly, the gown had been christened "temptation" by its aspiring creator. Not, she thought, as her eyes traced the clinging top and billowing skirt, that Jordan Kerr would be "tempted". Despite all outward appearance of his attentiveness, he had adroitly managed to keep his distance as far as physical contact was concerned, and Serena, recalling the painful hold he had clamped on her on the ship, was devoutly grateful for this small mercy; she was also grateful for the fact that the "engagement" plan had not been put into operation, although she knew it was only held in abeyance to be used as and when necessary to ward Roger off.

As she picked up her evening bag, Serena tried to imagine herself gazing up into Jordan Kerr's face with the adoration and love that would be required to convince Roger that she had fallen hopelessly in

love with the masterful owner of the island, but
found her imagination didn't stretch that far! It
might have helped if she had liked the man, but she
heartily disliked him. Quite apart from the rough
treatment he had meted out to her, she was sure she
wouldn't have liked him anyway, even if they had
met in different circumstances. He was too sure of
himself and too used to getting his own way. No middle way for such as he, she thought bitterly. There
was but one way, Jordan Kerr's way; right or wrong,
and in her case—wrong.

Serena was half-way to the lounge to join Mrs Tonetti when the thought hit her making her stop suddenly in her tracks. The engagement! She frowned;
really, her wits must have gone begging! Once it was
announced Mrs Tonetti would have to confess to
Jordan Kerr that Serena was not her granddaughter!
He hadn't believed Serena, but he would have to believe Mrs Tonetti! Her thoughts whirled on; as much
as she dreaded Roger's arrival his appearance now
was her only salvation.

Her frown deepened as she thought of the humiliation Mrs Tonetti would suffer should her deception
ever get to Mrs Simpson's ears, then she relaxed
slightly; Jordan Kerr might not care what happened
to her, but he did care for Mrs Tonetti; he would
keep the information to himself—and Myrna? Serena's eyes narrowed speculatively; she hadn't been
sure before but she was now. Myrna knew
nothing—she couldn't do! The knowledge gave her
a little shock and for a moment her attitude towards

Jordan Kerr softened, then her lips firmed. He was not a fool; knowledge like that in the hands of a jealous woman was pure dynamite! He wouldn't risk it and remembering Myrna's vicious glances in her direction, Serena heartily agreed with him.

Her step was a little lighter as she joined Mrs Tonetti in the lounge and noticing her pallor commented, "Don't you think you ought to give this evening a miss? I'm sure Jordan will understand."

Mrs Tonetti smiled. "It's only excitement, dear," she said. "So tiring when you get old, you know." She glanced down at her finely veined hands that trembled a little in her lap. "Perhaps it would be wiser to stay and rest. However, I shall only do so on your promise that you attend—not," she added mischievously, "that Jordan will hear of you doing anything else."

Serena smiled at her. "You have my word," she promised, then she fetched a footstool and placed it under Mrs Tonetti's feet. "I'll just tell Molly you're staying," she said, and walked to the door.

"No, dear, not just yet. I want to talk to you; you can tell Molly just before you leave."

There was something about Mrs Tonetti's expression as she made this request that alerted Serena. Had she decided to tell Jordan the truth? Serena's hopes soared—she would catch that plane after all!

"Come and sit down, dear," coaxed Mrs Tonetti in the sort of voice that suggested that she had bad news for her, and Serena wondered whether she had thought Jordan would lose interest in her once he knew the truth and was preparing her for it.

"I want to tell you about Jordan," the old lady began hesitantly. Serena could have cheered; she had decided to confess! However, it soon became apparent that no such thought had entered her mind. A very deflated Serena listened to what Mrs. Tonetti was telling her. "Don't get too fond of him, dear," she said slowly. "Not at least until you're sure, that is. You see, I know him very well, and although he doesn't deliberately set out to hurt anyone, I'm afraid it's quite possible it might happen to you." She sighed. "Not that I've any sympathy for the others; as a very wealthy man he's a target for the fortune-hunters," she lifted her hands expressively. "And there's no denying he's a very good-looking man," she half-smiled at this comment. "I'm not too old to appreciate that," she murmured, then sighed again. "It's very sad, but I don't think he's ever stopped loving Maria. They were almost engaged, you know, and she died. She was only nineteen and the loveliest thing you ever saw—blonde, with huge baby-blue eyes." Her voice softened as she spoke of the girl and Serena sensed that he had been very fond of her.

In spite of herself Serena was interested. "How did she die?" she asked quietly.

Mrs Tonetti started as if she had been brought back from her memories as indeed she had. "Drowned, dear." She frowned. "No one knows why she was swimming in that particular spot. It was a well-known danger zone, the currents are treacherous, and Maria should have known it was dangerous;

she had been coming to the island for years. Her parents were close friends of Jordan's parents and although they lived in New York they were always here for weekends." Once again she lapsed into reverie and Serena wanted to hear more, so she gently prompted her.

"How long ago did this happen, Mrs Tonetti?" she asked.

Mrs Tonetti frowned and concentrated on the question. "Seven years, I think," she answered musingly, and looked at Serena sadly. "He's never bothered since to really look at any woman, not in that light, I mean. Oh, he flirts with them, of course, he's human after all, but they're just ships that pass in the night as far as he's concerned. You know, sometimes I wonder if he resents them because they are living and his love's dead." She shook her head slowly. "So you see, my dear, why you must be on your guard. He wouldn't deliberately set out to hurt you, he wouldn't see that you're not like the others, and the fact that he thinks you're my granddaughter wouldn't make the slightest difference either, I'm afraid. So do be careful, Serena. Hold on to your heart until you're certain he's not just having a fling with you."

There was not the slightest danger of Serena being in any such predicament, but she appreciated Mrs Tonetti's confidential advice. For one thing it explained why his persecution of her amounted to a vendetta! Serena's fingers clenched into a fist. She couldn't wait for Roger's arrival and to be able to tell Jordan Kerr just what she thought of him!

The cablegram came just as Serena was leaving. It was from her mother and just stated that she would be arriving at noon the following day. Serena pushed the message quickly into her bag, and hoped Mrs Tonetti, who had gone to bed earlier, had not seen the messenger arrive. It was just another complication for Serena to deal with. For goodness' sake—why her mother and not Roger? She simply couldn't see Roger allowing her mother to chase after her; he would consider it *his* duty.

Stepping out on to the tiled porchway of the chalet, Serena watched the Rolls glide to a graceful halt beside her and her spirits sank as she saw who had collected her. He didn't even bother to get out but leaned over and opened the door for her, even Jake, she thought scathingly, had more manners than his autocratic employer.

As she sat stiffly beside him she felt the slight rustle of the paper under her fingers. Well, there was no time like the present, she thought. "My mother's arriving tomorrow," she announced airily. "Try convincing her I'm Lisa Tonetti!"

He thrust her a glinting look. "Boy-friend backed out?" he asked with grim amusement. "Your mother died six years ago," he said harshly. "I can even tell you how; in a car crash after having imbibed a little too much of her favourite beverage. Now this—er—mother," he said musingly, "she'd be genteelly bred, of course, down on her luck, probably through gambling losses and just right for your proposition. Of course, it wouldn't work unless you had some sort of family, would it? You needed a respectable background—could be tricky on your own home ground, though, so she probably resides elsewhere, called in as it were when necessary. It's been worked before, of course, quite successfully too. When the fish is landed there's a share-out and little monthly payments, not too much, but just enough to keep the bogus parent happy." He gave the stunned Serena another glinting look. "You didn't really think I'd fall for that, did you?"

It occurred to Serena that if she ever did break free from Jordan Kerr's pernicious hold, she might well take to a life of crime; it would be a pity to waste the first-class training she was receiving! Answering his last taunt, she said abruptly, "No, Mr Kerr, I can't say I can see you falling for anything, particularly when it doesn't suit your convenience. You've got it all taped, haven't you? I must say I'm a little intrigued over what sort of an apology you'll give after meeting my mother. After the treatment I've received, it had better be a good one," she muttered darkly.

As he swung the car into his drive, he answered casually, "As it's such an unlikely event, I shouldn't worry your head about it. Why didn't you mention this mother of yours before? It's a little late to bring that tactic into play, isn't it? Or is she likely to make trouble if she thinks you're running out on her?"

Serena did not answer simply because what he had said was partially true—she ought to have told him about her mother; it might have helped earlier—

now it was too late. She now wished she had never mentioned her, for she could have arranged to slip out and meet that plane and apprise her of the facts. It was a situation that would appeal to her immensely, and Serena knew she could rely on her to come up with some story to fob off a visit from Roger in the near future. Serena sighed. She always seemed to think of these things afterwards. If Jordan Kerr hadn't had such a chip on his shoulder he might have seen that she wasn't half so bright as he credited Lisa Tonetti with being.

The car slithered to a halt outside the house and Jordan got out. Serena, not waiting to be assisted, also got out and walked towards the steps to the house. To her intense irritation he placed a hand on her arm in what could hardly be called a lover-like hold and she shrugged it off furiously.

Giving a low laugh, he then placed an arm around her slender waist and clamped her to his side. It was a hold Serena couldn't break and she knew this was only the start of the evening. "Must you be so brutal?" she said in a low voice. "It doesn't help, does it?"

"It's the only way I can stomach the whole business," he replied curtly. "I haven't your experience in double-dealing. I must say I'm a little disappointed in you," his eyes held hers mockingly. "You're passing up a golden opportunity. I'm rich and fancy free." His hand increased its pressure and Serena winced. "You never know," he said silkily, "there just might be something in it for you."

Serena had a cold feeling again—he was challenging her, and she only wished she had the courage to take him up on it, for she could make things very unpleasant for him as she recalled his barely disguised distaste of her nearness when she had danced with him the previous evening. Her eyes sparkled; she would do it! This time the idea hadn't come too late! She would positively drool over him! He had wanted to create the impression that they were in love, hadn't he? And there was absolutely nothing he could do about it while they were in company. Afterwards . . . Serena decided she wouldn't dwell too much on that part of it. No matter what happened it would be worth it!

CHAPTER NINE

LONG afterwards, Serena wondered how she had found the courage to carry out her plan of discomfiting Jordan Kerr, for it was one thing telling herself she would do so, quite another carrying it out!

She did not attempt to bring the tactic into play until they were in full view of the assembly, then she shamelessly clung to his arm and almost chuckled at the start he gave. With no little satisfaction she watched his jaw harden and a glint appear in his eyes that promised retribution at no late date; but Serena refused to be intimidated.

As his arm pinned hers to his side he murmured in a low undertone, "There's no need to overdo it. I abhor clinging women."

Smiling at one of his guests standing a little way beyond them, Serena replied sweetly, "I'm only following your advice. Stupid of me to waste such a golden opportunity. Remember, Jordan, darling, I know all the tricks."

She knew by the indrawn breath that she had infuriated him and there was simply nothing he could do about it.

Myrna and her partner, a Mr Canning, an elderly

retired colonel, left the dance floor and joined Mrs Simpson just as Serena and Jordan approached. Myrna was looking particularly stunning in an apricot velvet off-the-shoulder gown that highlighted her fair colouring, and it occurred to Serena that she might well have reminded Jordan of his lost Maria. Men, she mused, were apt to be attracted by one particular type of woman—not, she thought, looking at Myrna's cold blue eyes, that anyone in their right mind could call her eyes baby blue, more like ice blue, she thought, as they rested on her for a brief second.

Completely ignoring Serena, Myrna placed a proprietorial hand on Jordan's free arm and gazed up at him coquettishly. "I absolutely demand the next dance, darling," she murmured throatily to him.

Serena almost felt sorry for Jordan. He must have longed to accept the invitation so seductively offered, but could hardly do so with Serena clinging to his other arm. Taking pity on him, she removed her arm and giving him what she hoped was a brilliant smile murmured with the same throaty intonation as Myrna, "Do go ahead; I've no right to monopolise your company."

Having seen Gerald approaching, Serena was confident she would at least be able to enjoy one dance and smiled at him as he joined them. To her fury Jordan decided the matter by firmly taking her arm and smiling half apologetically at Myrna, suggested, "Later, perhaps?" and led Serena on to the dance floor.

While she waited for Jordan to take her hand and place his arm round her waist for the opening steps of the dreamy music Serena consoled herself that he was not likely to ask her to dance again—she would see to that.

As before, his clasp on her hand was light, and she had no difficulty in disengaging it and placing it on his shoulder to enable her to move closer to him; a move she had seen carried out by her more uninhibited friends and one Serena would never have dared to imitate not even if she had felt attracted to the man in question—and when the man was Jordan Kerr . . . She felt him stiffen and knew he was appalled at the bold move. Again, there was nothing he could do about it; they were in full view of the whole room and any attempt to thrust her away from him would not fail to be seen.

His free arm now had to go round Serena, completely enclosing her, and she winced as he jerked her closer and made herself go pliant in his arms.

His voice was harsh as he spoke close to her hair. "Is this part of the softening-up process? Pity it's going to be wasted, isn't it?" he jeered softly as he swung her round swiftly so that she was jerked against his hard lean body in quick succession.

When Serena had partially recovered her breath she threw caution to the wind and muttered, "Just try and get me to dance with you again—I'd rather go to jail!"

His answer was a low chuckle. "Nice to know you're enjoying it as much as I am, but you asked for it."

Miserably Serena had to acknowledge the truth of this, but for once Jordan Kerr was as uncomfortable as she was, and that fact alone gave her some consolation.

However, it did serve to achieve her aim, for although the band immediately struck up another melody, Jordan did not request an encore but suggested they seek refreshment, a suggestion Serena was only too happy to agree with. Her waist felt as if it had just been released from an iron band and she wondered if the bruises would show later.

If Jordan was hoping for a short respite from the outward appearance of dancing attendance on her, he was doomed to disappointment, as the first people they encountered as they entered the supper room were no other than Mrs Simpson and a friend of hers. Mrs Simpson immediately pounced on him.

"Jordan! Margaret has just told me she hasn't seen the portrait of the first Jordan Kerr. I was just telling her of the likeness. Do you think we could go and see it now?"

Sensing that it was a move on Mrs Simpson's part to detach her from his side, Serena was all for it; she was almost sure he would accompany the ladies and not waiting to hear his answer walked towards the buffet in search of a long cold drink.

"Serena?"

To her extreme annoyance Serena found him beside her before she had swallowed a mouthful of her drink.

"I'm sure you'll find the portrait interesting," he

said smoothly, not giving her a chance of refusing. "Shall we go?"

Putting down the drink, Serena forced herself to sound interested. "Of course," she said airily, meeting Mrs Simpson's snapping black eyes.

"We're honoured, you know," Mrs Simpson commented casually. "Myrna's the only one so far to be given a private viewing."

Serena wondered if she felt better after having got that broadside in.

Staring at the life-size painting a few minutes later, Serena had to steel herself to suppress a shiver as she gazed at the cold eyes of the man in the portrait—and not only in front of her, she thought nervily, but at the side of her as well. The likeness was uncanny, the only physical difference being in the colour of the eyes. The pirate's were a dark blue, whereas Jordan Kerr's were that curious light green. It was hard to believe that the man she was looking at had lived centuries ago, yet the man whose eyes she could feel boring into her and standing by her side dressed immaculately in a dark tuxedo could have stepped straight out of the picture.

Her thoughts were echoed by Margaret, who exclaimed, "It's uncanny, isn't it?" in an awed voice.

Serena knew Jordan's eyes were still on her as he answered casually, "I believe the resemblance is there in more ways than one."

"What nonsense, Jordan!" simpered Mrs Simpson. "From what I hear of the island's history that gentleman gave no quarter. Of course," she added magnanimously, "things were different in those days. He had to be hard to survive."

"Precisely," murmured Jordan, and again Serena sensed his eyes on her. "Given the same circumstances, I, too, would give no quarter." He dismissed Mrs Simpson's eager attempt to refute this sweeping statement with a careless wave of the hand towards the portrait. "Believe me, my ancestor and I have a lot in common. Now, shall we join the other guests?"

After this little interlude it was doubly hard for Serena to revert back to the clinging stage with Jordan. Her every instinct cautioned her to keep her distance; she knew his words had been for her alone, a veiled warning to her not to cross him.

Ushering Mrs Simpson and her friend out of the library, he mockingly held his arm out for Serena's hand and she was forced to accept it, but he did not miss her reluctance, and as they followed the others back to the ballroom he inquired softly, "Lost your enthusiasm? I would have thought my worthy ancestor would have suited you admirably—in a way he had a lot in common with you, he took what he wanted, too."

"Yet you persecute me and glorify him," Serena grated back in a low voice. "How many lives did he take in getting what he wanted? I would rather my conscience than his!"

She found herself swung round to face him. He held her in a biting grip close to him and had either of the two ladies in front chanced to turn round at that precise time, they would have gained the impression that Jordan was kissing her. However, no such thought was in his mind as he surveyed her through hooded lids. When he spoke his voice was harsh.

"What he took, he took fair and square. Fought for it. He didn't wait until the coast was clear and sneak in the back way, nor," he added scathingly, "did he rob his friends."

He released her abruptly and Serena turned away from him quickly. There was nothing she could say to that—nothing he would believe anyway, she thought dully.

As she wearily prepared for bed later that evening, Serena's thoughts were centred on her mother and her proposed visit the next day. As no further mention of the subject had been made by Jordan Kerr, she presumed he had dismissed it as a story she had thought up to gain her freedom. It looked as if it was the first piece of luck she had had for some time, and she was determined not to make a hash of it. Her mother must be told of the bizarre situation she had landed herself in and go back to New York by the next plane if necessary, and apprise Roger of the facts. He could then come armed with all the necessary information to outflank Jordan Kerr. Serena, banging her pillows into a more comfortable shape, dwelt on this happening with relish. Why, she would be so grateful to Roger she might even consider marrying him!

Her brow creased as she thought of Mrs Tonetti. An excuse would have to be found to cover her absence. She would say she had some shopping to do—of course, she could tell her the truth, but on thinking it over, Serena decided against this. It might worry the old lady, and she might feel duty bound to invite her mother to the chalet and that would mean all sorts of complications. Serena felt the situation was complicated enough without adding more!

During her solitary breakfast the following morning, she rehearsed in her mind what she would tell her mother. There wouldn't be time to go into details. Roger had to be made to understand that his visit concerned only Jordan Kerr, and no one else, and that the information Mrs Belmont gave him should remain strictly private.

Having got everything clear in her mind, Serena was able to greet Mrs Tonetti with a bright smile when she joined her later and answer her query as to whether she had enjoyed herself the previous evening and whether Jordan had brought her back.

Serena knew Mrs Tonetti was trying to gauge just how interested Jordan Kerr was in her and felt it wise to play it down. In the not too distant future the "interest" would be non-existent and Serena would be sunning herself on the deck of a luxury yacht and wondering why she had allowed herself to be pushed around by a modern version of Long John Silver!

Her musings were interrupted by the appearance of Molly, who told her she was wanted on the telephone. Feeling a stab of apprehension, Serena went to take the call. Had her mother taken an earlier flight? Giving a cautious "hallo", she was half relieved to hear the deep voice of Jordan on the other end of the line—relieved, that was, until she heard the reason for the call.

"I'm picking you up at eleven-forty-five," he said curtly.

Serena did a double-take; whatever happened she didn't want Jordan Kerr around today of all days. "I've decided to spend the day with my grandmother," she said sweetly. "Tomorrow, perhaps?"

"Liar," he said softly. "You didn't think I'd forgotten your—er—mother's arrival, did you? Eleven-forty-five," he repeated slowly, and put the phone down on her.

"Jordan has other plans, I take it?" said Mrs Tonetti behind her.

Serena forced herself to sound gay—not easy when she wanted to shout and rave, either that, or howl her eyes out, but she was even denied this luxury. "I'm afraid so," she managed to say with a weak smile. "He's calling later."

Mrs Tonetti nodded happily. "I thought so," she smiled.

Serena looked at her as she settled herself in her chair. If only . . . "Mrs Tonetti—Nan," she began quickly. "Oughtn't you to tell him?" she pleaded gently. "It makes me feel such a fraud."

Smiling fondly at her, Mrs Tonetti replied softly, "If he loves you, dear, it won't make the slightest difference, you know." Her smile faded and a frown creased her finely lined forehead. "It's just that I'm not entirely convinced . . ." She was silent for a moment as if weighing the matter up, then she looked up suddenly to find Serena worriedly watching her and smiled at her, "I promise to tell him should it become necessary—don't look so worried, dear." The faded blue eyes now held the pleading look. "In my own way, Serena. It's not going to be easy, but if it's making you unhappy . . ."

"No," Serena replied hastily. "It's not that, it's just that I felt he ought to be put in the picture." She managed to bring a light note into the conversation. "As you say, there's time enough for that if things get out of hand—and I can assure you," she added firmly in order to take that anxious look away from Mrs Tonetti's expression, "that I'm still heart-free and likely to remain so. Your Jordan is a bit too dominant for my liking. I much prefer the easy-to-manage types, saves a lot of arguing in the long run, you know."

Watching Mrs Tonetti's frown replaced by her delightful smile, Serena breathed a sigh of relief. She might be in trouble, but it was infinitely preferable for things to remain as they were than to cause her kind hostess further misery.

SERENA WATCHED THE PLANE touch down with mixed feelings. It was now up to her mother; she was very conscious of Jordan Kerr's grip on her arm in case she made a bolt for it or attempted to forewarn what he thought was her accomplice.

As the passengers streamed down the gangway, Serena had no difficulty in picking out her mother. Her ridiculously flimsy hat with layers of chiffon would not have looked out of place at Ascot, come to that, nor would her dress of shantung silk, Serena thought, and in spite of her anxiety she felt a spurt of pride. Who else but her mother would have dared to wear a hat like that?—not only dared, but carry it off so magnificently. She heard Jordan Kerr give a derisive snort as Mrs Belmont, spotting Serena, held her hands out towards her in an affectionate welcome as she approached them.

"My congratulations," he said softly. "You've got her well trained, but I should imagine she's a little on the expensive side. I hope she's worth it!"

Moving forward to greet her mother, closely followed by Jordan, Serena did not bother to answer.

"Darling!" breathed Mrs Belmont as if it were six months since she had seen her instead of only one week.

As her mother kissed her cheek, Serena knew she was sizing up the man standing by her side. Nothing would go unnoticed, Serena knew. From his fine linen suit to his hand-made shoes, for Mrs Belmont was a snob—in the nicest possible way, of course. The only daughter of an impoverished Irish peer, she was used to moving in the right social circles and not unnaturally had high ambitions for Serena.

Having decided Jordan was "acceptable", Mrs Belmont flashed him a brilliant smile and Serena was furious. Before she could speak Jordan said coldly,

"Shall we adjourn to a more private spot?" and placing a hand on Serena's arm shepherded them towards the airport lounge.

Mrs Belmont's eyebrows lifted slightly at this autocratic treatment and she glanced swiftly at Serena. Interpreting the look, Serena knew she was saying "Well done", and it appeared her mother was labouring under the impression that Jordan Kerr was an impatient lover who intended to lose no time in making his intention clear to his beloved's only relation. She was, thought Serena grimly, in for a bit of a shock!

Reaching the lounge, he led them past the groups of people standing around and ushered them into a small office off the main ticket office.

As soon as the door was shut, Serena began hastily, "Mother, would you..."

"I'll do the talking," cut in Jordan curtly. "And you can drop the 'Mother' stunt for a start."

Had Serena not been so anxious to prove her identity the sight of her mother's bewildered face might have given her hysterics; as it was, she was tired of being bullied by this detestable man. "No, you will not!" she replied furiously. "You've had your say, Mr Kerr, now it's my turn. Mother," she demanded, "tell this man who I am!"

Mrs Belmont raised expressive eyebrows at this odd request. She was not, Serena noticed, a bit put out—almost, Serena thought crossly, as if this sort of question cropped up regularly!

"Who does Mr Kerr think you are?" Mrs Belmont inquired innocently.

Serena stared at her, not failing to note the grim expression on Jordan Kerr's face. "For goodness' sake!" she exploded. "This is serious, Mother!"

Jordan intervened swiftly with, "It appears your friend catches on a bit quicker than you do," adding silkily, "When I tell her there isn't a hope of an inheritance perhaps she'll catch on even quicker."

Serena had to hand it to her mother, she didn't bat an eyelid! "Where's Roger?" she asked quickly, thinking if she didn't get some assistance in the very near future, she would scream the place down.

"That, darling, is the reason I've come," replied her mother, keeping a wary eye on Jordan. "The poor dear's had an accident. The driver of the other car was drunk, and Roger couldn't avoid hitting him. He's not seriously hurt, though, slight concussion and a suspected broken ankle. We've had to cancel the cruise, I'm afraid, for a week or two at least." She cast another look at Jordan. "We couldn't think what was keeping you. I've strict instructions to bring you back with me."

"I regret that is out of the question," cut in Jordan swiftly. "I have no intention of releasing her."

Mrs Belmont gave these words a little thought and Serena had a nasty feeling that she was well aware of Jordan Kerr's status, and in that respect he was certainly in the "right" category as far as she was concerned! She made another desperate attempt to get through to her mother. "When you've heard..."

"There's nothing to hear," interjected Jordan, "nothing she doesn't already know, or has guessed."

His next words clinched the matter as far as Mrs Belmont was concerned. "You can give Mr Alton my regards; you can also tell him Miss Belmont regrets she will be unable to join him on the cruise. She is going to be—er—rather tied up for the next few months." He glanced at his watch and fixing a steely glance on Mrs Belmont, added haughtily, "I suggest you take the next flight back. There's one in precisely ten minutes."

Serena's mother blinked, then smiled knowingly at Serena. "Your dear father was just the same," she murmured mistily. "He would brook no interference." She smiled confidingly at Jordan. "I'll forgive your obvious manoeuvre to get rid of me. You've nothing to worry about, you know, I'm quite harmless. However, I didn't intend to stay long anyway, someone's got to look after Roger. He's bound to fret until he knows Serena's all right." She gave Serena a light kiss on the cheek. "You will keep me informed, won't you, darling?"

Serena really didn't see the point of answering. No matter what she said it was bound to be misinterpreted, if not by her mother, then by Jordan Kerr, in any case she was saved the necessity.

"You need have no worries on that score," Jordan assured her steadily as he opened the door to indicate the end of the discussion.

CHAPTER TEN

SERENA sat in a half dazed condition in Jordan Kerr's car as it glided smoothly out of the airport precincts. Bewilderedly she thought that if someone had told her of the position she would one day find herself in, she would have told them such things did not, could not, happen. People just did not behave like that—but they had! Her mother had for a start! She had gaily waved her farewell before boarding the plane back to New York.

For all she knew, Serena thought bitterly, she might have left her daughter to the tender mercies of a white-slaver. She sighed heavily; anyone else but the autocratic and wealthy Jordan Kerr would not have got away with it. The fact that her daughter had not only made the acquaintance of such an august personage, but apparently captivated him, had tipped the scales. Mrs Belmont, like Mrs Tonetti, was a firm believer in fate—in fact, they had quite a lot in common, Serena thought crossly; neither had proved exactly reliable in a crisis.

Gazing out at the waving palms that lined the road they were travelling down, Serena tried to cheer herself up with the thought that at least the worry of Roger suddenly descending on her had been effectively removed and she was now free to enjoy Mrs Tonetti's company—or at least she would be, if a certain character stayed out of her hair!

Serena was quite sure that if it had been anyone esle but Jordan Kerr holding the whiphand she would have been more than willing to play the part allocated her; she was very fond of Mrs Tonetti and it would be no hardship seeing to her welfare. It was just that something about this man caught her on the raw. She didn't even mind his insults—he would be the one making the apologies later; no—it wasn't that. Serena frowned; in some ways he'd reminded her of Roger. Dominant was the word, she thought. Perhaps what she'd said to Mrs Tonetti that very morning was the truth? That her type of man was the meek and mild type? She gave an impatient shrug. Well anyway, it certainly wasn't the Jordan Kerr model!

"Worrying about the boy-friend's reaction?" Jordan asked smoothly. "If so, I shouldn't. I've an idea your friend will think up some ploy to keep the pot boiling. Leave a bolthole open, as it were, in case things don't pan out this end. As I think I said, a very enterprising woman, that. I'm pretty sure she knew of me, not to mention what I'm worth." He threw Serena a mocking look. "Made no bones about leaving you, did she? Been in a similar situation, no doubt, and has every confidence of your coming home with the bacon again."

"Do you mind if we drop the subject?" snapped

Serena. "You've got what you wanted. I stay and be a dutiful granddaughter. Just promise me one thing," she ground out, "to stay away from me from now on."

"Come, Lisa," he all but purred the words. "We're almost engaged, aren't we?"

"You can drop that charade, too," Serena replied furiously. "It wouldn't be the first time you've suddenly lost interest, would it? I hear you're quite adept at it. My—er—grandmother thought it wise to drop me a hint on that score." Her eyes flashed shoots of violet rays. "Just say you've lost interest, I'll even play the part of the spurned woman to get you out of my vicinity. Say what you want—I don't care! Just leave me alone. It's not as if I can go anywhere, is it? You've got my passport," she added bitterly.

He slowed the car down and pulled up in a layby and sat studying her for a moment or so with narrowed eyes. "You seem to forget who's calling the tune," he said in a dangerously soft voice. "I like things as they are. That way I can keep an eye on you. No doubt it would suit your purpose if I drifted off the scene, but I'd never be certain, you see, that you hadn't hastened your grandmother's end."

It took a moment or so for her to grasp the full implication of these words and when it did her eyes opened to their full capacity. "You think I'd . . ." She couldn't go on.

His eyes registered the shock he had given her and he shrugged casually. "Oh, not consciously, perhaps," he said curtly. "But I wouldn't put it past you to vent your frustration out on her. No, Miss Tonetti, I'm not taking any chances. I'm going to be around for as long as it takes." So saying, he started up the engine and steered the car back on to the road.

The rest of the journey was spent in silence, Serena was too shocked to attempt to break it. She was partially recovering when he threw the second bombshell. Arriving at the chalet, he accompanied the silent Serena to the lounge and before she could guess his intention said casually to Mrs Tonetti, "I'm making Serena's stay permanent."

There was no mistaking his meaning and Serena stood helplessly by his side trying to look deliriously happy, but she was absolutely stunned, and fortunately for her so was Mrs Tonetti. After a fractional pause she moved towards them, and with tear-dimmed eyes caught both of their hands in hers. "Oh, my dears! I'm so happy for both of you," she smiled.

Why doesn't she say I'm not Lisa? Serena thought frantically and tried to catch her eye, but Mrs Tonetti was too overcome to consider such mundane information suitable at this time.

Serena longed for Jordan to go so that she could get through to her the absolute necessity for the truth to come out, but her new-found fiancé had other plans. Giving her no respite, he pulled her up out of the chair she had thankfully sunk into, remarking cheerfully, "We've got to get organised, darling. Come on!"

SITTING IN JORDAN'S STUDY a short while later, Serena watched dully as he twirled the knob of a heavy wall safe. "This is one combination you'll not get," he remarked caustically. "The ring's insured too, but then you wouldn't be stupid enough to try and hang on to it, would you?"

Serena had not said a word since they had left Mrs Tonetti, but now, watching him remove a small leather box and carefully lock the safe after him, she whispered bitterly, "Why?—why do you insist on going on with this farce?"

He had opened the box and stood looking at the contents. She saw his mouth twist slightly, and she thought she knew why; he was obviously thinking of the girl he had hoped would one day wear the ring. The small ornate box spoke of antiquity; the ring had probably been handed down through the centuries to prospective brides. Suddenly he glanced up at her, catching her unawares, and for a moment in time glinting green eyes pierced violet ones. Serena couldn't define that look, but it was as if they had gone back in time, not years, but centuries, and she felt the familiar tingling along her spine.

Whatever had affected her had touched him, too. She was sure of it as she saw him mentally shake himself, and watched the familiar hardening of the jaw as he answered her earlier question.

"Because your grandmother is not a fool," he said harshly. "I'm afraid she knows me a little too well," his glance was now mocking. "As you so kindly pointed out when we left the airfield, I have been known to be somewhat fickle in my attentions to the fair sex." His glance hardened. "If she thought fit to warn you that could mean only one thing—she was worried about you. And that's not the only thing I suspect she had on her mind. She knows she's nothing to leave you, and it's my guess she's worrying about how she's going to tell you. Well, this little charade will set her mind at rest. Come here," he ordered curtly.

Serena remained where she was. She guessed he wanted her to put the ring on and wondered why he didn't just throw the box at her. He certainly didn't intend to put himself out, she thought scathingly, and although what he'd said about Mrs Tonetti made sense, Serena was loth to commit herself to such a man, charade or no charade!

In three quick strides he was beside her and in no gentle fashion had grasped her left hand and held it up. Thrusting the ring into her right hand, he commanded, "Put it on," adding scathingly, "I have no doubt it will have to be altered."

Having no choice in the matter, Serena slipped the ring on the third finger of her left hand, still held hard by Jordan.

It was a perfect fit; Serena was slightly surprised and a little disappointed as she had hoped fervently it wouldn't be.

Her surprise was nothing compared to Jordan's. His autocratic brows rose and he turned the hand towards him as if to certify the fact that the thick band of gold was not biting into the flesh of her finger.

Then as if the contact stung him he withdrew his hold on her, leaving Serena staring at the imposing ring, its huge diamond centre piece flashing scintillating lights that screamed its value.

"I can't possibly wear it!" she exclaimed in a shocked voice. "It must be worth a fortune!"

Jordan smiled cynically. "It is," he assured her grimly. "Afraid you'll be tempted? Don't worry, before you've done your stint, you'll be glad to see the back of it. That ring," he said silkily, "gives me the right to seek you out at any time of my choosing."

Serena's eyes spoke her thoughts, but she did not give way to anger; she had no wish to feel his iron hold on her again, so she took refuge in sarcasm. "Surely you have some other little bauble that would do the job just as well?" She narrowed her eyes calculatingly as she held her hand up and studied the ring. "You know, I could use this to bribe someone to get me off the island. Have you thought of that?" she queried innocently.

For a few seconds it looked as if he might well throttle her, but he mastered his emotions and shrugged casually. "There isn't a soul on the island who would dare to cross me, Miss Tonetti. And," his eyes were hooded as he added softly, "I wouldn't advise you to try. You see, I might decide to save Alton from himself in spite of all the spade work your friend is putting in at her end, leaving the way clear for you to make a comeback. In your case, two birds in the bush is better than one in the hand, isn't it? Believe me, you accept my ultimatum or take the consequences. I can assure you Alton wouldn't touch you with a bargepole by the time I've finished with you. Nor would any self-respecting man!"

CHAPTER ELEVEN

WHATEVER reaction Serena might have given to Jordan Kerr's threats was never enacted, as a telephone call was received by him while she was busy gathering her forces for the onslaught.

His curt, "We'll be right over," told her he was in no mood for verbal battle, and his next words wiped out any inclination she had had to retaliate. "Your grandmother," he said tersely as he all but threw her light linen jacket she had left lying on a chair at her, and made for the door.

Serena barely had time to fling herself in the car seat before he took off. She wanted to ask what had happened, but something in Jordan Kerr's expression stopped her.

Within minutes they were sweeping up the drive to the chalet and, not waiting for Serena, Jordan was out of the car and into the chalet while Serena was still collecting her senses.

Although she had by now realised that whatever it was it was serious, she was still not prepared for what she heard the doctor tell Jordan as she came upon them in the hall. "There's not much time, I'm afraid. She's asking for you and someone called Serena—her granddaughter, I believe."

The doctor then caught sight of Serena standing hesitantly behind Jordan. "Go in, my dear," he said gently. "It's a door we all have to pass through and she's quite ready to go. Don't be afraid."

Serena was not afraid; the doctor had mistaken her hesitancy for fear. In fact, she did not feel anything; she was mentally and physically numb.

As she entered the cool shuttered room Mrs Tonetti lay in Molly raised tear-stained eyes towards her and put down the linen cloth she had just wrung out to place on Mrs Tonetti's forehead. She shook her head sadly as Serena's eyes met hers and mutely handed her the cloth, then softly left the room.

Gently wiping the perspiring face, Serena realised the old lady had sunk into a coma and was delirious. Suddenly her hand was caught. "Lisa? Is that you?" Then came a subsided muttering and, "Why did you leave? You didn't write. I was so worried." The breathing quickened and again she asked, "It is you, Lisa, isn't it? You've come back?"

Serena's eyes misted over; she patted the frail hand that moved restlessly across the linen sheet. "Yes, it's Lisa, Nan," she said softly. "I'm here."

A sigh of contentment followed this assurance and for a moment Mrs Tonetti clung to Serena's hand, then as if she hadn't the strength to keep it there it sank back on to the bed. Serena turned to the bowl of water on the side table to wring out the cloth once more and met the cynical eyes of Jordan Kerr standing just inside the door; something snapped inside her. His eyes were congratulating her on a fine performance. She looked back at Mrs Tonetti, who appeared to be sleeping peacefully, and unable to stand his presence, Serena walked past him out to the kitchen where Molly was hovering anxiously.

"I'm going to get some fresh air, Molly," she said quietly. "She's sleeping at the moment. I'll only be in the garden if she calls for me."

The cool breeze from the bay fanned her face as she stood gazing out beyond the breakers clearly seen in the light of a brilliant tropical moon. The soft lapping of the waves as they met the shore lulled some sense of proportion into her, and she knew an infinite sadness. For a brief minute she hated Lisa Tonetti for what she had done to her grandparents. Where was she now? Serena wondered. Living it up as Jordan Kerr had intimated?

"It's a little late to be sorry for what you did, isn't it?" said the goading voice directly behind her. "Or are you sorry? Or is it that you're missing the high life and wishing you were taking cocktails with another poor dupe?"

Serena would have liked to ignore him, but something spurred her on. "What if I did feel compassion for her?" she said in a low voice that vibrated with pent-up tension. "You wouldn't understand, anyway. Compassion is not an emotion you've ever felt. What if I were Lisa? Wouldn't I feel something? No one," she said bitterly, "is all bad, but you're so twisted inside you can't even entertain the thought that she might have stayed away because she was ashamed of what she had done."

"And are you?" he said softly, then sighed elaborately. "You know, I sometimes wish I had more faith in human nature, for you might have fooled me."

A stifled sob behind them made them turn, to find Molly walking slowly towards them. Both were aware of the tidings she had to convey to them, although it was no less of a shock.

Jordan, laying a comforting arm around Molly's shoulders, escorted her back to the house, but Serena stayed where she was. A sob escaped her and the tears slid down her cheeks. She had never known her grandparents and she couldn't have been more fond of them than she had been of Mrs Tonetti.

"There's no need to overact the grieving relation bit," Jordan's cold voice spoke behind her. "The doctor's gone and Molly's lying down with a sedative."

Serena turned towards him. He was so close she had only to lean forward and her head would rest on that strong shoulder so invitingly near. In her need for solace her bowed head rested wearily against him. "Please, Jordan, not now," she whispered.

For a brief second he stiffened, then with a soft groan his arms crushed her to him and his lips found hers.

The kiss was savage, but it awoke an answering echo in Serena. It also awoke her to a world of beauty, of giving and taking, of desire and a certain knowledge that until this moment she had lived in a vacuum not really knowing what life was all about.

She could even understand the brutality as her soft lips were ruthlessly pounded.

She knew that as she had sought consolation, so too did he. For one brief flight in time they met on another plane, each desperately needing one another.

Then she was flung from him and the fury in his voice brought her back to cold reality.

"So that's how it's done, is it?" he ground out. "What am I supposed to do now—compensate you with a fat cheque? And be besotted enough to collect on the dividend? Well, it didn't come off. You couldn't even wait until after the funeral before trying your charms out on me, could you? Well, get this, and get it good. As far as I'm concerned you're a tramp—a high class one, maybe, but still a tramp. I'd sooner tangle with a scorpion! Now we've got that little business out of the way I suggest you go and pack. You've got thirty minutes in which to do it. I want you on that plane and off my land in the shortest possible time."

Serena tried to collect her scattered wits. She was being allowed to leave? Her start did not go unnoticed.

"Yes," he jeered. "Back to New York and your fancy friends, and they're more than welcome to you!"

"The funeral?" Serena asked hesitantly, thinking how odd it would look if she weren't there.

"Fancy yourself in black?" he inquired silkily. "Or were you hoping there might still be a little something for you in the will? I'm sorry, but that's just not on. I want you off my land, pronto!"

He turned to go, then swung back to her. "Haven't you forgotten something?" he asked in that hateful soft voice of his, and held his hand out. "The ring, if you please."

Serena gave another start. She had forgotten the ring, and with a quick movement she slipped it off her finger. She was about to hand it to him when he said, "Did you hope I'd forgotten it? Or was that what the kiss was for?"

Goaded beyond all reason, Serena flung the ring at him. It landed at his feet, its brilliant stone picking up the rays from the moon lay flashing on the ground.

He made no move to retrieve it but looked at her. "Pick it up," he said in a dangerously soft voice.

In a voice that slightly trembled Serena replied, "Pick it up yourself!"

Her arm was caught in that familiar iron hold and was forced down to where the ring lay. "Now pick it up," he said in a voice that brooked no argument.

This time he did leave, and Serena stood staring after him with the nails of her fingers digging into her palms.

CHAPTER TWELVE

SERENA'S abrupt arrival in New York was met with surprise by her mother and barely concealed triumph by Roger, who adopted a "you may kiss my hand" attitude, indicating to Serena that although she had hurt him he was quite willing to forgive her.

However, Serena was in no mood to respond to this kind of tactic; she was heartsick and incredibly weary; and the thought that her whole life had been turned upside down in such a short period of time seemed barely conceivable.

With a tact that Serena didn't know her mother possessed, she ushered her out of the room and into Serena's. Helping her unpack and ringing for a tray of tea, she chatted on about this and that, never once mentioning a certain person's name, although Serena knew she was consumed with curiosity. Come to that, so was Roger, but it was a curiosity that would have to remain unsatisfied until Serena was more in command of herself. She didn't want to think about it, but she knew she would; she also knew she ought to be thanking her lucky stars that it was all over.

No more worrying about saying the right thing or

being treated as a second class citizen. No more Mrs Tonetti; she hastily blinked away the mistiness this thought brought. She had to remember she had died happy; and she had been happy, Serena thought sadly, remembering her unconcealed delight at the news of the "engagement". Serena suspected it was this very event that had caused the collapse—too much excitement after years of loneliness.

She also suspected that Jordan Kerr had come to the same conclusion. It would, she thought wearily, account for that one weak moment when he had kissed her so savagely. Hastily she brought her thoughts back in an effort to try and concentrate on what her mother was talking about. Tomorrow, she told herself, she would see things in a different light, even be able to enjoy herself.

Serena hadn't even noticed that her mother had left the room until she came back and remarked happily, "I've just left Roger organising the cruise. We leave as planned on Monday. He's sick and tired of being tied to the hotel room. Said he might as well collect a tan while he has to stay put until that ankle's stronger. He didn't break it, by the way."

Giving her mother a wry smile for the tactful hint, Serena exclaimed, "Oh dear, and I didn't even inquire how he felt!"

Mrs Belmont patted her daughter's hand. "Well, you can make up for it during the cruise," she said soothingly. "I must say it's nice seeing him in good humour again." She gave Serena a considering look. "You know he's very fond of you, dear, don't you?"

Serena nodded dumbly, thinking Jordan Kerr hadn't been all that far off the mark where her mother was concerned. She wanted to see Serena happily married, but it had to be to a rich man, it would never occur to Mrs Belmont that the two might not go together. Poverty was a nasty word where she was concerned and happiness out of the question if the bank balance was slender.

On her own once more, Serena thought about the coming cruise and wished she could work up a little more enthusiasm about it. Roger's excuse about getting a tan was a barely disguised ruse to keep her safe in close proximity. He was taking no chances of her doing the disappearing act again. Serena knew she ought to have been grateful that someone cared enough about her to adopt such strategy.

TWO DAYS LATER, while sunning herself on the deck of the luxury yacht, Serena came to a decision. If Roger asked her to marry him again, which she was certain would be any day now, she would agree.

Not because she loved him but because she had made the catastrophic discovery that she was hopelessly and irrevocably in love with Jordan Kerr. She did not try and delude herself that that love would ever be returned. He was as far out of her reach as he might have been had they never met; more so, she thought wearily, for he would never know the truth, and even if he did, he would only at the best feel apologetic, and in spite of her earlier thoughts on the matter Serena could not have borne that. She would far rather he went on hating her for what he thought she was.

She turned over on to her back and lay gazing up at the bright blue cloudless sky. Maria, she thought miserably. It all came back to Maria; how Jordan must have loved her! Serena's eyes moistened; whoever he eventually married would have to contend with a ghost. Would Myrna lay the ghost? Blinking the moisture away from her eyes, Serena couldn't believe that she would. She had only seen the hard side of his nature, but she was certain he was not a man to give his heart lightly. He would swear allegiance to but one woman, there would never be a second-best for him.

Mrs Tonetti had loved Maria too, and that, Serena thought, would endear Jordan to her. She felt a touch on her arm and glanced up to meet Roger's probing eyes.

"Ready to name the day?" he asked casually as he dropped down beside her.

Serena's voice was calm as she answered. He knows, she thought, he knows I'm in love with someone I can't have, but he doesn't care; he wants me enough to accept me on any terms. "Ready when you are," she replied just as casually.

Roger's breath caught and he pulled her up into a sitting position to face him. Slowly his eyes went over her face and met her eyes. "Finished careering off into the blue, have you?" he asked steadily.

Serena knew what he meant. He was asking if it was all over—or rather telling her it had better be, she thought wearily, and nodded mutely.

Satisfied, he drew her into his arms and held her possessively close to him. With his lips on her hair he murmured, "You'll never regret it, darling."

She had to steel herself to meet the kiss he gave her. His lips were firm and the kiss was not distasteful, but her whole being cried out against his touch. She tried hard to respond but failed miserably.

When Roger released her his eyes were narrowed and on her lips, then he said slowly, "You'll have to do better than that, Serena. I've waited a long time for this moment. You gave your word and I don't intend to release you, so don't have any second thoughts, will you?" He got up stiffly and picked his stick up. Before he limped away, he said, "I'm announcing the engagement at supper tonight; meanwhile, think about what I've just said."

Serena couldn't help obeying these instructions; for one thing she was appalled by the change in Roger's attitude to her. Although she knew he was dominant and liked his own way, he had been very careful in the past to wield the velvet glove where she was concerned. By those few but devastating words she had been given an insight of the future that stretched before her as his wife.

He would not only be domineering, but a jealous and possessive husband. She swallowed. It was too late now to back out—not that he'd let her; he'd told her that, too.

The sound of laughter came from the bar in the cabin beneath where she was lying. Soon, she knew, her mother would come in search of her to congratulate her. Roger would, of course make a point of informing her first. The other members of the party that numbered a dozen, mostly business acquaintances of Roger's with either their wives or their girlfriends, would be advised of the event as Roger had intimated, at supper that evening.

He would probably arrange a fanfare of trumpets, she thought miserably; Roger was all for pomp and ceremony, and the ring he would slip on her finger in front of the gathered assembly? She narrowed her eyes. It would be ostentatious and very, very costly.

Thinking of one ring, another was invariably brought to mind and Serena could still feel the weight of it on her third finger even it was no longer there. The tears pricked dangerously near the surface and making a vain effort to shake off these sad memories, she told herself with bitter humour that not every girl got engaged twice in one week and she really ought to feel honoured!

Mrs Belmont, when she had managed to tear herself away from a Mr Janson, a widower and rich industrialist, who had formed a predilection for her company, finally located her daughter in her cabin preparing to dress for the supper party.

"Darling!" she exclaimed, pulling Serena close, "I'm so happy for you. I knew you would say yes eventually, but I was so afraid you . . ." she hesitated as she met Serena's eyes. "Well," she went on lamely, "money isn't everything, is it?"

Serena started to laugh, but she wasn't really laughing, it was more in the nature of a mild attack of hysterics. Of all the people to make such a profound statement...!

"Serena?" asked Mrs Belmont uncertainly, not liking the lost, haunted look in her daughter's eyes.

Wiping her eyes, Serena smiled wanly. "It's all right, Mother. I suppose the past events have caught up with me. I know it's for the best, and I suppose one day I'll . . ." she choked on the last few words, then pulled herself together. "You'd better get ready, hadn't you? And I must hurry or Roger will be pounding on the door demanding to know what's keeping me."

Mrs Belmont had never known her daughter to be unhappy, and she loved her very much. For the first time she realised, somewhat belatedly, that what she had been urging Serena to do for months might not bring her the happiness she so desperately wanted for her. "Darling, you don't have to . . . Roger will..." she began hesitantly.

Giving her a wry smile, Serena pushed her to the door. "I said it's going to be all right," she said firmly. "Stop worrying and let me get on and dress."

Mrs Belmont did leave then, but it was obvious she had a lot on her mind, and Serena, wearily closing the cabin door after her, knew she wouldn't leave it at that. As for what she had said about Roger understanding, or would have said if given the opportunity, Serena sighed; her mother didn't know Roger half as well as she thought she did, and if she made any attempt to talk him out of the engagement she was in for a rude awakening.

Serena wore the white organdie gown she had worn at Jordan's ball. It brought back painful memories, but so would her blue velvet, she thought miserably. She couldn't discard them, they were the only evening dresses she had brought with her. A tap on the cabin door told her Roger was waiting for her and the look he gave her brought his last words sharply into focus again, and Serena almost shivered as he silently pulled her into his arms before escorting her to supper.

His kiss was fierce and demanding and again she tried to respond, and once again failed. The little smile he gave at her quick withdrawal from his arms worried Serena even more than his words had done. It promised firm action later that evening when they were alone.

She knew a moment's panic, then firmly took herself in hand. She was only getting engaged, after all, not married. She could still break it off if Roger persisted in treating her as if he owned her body and soul.

The small but luxurious dining room was as yet half empty when they arrived, and two stewards stood by waiting to serve the meal. The others would be taking their aperitifs in the bar and Serena, knowing Roger would wait until they were all seated before making the announcement, fervently hoped they would take their time.

She wondered if she were dreaming when the cry went up. "Pirates!" shrieked a feminine voice. Then there were more shrieks and then laughter. Serena glanced at Roger, but he was as nonplussed as she. His eyebrows rose a fraction, then one of the guests, meeting his eyes, grinned. "It's a stunt, I expect. We're not far from Blue Island, I believe it's one of the attractions there."

Blue Island! The very name started Serena's heart palpitating. What if Jordan were one of them? Her mouth felt dry. She prayed that if he were present he would stay on deck and having made an appearance, make his departure with equal speed! Only too well could she imagine his reaction on seeing her on board, and with Roger! As usual, his eyes would say it all.

Suddenly the laughter and shrieks grew louder, and the next moment the room seemed filled with "pirates".

Against her will Serena's eyes were drawn to their leader, standing so straight and tall in front of his men. Almost as if he knew I was here, she thought bewilderedly as his eyes met hers and stayed on hers as he walked slowly towards their table.

Feeling a distinct urge to run, Serena gripped her serviette tightly and tried to break that mesmeric hold he had on her.

Reaching their table, Jordan gave them a mocking bow and Roger, entering into the spirit of the thing, said, "I'm afraid we've no treasure on board, old man, but you're welcome to as much rum as you can sink."

Jordan's eyes slowly left Serena and turned to Roger. "Oh, but you have treasure," he murmured softly, his eyes returning to Serena. "And I'm afraid I'm going to relieve you of it."

Even if she had wanted to move, Serena couldn't. It was as if her limbs were turned to jelly. He's playing with me again, she told herself wildly. She couldn't go through that again, anything was better than that. "Roger—" she began desperately, but the rest of the sentence was never uttered as she found herself firmly caught and slung into a vaguely familiar position over Jordan's broad shoulders.

In sheer panic she struggled to release herself, but she knew from past experience that she was not going to be successful.

The action had so surprised Roger it had taken a second or so for him to recover and he made an attempt to free the struggling Serena, but he was handicapped by his ankle. "I think the joke's gone a little too far," he commented caustically. "Would you mind releasing my fiancée?"

Jordan's grasp on Serena tightened as he looked back at Roger. "I saw no ring," he commented casually. "Besides, she makes a habit of getting engaged, didn't you know? I intend to cure that tendency!" he added as he turned towards the door with his unwilling captive.

Roger made a grab at his stick and glared at the grinning men around him. "John!" he commanded to one nearest him. "For heaven's sake, do something! Don't just stand there grinning!"

"It's okay, old man," replied John. "I've seen it all before. He'll return her within a short while."

Jordan stopped in his tracks and turned back to the company. "I regret I must disabuse you. This is one prize I shall not be returning." This assertion, though quietly said, set up shock waves.

Serena, still struggling, saw a general surge forward in a late effort to rescue her, but Jordan's men formed a line between them and the door.

The last person Serena saw before she was so unceremoniously bundled out of the dining room was her mother, and she was certain she had given her a wicked wink!

CHAPTER THIRTEEN

JORDAN did not release her until he had watched the rearguard of his men leave the yacht and join what looked like a small flotilla of motor boats stationed alongside. Then his deep voice gave the order, "Let's away, Jake!" and the air was filled with the deep throbbing of the engines and one by one the small fleet swept out to sea.

Serena felt herself lowered to the deck of the powerful motor boat now making fast headway in the lead of the other boats, and she watched the twinkling lights of the yacht dwindle into dimness as the distance between the boat and the yacht was lengthened.

She was only too aware of Jordan standing close beside her, ready if need be to lay a restraining hand on her should she try to make a break for the side. Tensely she wondered what nasty little surprise he had up his sleeve for her this time. He must have decided she had got off a little too lightly and thought up some other way she could pay her debt to society.

When his voice spoke close to her ear she started and moved slightly away from him. "Shall we go below?" he suggested.

The heavy throb of the boat's engines made normal conversation impossible, but whatever he had to say Serena preferred to hear it right there and then; the breeze playing over her face and the spray sending up white plumes of water that sprayed over the deck would, she felt, help lessen the shock. "I'm quite happy where I am," she replied, trying to sound casual.

His reply was to sweep her off her feet and carry her down the two shallow steps leading to the cabin. "As I believe I told you once before," he remarked airily, "Milady has no choice in the matter."

As if she had no power left in her legs he put her down gently on one of the leather-covered chairs in the small salon, then sat down opposite her.

Serena watched him warily as he slipped the bandanna off his head and solemnly laid it on her lap. Without taking his eyes off her he said slowly and very distinctly, "Marry me, Serena Belmont."

A slightly stunned Serena realised he was telling her he now knew who she was. Her dazed eyes left his and rested on the bandanna.

"It's a custom of ours," he said gently. "Another way of laying our heart at the feet of the woman of our choice."

Hardly recognising her own voice, Serena whispered huskily, "Why?"

"Why the custom—or why the proposal?" he replied lightly. "I'll tell you about the custom some other time. As for the proposal—well, there's only one reason a man asks a woman to marry him, and I'm no exception to the rule."

He got up suddenly and pulled her into his arms. "We're wasting time," he said in a voice even deeper than its normal tone as he drew her closer into the circle of his arms.

With all her heart Serena wanted to respond; the love she had thought was denied her was hers for the taking. Why then did she hesitate? What perverse streak of nature held her back? Afraid to meet his eyes, she concentrated on his broad chest and noted absently how a thread of her dress had got entangled in the fine stitching of his jerkin. Then she had it: Maria! Maria was, had been, his woman; there would be no other. The thing she had been so afraid would happen had happened. He was now sorry for her—that kiss, she thought bitterly, remembering how she had melted in his arms and the shameless way she had clung to his lips. He knew she loved him! There could be no other answer for his gallant but heartbreaking offer.

Somehow she summoned up the strength to release herself from his hold and rushed to the door. She needed to get as far as possible from him; she didn't trust herself not to break down and be coerced into accepting his offer and spending the rest of her life competing with Maria's ghost.

Her hand was on the door when he reached out one long arm and hauled her back again. This time there was no escape from those strong arms of his. He caught the back of her head and made her look up at him.

"Leave me alone," she whispered pleadingly.

"I'll never leave you alone," Jordan answered harshly. "And you might as well accept that fact. I meant every word I said back there. I've got you and I'll keep you. You've got a lot to atone for. From the day you agreed to become Mrs Tonetti's accomplice you turned my well-ordered existence into a living hell. Can you," he said in a dangerously soft voice, "imagine my feelings when the one and only woman I could ever care for descends on me in the guise of the woman who had caused so much unhappiness to two very dear friends of mine? And there you stood looking like a Raphael painting. I loved you the moment I set eyes on you and spent the rest of that hellish time trying to hate you."

He pulled her fiercely closer and sought her lips saying as his met hers, "Don't try and deny me, my love. I won't be denied."

There was still Maria, she thought miserably as his lips at last released hers. Even now, as weak as she was in his arms, she couldn't forget Maria.

Holding her away from him, Jordan saw the hesitation in her eyes and mistaking it for uncertainty of her feelings for him, said softly, "I remember someone turning to me for comfort. I also remember lips wanting mine as much as I wanted them."

Serena could have wept, instead she gathered her forces for her last defence. His words had given her the spur she so badly needed. Her lovely eyes met his levelly as she said, "And Maria?"

Her heart leapt painfully as she watched his start at the name. That was one little fact he hadn't accounted for, she thought bitterly, and one that made a nonsense of his declaration that she was the only woman he had ever cared for. Serena thanked providence that she had kept her head and had not given way to her feelings. Now he would have to take those words back and the bald truth would at last come out.

She shivered; she didn't want to hear them, it was enough that she had been saved the painful knowledge before she accepted his proposal. She jerked herself away from him and walked over to the porthole and stood gazing out vaguely wondering where they were and whether he would take her back to Roger afterwards.

"How did you know about Maria?" he began.

Serena cut in wearily, "Does it matter? I know, that's all. And I'd be grateful if you would return me to the yacht."

She shivered again as she felt his arms slide round her waist and pull her close to his hard body. "We'll forget that last request, if you don't mind," he said firmly. "Now about Maria," he went on as he forced the struggling Serena to subside her efforts to release herself. "Whether you like it or not, you're going to hear. There's going to be no skeletons in this family cupboard." Then musingly he added, "Mrs Tonetti, of course—I ought to have known!"

He turned the now weak Serena round to face him and because she had no strength was able to coax her to lay her head against his shoulder. "That's better," he said gently. "Now let me tell you about Maria, who was beautiful and very spoilt. She was also born with the unfortunate knack of wanting what she couldn't have." He paused for a second or so as his lips touched Serena's hair. "As she grew older she had many admirers, but I'm afraid I was not among them. It might have been better if I had been. You see, I presented a challenge to her. At first it was slightly amusing; she would try little tricks to gain my attention; later, however, it became a downright embarrassment. It didn't help when my father encouraged her. He wanted to see me settled and thought Maria would make the ideal wife for me. He was of course slightly biased because of the long-standing friendship between our two families.

"After my father died I was able to avoid the get-togethers that occurred every weekend. Because of business connections I had to do a lot of travelling and that way was able to partially sever old commitments. However, I'm afraid Maria was a very determined girl and whether I was on the island or away on business, she would still spend her weekends here."

Serena stirred in his arms. She had heard enough, now she was able to understand. Jordan's eyes met hers and the love she saw in them made her catch her breath. Then he pulled himself together sharply and went on. "That's how she became acquainted with Mrs Tonetti," he said quietly. "She used to stay with her when they came over on holiday."

There was another pause and Serena sensed he was coming to the part he most disliked, but she knew he would not be put off from relating it. "I was here the weekend she died," he said slowly. "One of her manoeuvres to get my attention backfired with the tragic result of her death. It wasn't the first time she would do something crazy and land herself up in a position from which she had to be rescued, always of course with the knowledge that I was in the near vicinity, for that was the sole object of the exercise, and in spite of repeated warnings that the next time I'd leave her to get herself out of trouble, she still persevered." His voice deepened and Serena wound her arms round his neck. She could guess what came next.

"Not that I ever would have done," he said wearily. "It was just that I wasn't where she thought I was. There's a special spot on the southern point of the island where I used to go fishing. It's pretty inaccessible unless you know the way, and for my own peace and solitude I made pretty certain it stayed that way. Jake is the only other one who knows. Well, Maria couldn't get that information, but she did know approximately where my line would reach the water, and although she knew full well the dangers of swimming in that area it didn't deter her. She was a pretty strong swimmer anyway.

"I don't know what actually happened, but my guess is she called for help—which I might add she had done on several other occasions when she wasn't in the slightest danger. No matter, had I been there no doubt I would have gone in to rescue her. That's the trouble with a joker, you can never tell whether it's the real thing, or not. Having acted as though she were in trouble, I believe she found she had underestimated her own strength to battle with the elements."

For a while he was silent and Serena hoped he had finished, but there was more.

"Afterwards, I found out that she had deliberately misconstrued our relationship. Goodness knows what she had told Mrs Tonetti, but it was a plain fact that the whole island had been waiting for our engagement to be announced. To contradict the fabrication after her death would have looked callous—besides, it served no purpose."

His arms tightened around Serena. "So you see, my love, why I kept a healthy distance from any other designing female. I learnt a hard lesson and one that kept me safe until I met my destiny."

After his lips had hungrily reached once more for hers, he said huskily, "After I kissed you that night I knew my feelings were too strong and that I'd never be able to keep you at arm's distance. I also knew, or thought I knew, how quickly you'd catch on to that fact and would capitalise on it. As much as I hated you for what I thought you were, I wanted you so badly I would have been lost in the end. I had to send you away from me. When you'd gone I wandered back to Mrs Tonetti's. It was as if I couldn't keep away. I wanted to see the room you'd slept in, to touch the pillow that your head had lain against. I think I was half crazy." He drew a deep breath. "Then Molly gave me a letter, a letter that brought a rainbow into the room and that made me want to shout for joy. I was impatient to claim my one and only love, and the thought that I'd sent you back to the arms of Alton was almost unbearable." He ran his hands through her long silky hair. "But I couldn't leave right then. There were things to be seen to."

Serena knew he was referring to Mrs Tonetti's death. "Jordan, did we..."

He understood the question. "I don't know, my love. Perhaps; but one day I'll let you read the letter she left for me. One thing I can tell you, my darling, she died happy." There was another pause, then he said softly, "You know, I think it would be rather nice if we named our second child after her."

Serena's heart turned over and meeting his eyes she stammered, "Second child?"

He nodded autocratically. "Of course; the Kerrs' first-born is always a boy, and you won't need three guesses to know his Christian name!"

So saying, he swept her back into his arms. "You're too far away," he complained.

MASTER OF BEN ROSS

Master
of Ben Ross
Lucy Gillen

Melodie was enchanted—Scotland was even more beautiful than she'd imagined. John was right: if this country didn't inspire her to paint as she'd never done before, nothing would.

Her painting did go well, but soon Melodie discovered that there was more to inspire her here than just the countryside. There was her handsome host, Neil McDowell.

But once again John had predicted correctly, for Neil loved the estate and his work far more than he could ever love a woman. Melodie wondered if she should leave Ben Ross before it was too late, before she fell in love with Neil. Then she realized that it had been too late from the day she met him. . . .

CHAPTER ONE

GLEN ROSS station was more or less as Melodie expected it to be, and she smiled to herself as she stepped down from the train and stood looking around her for a moment or two. The simple concrete platform ran one side only and scarcely merited the title of station, but there was also a little stone hut built at one end of it and an elderly man was just emerging from the door to speak to another, younger man. If her information was correct Jamie McClure, the stationmaster-cum-ticket-seller, was much more helpful and kindly than his somewhat austere appearance suggested, and she approached him fairly confidently.

It had been suggested that someone would meet her when she arrived, but being fairly familiar with the vagaries of British Rail she had decided to take a taxi instead in case she missed the connection. The idea of keeping a stranger waiting around for her did not appeal at all and since there was a taxi on call she might as well make use of it.

The stationmaster was at present busy in conversation, but both men turned when she approached carrying her suitcase, and it was easy to guess that new arrivals were few and far between at Glen Ross. The younger man watched with a certain air of anticipation as she walked along the tiny platform, and made no secret of the fact that he liked what he saw, while the older one viewed her arrival with more plain curiosity.

Melodie was not very tall, but she had enough good dress sense to make the most of a softly rounded figure and slim legs, and with long black hair and wide blue eyes she was pretty enough to be used to admiration without being self-conscious about it. Consequently when she put down her suitcase and hovered discreetly, it was with the confidence that she would get someone's almost immediate attention.

Although the older man was not impressed in the same way as his younger companion, he was nevertheless curious enough to look across at her inquiringly. The younger one was quite attractive, although he was not, strictly speaking, good-looking. His features below a thick thatch of brown hair were open and friendly, and he had brown eyes that smiled when he did, and looked warm and encouraging, as if he might prove helpful should the stationmaster not be as co-operative as promised.

"Oh, please, don't let me interrupt," Melodie begged when their conversation ceased, but the younger man was shaking his head.

"Oh no, that's O.K., you're not interrupting anything. I'm about through now—please go ahead."

His accent had a definite transatlantic twang and

was not even vaguely Scottish, which surprised her, for she had already decided that he was a local, largely because of his features, she had to admit. He had what she had always thought of as a Scottish face—rugged but friendly, and rather attractive.

"I understand it's possible for me to get a taxi from here." She addressed herself to the older man, and he nodded.

"Aye, that's right. He disna stand in the yard, but if you're needing him I can ring for him tae come. Would you be wantin' me tae call him?"

"Well, I have to get to Ben Ross," Melodie explained, "and it's quite a distance, I believe." She gave him one of her best smiles, shamelessly seeking to get on the right side of him. "You must be Mr McClure?" she guessed.

For a moment she had the awful feeling that her efforts were going to be met with a firm snub, but then she realised that there was a faint smile barely noticeable on the dour face, and he was nodding. "I am that," he admitted, plainly puzzled by her knowledge. "You say you're wantin' to get to Ben Ross?"

"That's right." She was so thankful to have broken the ice that she gave him another smile. "I think you knew someone who lived there for a while, some years ago now. Catriona Holland—do you remember her?"

The old man's smile broadened and he nodded more firmly now. "Oh aye, I remember the lassie well! Miss Ross, she was then, o' course. She inherited the old house when her uncle died, then married and went off to Australia—I mind her well." His shrewd old eyes scanned her face once more curiously. "You'll be a relation, nae doubt?"

"Not a relation," Melodie denied, "only a friend. I'm to stay at the lodge cottage for the next couple of months, and I'm really looking forward to it."

"Ooh aye?" It was plain that the information surprised him, although it was difficult to imagine why, unless there was something about the place that she had not been told.

"You seem—surprised, Mr McClure." She looked at him both anxiously and curiously. "Is there any reason why I shouldn't stay at the cottage?"

"Och, no, no." He was shaking his head again. "Yon's a fine quiet and peaceful place for a holiday, though it's mebbe a wee bit isolated for a young lassie like yourself."

"Oh, I don't mind that!" Melodie laughed, dismissing the problem of isolation. "I'm not exactly on holiday, you see, I'll be working—at least I hope I will. My name's Melodie Carne, I'm an artist."

Once more the old man looked vaguely surprised, but it was evident he thought it none of his business to show anything more than a polite interest. "Well, it's a grand place for scenery too, and if you're to be busy you'll not be minding the isolation so much."

"It will make sure I work, at least," Melodie agreed. "Now if you would be so kind, Mr McClure—"

"Oh aye, your taxi. If you'll just wait a wee while, Miss Carne, I'll get him to come and fetch you."

"Hold it!" She had almost forgotten the young man busily stowing boxes in the boot of his car, but he was evidently still within earshot and interested in what was being said, for he put the last box in the car, then came to join them. His brown eyes were smiling at Melodie warmly and it was to her that he spoke. "I'm going out that way in just a minute, if I can be of any help," he said.

It would be an easy solution and it was one that appealed to her, Melodie had to admit. "That's very kind of you—but are you sure it isn't taking you out of your way?"

"Not in the least—I'm actually going to Ben Ross."

"Oh!"

She glanced at the boxes he had been putting into his car. Somehow he did not strike her as a delivery man, and he was not Neil McDowell. Her friends had described the Ben Ross estate manager as being almost blond, and this man had dark brown hair, apart from the fact that he wasn't old enough—Neil McDowell should be in his mid-thirties, and this man was not much older than herself.

"You may as well save the cab fare," the man beside her suggested, and she laughed, ready enough to fall in with the mildly joking reference to Scottish thrift.

"In that case, I will—thank you."

"My pleasure!" He offered a hand and with a smile she put hers in to it. "I'm John Stirling—my uncle works on the Ben Ross estate."

"Oh, I see." His identity was clear at last, although judging by the size and opulence of the car he was driving, either it belonged to the estate or else Neil McDowell paid his men very well.

"O.K.?"

He waited for her nod of consent before lifting her case into the boot of the car with the boxes he had been stowing, and Melodie turned back to the little stationmaster and smiled. "It seems I won't be wanting a taxi after all, Mr McClure, thank you." Impulsively she offered him her hand. "Goodbye, it's been nice meeting you."

John Stirling saw her into his car and the old man was still watching curiously when they drove out on to a crunchy stone road that led steeply uphill. Looking back through the car window Melodie could see the hill continue on its way, this time sloping steeply downwards into what could be the village of Glen Ross—a collection of small cottages about a mile distant from the station.

The road continued to rise just as steeply and she felt her heart beating faster all the time as excitement and anticipation mounted the nearer they got to Ben Ross. She looked forward to the next two months with growing confidence now that she was here, and it was obvious that she wasn't going to be disappointed in Scotland. It was going to be all it was said to be if her first experience of it was a true indication.

The scenery was breathtaking and she tried to take in everything as she was driven up the hill. She

caught fleeting glimpses of distant horizons sometimes, between the trees; vistas of mountains with
their heads in the mist, and broad sweeps of blue sky
as a background. There were trees either side of the
road, young rowans for the most part and not yet
fully grown, and immediately behind and between
them a mass of wild roses was hung with small pink
faces that peered from a tangle of green briars and
leaves.

Beyond them the ground sloped steeply in another
direction, down to what looked like a rocky glen of
some kind, where a river or a stream flowed around
the foot of the hill and glinted and gleamed in the
sunlight. The hillside itself was dotted with stunted
elder and with goat-willow, and the water could be
seen only as tantalising glimpses between them.
What she could see looked so enchanting that she
promised herself a much closer look before too long.

"Did I hear you tell the stationmaster that you're
an artist?"

John Stirling's pleasant voice snatched her back to
the present, and Melodie nodded. "I'm hoping to be
one day," she told him. "I'm supposed to be—well,
quite good, but I'm still only a beginner, and lately I
haven't been getting on very well. I'm hoping Scotland will inspire me."

"If it doesn't, nothing will!" he assured her.

Melodie looked out of the car window again, and
could only agree with him. "It's so beautiful, I can't
quite believe it's true," she said. "I've never seen
anything like it."

"It's very like parts of Canada." He spoke with such confidence that she felt she could safely confirm that transatlantic accent, but before she could ask, he forestalled her by asking her about her own origins. "Where are you from, Miss Carne?"

"From Surrey originally, but we moved as a family to Australia a couple of years ago."

"And now you're back in the U.K.?"

"Only me." She laughed and pulled a face, wondering why she felt she had to offer an excuse for her returning. "The others settled down quite happily."

He did not take his eyes off the road, and she thought he was not asking the question out of mere curiosity—he was interested. "But you *weren't* happy?" he suggested, and she laughed and shook her head.

"I wasn't exactly unhappy, just—restless. It's a wonderful country, but I simply couldn't settle down over there. I happened to mention at a party one evening that I'd like to go back—come back, and some friends of mine suggested I had a couple of months up here in Scotland to see if I could get back to working the way I used to."

John Stirling smiled at her over his shoulder, a warm encouraging smile. "I warn you, this place works spells," he said. "You might find when your couple of months is up you won't want to leave."

Melodie looked out at the hills in the distance, and the clouds scattered like flakes of snow in the summer blue sky and smiled. "I might at that," she agreed.

It was something of a surprise when he sounded more serious suddenly. "Do you know Neil McDowell?" he asked, and she shook her head.

"No, I don't know him, only about him." He hesitated, or so it seemed to her, as if he was in two minds about something he had to say, and she looked at him curiously. "Why do you ask, Mr Stirling?"

"Oh—no reason!"

His shrug and the tone of his voice were enough to put ideas into her head; discomfiting ideas that disturbed her present rather complacent satisfaction, and she continued to look at him while she sought for reasons. If there was something about Neil McDowell that she should know, she would rather learn it now, before she arrived, than have whatever it was sprung on her after she got there.

"Tell me about him," she said, and put on her most persuasive look when he turned his head for a moment. "I'd like to know what I'm up against, Mr Stirling, and at the moment I have a strange feeling that I might not be as welcome as I'd hoped."

John Stirling made no reply for a moment or two, then he shrugged. "It's nothing much," he confessed. "It's just that I'm rather surprised that he's having someone stay there, that's all, though of course if his boss said you were coming there wouldn't be much he could do about it, I guess." He laughed and shook his head as he glanced briefly at her, and Melodie looked at him curiously.

"You mean—he doesn't like anyone staying

there?" It was a possibility that had not occurred to her, and she viewed it with dismay.

"I can't honestly say that, because I've never heard his opinion on visitors," John Stirling admitted. "But he guards Ben Ross as jealously as if he really was the laird."

"That's the Scottish equivalent of a—a lord of the manor, isn't it?"

He nodded. "The locals refer to him as the laird of Ben Ross, though I've always taken it as rather a joke, but—I don't know. Maybe I'm wrong and they really look upon him as the laird; I guess he is to all intents and purposes, for he's looked after the estate since the days when old man Ross was still alive, and he must feel a kind of possessive love for the place."

More than that, Melodie thought, from the sureness of inside knowledge. She had a letter in her handbag, and papers that would put Ben Ross completely into the hands of Neil McDowell once all the legal formalities had been completed. His former employer and benefactor had left him a wealthy man and he had at last achieved his ambition to own the old house he was so fond of by persuading the old man's niece to sell it to him. All this she knew because Catriona Holland had entrusted her with the precious papers—but she knew nothing of the man himself, or almost nothing, and perhaps John Stirling could enlighten her.

"You know him quite well?"

He shrugged. "I know him," he said. "I doubt if

anyone knows him really well, he isn't a man it's easy to get close to, but he's not as dour as some folks think he is either." He laughed and looked at her briefly. "Dour is a Scottish word," he informed her. "It means kind of—forbidding, stern, if you like."

"Oh dear!"

It was obvious he regretted the impression he had given, and he was shaking his head. "I'm sorry, Miss Carne, I guess maybe I've put you against the man before you've even met him, and I didn't want to do that." He turned the car into a gateway as he spoke, then put on the brake and turned in his seat to look at her. "This is the lodge cottage," he told her. "Do I drop you off here, or shall I take you up to the house?"

To one side of the drive, hidden by tall shrubs for some half of its height, was a small stone cottage. It looked quite homely for all it was obviously empty, and Melodie felt vaguely out of her depth for a moment or two, until she remembered that she had no way of getting into her new home, even if she wanted to.

"I have to get the key from the house," she said, "so if you could—"

"Nothing simpler!" He was smiling and somehow that was very reassuring, then he started up the car again and drove between high borders of shrubs which gave glimpses of steep hillsides on either side and a loch far down in a valley, shining like a blue silk patch amid the soft drabness of heather. "Please don't take me wrong about McDowell," John Stirling begged. "He isn't as dour as he's reputed to be, and anyway—" he turned and smiled at her "—one look at you and he'll be charmed to welcome you."

"I hope so."

Melodie was recalling another opinion of Neil McDowell—a woman's opinion, and probably one that was mellowed by time and pleasant memories. She always suspected that there might have been something between Catriona Holland and her estate manager at one time, although nothing had ever been said to encourage such a suspicion. It was just something in the way she spoke of him, and in the way Nick Holland looked at his wife sometimes when she spoke of him. Maybe Neil McDowell nursed an unrequited love, in which case he was unlikely to be charmed by another woman even after eight years.

She looked at John Stirling again from the corner of her eye, and hoped she would see something of him while she was here. He seemed pleasant and uncomplicated, and he might prove a welcome means of support if Neil McDowell should prove as dour as he suggested.

"You don't come from around here either, do you, Mr Stirling?" she asked, dismissing her prospective host from her mind for the moment, and John Stirling shook his head.

"I was born not far from here, but my folks, like yours, emigrated, only in their case it was to Canada. We went just after my fifth birthday, so I guess you could say I'm practically one hundred per cent Canadian after twenty years. My folks still have a Scottish burr in their speech, but not me, I'm afraid!"

"So you're just visiting, like me."

"Not quite like you," he denied with a laugh. "I've no intention of doing anything remotely like work while I'm here."

"Are you here for long?"

He shrugged carelessly, then cast her a smile over his shoulder. "I arrived last week and I figure to stay at least another couple of months."

"Oh, I see." She didn't like to ask outright, but it was difficult to imagine him wealthy enough to take such a long holiday if his uncle was an estate worker. "You don't have to worry about how long you stay away, then?"

"I can't quite say that." He pulled a face, as if he found what he was about to say a little embarrassing. "Don't be misled by Uncle Jamie working for the Ross estate, Miss Carne—I guess you could say we're kind of—rich relations. Isn't that the term they used to apply to the wild colonial boys who made good?"

"Something like that," Melodie agreed, frankly interested.

"My pa made good in a big way out there and he built up a business that by now runs like clockwork, but he still puts in ten or more hours a day, would you believe?" He laughed and shook his head, evidently finding his father's passion for business beyond his comprehension. "I've been put through the processes from A to Z and I guess I know it pretty well by now, but—" He shrugged and once more turned a smile on her. "I like to unwind a little now and then and when I do I take off and come and stay with Uncle Jamie."

"It sounds marvellous!"

He laughed and shook his head. "It is, believe me! I ride sometimes, McDowell makes his stables available to me, and I fish and generally laze around." The brown eyes smiled their warmth at her once more. "Maybe I could persuade you to join me instead of working, huh?"

"Maybe you can—sometimes!"

He braked the car in front of a big brick house with tall windows and huge wooden doors, and Melodie sat for a second taking it in. "Well, here you are, Miss Carne—Ben Ross."

Five wide and impressive stone steps led up to the front doors and Melodie had the strangest sensation of having been delivered rather than merely being given a lift. It was a moment or two before she took advantage of the car door being opened for her, and she thought John Stirling was watching her curiously as he waited.

"Thank you." She accepted his help and stood on the gravel drive looking up at the old house. "I—I suppose there's someone home?"

"Sure to be," John Stirling assured her confidently, then slid a hand beneath her arm and bent his head slightly as he lowered his voice. "Would you like me to come with you, at least as far as the door?"

She accepted the offer gratefully. "I'm an awful coward," she confessed with a faint smile. "But I keep thinking of Neil McDowell as stern and forbidding ever since you described him."

"Oh, gee, I'm sorry!" He looked dismayed at the idea of being the cause of her nervousness. "I wasn't trying to scare you off, and he really isn't too bad when you know him, honest!"

He kept hold of her arm while they walked up the stone steps together, carefully avoiding the dangerously worn parts in the centre. An ancient iron bellpull clanged somewhere inside the house, and they waited in silence while Melodie looked around at the garden behind them.

"Miss Carne's here to see Mr McDowell, Mrs McKay." John Stirling's voice recalled her, and she spun round quickly when she realised the doors had been opened.

She had heard of Jessie McKay too, and her reputation was less guaranteed to inspire confidence, a reputation seemingly confirmed by a pair of shrewd and distinctly unfriendly brown eyes. She was plump and her round face wore a slight frown, as if she did not welcome strangers on her doorstep. A plait of grey hair encircled her head like a coronet and made her appear yet more severe as she took stock of Melodie before she spoke.

"Come away in, Miss Carne, and I'll tell Mr McDowell you're here." She acknowledged John

Stirling with a slight nod of her head, and made it plain that he was not included in the invitation. "You'll not be wanting to see Mr McDowell as well, Mr Stirling?"

If she expected him to take the question as a dismissal she must have been disappointed, for he was not as easily put off as she obviously expected him to be. "I have Miss Carne's luggage in my car," he explained, unabashed by his chilly welcome. "I brought her up from the station, so I guess I'll hang around until she's ready to go back to the cottage."

"You'll wait in your car?"

It was clear what she expected the answer to be, and Melodie saw a hint of a smile appear on his mouth. "Sure, I'll wait outside!" He smiled at Melodie reassuringly and partly closed one eye in a suggestion of a wink. "See you later, Miss Carne!"

"You're sure you don't *mind* waiting?"

It seemed rather an imposition after the way he had been treated by the housekeeper, but he was apparently untroubled by it and grinned cheerfully. "Not in the least," he assured her. "I'll still be here when you come out again."

"Thank you."

When Melodie stepped in through the doors it was like entering another world, different from any she had known before. The hall she found herself in was enough to make her stare about her in frank amazement, for it was so exactly what every stately home is reputed to be like that she could scarcely believe it was real.

Above her head it soared upwards almost out of sight in the shadows, dark-panelled for the first few feet, then painted starkly white the rest of the way up to the vaulted ceiling. A staircase occupied the whole of one wall and a huge portrait hung about half way—a huge portrait of a man whose dark visage seemed to dominate the hall and whose sharp dark eyes appeared to watch her with discomfitingly lifelike sternness.

Yet strangely enough there was an air of homeliness about the place, despite its grandeur, an atmosphere of quiet that she found encouraging. She thought the housekeeper was regarding her curiously and she hastened to explain her interest.

"I've heard so much about Ben Ross," she said, "I've been dying to see it." She indicated the portrait on the stair, pressing on impulsively as she was prone to do. "That's Mr Duncan Ross, isn't it?" she asked. "It's a wonderful painting."

"It's a guid likeness," Jessie McKay allowed, and spoke with the authority of familiarity.

"Mrs Holland told me about the painting," Melodie explained. "I have an interest, you see, being an artist."

"Oh aye, you would."

It was scarcely an encouraging response, but Melodie hoped her manner was not an indication of what she could expect from her employer. She led the way across the hall to one of the doors that gave on to it, and indicated that Melodie should follow. "Mr McDowell's in here."

"Here" proved to be a library as grand as the hall. It was huge and furnished with rich leather furniture, and leather-bound books lined the walls on three sides. A massive fireplace, screened for the summer with a huge wrought iron screen, seemed to span half one long wall. Tall, arch-topped windows admitted the sun, but the room was cool, and she barely had time to notice very much before her attention was drawn to the man who stood in front of the fireplace.

It was a curious sensation to see someone she had had described to her and to find nothing at all recognisable about him. For one thing Neil McDowell was taller than she expected, and less handsome than she had been led to believe. He might have been very good-looking at one time, Melodie thought, but at thirty-three or four he was lean and rugged and looked every bit as dour as she feared.

At the same time there was a curious magnetism about him, a suggestion of power and self-confidence that sat well on the broad shoulders. His hair was fair; thick and glossy and falling over part of a broad brow, and he had grey eyes that were steady and confident, but not especially friendly as he looked across at her while she followed his housekeeper over to where he stood.

He wore breeches and boots and a shirt that was open at the neck to show a brown throat, and he looked so completely at home standing there with his feet just slightly apart in front of that huge fireplace that it was difficult to believe he was not already the owner of Ben Ross.

"Thank you, Jessie." A brief nod dismissed the formidable Mrs McKay and she went out again, leaving Melodie alone with her supposedly unwilling host.

"Miss Carne—I'm Neil McDowell." He extended a hand and she took it a little cautiously, wincing slightly when the strong brown fingers curled over hers for a second only. "Please sit down." She did as she was bid, perching herself right on the edge of one of the big wing armchairs. "Did you have a good journey?"

His voice was pleasantly low and the softness of the Highland accent made it more attractive, but he asked as if she had come only from somewhere just south of the border, instead of several thousand miles from Australia.

"Yes, thank you, Mr McDowell. It's a long way, of course, and I'm rather tired what with the jet-lag and—"

"You need the key to the cottage, of course."

She nodded and opened her handbag, pulling out the bulky envelope she had been charged with delivering. "I also have a letter and some papers for you from Mrs Holland."

"Ah yes." A large hand took the packet from her and he nodded his satisfaction. "Thank you, Miss Carne." He looked down at the envelope in his hand for a moment, as if he was impatient to open it and study its contents, and she had the feeling he was waiting for her to go as soon as possible. "I'll get the key for you!"

He strode across to a big bureau and pulled down the front of it, returning a second later with a key which he handed to her. "Thank you."

The grey eyes spared her a moment and she was surprised to see a quite unexpected glimmer of speculation in them. "Do you ride, Miss Carne?" She nodded and he smiled. "Ah yes, of course, you're Australian, aren't you—brought up to ride horses!"

"I'm not Australian, Mr McDowell, I'm English, though I've spent the last two years in Australia." She was afraid she might have sounded rather sharp when she contradicted him, so she smiled to take any suggestion of criticism out of the words. "That's not long enough to make an Aussie," she told him. "But I do ride, as it happens, though not very well, I'm afraid."

From the way he was dressed it was obvious he rode, and probably very well, and she half expected an invitation to join him, despite the reputation for dourness. Instead he nodded, tapping the packet he held against the thumb of one hand in a way that hinted at impatience.

"Please feel free to use any of the horses in the stables while you're here, except Black Knight, he's not a woman's horse and he can be hard to handle."

"I'll remember." She smiled at him again, wondering whatever had possessed John Stirling to suppose that one smile was enough to charm him. "And thank you." She got up from the edge of her chair and indicated the package he held. "I'll go and unpack, and leave you to read your letter."

"Aye, thank you." He held her gaze for a moment and she found the grey eyes unexpectedly warm when he smiled. "Enjoy your stay, Miss Carne." Something seemed to occur to him suddenly and he frowned. "I should have thought," he said, "have you left your luggage at the cottage, or have you now to carry it down there? If you have I'll have the car out in a moment and run you down there."

"Oh no!" She felt curiously uneasy suddenly when she came to tell him about John Stirling, though heaven knew why. "I—I had a lift from the station, and Mr Stirling's waiting for me with my suitcase in his car, the rest of my stuff will be coming some time soon."

"Jamie Stirling?"

There was something about the way he asked the question that told her he knew who she referred to quite well. "No," she said, "John Stirling. I believe his uncle works on the estate."

He neither confirmed nor denied that fact, but merely nodded his head as if the matter was of no further interest to him. "You'll not be needing my help, then," he said, and Melodie took that for her dismissal.

She looked at the key in her hand, and turned to go, still with a strangely dissatisfied feeling that made her unwilling to go yet. "I—I'll remember about the horse," she said. "I mean, not to take the black one."

For a moment the grey eyes held hers again, and she thought the wide mouth was touched by a hint of

smile for a second. "You'll likely have no need to remember," he told her, "unless you're a very early
riser. I'll have Black Knight saddled and away before you come on the scene, I daresay."

"You—you ride every day?"

He showed no surprise at her interest beyond a
brief elevation of one fair brow. "I ride round most
of the estate every day," he said. "It's part of my
job, Miss Carne."

"Oh yes—yes, of course." She hastily recalled
John Stirling sitting outside in his car and waiting for
her, and she gave a short and slightly uneasy laugh as
she turned away. "I'd better go before my voluntary
chauffeur decides to go without me!"

Neil McDowell was shaking his head, and she
stopped in the act of turning to look at him over her
shoulder. "Oh, he'll not do that!" he assured her,
soft-voiced, and she found it hard to explain the sudden flush of colour that warmed her cheeks as she
turned swiftly and headed for the door.

"Goodbye, Mr McDowell!"

CHAPTER TWO

I⊤ was a pleasant surprise for Melodie to find that the cottage she was to occupy was not merely habitable, but brightened with one or two unexpected touches that suggested a welcome. A vase of flowers, obviously fresh picked from the gardens, stood on the table in the one small sitting-room and dining-room combined, and another on the windowsill of the bedroom.

On exploring her new domain she found that even more practical matters had been thought of. There was a supply of groceries in the kitchen cupboard which would be enough to last her for a day or two, at least until she had time to do some shopping. The unexpectedly thoughtful gesture both surprised and delighted her, and she felt lighthearted enough the following morning to sing to herself while she prepared her breakfast.

She would go for a walk, she decided while she was washing up her breakfast things, and earmark a few likely places where she could work. The whole area around Ben Ross as well as the estate itself seemed to be one big scenic canvas and, as John Stirling had said, if this scenery did not inspire her to produce some good work, then nothing would.

Even the view from the tiny kitchen window was enchanting for all its limited scope, and she felt rather as if she was at the very edge of the world. If she looked to the left, she could just see the way in to Ben Ross. The gates had long since disappeared, but the two broken stone gateposts still remained, although almost completely covered by a cloak of shiny-leafed ivy and buried in the overgrown shrubs that lined the drive to the house. Immediately in front, more low-growing shrubs allowed a view across seemingly endless landscapes of hills and valleys, still misty in the morning sunshine and alternately shadowed and brightened as billowing white cumulus drifted across a pale sky.

It was an unmistakable sound of horses' hooves on the crunchy gravel of the drive that brought her out of her daydream, and she put down the drying up cloth she was using, when she recognised it, and went into the little sitting-room. John Stirling had mentioned that he sometimes rode, and he might have taken it into his head to call on her to see how she was getting on.

It was possible from the sitting-room window to see some distance along the drive and the rider was closer than she realised when she looked out. Unsure just what her reaction was at first, she recognised him not as John Stirling but Neil McDowell. Had it been John Stirling she could have been sure that he was coming to see her; in the case of Neil McDowell she thought it less likely, for recalling his reception of her yesterday she thought it unlikely he would be troubled with whether she was settled in or not.

Whatever his reason for riding along the drive towards the cottage, she found the sight of man and horse fascinating enough to spend a moment or two watching them. He had mentioned that he rode over the estate every day as part of his job, but it was more than a diligent application to his job, she thought, that gave him that air of possession, and reminded herself that he *would* soon possess the estate he had loved and worked for for so long.

He sat well in the saddle, with an ease that suggested long practice, and mounted on a shiny black stallion, who she assumed was the notorious Black Knight she had been warned against, he looked every inch the lord of the manor that John Stirling had dubbed him. The horse was a magnificent animal and it was obvious from the way he arched his neck and occasionally tried to shake his great head that he was impatient to indulge in something more exciting than the quiet trot that was all he was being allowed at the moment. Only the man's firm hand on the rein kept him in check, and Neil McDowell held him confidently and with deceptive ease.

He was a man who suggested strength, perhaps even a certain ruthlessness, which was not at all as he had been described to her before she left Australia, and she wondered how much he had changed in the eight years since her friends had seen him last.

He was dressed very much as he had been yesterday, in breeches and boots, but today a blue shirt seemed to lend emphasis to the contrast between fair hair and a skin tanned to a deep golden brown by years spent outdoors in all weathers. He was not at all as she had visualised him, but she found him rather intriguing all the same, and enigmatic enough to arouse her interest.

So convinced was she that he intended to ride straight past with possibly a polite acknowledgement of her as she stood at the window that when it became obvious that he meant to call at the cottage, she was caught unawares. She heard the violent and indignant snort of the stallion when he was brought to a halt, and hastily brought herself back to reality, brushing a hand over her hair as she hurried across the little room to open the door.

Neil McDowell was tethering his mount to one of the trees that half-buried the cottage on the side furthest from the drive, and he turned when he heard the click of the latch, his grey eyes regarding her with the same disconcerting steadiness she had noticed yesterday.

"Good morning, Mr McDowell!"

Three long steps brought him to the door, but he made no attempt to accept the invitation she conveyed by stepping back and smiling in a vaguely uncertain way. He put one hand on the jamb of the door and leaned on it, while a hint of smile touched his mouth for a moment. "Good morning, Miss Carne—are you settling in? Is everything all right for you?"

"Oh yes, thank you. It was very kind of whoever

was responsible for the flowers and the supply of groceries. I should have thought of bringing *some*thing to somewhere as isolated as Ben Ross, but I'm afraid it just didn't occur to me until it was too late."

"You'll not be too uncomfortable, then?"

For a moment she wondered if he hoped she was uncomfortable enough to decide not to stay, and she hastened to disillusion him. "On the contrary, I'm very comfortable!"

His manner suggested not so much terseness, as a desire to be away as quickly as possible, and she did not profess to understand him. "If you need anything more, I'm sure Mrs McKay will be able to find it for you."

"Oh no, I'm fine, thank you." She wished he would come inside instead of standing on her doorstep, as if he was merely making time to call because he felt he should. "Won't you come in for a moment?"

He was shaking his head almost before she had finished asking, and he looked decided enough not to change his mind. "I'll not trouble you, Miss Carne. Now that I know you're settled and not needing anything, I'll be away."

He had already unhitched the black and was preparing to remount before she found her tongue again.

"Oh, Mr McDowell—thank you for coming to ask after me."

He turned and looked at her over his shoulder and

for a second the grey eyes held hers steadily. Then she caught another glimpse of that faint smile on his mouth as he shook his head. "You're a guest of the estate, Miss Carne; Ben Ross is not lacking in hospitality, I hope."

"No, of course not." She tried not to feel as if she had been put in her place, and made another effort to let him know that she appreciated what had been done for her. "Were—were you responsible for the flowers and the groceries?"

He seemed to take a minute to consider whether or not to admit responsibility. "I guessed a young girl who was—arty by nature would not have the practical good sense to think to fill the store cupboard," he told her with unabashed frankness, and hastened to remind her how right he was. "And you said yourself you'd not thought of it until it was too late, did you not? The flowers must have been Mrs Stirling's touch; I have to confess I'd not thought of that."

"Mrs Stirling?" Surprise at the name overshadowed any objection she might have had to his opinion of her, and her reaction evidently amused him, for it showed in the grey eyes for a moment.

"John Stirling's aunt."

"Oh! Oh, yes, of course." She recovered herself hastily. "He told me he was staying with his uncle on the estate, I hadn't thought of an aunt too. Maybe I'll see her some time and be able to thank her for the flowers."

He said nothing for the moment, but swung himself up into the saddle and held the restless black with the same apparent ease that had impressed her so much when she watched him ride down the drive. He turned the animal and held it in check a moment longer while he looked down at her.

"I dare say John Stirling will be glad to pass on your thanks," he told her. "I've no doubt you'll be seeing him before long!"

He put his heels to the black stallion's glossy flanks, and Melodie followed their progress for as long as she could see them along the drive towards the house, her feelings strangely mixed. There was a consummate skill in the way he rode that was exciting to watch; the satiny black horse, streamlined for power and hard to handle, and the tall, fair man who controlled him so skilfully. It was an exciting and curiously disturbing combination, and her expression was thoughtful as she turned back into the cottage.

JUST AS NEIL MCDOWELL HAD SUGGESTED, it was not very long before she received a visit from John Stirling, not riding on horseback, as she half expected, but driving the same car he had brought her from the station in. He arrived a little after eleven and asked her out to lunch with him.

It was an invitation she would have liked to accept, but she had not gone for her walk after all the previous day. Various small jobs around the house had demanded her attention and she had still not made that necessary tour of reconnaissance, and she had to remind herself, as well as John Stirling, that she was there primarily to work.

"I'd love to go with you, Mr Stirling," she told him, hoping he would not put her resistance to the test by insisting, "but I really do have to try and get down to some real work. Yesterday I promised myself I'd take a walk and get the lie of the land, but I didn't go and I simply can't allow myself to be—sidetracked again today, much as I'm tempted."

He looked so genuinely disappointed that Melodie felt vaguely guilty about refusing to go with him. He was a nice, friendly young man and he felt towards her, much as she did towards him, she guessed. They had taken a mutual liking to one another from the beginning and so far there had been no suggestion of anything other than liking, though almost inevitably something more would develop before too long, she was not naïve enough to suppose it wouldn't.

He had perched himself on the edge of the sitting-room table and he regarded her for a moment or two with bright speculative brown eyes, then he smiled. "Do you think you could call me John?" he asked, and Melodie stared at him for a moment, then laughed and shook her head.

"I don't see why not," she agreed. "Could you manage to cope with Melodie? It's rather more of a mouthful, I'm afraid."

"It's beautiful, and I guess I could cope very nicely, thanks!"

She smiled at him, feeling she had in some way compensated for refusing to lunch with him, and walked into the tiny kitchen at the back of the cottage. Taking a coffee pot from the cupboard on the wall, she looked over her shoulder.

"Can I persuade you to have coffee with me?"

He had followed her into the kitchen, and it was plain that he was as tempted to accept as she had been, but he pulled a rueful face as he leaned against the door jamb with his arms folded one over the other. "I wish I could," he said, "but I promised Uncle Jamie I'd fetch some stuff for him from Corrie by early this afternoon. In fact I was hoping to kill two birds with one stone when I asked you to have lunch with me."

"I'm sorry, John."

"You insist on working?"

She probably imagined a hint of impatience in his voice, but it was possible he was not often refused, and disliked the experience. Dislike or not, she must be adamant if she was going to achieve as much as she hoped in the next couple of months.

"I must, John. I'm here to work and so far I haven't done a thing about it. I know it's only one day," she added hastily when it appeared he was going to remind her, "but with someone like you around it could be all too easy to slip into the habit of going out and about when I should be painting, so I mustn't let myself be persuaded."

The smile she gave him suggested flattery, as much as the words did, and she used both, shamelessly, for her own ends. Apparently with some success too, for he stood and watched her for a moment or two while she put coffee into the pot, then shrugged and sighed. Heaving himself away from the doorway, he came and stood beside her while she busied herself at the kitchen dresser.

"O.K.—I guess I've got the idea, but you surely don't intend working all the hours God made, do you, Melodie?"

"Not quite!" She smiled up at him. "If you still want to take me out somewhere, ask me at a weekend. I'd really *like* to go with you, you know, it's just that I really must try and do something now that I'm here—start off on the right foot, so to speak."

"Yeah, sure!"

She paused in the act of taking a cup and saucer from the cupboard, and looked at him over her shoulder for a second before she spoke. "You are *going* to ask me again, aren't you?"

An arm slid around her waist, drawing her against him, and the move was so unexpected that she caught her breath, then he bent his head and his voice murmured close to her ear. "You bet your sweet life, I am!"

Melodie eased herself away, using the near boiling kettle as an excuse to make the break. She wished he had not made such a move so soon, especially when she had not been expecting it, but she still treated the matter lightly. "I'll hold you to that!" she threatened.

While she made the coffee he watched in silence, then he shrugged resignedly. "You won't change your mind, I guess?"

"Not at the moment, John."

She put all the things on a tray and he carried it into the next room for her. "O.K." He shrugged again, obviously not happy about being refused, but resigned to it for the moment. "I'll see you, Melodie!"

"I hope so!"

The brown eyes regarded her for a second, seemingly in some doubt. "So do I," he said.

WALKING HAD NEVER SEEMED SO ENJOYABLE before, and Melodie found every aspect of the vast Ben Ross estate, and its surrounding countryside, well worth recording on canvas. The whole place was completely irresistible, and she found so many views and impressions that just begged to be painted, that she was almost confused with a surfeit of good things.

A rather hair-raising drop from the side of the drive seemed to be her only means of access to a lush and fertile glen, and while she debated the wisdom of making such a hazardous descent she stood looking at the country around from her vantage point.

Rolling hills, their craggy outlines softened by a seemingly permanent mist caused by the summer warmth, and sweeps of dusty mauve heather and soft green turf—all soft muted colours that delighted the eye of an artist and made her positively anxious to start working. Not a breath of wind stirred, and the surface of a small loch below in the glen reflected the sky like mirror glass.

A river ran like liquid silver across in the distance, skirting the nearer hills, and great grey granite boulders thrust up through its racing waters, overwhelming the wind-dwarfed scrub that lined its banks. There were salmon, she knew, and she dwelt on the thrill of seeing them thrust their silver-grey bodies against the wild river.

It was an irresistible challenge to climb down to the glen below where she stood, and she managed with less effort than she expected, although it took every trick she had learned with two rock-climbing brothers to get her safely to the bottom without mishap. It was well worth the effort when she stood at last by the smooth stillness of the little loch, and it was so quiet that the silence was almost tangible.

The waters of the loch were green and clear, backed by more hills, softly rounded and draped in green and purple. She had never felt more at peace in her life, she thought, and closed her eyes for a second as she took in a long, slow breath. Just imagining spending the next two months here was enough to convince her that she would be able to work as never before, and it gave her a sense of excitement just to think about it.

"Miss Carne—good morning!"

Startled by the sound of a voice behind her, Melodie spun round quickly, her eyes wide open now, and blank with surprise, then blinking rapidly back to reality when she met the disconcerting steadiness of Neil McDowell's gaze. He was mounted on the black stallion, and before she could return his greeting, he swung himself down from the saddle and draped the rein over his arm as he came to join her at the edge of the loch.

"Did I startle you?"

Her immediate instinct was to deny it, and she shook her head, at the same time hastily avoiding that steady gaze that she found so disconcerting. "No, not at all," she said. "I just wasn't expecting anyone else, that's all—it's peaceful here and I didn't see anyone coming."

"You'd be too busy contemplating the loch; and I came down the hill from the house."

She glanced up at the steep hillside automatically. It was strewn with outcrops of rock that looked dangerously hazardous for both horse and rider, and he must be a quite remarkable horseman to have achieved it without mishap. He had apparently noticed the direction of her glance and from the faintly amused smile that touched his mouth for a moment, she gathered he followed her train of thought quite easily.

"It's not as dangerous as it looks when you're used to it," he said, and Melodie felt somehow that she had been gently chided for being over-anxious.

In truth she had been snatched from a reflective mood of pleasant tranquillity, and plunged into conversation with a man who she freely admitted made her curiously uneasy. There was no good reason for her uneasiness, but nor was there much she could do about it. Whenever she came into contact with Neil McDowell she felt the same reaction to him, and it irritated her without her being sure why.

"You ride very well," she said, attempting an off-hand compliment. "I wouldn't like to tackle that slope even on the best horse there is."

"I would hope not!"

Something in his voice brought a reaction from her, though she could not have said why. "You feel a woman isn't capable of it?" she asked, and the grey eyes swept slowly over her face before he answered.

"Some women might be," he said in his quiet voice. "Not you, I think, Miss Carne, you're too much a—a womanly woman."

It was a compliment, Melodie recognised a little dazedly, though it was doubtful if even he fully appreciated the fact. "I'm not a very good horsewoman either," she said, "I have to admit it."

He looked around at the gentle beauty of the glen, and then looked at her with a raised brow. "Were you finding subjects for your paintings?" he asked, and Melodie nodded. "You'll find plenty to please you here."

"I'm—overwhelmed by it!" She too looked around her and smiled, touched again for a moment by that sense of peace and satisfaction she had felt earlier. "I could live here for ever, and never run out of subjects. It's all so unbelievably lovely, and the most marvellous thing, I think, would be the way it must change with every season—show a different face all the time. I'd love to see it in winter, in the snow!"

"You'd not be standing here in winter!" He was smiling, and the difference it made to his normally serious features was stunning. It gave a glimpse of the man he might be, and warmed the grey eyes to a more gentle expression. "The water literally floods down from the hill when the snows melt," he went on, "and this glen, often as not, becomes a loch, for a while at least."

"But it must be exciting, even then," Melodie insisted. "It's part of the character of the place, isn't it?"

He was watching her with a more thoughtful look in his eyes, as if he found her views surprising in some way. "You've a feel for the country, Miss Carne, you should do it justice."

"I shall try!"

His approval was somehow both unexpected and oddly gratifying, and it occurred to her for the first time to wonder whether his breakneck ride down that stony steep slope had been specifically so that he could join her, or if he would have undertaken it anyway. He must surely know the estate as well as anyone, and she speculated on just how willing he would be to help with names and location, if she asked him.

"Were you thinking of painting Loch Lairdross?" he asked, and she nodded, looking at him curiously.

"Is that its name?" She glanced up at the lean and sternly attractive face through the thickness of her lashes for a moment. "I don't know the names of anything," she ventured. "That fall, for instance." She looked across to where a stream ran like a swift silver ribbon between ragged rocks, fed from above

by a glittering waterfall that seemed to spring suddenly from nowhere, way up in the hillside. "That
waterfall's beautiful with the stream at the bottom—
has it a name?"

"The Ghyll burn." He provided the information
willingly enough, and it gave her encouragement to
ask more questions.

"Ghyll's a local name?"

"It's from an old Nordic word meaning a ravine or
narrow valley with a stream running through it—
there are many such names about here." His matter-
of-fact presentation of the information surprised her
rather, and she looked at him curiously.

"That's interesting," she said. "Are you an expert
on such matters, Mr McDowell?"

"Not an expert, no." The grey eyes watched the
glinting fall of water down the hillside rather than
her, and once more she felt a desire to know more
about him, to break through that enigmatic barrier
and find the man behind it. "I know a little about
Ben Ross because it interests me."

"You love it."

She had not meant it to sound anything other than
a statement of an obvious fact, and yet she saw a
swift flick of surprise show on his face for a moment
before he spoke. "Aye," he said in a voice that was
low and soft, "I love it, and I've no doubt you'll be
fully aware of the fact that it's going to be mine before long."

Melodie nodded, more touched by his confession
to loving the place than she would have believed

possible. "I know," she agreed, "and I'm sure it couldn't be in better hands."

The grey eyes held hers for a second and she felt compelled to look away, disturbed by something she could not quite understand. "I agree, Miss Carne," he said, "but then, of course, I'm biased!"

It occurred to her suddenly to wonder how soon he was to become the legal owner of Ben Ross, and if his taking over was likely to affect her own position. "How soon will it be?" she asked, and added hastily, "before you take over, I mean."

"Does it matter?"

It was a polite way of telling her to mind her own business, she realised, and felt the colour that warmed her cheeks suddenly. "I—I suppose not," she allowed. "Unless you're likely to evict me from the cottage the moment you take possession."

He regarded her again with that hint of smile on his mouth, but said nothing. Climbing once more into the saddle, he held the restless stallion with a firm hand while he looked down at her from his superior position. "I'll not do that," he said, and Melodie heaved a sigh of relief, more pleased than she would have believed to know that he was not anxious to be rid of her. "You're a guest, Miss Carne, I cannot turn around and send you packing the very minute I take possession—even if I'd a mind to."

He gave her no time to reply to the somewhat discomfiting assurance, but put his heels to the black stallion and sent him galloping off across the springy turf with Melodie watching him, trying to decide

whether or not she had been snubbed. It was going
to take a great deal of patience and perseverance to
understand and know a man like Neil McDowell,
but it never for a moment entered her mind to wonder whether it would be worthwhile.

MELODIE WOULD NOT HAVE DREAMED of intruding
into the privacy of Ben Ross itself, but by walking in
the gardens that were furthest from the house, she
felt, she could not be accused of intruding, and the
view from the front of the house was breathtaking.
There were hedges of tall sturdy evergreens that
shielded the terraced walks on the upper level from
the searing winds of winter, and steps between the
two levels.

It was on the intermediate steps that she stood at
the moment, her eyes on the vast expanse of the
landscape visible to her from that vantage point. The
gravel drive beside which her own cottage stood, was
to her left, sloping steeply down towards the narrow
stony road. It wound like a ribbon across the foreground of her vision, leading in turn to the tiny station of Glen Ross, and beyond that to the village
itself.

Mountains, road, river and streams, and acres of
rolling open country seemed dominated by the towering situation of Ben Ross, and as she looked out
from her lofty viewpoint she found herself well able
to appreciate Neil McDowell's arrogant pride in the
place.

Even on such a warm sunny day there was a breeze to temper the warmth of the sun. A light, soft wind that was just strong enough to stir the strands of black hair around her face, and mould the thin dress she wore to the soft contours of her shape. The sun was bright enough for her to need a shading hand over her eyes, and she was unaware of anyone else near until someone spoke from the lower level of the terraced lawns.

"Beautiful!" John Stirling's pleasant voice declared softly. "Just beautiful!"

Melodie looked down at him, momentarily blinded by the sun in her eyes, and smiled. "That's why I'm admiring it," she told him, deliberately misunderstanding. "Good morning, John!"

He shook his head, taking the brick-edged steps in a couple of strides to stand beside her. "You know I wasn't talking about the view," he chided, and his brown eyes glowed earnestly in his nice friendly face. "You're easily the loveliest girl I know," he assured her, "and I'm not just saying that, Melodie."

She found his unexpected earnestness a little disconcerting, and sought to hide her reaction to it, by looking at the view once more. "Did you come to find me especially to say nice things?" she asked, treating it with studied lightness. "You're very good for my ego, John."

"I was hoping you'd do something for my ego by promising to come with me into Corrie," he confessed. A firm but tentative hand was placed on her shoulder, and persuaded rather than obliged her to turn and face him. "I know you said not to ask you until the week-end, but can't you change your mind and come anyway?"

He was much harder to resist than he probably realised, but Melodie had in mind to try and paint the whole exciting scene laid out down there before her, and at the moment it filled her head to the exclusion of almost everything else. She pointed to her easel and the rest of her equipment leaned against the hedge that sheltered the upper terrace.

"I came up here to work, John, I'm sorry."

The hand on her shoulder remained, though its pressure was more caressing than firm now, and infinitely persuasive. "Ah, come on, Melodie, who's going to complain if you take a few days before you start working, hmm? Nobody's pressuring you, are they?"

"No, of course no one's pressuring me, but I can't *wait* to start!" She laughed and half turned to indicate the scene behind her. "You said yourself that if Scotland didn't inspire me, nothing could, and I have to agree with you."

"Oh, Melodie!"

He put his other hand on her right shoulder and held her for a second facing him, his fingers tightly pressed into her flesh under the thin dress she wore. His face was closer suddenly, and his mouth only a warm breath away, and she would probably have allowed herself to be kissed without protest. Except that when he was about to kiss her some sound behind them on the gravelled walk brought both their heads round swiftly, and John muttered something under his breath, his hands dropping quickly to his side.

"Good morning, Miss Carne."

"Mr McDowell."

She sounded breathless, but she could do nothing about it, she was startled, perhaps even more so than John, and it probably showed on her face. Neil McDowell had been riding, or was about to go, for he was dressed the only way Melodie had seen him dressed so far—in breeches and boots, with a cream shirt in stunning contrast to the golden tanned colour of his skin.

It must have been evident what he had interrupted, but he showed no sign of reaction beyond the faintest tightening of his mouth just before he spoke, although Melodie felt more embarrassed than she would have believed possible. She had been brought up in a fairly free and easy atmosphere and she had gone with a number of boy-friends during her twenty-two years, so there should be no reason why she felt the way she did.

The teasing affection of two older brothers had also done a lot to overcome any tendency towards shyness, so that she was for the most part quite at ease in men's company. It was only when she came into contact with the curiously stern detachment of Neil McDowell that she experienced these qualms of uneasiness, and because the sensation was new to her, she not only found it discomfiting, but she resented it too.

"I'm sor—" She stopped herself hastily from apologising, but it seemed as if her attempt went unnoticed anyway, for he was addressing himself to John.

"Good morning, John, aren't you riding this morning?"

The informality of the Christian name surprised her, but then she recalled that John had sounded as if he not only knew him fairly well, but liked him too. His brown eyes showed the same suggestion of uneasiness she was experiencing herself, and he ran a hand through his thick hair as he answered.

"Not this morning—although I guess I might as well have done since I had a fruitless walk up here."

Neil McDowell said nothing, but neither did he make any move to leave them. He was quite within his rights, of course, Melodie was forced to recognise, for after all, he was on the verge of becoming the new owner of Ben Ross, and both she and John were standing in his grounds.

He looked at her in that steady and very disconcerting way he had, and a slight tilt to his mouth suggested a smile. "You'll be ready to start painting, Miss Carne?"

"Yes—at least, I'm hoping to."

"You'll need peace and solitude for that, I'm thinking?"

His meaning was obvious, and John Stirling's brown eyes looked at her reproachfully when she replied, "Ideally, yes."

She felt sure he was waiting for Neil McDowell to

leave, and when it began to look as if he did not mean to, he shrugged his shoulders and thrust his hands into the pockets of his slacks. "I guess I may as well take that ride after all," he said. "I'll see you, Melodie, huh?"

"Yes, of course."

Neil McDowell registered a barely perceptible flicker of surprise at the use of her name, but he made no move to follow suit when John turned and walked back across the lawn to the drive. He was still standing there beside her when John turned, hopefully she guessed, to wave a hand to her.

"I hope it's all right for me to sit here and paint," Melodie ventured after a second or two. "It's such a wonderful view, I can't resist it."

"Of course." The softly accented voice gave no indication of his personal feelings in the matter. "You're to have the free run of the estate, Miss Carne, those are my instructions."

The irritation she felt at his having stressed the fact that he was merely following instructions in allowing her to sit there, was perhaps unreasonable, but she could do nothing about it. She did frown, however, and tilted her chin slightly when she replied.

"Good—then I'll set up here at the top of the steps."

He seemed not to have noticed her reply, but was looking across the lawn at the now distant figure of John Stirling as he walked away along the gravel drive rather quickly, his shoulders hunched in a way that suggested he was still smarting from her refusal to be persuaded.

"You *do* prefer to be alone while you're working, do you not?" he asked, and Melodie shrugged.

"On the whole," she agreed, "but I hardly think *you* encouraged John to stay, Mr McDowell."

He said nothing more for several seconds, and Melodie wished she felt less small and at a loss. He really was the most disconcerting man. "I'm sorry, I'd no idea you were so—close." The quiet voice with its gentle accent was not even slightly raised, and yet she felt sure he was at least annoyed by her remark. "I thought you were virtually strangers, until a few days ago."

"We are—virtually strangers, as you say, but we're friendly."

She looked at the stern, uncompromising features and wondered if he had any idea of the kind of relationship she had with John Stirling. A kind of easy, natural friendship that could, or need not, turn into something more serious in time.

Neil McDowell, she felt sure, was a man of more deep and enduring feelings, capable of a depth of emotion she was neither used to nor could yet understand, and for that reason he disturbed her, if for no other. To reach her painting gear she had to get past him, and she did not have the immediate nerve to do so, so she stood beside him for the moment, on the top step, with that breathtaking vista all around, and tried to keep her firm hold on her patience.

"I interrupted—something, did I not?" He gave

her no time to either confirm or deny it, but went on in the same quiet, matter-of-fact voice. "I'm sorry if I appeared at an inconvenient moment, but I wasn't to know what the situation was, of course."

Melodie looked up at him swiftly, her eyes bright with some reaction she was not quite sure of, bright as jewels, and faintly challenging. "There is no— situation, as you call it, Mr McDowell!"

The grey eyes scanned slowly over her flushed face, and came to rest on the softness of her mouth, reminding her of how close John had been to kissing her when he appeared; then he shook his head. "But you're angry," he declared with certainty.

"Angry?" She laughed, a short unsteady sound that betrayed her uneasiness. "Why on earth should I be angry?"

Once more he took his time answering, and as before his eyes made a slow searching survey of her face, noting how her thick lashes hid her gaze from him. "Maybe because you were about to be kissed," he suggested, soft-voiced, "and you're disappointed." For a heart-stopping moment she was sure he meant to soothe her disappointment by kissing her himself and she held her breath. Instead he simply stood for a moment with that steady gaze fixed on her mouth, then he shook his head and half-turned away. "I'll leave you to your painting," he said. "If you've a need of anything, Miss Carne, don't be afraid to ask—we're not lacking in hospitality, I hope."

CHAPTER THREE

AFTER two weeks of near-perfect weather, the sky was overcast and threatened a storm. Heavy black banks of cloud loomed in over the hills and there was a warm smell of rain in the air. From her kitchen window in the little cottage Melodie watched the storm gathering and debated whether or not to yield to the threat and stay at home, or whether to take a chance and walk down to the river as she had promised herself she would.

It was a very long walk and there was virtually no shelter if the storm should break while she was out on the open moor, and yet the temptation to go was almost irresistible. The idea of borrowing a horse from the Ben Ross stables, as Neil McDowell had invited her to, had crossed her mind more than once, but so far she had never taken up the invitation, yet that would seem to be the solution at the moment.

She would still get very wet if the storm broke, but at least she would have a faster means of gaining shelter than if she was on foot. Another few minutes spent hovering uncertainly by the window, and she finally made up her mind—she would ride.

A pair of fawn trousers and a white blouse served,

for it was all she had in the way of riding clothes, and she set off along the drive to the house with a curious little flutter of excitement in her breast. It was some time since she rode last, and she hoped there would be a mount available to her who was less temperamental than the glossy black stallion that Neil McDowell always rode.

When she neared the old house it occurred to her how it always seemed so still and silent, as if it was completely deserted; it had seemed so when she arrived and it still did, so that she sometimes wondered just how lonely its solitary occupant must be with no other company than the housekeeper, Jessie McKay.

The company of an elderly servant, no matter how devoted she might be, was surely no substitute for a wife and family, and yet so far as she knew Neil McDowell had lived that way for the past eight years. Ever since the Hollands left him in charge of Ben Ross and went to live in Australia.

He was an attractive man for all his dourness, and when he smiled it made such a difference that the pity was he did not do it more often. John liked him, though with reservations, she thought, and she wondered if it was that apparently impenetrable barrier of reserve that kept Neil alone in the vastness of Ben Ross.

As always there was no sign of life when she walked past the front of the house on her way to the stables at the back, except that she thought she detected a brief flutter of movement at one of the

ground-floor windows as she passed. Once at the
rear of the house she stood for a moment, undecid-
ed, for she was on completely strange ground and
very unsure of herself.

It was all very well to receive an invitation to ride
any time she felt like it, but it had not occurred to
her until now that the invitation might possibly have
been made simply out of politeness and with no
thought of its being taken up. There was no sense in
turning back now, she supposed, for the invitation
had been issued, whether or not it had been intended to be taken seriously, so she took a swift
glance round then walked on boldly, a hint of defiance in the angle of her chin.

A wide cobbled yard spanned the distance between the back of Ben Ross and a small stone cottage with green shutters, and stable buildings took
up two whole sides of the yard. They were spacious,
she noted with some surprise, and were probably capable of stabling ten or twelve horses, though it was
doubtful if Ben Ross supported that number at the
present time.

The first two stalls were unoccupied and suggested
from the state of them that they always were, but in
the third one along she found a stocky, rough-coated
chestnut gelding who looked up inquiringly at her,
which was all the encouragement she needed. From
the stall next door the restless sound of hooves on
the straw-covered floor and an impatient snorting
suggested that it housed a more lively animal, and to
be on the safe side she decided on the seemingly
quiet and docile gelding.

There was bound to be a tack-room somewhere, but she found a saddle and everything else she needed either hanging on hooks on the wall or slung over the wooden screen between the stalls. Hesitating before she took it down, she puzzled over her right to use it, but then decided that, since it was in the chestnut's stall, it would seem to imply that it was what the animal usually wore.

Lack of practice made her clumsy, but the chestnut co-operated well and although it took a lot of effort and concentration, she eventually had him ready and she stood for a moment getting her breath back, stroking the gelding's nose and brushing back a wisp of hair from her own forehead.

She quickly dropped both hands when she heard footsteps on the cobbled yard outside and seconds later a tall shadow fell across the opening. The shadow became suddenly and curiously still when she was seen and, feeling quite ridiculously guilty, Melodie looked at the newcomer with wide, uncertain eyes.

"Miss Carne."

"Good morning, Mr McDowell—I hope it's all right my being here. You did say—"

"Yes, of course it's all right."

He was taken as much by surprise as she had been herself, she thought, and she was aware that his eyes were registering every inch of her slim rounded figure in slacks and a short-sleeved blouse. As always happened his scrutiny made her inexplicably nervous and she once more felt a flick of annoyance for her own reaction, though there seemed nothing she could do about it.

Turning back to the gelding, she rubbed the soft nose while she tried to keep her voice as light and matter-of-fact as possible. "I found the saddle and the rest of the gear in the stall—I hope it's all right for me to use it." He nodded without speaking, and she hurried on. "And is it O.K. if I take the chestnut?"

"Yes, of course. The only one I wouldn't let you take is Black Knight, he's too dangerous for a woman to handle."

"Yes—I remember you told me." Once more she gave her attention to the chestnut rather than look at him. "This fellow seems rather sweet and docile."

"His name's Rusty."

She patted the rough chestnut coat and smiled. "It suits him. I'm so badly out of practice that I don't want anything too lively, and he'll suit me fine."

"You'll find him quiet enough," Neil McDowell agreed, and looked at her thoughtfully for a second before he added, "but if you're very much out of practice maybe it would be better if you rode out with me for a wee while, until you get the feel of riding again—we'd not want you being thrown or falling off."

Melodie was still staring at him over her shoulder. The invitation had taken her so by surprise that for a moment she made no response. When she came to find herself a mount she had not expected to see him at all. She had been quite certain that by now he

would be out somewhere on the estate, making that
tour of inspection he had mentioned, and that he
would be gone for most of the morning. His sudden
appearance threw her rather off balance, the more
so because he had suggested they ride together with
the apparent intention of seeing that she came to no
harm. She was unsure at the moment just what her
reaction was, and she looked up at him and smiled a
little uncertainly.

"Are—are you sure I won't hinder you?" she
asked, and added hastily, "You did say that you
rode around the estate as part of your job, and I
don't want to take up your time if you're busy."

The disconcerting steadiness of the grey eyes was
something she was beginning to expect, and his
mouth twitched into a half smile as he walked past
and turned into the neighbouring stall. "You'll not
hinder me, Miss Carne. I'm not just setting out on
my daily inspection, I did that some time ago! I
merely returned to the house for a few minutes,
that's all."

"Oh, I see."

When he emerged a few seconds later he was leading the black stallion, his glossy coat gleaming, already saddled and anxious to be off again. For a
moment Neil stood stroking the animal's nose while
he regarded her in that same steady way as she stood
in the dimly lit stall. "If it's simply that you'd rather
not ride with me, you've only to say so," he told her
quietly.

"Oh, that's silly!" The flush in her cheeks annoyed

her, because it was so seldom that she blushed, and
yet Neil McDowell seemed to have the ability to get
under her skin in a way she could not understand.
"I'd like to ride with you," she went on, keeping her
voice coolly matter-of-fact with a determined effort.
"I just don't want to hinder you, that's all."

He said nothing, but turned to tighten the stallion's girth, then led both animals out into the yard,
dropping the rein for a moment while he helped her
to mount. She thanked him, more demurely than she
would have believed possible, and he swung himself
up with the same easy grace she had noticed before.
Everything about him was firm and confident, and
he was undoubtedly an excellent horseman, so that
she feared her own prowess would fall far short;
however, if he was prepared to make allowances,
then the ride could prove quite enjoyable.

"Did you have anywhere special in mind to go?"
he asked as she clucked the chestnut gelding into
motion, and Melodie shook her head.

"Not exactly," she said. "Though I had thought of
riding over to take a closer look at the river I've seen
from a distance. Would that be possible, do you
think?"

"Of course!" They had left the yard and the anvil
sound of the horses' shoes on the cobbled yard gave
way to the softer, sound-deadening turf. Turning,
Neil looked over his shoulder and once more that
suggestion of a smile touched his mouth for a moment and warmed the sober grey eyes. "We'll take
the long way down, it's a better ride."

"Whatever you say."

There was no point in presuming to suggest a route, for he knew every inch of Ben Ross, better than any man alive, and she was in no special hurry, for all it looked very much as if there would be a storm before too long. As if he was thinking along the same lines Neil too looked up at the gathering clouds as they rode down a gentle slope towards open moorland.

"You'll not mind getting wet?" he suggested. Briefly his eyes scanned her fawn denim trousers and the thin cotton blouse that in the event of a storm would offer very little protection. "You should mebbe have worn a jacket."

The storm seemed to be hovering only a few feet above their heads, dark and heavy, and already the wind stirred restlessly beneath it. Melodie pulled a rueful face, shaking her head. "I should have done," she agreed, "but it's too late to worry about it now, and I don't suppose a drop of rain will hurt me."

"You'll see yourself as a tough woman, hmm?"

He did not mean it seriously, she felt sure, and she smiled in response to the suggestion. "Not really," she demurred, "but I've been rained on before."

He said nothing, but gave his attention to keeping the black at the same speed as her own mount and made it look much easier than it was. He looked at ease and relaxed as they rode across the open moorland; a man in love with the country he belonged to. It was a country to inspire devotion too, Melodie thought, for it was breathtaking in its splendour, and beautiful rather than pretty—a rugged country, made for men like Neil McDowell.

Huge grey boulders thrust their way through springy turf and dark shaggy heather, adding to the air of rugged grandeur, and the sound of the river gabbled through the still air even before they could see it properly. The scowling clouds seemed to magnify every sound, cutting off the tops of the hills and turning the landscape into a mass of shifting shadows that flitted darkly among the rocks.

"It's magnificent!"

Neil turned his head when she breathed the words almost involuntarily, and she could feel the intensity of his feeling for the place—a kind of electric excitement charged by the nearness of the storm. "Aye," he said with deceptive quietness, "it's magnificent."

"And it's yours!"

She looked across at him, the gelding having for the moment drawn dead level with his faster companion, and she saw the unconscious lift of Neil's chin and the look that passed across his lean features suddenly. "Not yet," he said in the same quiet voice. "Not quite yet, but soon."

They approached the river more slowly, and Melodie could see how fast it flowed over its stony bed. Frothing and sparkling, it raced around the outcrops that pierced its surface and it seemed deep even quite near to the banks; louder now, too, and competing with the encroaching thunder. They rode almost to the very edge before she dismounted, aware that Neil had followed suit, and drawn to the brink by the hypnotic fascination of swiftly flowing water.

"Take care!"

A hand on her arm brought her round swiftly, her eyes still vague and bemused, and her pulse responded rapidly to the soft quietness of the warning voice. "Yes. Yes, of course, it's very deep, isn't it?"

"And fast—you'd have no chance at all among those rocks if you fell in."

With the idea of moving to a safer distance, Melodie gave a light pull on the rein to persuade the gelding to turn, but either he misunderstood her intention or the liveliness of the water made him frisky. Instead of turning so that she could lead him to a safer distance, he tossed his head and gave a whinny of protest, then nudged her nearer to the edge of the bank.

The stones at the very edge of the water were wedged only into sandy soil, and when her weight was put on them suddenly it was inevitable that they gave way under her. She was never quite sure exactly what happened, but one minute she seemed to be stepping back into empty space, and the next she was pulled hard against the reassuring solidity of a masculine body, with a hard left arm tight about her waist.

She made no sound, for surprise had followed surprise so rapidly that she had no time to cry out, and neither did she offer any kind of resistance to the arm that held her so tightly. The thudding beat of her heart almost deafened her to even the noise of the water, and for a second or two she pressed her face to the softness of a cotton shirt and the warmth of the body beneath it, letting relief envelop her as well as other reactions she made no pretence of understanding.

"I warned you to take care, did I not?"

The quiet voice was muffled and it took her a moment to realise that it was because his face was buried in the softness of her hair. The black stallion, his rein trailing, tossed his head at the rumble of thunder and snorted impatiently, followed closely by a whinny of protest from the gelding when a vivid flash split the overhead blackness.

Two hands curled their strong brown fingers around her soft upper arms and held her away while still keeping a light tenuous contact between her own rounded shape and the firm hardness of Neil's body, and she raised her head at last. There were fine lines from the corners of the grey eyes, she noticed as she tipped back her head, and a suggestion of tension in the straight firm mouth so close to her own, an urgency in the lean brown features that brought a sudden and unexpected shiver.

She was trembling and she could do nothing to stop it, her emotions shattered by surprise and uncertainty, and in that moment it began to rain. Huge splashes hit the dry ground and made dark patches on the rocks, and the storm was right overhead suddenly—jagged flashes overtaken by rolling thunder.

The mouth that took hers was fierce and hard, almost savage in its demands, and she was so stunned by its savagery that she never even thought to offer resistance, but yielded her mouth and the soft curves of her body to his steely hardness. His arms were inescapable and in a half-conscious, dazed way she was aware of not wanting to escape, although her heart was beating so urgently that her head was dizzy with it.

She did not even realise the storm had overtaken them until Neil released her at last and she saw how the rain had darkened his fair hair and gave his skin a golden glowing look, like burnished bronze. Her own hair clung wetly to her head and the thin blouse she wore was no protection from the downpour but moulded to her like a second skin as she slipped out of the arms that let her go more easily than she anticipated and left her exposed to the full force of the deluge.

The surface of the river frothed and spumed with even more fury as it was lashed by the downpour and the noise of the storm with that of the river made such a cacophony that it was impossible to speak above it. By signs Neil indicated that he would help her to mount and she hastily brought herself back to earth when she realised the moment was ended that had brought them close for those few seconds of excitement. She nodded silently, but her heart was still racing when she sat in the saddle again, and she flung back her wet hair in a gesture that was vaguely defiant.

"Let's go!"

He put his heels to the stallion and the animal took off like a streak of shiny black jet, thundering across the wet turf like the wind and leaving the slower gelding behind. Melodie used her heels, but to less effect; the beast was slower and less spirited and she knew he could never hope to catch the stallion, no matter how he tried.

Resigned to following, she rode with her head down, her heart rebelling against being deserted so soon after those few moments of fierce passion, and she felt more wildly angry with Neil McDowell for leaving her than she would have believed possible. Resentment, confusion, anger—all played a part in the seething emotions that kept her taut and stiff in the saddle as she rode before the storm.

"Come on!"

The first indication she had that Neil had come back for her was his voice as he came up beside her, the sound of it almost drowned by the roar of the storm, and blown away on the wind. He took hold of the gelding's rein and brought the two animals close together, the black stallion running level, held back by the slower speed of his stablemate and resenting it.

"I can manage!"

His coming back should not have surprised her, but she was not thinking very rationally at the moment. She still resented his action no matter if it was an oversight and understandable in the circumstances. Neil let go the rein but kept the stallion to the same pace as the gelding, and both riders kept their faces forward, not once looking at one another until they rode into the yard.

Their hooves clattering on the wet cobbles, the horses galloped into the yard and, even before Neil had dismounted, the back door of the house opened and Jessie McKay's short, stern figure stood there. Taking the rein from Melodie's hands, Neil indicated the open door with a nod of his head.

"Get away in and take off those wet clothes," he ordered brusquely. "I'll see to the animals."

"But you—"

Her protest was instinctive and he cut it short impatiently, his normally quiet voice a note or two higher than usual. "Go, woman, and make yourself dry before you catch your death! Jessie'll find you something to change into—now, away in with you!"

Only once before had Melodie been inside Ben Ross, and Jessie McKay looked no more welcoming on this occasion than she had the first time. She held the door open wider and stood back, but her eyes were on Neil while he led the two horses into the stable, and it was clear that she at least considered the job of rubbing down and stabling should have been shared.

Melodie looked at the round austere face and wondered if it ever smiled, or if the shrewd brown eyes ever showed a glimmer of warmth. She looked a woman who judged the world a harsh place and an unjust one, though it was clear in the few times Melodie had seen her near Neil McDowell that she had not only a high regard for her employer but a quite deep and genuine affection too.

Melodie let the wetness drip on to the floor of the

passage rather than shake it off as she followed the
housekeeper through from the back of the house to
the hall and the stairs. "Mr McDowell said you'd be
able to find me something to change into," she ventured. "I'm afraid I'm very wet."

"I'll show you upstairs, there's a robe of Mr
McDowell's you could borrow until your own things
are dry."

She made it clear that she complied only with reluctance and because she had more or less been in-
structed to provide temporary replacements. She
would have liked it a lot better if Neil had not still
been out there dealing with the horses while the
stranger was already on her way to drying off.

The house was evidently much bigger than Melodie had thought and very grand in its manner too.
Like that wonderful hall she had first seen, the upstairs suggested the traditional stately home and the
landing was dark-panelled too, with any number of
doors opening off, presumably into bedrooms.

The place was huge, far too big for one man and
an old housekeeper, and Melodie once more speculated on the lonely existence of Neil McDowell. He
would surely be much better off and far less grim if
he married and had a family. It was the sudden rec-
ollection of that fierce hard kiss and the strength of
his arms around her that made her pull herself up
hastily and put such thoughts out of her head. It was
purely speculation on her part—maybe he was neither as lonely nor as solitary as she supposed.

The bedroom she was shown into was exactly what

she would have expected from what she had seen of the house so far. Half-panelled in dark oak, it had a high ceiling and tall windows against which the rain hissed and rattled in its fury. Thick carpet deadened her footsteps and there was a big four-poster bed on one wall with a yellow silk cover that gave an added touch of luxury.

It was a beautiful room, though it gave the uncomfortable feeling of not having been slept in for a very long time, and she shivered involuntarily as the rain continued to beat at the window, like someone tapping. Jessie McKay said nothing, but withdrew at once, presumably to find the robe she had promised to provide, and Melodie took the opportunity to look around her. It was the kind of room that suggested secret panels and family ghosts, but she had scarcely time to indulge in a small shudder at her own fancies before the housekeeper returned.

The promised robe turned out to be a big red dressing-gown of thick towelling, the type that fastens with a sash at the waist, and she took it with the thought that it would probably smother her, but at least it would serve to preserve her modesty while she was wearing nothing else.

"If you bring your wet things down with you when you come, I'll see to drying them for you," Mrs McKay told her, and Melodie smiled, hopefully trying to establish a less unfriendly atmosphere, though not with much optimism.

"I just hope I'm able to find my way back," she said, with a rather unsteady little laugh. "It seems like a very big house and there are so many doors."

Her laughter inspired no more than a brief lift of one sparse grey brow, and Melodie suspected Mrs McKay was virtually without a sense of humour at all. "You'll not go far wrong if you turn right when you leave this room and walk along to the top of the stairs," she told her. "From there it'll not be possible for you to lose yourself."

Not even for you—Melodie added silently, but she nodded her thanks for the guidance all the same. "Thank you, Mrs McKay."

She stood watching the stocky and faintly disapproving figure of the housekeeper walk to the door, waiting to see it close, but she blinked hastily when Jessie McKay turned in the doorway and her shrewd brown eyes looked at her once more. "You'll be chilled from the rain," she stated in her flat voice. "I'll have you something hot to drink that will take the chill from you."

Dazedly Melodie nodded and smiled. "Oh, that would be lovely, thank you!"

This time the door closed behind her, and Melodie watched it with dazed eyes. Such an offer of hospitality was the last thing she expected from that dour and uncompromising woman, and she felt a momentary twinge of guilt at the thought of possibly misjudging her. When she unrolled the dressing-gown too, she found a large bath towel in the middle of the bundle, and she once again wondered at the unexpected thoughtfulness of Jessie McKay.

Her skin glowed after a vigorous rubbing with the towel, and Melodie felt much more comfortable as

she shrugged herself into the thick towelling robe
and tied the sash at her waist. As she expected, it
covered her completely from head to foot, but at
least it allowed no glimpse of her nakedness, and she
rolled the sleeves back as she surveyed herself in a
long cheval mirror.

The red colour suited her and added to the rather
wild gypsy look that was suggested by her black hair
roughly towelled dry and left to riot around her face
because she had no means of combing it into any
kind of order. There was laughter in her blue eyes
that appreciated the sight, and she could not restrain
a rather nervous giggle as she faced the prospect of
appearing in such a state.

There was no one about on the landing when she
looked out, and she padded out on her bare feet,
then turned to carefully close the door behind her. It
was as she straightened up that she found herself
looking directly along at Neil McDowell, and for a
moment she hesitated.

Evidently he had come from the stairs while she
was closing the door, and his hand was on the handle
of a door immediately at the top of the stairs, presumably his bedroom. For some reason she expected
him to simply acknowledge her being there and then
carry on into his room, and with that in mind, she
waved a hand. But although he acknowledged the
wave he made no other move and she was more or
less obliged to walk along the landing towards him,
feeling more self-conscious than she had ever done
in her life.

Seeing him again she was reminded of the way he had held her in his arms, such a very short time ago, and the sight of his bare brown arms, still glowingly damp, brought a swift and disturbing reaction from her senses. Giving herself a mental shake, she smiled and walked over with as much confidence as her attire allowed.

Neil had kissed her, that was all, and it was hardly such an unusual event in her life that it should mean so much—she had been kissed before. Not with such intensity, it was true, but she had been kissed by men before, and it made no sense at all that Neil McDowell should have left a so much deeper impression on her emotions than anyone else ever had.

Grey eyes swept over her modestly covered length and registered the tumbled mass of her hair then he smiled, and she was once again startled by the difference it could make to that rather stern face. "I'd no idea I was so much bigger than you," he said. "That dressing-gown is mebbe a wee bit big for you!"

Melodie laughed because, despite her efforts at self-control, she felt curiously excited suddenly; the way she had down by the river, though she did her best to quell the feeling as she pulled the red robe about her more tightly. "It drowns me!"

"That colour suits you."

"A red rebel! That's what my brothers sometimes call me!"

"You've brothers?"

She nodded. "Yes, two of them, for my sins!"

He nodded, but he was remembering those few

moments beside the river; she knew it, even though he said nothing. She could sense it in his manner and she felt herself shiver at the possibility of the scene being repeated. She looked down at the thick red dressing-gown, anything rather than meet his eyes, then once more that small and slightly unsteady laugh betrayed her nervousness.

"Well, I'd better let Mrs McKay have—" She stopped, looking down at her empty hands for a second until the truth dawned, then she shook her head. "Oh, what an idiot I am—I've forgotten my clothes!"

Turning quickly, she started to run back to the bedroom she had used, vaguely aware as she did so that Neil was calling something after her, then suddenly she went sprawling, tripped by a corner of the too-long dressing-gown that had caught under her foot.

Too breathless for a moment to get up, she lay full length until two large hands reached down for her and raised her from the floor. He said nothing, but held her for a moment while she recovered, and her cheeks were flushed, her eyes downcast because she felt she had made a fool of herself. Then the strong hands on her arms and the masculine scent of his warm, damp body seemed suddenly much too affecting, and she glanced up suddenly and shook her head, laughing unsteadily to cover the way she felt.

"It's just not my day, is it?"

"No harm done." The hard fingers on her arms pressed into her soft skin for a second before he released her. "But Jessie will fetch your things—you'd best have two hands to cope with that long dressing-gown while you go downstairs."

"Won't she mind?"

The question was instinctive, but she did not really know why she asked it, except that Jessie McKay's stony manner was still too easily recalled. But she saw Neil's brows rise as if it surprised him. "I should hope not," he said quietly, and glanced down at his own wet clothes. His shirt clung to his broad chest and showed the tanned skin through its thin texture, and his fair hair was still darker than normal, though already starting to dry. "I've to change my own things first, then I'll be down too."

Something else occurred to her suddenly, and she looked up at him. "I haven't thanked you for taking care of both horses—I should have remembered."

That too appeared to surprise him, for he was looking at her between thick fair lashes, and his head was angled in query. "Would you not expect me to take care of them both?" he asked, and Melodie shrugged, vaguely uneasy without quite knowing why.

"Yes. Yes, I suppose so, but I'm still grateful."

The grey eyes studied her for a second or two, and she found the scrutiny oddly disturbing, then he shook his head slowly. "You'd best away downstairs," he said, "and mind and lift that robe when you go."

The warning reminded her so much of the way her brothers sometimes spoke to her that she responded in much the same way she would have done to one of them, letting him know that she was not baby enough to need to be told.

"*Yes*, Mr McDowell!"

It was a pert answer, but meant only to tease him for the way he was instructing her and she wondered if she had been too rash when she saw him raise a brow as he regarded her steadily for a moment. "You don't have to be sassy," he told her, and the slang expression spoken in that soft quiet voice brought a swift flush of colour to her cheeks.

"I'm not *being* sassy!"

She looked up at him, her blue eyes unconsciously provocative between their thick black lashes, and she was at the same time tinglingly aware of her own body and of the man facing her. The air was electric, just as it had been down there beside the river, with the storm venting its fury all around them. A vivid flash barely preceded the snarling roar of thunder that shook the house, and she saw a glimpse for a moment of the same kind of fierceness in the eyes of the man beside her, before it was hidden from her.

"Jessie has some hot toddy ready that will take off the chill," he said in that cool voice. "I'll be down for my share as soon as I've changed my clothes."

Her mind could not immediately cope with the matter-of-factness of what he was saying, and she shook her head slowly and vaguely. "Mr McDowell—Neil—"

"Have you not heard that silence can be golden?" he inquired softly. "I suggest that this is one of those occasions, Melodie."

He turned and went striding back to his room and Melodie watched the tall figure in clinging wet clothes with dazed eyes. Pride and even arrogance showed in the way he walked, and she watched him go with a strange feeling of regret that she was not altogether sure she could explain.

CHAPTER FOUR

MELODIE had said nothing to John as yet about riding with Neil, or that they had been caught in a storm and she had been obliged to take shelter in Ben Ross. It struck her as odd that she was so diffident about mentioning it, and once or twice during the ensuing week she had questioned her own reasons.

John had become an even more frequent visitor to the cottage. He either came to see her in the mornings before she started work, or in the evening when she had finished for the day, and a couple of times he had taken her to visit his uncle and aunt in their cottage on the estate. The visits were not altogether a success, although it was pleasant enough chatting to his family, but the Stirlings had lived all their lives in the service of the family at Ben Ross and the idea of having a guest of their employer visiting as a friend of their nephew, made them uneasy, and did not fit in with their idea of how things should be.

She had seen Neil several times during the week, but had been given the opportunity to do no more than wave a hand as he passed, either from her cottage or from her chosen viewpoint at the top of the terrace steps. While he returned her greeting amiably enough he had not once stopped to say more than a couple of words to her, and deep down she resented the fact more than she cared to admit.

From his manner at present it might be supposed that he saw her simply as someone he could do no more than be civilly polite to, but in view of the way he had acted when they stood beside the river in the midst of a raging storm, it was not an attitude that was easy to either accept or understand. Neil McDowell continued to be as much an enigma as ever, and sometimes she lost patience with herself for being so intrigued.

On Saturday morning, John was a fairly early caller at the cottage, and when Melodie opened the door to him it was plain from the way he was dressed that he had it in mind for them to go riding. He wore dark denims and a blue open-necked shirt, and he looked irresistibly cheerful, grinning all over his pleasantly attractive face when she opened the door.

"Hello, John, you're an early bird!"

He gave her a mock salute and leaned a hand on the lintel of the door while he grinned at her hopefully. "How do you feel about exercising one of McDowell's horses this morning?" His grin was perhaps just slightly less confident at the moment and she wondered if the surprise she felt showed on her face. "Can't I tempt you, Melodie? I know you *can* ride because you've said so—so how about it?"

Her hesitation was purely and simply because she was remembering the events of the only other time she had borrowed a horse from the Ben Ross stables, but John did not know that and he was watching her with a curious anxiousness, as if he feared she might refuse. There was absolutely no reason why she should refuse to go with him, and she nodded after only a moment or two, glancing down at the summery dress she was wearing.

"You'll have to give me time to change," she told him, and stood back from the door to let him in. "Would you like to come in and wait for me—I shan't be very long?"

John's grin became broader than ever and, as he stepped inside the little cottage, he caught hold of her hand and gave her fingers a brief squeeze. "Take all the time you need," he said. "I'm in no rush now I know you're not turning me down flat."

Assigning him a chair with a careless hand, Melodie watched him curiously as he dropped into one of the cottage's rather battered armchairs. "Did you expect me to turn you down flat?" she asked, and he shrugged, as if he hated to admit that he had ever doubted his own powers of persuasion.

"I don't know," he confessed. "I guess I figured that as it's such a long time since you were on a horse you might think twice about it when it came to the crunch."

Of course, it was a long time as far as John knew, she thought, but rather than tell him that it was in fact little more than a week since she was last on a horse, she turned away towards her bedroom with a somewhat uneasy smile. "I'll go and change," she said.

When she reappeared a few minutes later she was wearing the same denim trousers and white blouse she had worn when she rode with Neil, and John got to his feet hastily. The way he looked at her, a swift searching scrutiny from head to foot, was reminiscent of Neil's reaction in similar circumstances, and the clarity with which she remembered the fact startled her for a moment.

Physically John was every bit as attractive as Neil McDowell, but there was something about the older man that left a deeper impression on her, although she could not have said why or what it was that made it so.

John's grin was in evidence once more as she came across the room to him and she responded to it instinctively. There was something about his almost schoolboy enthusiasm that appealed to her present mood. "Well," he drawled, "that must be something of a record for a quick change, and well worth the effort, believe me."

His car was parked outside the cottage, but they walked along the steeply sloping drive towards the house, and once more Melodie was driven to speculate, as they approached the big red brick building, on how lonely it must be for Neil living alone there. She did not say as much to John, but simply remarked on the air of solitude about the old place, and he nodded agreement, unhesitatingly.

"I can't think why it hasn't been turned into a hotel or something by now," he declared, and shuddered melodramatically. "It'd give me the creeps, living alone in a mausoleum like that."

"Oh, I wouldn't call it a mausoleum!" Her defence of the old house was quite instinctive, and she did not even notice John's vaguely surprised look when she made the denial. "In fact it's really quite homely inside, and—" She stopped herself there, before she made a statement that could very well complicate things. Betraying an inside knowledge of the bedrooms in Ben Ross was bound to make John more curious than she was prepared for at the moment.

"I can't think why anybody would get so attached to it," he observed, glancing at the rather severe face that Ben Ross presented as they passed along its frontage. "Mind you, it must have something, I guess—the girl who inherited it from old man Ross hated leaving it, so Uncle Jamie says, though I'd have thought she would have been glad to see the back of it!" Only then did he remember at whose invitation she was there, and Melodie saw his suddenly rueful face. "Oh, heck," he said dolefully, "I forgot you're a friend of hers."

"You don't have to worry," Melodie insisted, intrigued anew about Neil's position at Ben Ross. "Catriona and Nick were more neighbours than close friends. We got along well socially, but I never knew a lot about them, only that Catriona inherited Ben Ross about eight years ago, but gave it up to marry Nick and settle in Australia." She looked up at the house again as they turned the corner and made for the stable yard. "Just the same, I can see how she'd hate leaving Ben Ross."

"And its manager, maybe?" John suggested softly, and Melodie turned to him swiftly, her curiosity fighting a certain loyalty she felt she owed to her ex-neighbour in Australia.

"Just what's that supposed to imply, John?"

He shrugged, obviously regretting having made that rash and somewhat malicious comment, but there was little else he could do, having gone so far, but go on. And Melodie wanted to know the rest with a compulsion that surprised her. "It doesn't mean anything very much really," he confessed uneasily. "It was just something that my uncle said once, about Neil McDowell having been keen on the girl who inherited this place."

"You mean he was in love with her?"

It fitted in so well with the kind of situation she had visualised for Neil, and her blue eyes had a distant, hazy look for a second or two as she pictured him in love with the owner of Ben Ross, then losing her to Nick Holland. She had known somehow that he had been a loser in a love-affair, and her heart beat faster suddenly when she thought of him living alone in that great house with memories that were possibly more painful than anyone realised.

John took a more prosaic view, and he shrugged lightly. "Who knows?" he said. "Uncle Jamie said he was keen on her, he didn't enlarge on it."

"I had a feeling there was something like that." She shook her head slowly. "He has that look about him somehow."

"Ah, come *on* now!" John laughed off her romantic notions with a determined practicality, and taking her hand he smiled down at her, his brown eyes glistening. "He's just a dour Scot, it has nothing to do with unrequited love! Don't get carried away with sentimental notions about him. Melodie—Neil McDowell isn't the type to take kindly to anyone feeling sorry for him."

"I wasn't *feel*ing sorry for him!" She denied it hastily and firmly, and yet she knew it wasn't quite true, and the flush in her cheeks made John raise a brow.

"O.K., O.K.," he soothed, and squeezed her fingers persuasively. "So let's drop the subject of McDowell and get ourselves a couple of horses, shall we?"

Melodie said nothing for the moment, but walked with him across the cobbled yard and into the stable, instinctively pausing beside the stall that housed the chestnut gelding she had ridden the last time she went out. Black Knight's stall next to it was empty, and she breathed an inward sigh of relief that Neil was unlikely to catch her unawares this time.

"I'll take Tarquin, the one I usually ride," John told her from further along, "and there's a nice little grey here you'll like. I'll saddle him for you since you're out of practice."

"Oh no, I'll take Rusty!"

Her response was unthinking and it was not until John walked back to her and she saw his curiously furrowed brows, that she realised what she had said. He came and stood by the chestnut's stall, resting one hand on the dividing screen and looking at her in silence for a moment before he spoke.

"Anything you say," he told her, but made no other move. "He's quiet enough at least."

"Yes."

He still made no move, but stood watching her, and she felt there was a certain tautness in his manner. "I get the feeling I've missed out somewhere," he remarked. "Or maybe it's none of my business."

It would have been so much easier if she had explained in the first place, Melodie thought; as it was he was bound to suspect her motive for keeping quiet about her ride with Neil. To cover her discomfiture she turned and took the saddle herself and started to put it on the gelding's broad back, but she had barely started when John took over, his usually sunny face showing the first hint of anger she had ever seen there, then he looked at her and his eyes were narrowed.

"I guess it's none of my damned business at that!" he declared forcefully.

It was difficult to explain, and she wished it wasn't, for there was no reason why she should find it so hard to tell him that she had been for a ride with Neil. Except that she thought of the ride simply as a prelude to what had followed, and that was what made her reticent.

"There's really no mystery," she said, taking the rein from him and soothing the gelding's soft nose while she talked. "I came up here about a week ago because I suddenly decided I'd like to ride, and— Neil was here, so we went together."

It sounded so simple and so uneventful, outlined

like that, and that was how it should have been. Only the advent of a storm and that fiercely passionate reaction of Neil's to her near ducking in the river had turned it into anything other than a perfectly ordinary ride, but it was the unexpected that made it so hard for her to forget the incident.

John's brown eyes scanned her face for a moment, then he reached out and took the hand that stroked Rusty's nose, drawing it into his hold for a moment while he spoke. "You don't expect me to say I don't mind, do you, Melodie?" he asked, his voice quiet but not quite steady. "I do mind, and I mind more that you felt you had to keep quiet about going with him, but as I said, it's none of my damned business!"

"John!" She looked at him with wide uncertain eyes, finding his reaction difficult to cope with. "I didn't keep quiet about it—not intentionally. I mean, I'd have told you if the opportunity had arisen, but there didn't seem any point in suddenly announcing the fact that I'd been riding with Neil."

"Not even back there at the cottage—when I spoke about how long it had been since you rode last?"

The suggestion that he was accusing her of something was not easy to accept, but she knew that was what he was doing, and she did her best not to resent it. "It didn't seem that important," she insisted, and he pursed his lips.

"Seems to me it was a whole lot more important than it should be from the way you're reacting."

"John, it's not—"

"O.K., O.K.!"

He gave her one long look before turning his back
to her and walking back along the stable to saddle
his own mount, and she watched him with vaguely
uneasy eyes while she stroked the gelding's soft nose
absently. It hadn't been important, she was sure Neil
would agree with that, but it crossed her mind to
wonder just how much more resentful John would
have been if he had known the full story.

"Shall we go?"

His sudden question brought her swiftly out of her
reverie, and she nodded hasty agreement, leading
Rusty out into the yard. Just as Neil had done, he
left his own mount to come and help her into the
saddle, but before he did so he stood with one hand
on the animal's neck, very close to her and looking
down at her steadily with serious brown eyes.

"I guess I'll have to watch my step," he told her
ruefully. "I could quite easily fall in love with you,
Melodie Carne, and I have a feeling I'd be wasting
my time."

"John—"

He put a finger over her lips to silence her, then
bent to help her up into the saddle. "Let's go," he
said, "before I start saying something I'll be sorry
for."

She watched him swing himself on to the broad
brown back of his horse, and tried not to compare
his style with Neil's, shaking her head firmly to dismiss the comparison. They were two very different
men, both in character and appearance, although

both had the same kind of rugged attraction. The difference was that John was open and extrovert, while Neil McDowell presented an enigma that she found an increasing need to understand.

OUT ON THE MOORS AGAIN, Melodie felt the same sense of being overwhelmed by her surroundings as always, and she wondered if it would ever be possible to grow tired of such an environment. Riding with John she realised that he was less a part of the countryside than Neil was, but that was only to be expected. Canada was his country and he probably had the same affinity with that vast continent that Neil did with this ruggedly grand country.

They had ridden so far at a steady walk, but John as well as his mount began to grow restless eventually at the slowness of their pace, and he turned to Melodie with the familiar grin and a hint of challenge in his eyes that she found hard to resist.

"How about seeing what these critters are made of?" he asked. "Do you feel up to taking a gallop?"

Melodie had no great enthusiasm for the idea, but neither was she completely averse to it, and it was certain that Rusty would be less soundly outclassed by John's mount than he had been by the flying black stallion. "Why not?" she said, and he studied her for a moment with a sudden concern.

"Don't say so if you'd rather go on at a steady pace," he told her. "I'd hate anything to happen, Melodie. If you got hurt I'd never forgive myself."

"I won't get hurt." She stroked the gelding's rough coat without looking at John as she spoke. "I'm quite capable of taking care of myself, John."

He leaned across and put his hand over hers for a moment, his expression serious. "I hope so, honey—I'd hate it if you got hurt just to prove something."

"I won't."

"O.K." He gave her one last look, then put his heels to his horse's flanks and set him off at a gallop, heading for a huge boulder that soared skywards from the turf and heather, some half a mile away. "Let's go!"

To Melodie it seemed the ground was more un-even than she remembered it from that wild gallop through the storm a week ago, but the gelding never once faltered, and she began to thrill to the speed of their gallop as her long black hair fluttered out be-hind her and the wind whipped a bright colour into her cheeks.

John was in the lead by about four yards as they raced the last few yards to the boulder and she had little hope of catching him, although her mount seemed quite willing to try, until a sudden high-pitched whinny of fear startled him into swerving from his course. It took all her skill and strength to pull him up and she saw what happened only from the corner of her eye when the horse ahead stumbled suddenly and fell, rolling over before it lay on its side, its belly heaving with recent exertion, while its rider rolled clear.

"John!"

She turned the gelding hastily and slipped from the saddle almost before he stopped moving, kneeling on the turf beside John. He was already raising his head when she knelt down, with a hand to his brow and looking as much annoyed as hurt. He hauled himself up on to an elbow and pulled a face at her.

"Of all the lousy luck!" he declared, and for some reason she could not explain, Melodie felt a sudden surge of anger.

"It's worse luck for your horse!" she told him, and got up from his side to go and look at his horse.

She soothed the glossy brown coat with a gentle hand and wished she knew enough to recognise an injury when she saw one, for the animal had made no attempt yet to get to its feet again, so she felt sure it must be more seriously hurt than its rider. Then she heard two new sounds at almost the same instant, and felt her heart thud suddenly hard in her breast.

John swore softly to himself, and the thud of a horse's hooves reached her quite clearly via the springy turf she knelt on. In the circumstances it had to be Neil, and the stallion that enabled him to cover the distance between them so rapidly that she had barely time to muse on his timely arrival before he was there beside her.

Nor did it come as any surprise that he gave his immediate attention to the animal rather than its rider, or that he said nothing until he had assured himself that the horse was not too badly hurt. He knelt beside her, almost sweeping her aside, and ran his big gentle hands over the animal's legs and the glossy flanks with a surety of touch that suggested he knew exactly what he was doing.

His voice murmured quietly all the time he was carrying out his inspection, soothing and reassuring the animal. Melodie got to her feet after a second or two, but still stood beside him, fascinated by his gentleness and unaware that John was watching with a frown.

Only when he was apparently satisfied did Neil get to his feet and looked across to where John sat with his knees hunched before getting stiffly to his feet. He could not be too badly hurt, Melodie felt sure, for he had rolled clear and the heather made a soft fall, but he evidently meant to make the most of his moment.

"Are you hurt, John?"

The belated inquiry from Neil brought a grimace, and John was running his hands through his hair, a frown suggesting that Neil McDowell was the last person he wanted to see at the moment. "I thought you'd never ask!" he retorted acidly. He came across to them, rubbing a hand over his back and grimacing as he walked. "I'm O.K., just bruised a bit—how's Tarquin?"

Neil gave his attention to the fallen horse once more before he answered, holding the rein lightly in one hand and coaxing the animal to its feet with soft words and a soothing hand until it stood up. "He's not much more than winded, as near as I can tell at the moment," he said, "but I'll need to look at him more thoroughly in the stable." He bent once more and ran his hand over the vulnerable fetlocks, then nodded as if satisfied. "At least he has nothing broken."

"Well, thank God for that at least!" John's voice was heavy with sarcasm, and Melodie looked at him in some surprise. "I don't have anything broken either, but I feel like I've been thrown out of a window!"

"John, you're *not* hurt are you?" She felt vaguely guilty suddenly, for both she and Neil, she realised, had given more attention to the well-being of John's mount than to him. "You didn't say—"

"You didn't ask!" John interrupted ruefully, and she realised that was true.

She had gone to him, prepared to sympathise, but his statement that his fall was lousy luck had incensed her for some reason she could still not quite explain, and she had left him almost at once to go and look at Tarquin. Neil, she thought, was probably more angry than he appeared at first sight. It showed in the darkness of his grey eyes and the tight look about his mouth.

"You're both a lot luckier than you've any right to be!" he said.

John's usually friendly face was flushed, and he was much less troubled about letting his anger show. He glared at Neil in a way Melodie would not have believed him capable of only days ago. "I get the impression that I'm taking the can back for this fall," he said, his voice harsh. "Dammit, how was I to know the fool horse would tread in a hole?"

Neil still would not allow himself the luxury of losing his temper, Melodie realised as she watched that stern and uncompromising face from the shadow of her lashes, but his eyes had a steely greyness that brought an involuntary shiver to her. So far he had said nothing to her directly, and she hastened to speak up before a more serious situation developed between the two of them.

"We—we thought we'd give them their heads for a change," she ventured, and Neil turned and looked at her at last.

"We?" He asked the single word question so quietly that it was doubtful if John even heard it, and Melodie flushed.

"I—agreed," she told him. "It's the same thing."

He seemed unprepared to argue the point, but after a brief steady survey of her flushed face he walked across and picked up the rein of his own mount again while both she and John watched him uneasily. It wasn't in John's interests to quarrel with him, no matter how much he felt inclined to and she thought, with sudden insight, that John was not the kind of man to do anything that would jeopardise his own comfort or convenience.

"Well, what happens now?" he asked, and Neil shook his head. His hand was on the stallion's saddle and he prepared to remount, but he still had possession of Tarquin's rein, and that worried John. He watched him with a curious mixture of suspicion and dislike, but said nothing more.

Safely mounted once more, Neil looked down at the two of them for a moment before he replied. "Give me your hand, Melodie!"

"Hey now, wait a minute!"

John found his voice again, but by then Melodie had obeyed the instruction more by instinct than conscious reaction, and Neil's strong fingers were closed around her wrist. "Now come away up!"

The grey eyes looked down at her steadily, challengingly, she might almost have said, and she did as he said, letting him use their clasped hands to help her on to the stallion's broad back, pillion-fashion—behind him. She slid her arms around him and felt the hard rapid beat of her heart as she pressed against the warm vigour of his body.

He gave her one brief glance over his shoulder, then looked down at John still standing, helplessly angry, on the ground. "Take Rusty, John," Neil told him, and countered any protest on John's part by posing a question. "I think Biack is better able to carry two than poor old Rusty, do you not agree?" he asked with deceptive mildness. "And Tarquin had best be walked until I've had the chance to take a better look at him."

"If you say so!"

John complied with very bad grace, and he pulled the patient gelding round quite roughly until he caught Neil's eye on him, then he frowned and swung himself up into the saddle, a picture of angry resentment. Neil handed him the rein of his erstwhile mount and he took it without a word.

"I need both hands for this fellow," Neil explained, "especially with a lady aboard."

They made a curious little procession as they rode back across the moor, with Neil slightly in front on Black Knight, as was to be expected, and John obliged to slow his pace to a walk because of the riderless horse's hurt. It was as they neared the house and the cobbled yard that Melodie ventured to speak to Neil about the incident.

Her voice was as low as she could make it and still be sure he heard what she said, for she did not want John to hear and resent her appealing on his behalf. "Please don't blame John for what happened." She put her face close to his, stretching to reach over his shoulder and conscious as she did so of the hard muscles that kept the stallion under control.

Neil half turned his head, his cheek brushing hers and showing her a brief glimpse of his mouth, just touched by a hint of a smile, as if her appeal amused him. "I don't blame John," he told her. "Whatever gave you the idea I did?"

It was not the answer she expected, and for a moment she was at a loss. "I—I don't know," she confessed. "Except that you seemed angry."

Once more he half turned his head. "I'm always angry when one of my horses is hurt," he informed her, as if she should have known his reason without being told. "I care for my animals, Melodie."

"More than you do for people!"

The retort was impulsive, and unforgivable, she realised when she felt the hard body she clung to stiffen in her arms, but his self-control was remarkable. His body was no less taut, but it was quite at variance with the cool and matter-of-fact voice, and she was once more forced to ponder on the complicated character of the man.

"I find them a lot more reliable than most people." He turned the stallion into the stable yard and his hooves clattered on over the cobbles in a way that aroused memories of the last time they had come back from a ride, so that Melodie half expected to see Jessie McKay in the doorway as she had been then. He reached round for her hand to help her down before he dismounted himself, and for a moment she met the steady, unwavering look of the grey eyes head on and at no more than a few inches distance. "You find that cynical?" he asked, and Melodie did not reply at once.

She slid down on to the cobbles and glanced at John just appearing on the far side of the yard. She recalled the story John had told her only that morning, confirming her early suspicions that Neil McDowell had been the victim of an unhappy love affair, and she shook her head.

"No," she denied. "I don't find it cynical."

She felt very small suddenly now that he stood beside her, looking down in that steady and infinitely disturbing way he had. He was close enough for the fine lines at the corners of his grey eyes to be clearly seen, and she could sense the vigorous tautness of his body, like a tensed spring. Raising her eyes, she looked at him as steadily as she was able, trying to convey to him that she understood his reasons for being the way he was, and the act of meeting his eyes brought a tingling awareness to every nerve in her.

"I—I understand," she said. "I understand your reasons perfectly."

Clearly he found her pronouncement puzzling, for he was frowning. He would quite probably have questioned her meaning, but by then John had joined them and he looked no less resentful and disgruntled—a definite discouragement to further conversation.

"I will ask you to explain that at some other time," Neil murmured, and Melodie wished she had not glanced over her shoulder the way she did, as if she feared John might have heard what he said.

POURING OUT SECOND CUPS OF COFFEE, Melodie looked across at John and felt a twinge of impatience for his continued ill temper. It was a new side to his character that she had not come into contact with before, and not one she liked very much. It seemed incredible that after such short acquaintance he could be acting the way he was because he was jealous, and yet there seemed no other explanation. If that was the reason she must do something about it as soon as she possibly could, for as far as she was concerned their relationship had not yet reached the stage where he had either cause or right to be jealous of anyone.

"I can't imagine why you're making such a big thing about this," she told him as she stirred her own coffee. Elbows resting on the table, she looked across at him, her own blue eyes showing the impatience she could not hide for much longer. "I've told you that Neil doesn't hold you to blame for whatever happened to Tarquin."

"That's big of him!" He took a gulping mouthful of hot coffee and held the cup between both hands, much more tightly than he needed to. "I don't know why you felt the need to put in a plea for me in any case, Melodie—damn it, the horse fell, he'd know that as well as anyone!"

"I just tried to help, that's all."

"And then to go riding off with you like—like he was the lord of the manor with every right to carry you off! I could have kicked him—more, I could have taken a poke at him and I darned near did!"

"Well, I'm glad you didn't, it would have been pointless and rather childish, and it wouldn't have served any useful purpose at all in the circumstances."

"It would have made *me* feel better!"

"And what about me?" The impatience she felt was evident in her voice at last, and she thought he took warning from it, for he leaned across the table and curled his fingers over her hand.

"Melodie, I'm sorry!" His brown eyes were anxious and questioning and it was very hard not to be affected by them. He shrugged uneasily and shook his head, pulling a wry face at her. "I guess that guy gets me into such a lather I can't think straight!"

It was something that he was backing down and showed signs of recovering his usual affability, but she was troubled by his sudden and open dislike of Neil. Looking down at their entwined hands on the table, she pressed her fingers to his, her voice quiet but undisguisedly curious.

"I thought you liked Neil, John. You gave me that impression when you spoke to me about him on the day I arrived."

John's smile was rueful, making it clear that he was about to confirm her suspicions. "But that was before I got so worked up about you, honey. Now I can't help seeing him as the other man in a triangle situation—and from that angle he doesn't seem so easy to like."

It was difficult, much more difficult than she had anticipated, and she did not look at him, but continued to study their clasped hands instead. "I wish you wouldn't see him in that light, John, there's really no cause for it."

Her heart was hammering hard suddenly and she could not imagine how this episode was going to end. Neil McDowell had done nothing to encourage her to think of him in any other way than as her rather unwilling host, except for one unexpected kiss—and she had been kissed before.

"No cause?"

John was watching her closely and she shook her head as firmly as possible to convince him. "I can't imagine why you think there's anything—like that."

He watched her for a moment longer, then shook

his head slowly, a small tight smile on his mouth. "Maybe something about the way he looked at you out there this morning." He turned his hand to enfold hers even more tightly, and his brown eyes were narrowed when he looked across at her, lacking their usual warmth and laughter. "And maybe because you took so long telling me about that last ride you took—with him."

"John, I told you—"

"Yeah, yeah, you told me!"

He held her hand tightly, then raised it to his lips suddenly and pressed his mouth to her palm, watching all the time as if he sought her reaction. She did nothing, but simply tried to still the urgent beating of her heart. She didn't want to get serious about anyone at the moment, and especially a man she had known only a few weeks, but it was gratifying to have him apparently so deeply attached to her, and she could not help feeling a certain satisfaction.

Looking across at him, she scanned his ruggedly attractive face for a second or two. "I don't know what you think has—happened, John, but—"

"No, don't!" He raised himself from his chair and leaned across the table to kiss her mouth, then laughed shortly and rather unsteadily. "Don't give me any explanations, honey. I don't want to hear them and I don't have the *right* to explanations. Most of all I don't want to quarrel with you, not about McDowell or anybody else. I guess you could say I'm prepared to sign an armistice on any terms, just so you don't throw me out on my ear!"

"Oh, John, I wouldn't do that!"

She was shaking her head, won over without ever being quite sure what the quarrel had been about, or even if they *had* quarrelled, and John held both her hands in his. His smile looked less tense and the familiar warmth was back in his eyes again as he looked across at her.

"Promise?" he asked, and she nodded.

"Promise."

CHAPTER FIVE

IT was hard to believe that a month had passed since Melodie first came to Ben Ross; since John Stirling had driven her in his car to meet the man who he said had a reputation for being dour, and who soon hoped to be owner of Ben Ross instead of just its manager.

She looked at the one completed canvas she had done since her arrival and studied it critically. The work was good, and yet somehow she felt she had failed to catch the essential character of the landscape, and it displeased her. Those elusive soft greens and blues, and the mellowness of the countryside, made it exclusive, she felt, and quite unlike anywhere else she had seen, and she had hoped so much to capture it, but not quite succeeded.

For some reason she had more than once felt the temptation to show the completed picture to Neil and seek his opinion of it. He would, she felt, be better able to judge whether or not she had captured the character of the country as well as she had hoped, but an unfamiliar shyness had held her back so far.

With the picture in her hands she studied it with

her head on one side and a small frown drawing her brows together. She was never a very good judge of her own work, but the distant view of Glen Ross village from the terrace steps was fair enough, she thought, and the little houses, squat and palely honey-coloured, looked as they did in the reality of the summer sun. The road straggled upwards in the near foreground, hidden for the most part by rowan trees that in autumn, when she was gone, would add the bright red of their berries to the softer hues of the hills and glens.

"Melodie?"

She looked up hastily and put down the canvas she had been studying as she brought herself hastily back to earth. She had heard no sign of anyone approaching—neither the unmistakable crunch of hooves on the gravel drive nor the light knock on the open cottage door, and she stared at the newcomer for a moment with the dazed look of absence still in her eyes.

A pale blue cotton top hung loose above a pair of well worn jeans, and her black hair showed that she had run her hands through it over and over while she tried to form a judgment of her work, and Neil took it all in in one searching survey as he stood in the doorway watching her.

"I'm sorry." Melodie shook her head to dismiss the last remnants of preoccupation and looked across at him curiously. "Please come in, Neil, if you don't mind it being rather untidy."

He smiled, and it was the same almost miraculous

transformation of that rugged face that it always was. "Is that not the privilege of the artistic temperament?" he asked, and Melodie pulled a face.

"I don't know about that," she demurred, "but it's a fact in my case, I'm afraid, I'm not as domesticated as I could be. Though I can *cook* rather well," she added with a hint of mock defiance.

"Can you now?" His eyes were warm with laughter. "Then I'll mebbe call on you when Jessie is away visiting her sister!"

"Any time!" It was odd how shy she felt suddenly, and the realisation brought a flush of colour to her cheeks and made her hastily avoid his eyes. "Was it to ask me to help out that you came to see me?"

Neil shook his head, serious once more. "I brought a letter for you that the postman left at the house by mistake, but I was coming this way, so I'd not to make a special journey."

As if he feared she might think he had put himself out for her, Melodie thought ruefully, and took the envelope from him, noting absently that it carried an Australian stamp and had been addressed by one of her brothers. "Thank you—it's yet another letter from the family."

"You'll hear from them quite often, I imagine?"

"Often enough!"

It was so difficult to think clearly when he was with her, and even the most commonplace remarks seemed significant when he said them. It was quite easy to see how he might have acquired a reputation for being dour, for he was mostly so serious, and there was an air of reserve about him that did not encourage confidences, yet only seconds before the grey eyes had been warm with laughter, and even now it was obvious that his interest was genuine.

"They worry about you, no doubt?" he suggested, and she hesitated to deny it.

"I don't think they exactly worry about me," she explained, "it's more that they don't trust me to eat as much as they think I should, or remember to buy things in—as I did when I arrived. You know what families are."

He nodded solemnly, as if he knew exactly what she meant, although as far as she had heard he had no family. "Catriona mentioned in the letter you brought with you that you'd not been away from home before and that your family were a little concerned about how you would fare on your own."

The information was such a surprise to her that Melodie stared at him for several seconds, scarcely able to believe him. "You mean—you mean they told—"

"They apparently suggested to Catriona that if someone this end could see to it that you settled in all right and looked after yourself while you were on your own, they would be grateful."

The implication was unmistakable and his matter-of-fact acceptance of it even more surprising. She felt incredibly small suddenly, and rather humiliated, though that was a rather too dramatic reaction, she realised. Just the same she felt angry to think that someone like Neil McDowell had been more or less assigned to see to her well-being. A quiet, reserved man who would find the request much more difficult to comply with than someone with a more extrovert nature would have done.

"I'm—I'm sorry, Neil."

It was clear that her apology puzzled him, for he was frowning. "For what?"

She shrugged, feeling helpless and slightly silly, when she thought of what his reaction must have been in the first instance. "It's rather a nerve to ask a complete stranger to—to act as nursemaid to a grown woman," she said, "and I wish Catriona hadn't passed on the request. It was a quite unnecessary chore to land you with, and I'm sorry."

A glimmer of that earlier warmth showed for a moment in his eyes, and he was shaking his head slowly at her. "I've not found it such a chore," he denied. "You've proved well capable of looking after your own interests so far."

"Well, of course I am!"

Once more he scanned her flushed face with a slow searching gaze that she found infinitely disturbing. "You don't like to think of me keeping an eye on you, mebbe?" he suggested.

"I don't like to think of *anyone* keeping an eye on me!"

His wide mouth hinted at a smile once more, and he shook his head as if to admonish her. "Nevertheless, I think I'll not relinquish my role yet awhile—if you don't mind." The rejoinder suggested a sarcasm that she would not have expected of him, and she frowned.

"I really don't need looking after, Neil, and I'm sure it isn't a job you relish!"

There was something in the way he looked at her that brought an unexpected flutter of response from her pulse, and she hastily looked away, even before he spoke. "I've not found it a particularly arduous chore so far," he assured her in his quiet and softly accented voice.

"Just the same I wouldn't have thought it was a job you would take to very willingly." Her voice was unsteady and a little breathless, and she avoided his eyes at all costs, though it wasn't easy. "You're not the type to—I mean," she hastily corrected herself, "you don't seem to me to be the sort of man who would take on such a chore with very much enthusiasm."

Once more she was made aware of a short, significant pause, as if he was watching her, waiting for her to look at him. "I think perhaps you've been labouring under a delusion concerning me, Melodie," he told her. "Maybe more than one."

"I—I don't think so."

"You claim to know an awful lot about me, it seems!"

"Oh, but I didn't mean—I mean I don't claim to know you at all well, it's just that—" She shrugged uneasily, her hands spread in a curiously touching gesture of helplessness.

There was a curious air of tension in the little

room that she could not account for at all, and she wondered vaguely if Neil was as aware of it as she was herself. She wished, not so much that he would leave her, but rather that the subject might be changed for one that was a little less personal to her. At the same time she could believe that if Neil had set his mind on following something up, her own feelings in the matter were unlikely to be taken into account.

Black Knight, tethered outside the cottage, could hear their voices and shifted restlessly, reminding them of his presence, and to Melodie the reminder brought other occasions to mind. Like the time when she had returned home riding pillion behind Neil, while John trailed them reluctantly on Rusty, leading his injured horse. And later, John's undisguised jealousy—his suspicion that there was something more between her and Neil than she was prepared to admit.

Neil had perched himself on the edge of the table with one booted foot swinging, and he seemed perfectly at ease, though she was far from being so herself. "I seem to remember that at one time you suggested I cared more for horses than for people, did you not?"

"And you agreed!" Her response was defensive, almost defiantly so, and she tried, a little dazedly, to remember how they had become involved in such a discomfiting exchange.

"I believe I told you that I found them more reliable than most people," he corrected her with confidence, and she nodded.

"It—it was something like that."

The grey eyes assessed her response and her seeming nervousness for a moment in silence. "You assured me then that you understood my reasons perfectly," he reminded her. "Isn't that so, Melodie?"

She was rather taken aback to realise that he had quoted her word for word as far as she could recall, and at the time he had implied the necessity to explain her words at some future time. This, she felt, was going to be the moment, and she spread her hands in a curiously helpless gesture of appeal.

"I might have done," she agreed.

How on earth could she tell him what she had learned from John? That she knew about his love for the woman he worked for and had lost to another man. It wasn't something she could put into words, and she looked at him with an appeal in her blue eyes that besought him not to pursue the subject.

"You've mebbe been—hearing things?" The soft voice persisted, but she simply nodded and looked down at her feet. Then a long finger slid beneath her chin suddenly and lifted her face, the touch of his hand bringing a tingling flick of excitement to her senses. "What tales have you been listening to, Melodie? Something John Stirling told you?"

"Not John!"

"Quick in his defence!" He spoke as quietly as ever, but she detected an unmistakable touch of hardness in his voice. "That tells me what I need to know, Melodie! What have you been hearing?"

"Nothing, I—"

"I'd rather you didn't lie to me!" The finger on her chin gave a short flick upwards and she caught her breath.

She could sense it again—that strangely taut atmosphere that filled the little room like a charge of electricity, and for several seconds Neil sat holding her with her chin supported on his finger while he looked down into her flushed face, dwelling longest on the soft, vulnerable tremor of her mouth.

"What have you heard about me, Melodie?"

It was incredibly hard not to tell him what John had told her, but she held her impulsive instincts firmly in check. There were enough uneasy meetings between him and John lately, without her making more cause for dissent, so she shook her head as well as she was able.

"Nothing I didn't know or—or guess before," she insisted, and raised her eyes briefly to see if she was believed.

"I see."

He quite possibly did see, all too clearly, Melodie thought, and wished she need not have been the cause of raising such uneasy memories. To Neil the intrusion of strangers into his private affairs would be a more deeply affecting thing than it would to someone less reserved, and she hated to think of herself as an intruder.

He stood up suddenly and for a moment looked down at her in silence, so that she felt herself trembling like a leaf because of his nearness—the light touch of his arm that barely brushed hers when he moved. "Since you already know so much about me," he told her in a tight, clipped voice, "you'll maybe already know what it was I came down here to tell you, so I needn't bother myself!"

"Oh, Neil, please!" She cared more that he was angry for the moment than about whatever it was he had to tell her, and she looked at him appealingly with a hand on his arm, its fingers pressed tightly into the firm brown flesh in her anxiety to convince him. Almost without being conscious of doing so, she used her wide blue eyes to persuade him. "I promise I haven't been discussing your private affairs with anyone, please believe me, Neil."

It took a moment or two, but then she felt him begin to relax and the taut muscles in the arm she held eased their tightness. He looked down at her for a moment, then shook his head slowly. "I can't quite believe that I became so involved with you that I forgot—momentarily at least—the news I have."

Melodie's heart was beating anxiously hard in her breast as she searched his face for some hint, then she found it in the bright, glowing darkness of the grey eyes suddenly, and felt an overwhelming surge of pleasure. A pleasure that banished the last shreds of their brief disagreement.

"Oh, Neil!" Her voice was husky with emotion and her eyes had the bright shining look of jewels as she searched his face. "You've got Ben Ross—it's yours, isn't it?" His expression was confirmation enough and she flung her arms impulsively around his neck and kissed him beside his mouth. "Oh, I'm so glad!"

His pride was such that she felt a momentary flick of jealousy for the vast acres of Ben Ross, because he loved them so much and so completely. "So am I," he said softly. "It's been quite a while."

Her curiosity was aroused, but Melodie did not propose to question him, only prod gently to satisfy some inner longing she felt to know all there was to know about him. "Have you always wanted to own Ben Ross?" she asked, and he did not immediately answer.

"For quite a long time," he admitted at last, then shook his head and half smiled. "It's a long story, but maybe I'll tell it to you one day."

Through her thick lashes, she looked up at his lean brown face and felt the sudden rapid urgency of her heart. "Not now?" she coaxed, and he shook his head.

"Not now—perhaps when you tell me how it is you understand my reasons for saying what I did about horses and people, hmm?"

She would have found some reply, though heaven knew what there was to say in response to such a provocative suggestion, but before she could even draw breath he had spanned his broad hard palm under her chin, and his fingers were stroking the softness of her cheek.

She half expected the gentle kiss he pressed on to her mouth to be merely a prelude to the same passionate and fierce caress that had stunned her on that earlier occasion, but instead he released her after that brief, light touch and she tried hard to stifle the sense of disappointment she felt.

The flush in her cheeks was even more pronounced, and she felt horribly vulnerable suddenly as she fought hard to remain matter-of-fact. "Whatever the story behind your wanting it, I'm glad you've got what you wanted, Neil."

That glow of warmth was in his eyes again, and he smiled. "Aye," he said, "I believe you are."

"What happens now?"

It was not her own situation that she had in mind when she asked the question, though obviously that was what Neil thought, and he raised a brow, a half smile teasing her gently for her anxiety. "Oh don't worry," he told her, "I'll not evict you from the cottage, Melodie. I promised, did I not?"

"I wasn't thinking about myself, I meant—" She shrugged uneasily, wondering suddenly if he would see her interest as an intrusion into his privacy. "I just wondered if it would make any difference to you, that's all."

"Very little."

"Except that you'll really be the laird of Ben Ross now."

His eyes narrowed slightly and he looked at her for a moment in silence. "Is that what he calls me?" he asked, and she did not have to question whom he referred to.

"Not only John, apparently—most people around here refer to you in that way." She looked up at him, seeking to put matters straight. "Not in a derogatory sense, Neil—after all, it's been true, hasn't it—even before today?"

Neil seemed to take a moment to decide, then he nodded, and she wondered if he saw himself in the part as well. "I suppose it has," he agreed. "For five years before Duncan Ross died he did little on the estate, but left it to me, and for the past eight years I've not even had anyone to oversee what I do. I've run the place for the past thirteen years—my way."

And how he had hated to see it go to a woman when old Duncan Ross died, Melodie thought. After five years of caring for the place as if it was his own, he had probably felt that he owned it already, although his fierce pride in Ben Ross was still puzzling to her in one way. How could a man give his life to a place when he had little or no hope of ever making it his own? Perhaps this day had been his goal all along—the possibility that one day he *would* own it.

"You deserve to have it," she told him, and Neil said nothing for the moment, but simply shook his head, as if he found it still too much to believe.

"We'll see," he said, and seemed to deliberately seek out another subject for discussion.

Picking up her painting where it still lay on the table, he held it at arm's length for a moment or two and studied it, while Melodie watched him from the concealment of her lashes, trying to decide what his opinion was. His expression gave no indication whether or not his opinion was favourable, and she waited for it with a certain amount of anxiety.

"I've been trying to decide about that," she told him with a slightly unsteady laugh, and when he spoke it was without turning round.

"Do you sell your work, Melodie? Are you a professional artist?"

It was not quite the answer she had expected, and she watched his face for a moment from the concealment of her lashes. "Why—yes. I've sold them at various times—whenever someone wants to buy them."

"I'd like to buy this one."

Melodie was too startled for a moment to quite realise what he was saying, and she stared at him with wide eyes. "You—you really like it?"

"I like it very much."

"You don't think it's—"

"It's fine—I like it."

She could not rid herself of the suspicion that for some inexplicable reason he was simply trying to please her, and yet there was no earthly reason why he should go to such lengths to please her, and she shook her head slowly. Nevertheless she had to be sure, and she touched his arm lightly with her fingertips to make him look at her.

"Neil—you *really* want it?"

After a moment he smiled, and it was one of those smiles that glowed in the grey eyes, and brought a hundred tiny lines to the lean contours of his face. "You're not a very good salesgirl, Melodie," he teased. "Yes, I really want it—the first thing I've got for Ben Ross since it became mine."

His reason touched her more than she cared to admit, and she reacted impulsively, as she so often did. Putting her own hands over his as they held the painting, she squeezed his fingers persuasively. "But won't you please let me give you the painting for a housewarming present, Neil?"

He hesitated, and she watched him almost anxiously, then after a second or two he smiled again. It was not as wholehearted as the last, but none the less warm for all that, and it expressed his appreciation of the gesture. "Maybe it'll sound a wee bit strange to you, Melodie, even ungracious since you've offered to make it a gift, but—I'd like to buy the picture for myself—for Ben Ross. Will you let me do that?"

She thought she understood, though she would gladly have given it as a present, so she nodded. "Yes, of course," she said in a small soft voice. "I understand."

It was a second or two before she realised that she had used those exact words once before, and when she glanced up at Neil, it was clear that he remembered too. The grey eyes held hers for a moment with that disturbing steadiness that shivered a thrill of sensation along her spine, and briefly, for a second or two, that glowing warmth was in their depths again.

"Aye, I think maybe you do," Neil said softly.

IT HAD BEEN A LONG AND QUITE TIRING DAY one way and another and, having seen John out, Melodie yawned lazily and thought about going to bed. She had been a town dweller all her life, including the time she spent in Australia, and the hours she now spent in the rich Highlands air made her pleasantly sleepy so that she was always a little heavy-eyed by late evening, and had slept like a baby ever since she came to Ben Ross.

John was still a regular visitor and came most days, so that she wondered if he as well as Neil had taken it upon himself to keep a caring eye on her well-being. John, in fact, had made it increasingly plain recently that he would like their relationship to develop into something much more intimate, although so far Melodie had done nothing to encourage him.

She thought it was doubtful if he knew about the official change of ownership of Ben Ross, or he would almost certainly have said something to her about it, but she had no intention of being the one to inform him. If Neil wanted it made public knowledge he would let John's uncle know—he probably would in time, along with the rest of the estate employees, although it would make virtually no difference to their positions at all.

Smothering yet another yawn, she went through into the tiny kitchen and on impulse opened the door of a cupboard tucked away in one corner. Normally it housed only brooms and dusters and the paraphernalia of house cleaning, but its prime purpose as far as Melodie was concerned was as a store for her painting equipment, and from the top of the pile she picked up the painting that Neil had asked to buy.

Frowning over it for a moment or two while she decided whether or not it was dry enough to varnish, she came to the conclusion that it was perhaps better than she had first thought. Maybe Neil was a better judge than she was herself—it really wasn't too bad at all.

There was still quite a lot of daylight outside, but inside the little cottage the small windows admitted only a limited amount of light, and she switched on the overhead light for a moment while she studied the painting further. The light flickered unsteadily for a second or two and she frowned up at it. It had been happening quite often lately and she supposed it was a technical fault—something to do with those huge skeletal giants of pylons that strode across the hills and spoiled so much of the landscape.

When it happened again she switched off and put the painting back in the cupboard, glaring impatiently at the light. "Stupid things!" she declared, condemning the pylons for being ineffective as well as ugly.

Tomorrow she would varnish the painting and then, after another day or two, Neil could have it and hang it in his newly acquired domain. She must ask him, she thought as she undressed for bed, just where he had in mind to hang it—it would please her to think he wanted it somewhere where he could see it often, but she was not going to fool herself to the extent of thinking that he really cared that much one way or the other.

Outside the last of the daylight glowed in the evening sky, and through her open bedroom window the sound of a light wind in the shrubs and trees that surrounded the cottage rustled and whispered in a comfortingly familiar voice, lulling her off to sleep almost at once. It was the last sound she heard as her eyes closed, until a sudden loud and urgent voice yelled quite close to her ear what seemed like only seconds later, and snatched her from her sleep.

Her brain was dull, deadened by sleep, and her eyelids refused to open beyond a narrow, hazy slit that unbelievably showed Neil McDowell's stern face bending over her, while his hands gripped her shoulders with bruising force as he tried to shake her awake.

"Wake up, Melodie, for God's sake—wake up and get out of here!"

"What—I don't—" She shook her hazy brain into as much wakefulness as it was capable of at the moment, and glared at him indignantly. "Don't *do* that! Stop it, Neil—leave me alone!"

"Oh, God in heaven, you're still half asleep!"

His voice seemed even closer suddenly and more urgent, and she cried out instinctively when the bedclothes were pulled back roughly and arms grabbed her up from the bed in one frantic movement, while she still fought to make him stop.

"Stop it, for heaven's sake, you little idiot! Stop fighting me!"

There was a curious and unfamiliar smell in the room, but she was incapable of recognising it for what it was at the moment, she could cope only with more immediate things. Like the strong, unyielding arms that she struggled against, blindly and instinctively, right up to the moment when they pushed her unceremoniously through the bedroom window and into the cool night air, and she cried out in indignant protest when she landed among the shrubs outside the cottage.

The shrubbery probably made a softer landing ground than the hard ground would have done, but its leaves and branches were prickly, and she had no better protection than her nightdress, so that the impact was sharply uncomfortable. Her skin was scratched and grazed as she struggled to her feet and she stared at the cottage, the last remnants of sleep driven from her brain by the realisation of what it was all about. Smoke and flame seemed to be pouring from every window in the cottage and even the bedroom where she had been sleeping was filled with smoke.

"Neil!"

The cry was as instinctive as her struggles had been earlier, and she gazed at the window through which he had pushed her to safety, with a cold sense of panic in her breast, for there was no sign of him. No matter if the stony ground hurt her feet, she went to the window and raised her voice above the angry crackle of flames consuming tinder dry furniture and rafters, the heat scorching her cheeks as if an oven door had been opened.

"Neil!"

Her voice cracked in panic and she felt a tightness in her throat when she spotted him at last, over near the door as if he had been trying to get through into the rest of the cottage and had been driven back by the fire. He managed to close the door while she watched and she saw him hesitate for a second before striding across to the old-fashioned wardrobe that took up nearly half of one wall of the bedroom. He turned the handle and nothing happened—the wretched thing always stuck when she tried to open it herself.

"Neil, please—get out of there!"

She gave a sudden sharp scream of terror when the door of the bedroom burst inwards before a long licking tongue of flame that came within inches of where Neil still struggled to open the wardrobe door and she shook her head in despair. A great billow of smoke followed and more flames, spreading rapidly through the dry timbers of the old cottage, and Melodie cried out to him again.

"Neil! Neil, please!"

She saw him start towards the window, then dart suddenly across to where her robe lay across the foot of the bed, snatching it up as he came. He was across the room in a matter of seconds after that with the fire at his heels, and Melodie stepped back quickly from the window for fear of hindering his escape.

Smoke billowed out behind him as he climbed over the sill, and he shook his head as if to clear it, brushing a smoke-blackened hand across his brow, while in the other he held her robe, carelessly bundled into a mere handful. It looked such a little thing to have risked his life for, even though it was probably all she owned in the world at the moment.

He held it out to her and she was trembling like a leaf while he helped her into it, for it afforded little more protection than her nightdress did, and she stood like a small pale ghost in the vivid red firelight for a moment. Dazed and suddenly chill, she turned to him instinctively when he reached out, and hid her face for a second against his shoulder, while his arms held her close.

"That damned robe was all I could get for you," he said, as if he needed to explain, and Melodie was shaking her head urgently.

"You shouldn't have taken such a risk—it wasn't worth it to get my clothes."

Limp and unresisting, she would have stayed where she was, in a curiously satisfying limbo of inaction, but Neil was taking off his jacket and wrapping it around her, his big hands strong and reassuring, and the grey eyes scanned her face in a swift searching scrutiny, as if he found it hard to believe she was unharmed.

"Are you all right?"

It seemed such a commonplace question in the circumstances, and she felt vaguely lightheaded, so that she almost smiled. Instead she nodded assurance and her eyes in turn searched his dark, smoke-grimed features for a sign of hurt.

"Are you?"

His nod was brief but reassuring, then he cast a swift downward glance at her flimsily clad shape, only partly covered by his jacket. "You'll be getting chill if you stand around in this night air," he declared with almost his usual matter-of-factness. "I'd best get you up to the house as soon as possible and let Jessie take care of you."

"The house?"

It had not yet occurred to her what was likely to happen now that she was virtually homeless, but taking refuge in Ben Ross was the last thing she could have foreseen, though the only possible one in the present situation, she realised. Neil was looking at her with raised brows and a hint of impatience, she feared.

"Of course," he said. "Did you think I'd leave you to spend the remainder of the night under the hedge?"

"Oh no, but—"

She got no further with her explanation, for she was lifted once more into his arms and carried round the end of the burning cottage to where his car stood on the drive. Neil put her into the passenger seat, then came round quickly and got in beside her, turning his head briefly to look over his shoulder at the blaze.

In the flickering red light his face had a curiously tired look suddenly, and his grey eyes appeared more black than grey, so that she tried to imagine what he was feeling. Then he turned back, a tight stern look about his mouth as he started up the engine.

"I'm sorry, Neil." From the way he glanced at her it was clear that her apology puzzled him, and she hastened to explain. "It's your property," she reminded him, "and it seems such a shame that your ownership should start off so badly."

They drove along the drive to the house, taking only minutes to cover the distance it took her quite a long time to walk, and between the shadowy darkness of the shrubs and trees she caught glimpses of the bulk of Ben Ross against the skyline ahead and of the shimmer of water where Lock Lairdross caught the pale moonlight in the glen below and to their right.

"I'll call the fire brigade," Neil said, turning the car around the last bend in the drive, "but there'll not be much they can do by the time they arrive. I'm sorry about your things."

"Oh, I can hardly blame you! You took too many risks as it was."

In fact Melodie did not altogether understand her own present reaction to the drama. She should have felt something for the loss of her clothes and the rest of her possessions, and yet her main reaction at present was one of incredible satisfaction because Neil had been there to rescue her. It did not make sense, and she would probably feel quite differently about it in the morning, but at the moment the fact that Neil had snatched her to safety was the only thing that seemed to matter.

"I haven't told you how grateful I am for getting me out of there," she told him. "I dare not think what would have happened if you hadn't been on the spot."

"Do you always sleep so heavily?" He offered no explanation for his fortuitous presence in the vicinity of the cottage, but looked briefly over his shoulder at her, as if he recalled the difficulty he had in waking her, and Melodie nodded.

"Ever since I came here, I've slept like the dead," she confessed, then realised how true that could have been and shuddered. "I really am grateful, Neil." Something else occurred to her then and without thinking she mentioned it. "I'm afraid you won't get your painting now, it'll be lost in that blaze."

Neil swept the car round the last few yards in front of the house and braked to a halt, turning his head briefly as he switched off the engine. It was difficult to see anything of his face for the moon was new and pale and only the diffused lights from the glass panels either side of the doors in the house gave it any illumination.

"Better the painting than the artist," he said.

CHAPTER SIX

IT took Melodie several minutes when she woke the following morning to realise just where she was. The bedroom window was open and the curtains drawn back, and the customary sounds of morning reached her, but the warm sunshine across her face that had woken her was something out of the ordinary and she lay there for a moment or two slowly remembering how she came to be sleeping in a big, oak-panelled bedroom, instead of the more familiar cottage room.

The huge bed she was in was soft and comfortable and at some other time it might have tempted her to stay in it for much longer. As it was there was a great deal for her to think about since the events of last night, not least the uncertainty of her future position at Ben Ross, and she was far too restless to remain inactive.

Dressing was an immediate problem, for she had nothing but the nightdress and flimsy robe she had escaped in last night, and she could not go far in them. At the moment she was not even wearing her own nightdress, but a voluminous cotton garment given to her last night by Jessie McKay.

It draped her slim form in shapeless folds, but Jessie had insisted that her own flimsy affair was far too smoke-grimed for anyone to go to bed in and she had provided one of her own. It had been a kindly gesture, Melodie felt sure, but once the donor had gone she had been reduced to a fit of slightly hysterical giggles at the sight of herself in yards of white cotton.

Backed by fat feather pillows, she sat hugging her knees and looking out of the window at a new aspect of the now familiar countryside. The dominant position of Ben Ross gave a much wider view and was all the more breathtaking than from her cottage windows, and before long she was drawn into daydreaming as she watched the day grow.

The hills and mountains were veiled in mist, as they always were at this time of the day, their shapes made indistinct and softer. Their blue-grey colour muted and patched with shades of dark, rusty green heather that varied its hues with the movement of the clouds billowing like rolls of cotton wool around their peaks.

The sun as yet was little more than a hazy suggestion of gold that dabbed little touches of light over the landscape and coloured the hovering mist with a promise of a hot day. It was not yet the hot, summer sun that would develop later in the day, but it was pleasantly warm when she turned her face towards it and closed her eyes for a second.

A short preliminary knock preceded the opening of the bedroom door, and Melodie blinked herself hastily back to earth to see Jessie McKay's short, stocky figure coming across the room, carrying a tray which she placed carefully across Melodie's knees before she spoke.

"Good morning, Miss Carne—had you a good night?"

The breakfast as well as the inquiry were unexpected, and Melodie nodded rather dazedly as she looked down at the tray. "Yes, thank you, Mrs McKay."

Shrewd brown eyes cast their gaze over her face and Melodie liked to think that they appeared a little less disapproving than usual, although it was probably no more than her imagination playing her tricks. "You've no after-effects from yon blaze, then?"

"None at all, I'm glad to say, though I dread to think what might have happened if Mr McDowell hadn't been on hand—I'm such a heavy sleeper I probably wouldn't have woken until it was too late."

"Aye, he'd a job to wake you, I understand."

Evidently Neil and his housekeeper were on the sort of terms that allowed confidences, and it did not altogether surprise Melodie to realise it. "He's probably told you that he had to throw me out of the window to wake me up," she said, and Jessie nodded.

The tray contained, as well as a plate of bacon and eggs, toast and marmalade and a pot of tea, everything necessary to a complete and very large breakfast, and Jessie McKay stood back with her hands clasped across her stomach, watching her as if she awaited some reaction.

"You'll be hungry," she guessed. "There's more if you need it."

Melodie lifted the cover from the bacon and eggs, shaking her head over the size of the meal and smilingly denying the need for more. "Oh, I shan't need more of anything, Mrs McKay, thank you, not after I've eaten this lot! Are you sure you haven't given me Mr McDowell's breakfast by mistake?"

It had been meant as a joke, but she remembered too late that the dour little housekeeper was lacking a sense of humour. Not a vestige of a smile crossed her face, but she answered her as solemnly as if the question had been a serious one.

"Mr McDowell had his breakfast long since," she told her. "He's away down to the McKenzie place to see about some clothes for you. Their Kirstie would be about your size."

Whoever Kirstie McKenzie was she was evidently not much in favour with Jessie McKay, judging by the tone of voice she used, though that was probably true of most people, except Neil. "It's very good of him to bother himself," Melodie told her, and wondered why Jessie had not undertaken the job herself.

The shrewd brown eyes were looking at her meaningfully. "You're in no fit way to be walking about in public in nought but a night shift," she reminded her. "You've no other clothes left."

It was the first time that the fact had been brought home to her quite so forcibly, and Melodie bit her lip as she looked at her anxiously. "Everything went? The whole thing?"

"Every stick and stone," Jessie stated flatly.

It was what Neil had expected, of course. The fire had had far too great a hold before it was noticed, and she supposed that to some extent, the fault was hers because she had not woken before. Neil had spent some time trying to get her out safely and then it had been necessary to drive up to the house before the fire brigade could be called, and the nearest one was at Corrie.

Everything had contrived to delay the arrival of help, and it was only to be expected that the little cottage would be a total loss—she was only thankful that she was not a part of the total destruction, and she shuddered at the thought of how close that had been.

She gazed out of the window for a second at the bright, golden morning and felt suddenly sad, as if something was ending, then she shrugged, not carelessly but resignedly. "Oh, well," she said to Jessie McKay, "I suppose that's it."

"You'll have lost everything," Jessie said, and Melodie noted the sympathy in her voice with another flick of surprise. "I'm sorry, Miss Carne."

Overwhelmed by a sudden sense of helplessness, Melodie looked up at her. "I don't quite know what I should do," she ventured, though with not much hope of being advised, and Jessie set her mouth firmly.

"First you've to eat your breakfast before it grows cold," she directed. "Then leave matters to Mr McDowell—as I've said, he's already seeing about some clothes for you."

Unable to think of an alternative suggestion at the moment, Melodie picked up the knife and fork on her tray and prepared to tackle that big plateful of bacon and eggs. "I'm not very practical when it comes to organising myself," she confessed. "It's very good of Neil—Mr McDowell—to take the trouble. And Miss McKenzie too, whoever she is."

"McKenzie has the croft over near Glen Bar." Jessie provided the information with apparent willingness. "They've just the one daughter, and she's away to work in Corrie."

"Oh, I see."

It came unbidden into Melodie's mind to wonder if Kirstie McKenzie was pretty enough to catch a man's eye, and if maybe that was the reason Neil had gone over to see her himself instead of despatching one of his staff on the errand. It was a discomfiting idea, more discomfiting than she would like to admit, but she had to remember that for all his dourness, Neil McDowell was capable of a depth of passion that was surprising.

It was almost as if Jessie followed her thoughts when Melodie looked at her again, for there was a slightly narrow look about the bright brown eyes and her mouth was pursed as if in dislike. "I've no doubt you'll be found all the clothes you need from that place where she works," she informed her. "A boutique they call it, though 'tis nothing more than a shop to my mind."

It wasn't the fact of Kirstie McKenzie that made Melodie stare at her, but the fact that Neil was arranging the purchase of new clothes for her when she was virtually penniless until she could obtain a new cheque book, and that was likely to take time.

"But, Mrs McKay, I don't have the money for new clothes. Not at the moment, at least; I—I shall have to—" She put down her knife and fork and gazed at the housekeeper with troubled blue eyes. "I didn't realise what he was doing; I mean, I thought he was borrowing some things for me."

"Oh, he'll borrow something for you first off," Jessie allowed, "but he'll know that a girl like Kirstie McKenzie will not have the kind of things you're used to, Miss Carne. She's not a tasteful dresser," she confided, and Melodie wondered what she could expect.

"Oh, but—"

"Pay it no mind for the moment," Jessie advised. "Eat your breakfast and then wait here in your bed until Mr McDowell gets back with something for you. As soon as he comes I'll bring you what he has."

"Thank you." The round head with its encircling grey plait nodded silently, as she turned away. It was only when she had the door open that Melodie realised just how much comfort and reassurance she had been given, and she called out to her impulsively as she stood in the doorway, "Oh, Mrs McKay!" When she turned and looked across inquiringly it was not quite as easy to say anything, for it was never easy to express thanks to someone like Jessie McKay. "You—you've been very kind and—and understanding. Thank you."

It seemed barely possible that she was smiling, and yet there was a distinct upward curve to the straight firm mouth, and the brown eyes showed a glimmer of warmth for a moment. "I think I hear someone," she said. "It's mebbe Mr McDowell with your things."

She closed the door behind her and was gone. In fact she was gone for so long that Melodie began to wonder if Neil's trip could possibly have been fruitless after all, and alternatives were being sought. She had eaten her breakfast and returned to gazing out of the windows again when Jessie came back at last, and she turned swiftly when she heard her come in, smiling a welcome.

"I think you'll find all you need in here," Jessie told her, placing a plastic dress-bag on the bed. "I hope they're to your taste, Miss Carne."

Anything would have been welcome, Melodie thought, as long as it enabled her to get up and throw off the feeling of helplessness that being confined to her room gave her, and she laughed as she plunged her hands into the bag. "Oh, I don't mind what it is, as long as I have something to wear," she said. "I was beginning to feel as if I'd have to spend the rest of my life in bed."

It was an impulsive, half joking remark and it never for a moment occurred to her that it could give offence until she saw Jessie's expression change, as if she suspected she was being criticised, and it dawned on Melodie again that she must remember not to joke with her.

"Mr McDowell's only this minute returned," she told her, edgily defensive. "I brought them straight to you, Miss Carne."

"Oh, please don't think I was complaining," Melodie assured her hastily. "It was just that you said you thought you heard Mr McDowell come in when you left me, and you were a long time—I thought he'd been unlucky with Kirstie McKenzie's wardrobe, that's all."

If she had been taking an interest in the contents of the bag instead of looking across to apologise, she would probably not have been told anything more. As it was she noticed a rather vaguely uneasy look on Jessie's face suddenly, and looked at her curiously.

"That was not Mr McDowell," Jessie said. "It was—a caller."

"Oh, I see." There had to be more to it than that, Melodie felt sure, and she was still watching her curiously without quite knowing what she expected.

"It was Jamie Stirling's nephew," Jessie went on in a tone that suggested she would rather not have imparted the information. "He came to see if you'd been hurt in the fire. They'd no notion there was a fire—they'd not hear the siren from the other side of the hill."

"John!" Melodie put her hands over her mouth and her eyes had a wide anxious look as she imagined John's reaction to finding her cottage completely gutted by fire. "Oh, how could I have forgotten that he was very likely to go down there this morning, and to find the cottage burnt out—Is he still here, Mrs McKay?"

"He is not," Jessie declared firmly. "I told him you were not able to see him at the moment, but that he'd no need to worry since you'd not been hurt at all. I also told him," she added with unmistakable relish, "that Mr McDowell was taking care of everything for you—and he left."

It was possible that John had been so stunned by the shock of finding the cottage burnt out that he had actually allowed Jessie McKay to send him away without leaving a message for Melodie, and she felt a twinge of conscience about him. She should have thought about the possibility of his paying a morning visit to the cottage, he often did, and anticipated his shock when he saw what remained of it.

"I'd like to have had a word with him," she ventured, but Jessie was pursing her lips in evident disagreement.

"I couldn't admit a young man to see you when you'd not a stitch of clothing to wear," she declared.

"I'm wearing your nightie and I could have borrowed that big red dressing-gown of Neil's again," Melodie argued.

She said what she did more for the sake of making a point than for any other reason, but Jessie's frown condemned the very idea. She set her features sternly and her short dumpy figure expressed disapproval when she drew herself up, and regarded her gravely.

"It would not have been fitting with yourself in no

more than a night shift and a dressing-gown," she declared flatly. "Mr McDowell would not have liked that at all."

Melodie rolled back the bedclothes and got out on to the carpeted floor, catching sight of herself in the voluminous borrowed nightdress as she did so, and she smiled at the very idea of its being considered even vaguely indecent.

"It's more than I was wearing when I sat drinking hot toddy with *him*," she reminded Jessie, "and I don't seem to remember him objecting then."

Jessie was making her way to the door with her head high and disapproval showing in every inch of her straight back. She turned when she got to the doorway and looked back for a moment, her eyes sharp and dark in her round face.

"That was different," she decreed, and closed the door firmly behind her, leaving Melodie wondering just why it should be considered so different—in Jessie's eyes, at least.

It was fortunate that Kirstie McKenzie's measurements were apparently identical with her own, except perhaps in the matter of height, for either the other girl wore her clothes quite long or she was some bit taller than Melodie. Otherwise the clothes Neil had borrowed for her fitted perfectly.

The tartan skirt that had been provided was longer than she would normally have worn, and it made her feel rather prim and proper as she made her way downstairs, but there was no fault to find with the blouse. The plain white shirt blouse suited her well and she left the two top buttons of it undone to make it look a little less severe, but with the neatly cut skirt it seemed to suggest that Jessie McKay's opinion that the girl lacked taste was more malicious than accurate.

Her legs were bare, but a pair of flat-heeled casuals were soft and comfortable, so that all in all she was well satisfied with her makeshift wardrobe. It was getting on for eleven o'clock when she went downstairs, and the house seemed curiously quiet and still, although before she reached the foot of the stairs she thought she could hear voices somewhere.

She was curiously reluctant to go down now that she was able to, and she looked up swiftly when she came under the scrutiny of that startlingly lifelike portrait that hung part way down the staircase. It attracted her without her quite knowing why, and she stopped in front of it for a moment or two, studying it with professional interest as well as curiosity about the sitter.

A plaque along the bottom of the gilt frame gave his name and the date it was painted, but the face itself attracted her. Duncan Ross, she felt, must have been a very strong-minded character, judging by his portrait, and yet there was a hint of laughter in the fierce dark eyes if one looked deeply enough.

Against the soft blues and greens of the background he looked an arrogant man, and yet he must have had a streak of sentimentality, for according to what she had been told he had loved and lost, but felt so sentimental about his lost love that he had bequeathed his house and a substantial part of his wealth to her daughter, Catriona.

It struck her too that there was something elusively familiar about the strong features, and yet she could not put a finger on exactly what it was. Hearing a sound of movement downstairs, she hastily shook herself out of her daydream and started down the stairs once more.

More than likely Neil was already out on his morning round of the estate, delayed by the need to provide her with something to wear from Kirstie McKenzie's wardrobe. He still followed the same routine even now that he was owner—Melodie could never imagine him delegating any of his usual tasks to others. He was much too concerned with the affairs of Ben Ross to leave the running of them to someone else, no matter how much work was involved.

As frequently happened when she became completely lost in her thoughts, she was unaware of anything going on around her, and she started almost guiltily when a door opened across the hall and Jessie McKay came out of the room she remembered was the library. Melodie was subjected to a short critical scrutiny in the time it took the housekeeper to meet her half way across the hall, and a slight nod of her head seemed to suggest that the outfit met with her approval.

"Kirstie McKenzie must have better taste than

you gave her credit for," Melodie suggested, unable to resist commenting. "These things are very nice."

"Sunday clothes," Jessie decreed, casting her critical gaze once more over the borrowed garments. "I've seen the girl wear them in the kirk."

"Oh, I see." Melodie smoothed her hands over the skirt, wondering if perhaps Neil had exerted his authority as laird to obtain the best for her, and hoping he hadn't. "In that case I'd better take extra care with them."

Jessie nodded, then glanced over her shoulder towards the room she had just left. "Mr McDowell's in the library," she told her. "You'll be wanting to have a word with him?"

Melodie tried to do something about the sudden and rapid increase in her pulse rate as she followed the older woman back across the hall. She had expected him to be out on the estate somewhere; instead he was waiting for her in the library and she found the knowledge more disturbing than she cared to admit.

She kept remembering that lean anxious face in her bedroom last night, bending over her and trying to shake her into wakefulness while she fought him as if his intention was something quite different; and then the comfort of those few moments when she had been held close in his arms. There were all too many occasions when Neil McDowell had played havoc with her usual bland self-confidence, and it troubled her sometimes that it should be so.

Jessie merely opened the door for her, she did not

come into the room, but there was a look in the shrewd brown eyes as she passed her that brought a flush of colour to her cheeks, and she hastily quelled any wild guesses as to the meaning behind it.

Neil was standing in exactly the same position as he had been the first time she ever saw him—before the huge fireplace, his feet slightly apart and with that slightly autocratic air of ownership about him. Only now, of course, he *was* the owner of Ben Ross, and she wondered what difference the fact was going to make to her own position in the present circumstances.

In riding clothes, as he most usually was, he wore a blue shirt that emphasised his tan and showed off muscular brown arms that were pulled back behind him by clasped hands. He came forward when he saw her, and the grey eyes scanned her face swiftly at the same time as he reached out a hand, instinctively, she thought, almost as if he thought she needed support.

"Good morning."

"Good morning, Neil."

There was something curiously and disturbingly intimate about coming downstairs to greet a man in his own home, and once more she wondered at her increased sensitivity where he was concerned. The hard fingers closed about her arm for a second, but released her as soon as he realised she was in no need of support.

"How are you feeling, Melodie?"

"Oh, I'm fine, thank you." She scanned the lean

shadowed face for a moment but avoided direct contact with the steady grey eyes, and she smiled. "And you? You took far too many risks last night, trying to recover my clothes."

A careless hand dismissed any suggestion of risk involved, and he cast his eyes over the rather schoolgirlish outfit he had borrowed for her. "Your borrowed plumes fit you well enough, do they not?"

"Very well indeed," Melodie agreed. "But it was very good of Miss McKenzie to lend me her Sunday best—I must try and thank her for them myself."

A glimmer of laughter touched his mouth for a moment and warmed the grey eyes. "Your thanks should go to the minister of the kirk—Kirstie's usual tastes are rather flamboyant for churchgoing and the Reverend suggested something a little more demure might be more in keeping with the Sabbath. Kirstie complied, but she'd as soon see them go as anything else, even though she's only loaned them."

"Oh, I see. Jessie did suggest that she was a bit—"

A light shrug conveyed her meaning, and Neil nodded agreement. "She'll likely grow out of it when she's a wee bit older," he suggested.

"I see—she's not very old, then? I thought perhaps—"

Remembering her own speculation on the subject of Neil's personal visit to ask the girl for a loan of some of her clothes, Melodie looked at him curiously. It was only when she saw his raised brow and the way he was regarding her so steadily with a hint of mockery in his eyes, that she realised at least something of what was going through her mind must have showed in that look, and she hastily glanced away.

"You thought she was older?" The soft-voiced inquiry almost taunted her. "Old enough to interest me, mebbe?"

"I'd no idea *how* old she was!"

She could not protest too forcibly, for he was too close to the truth for comfort and she feared he realised it. "Kirstie is sixteen," he informed her. "She's time enough to change, though I doubt she will." He indicated an armchair and Melodie sat down in it rather hastily. The trouble was that he could now look down at her from an even greater height, and she already felt dismayingly small. "You've had breakfast, so Jessie tells me."

"Yes." She ventured a smile. "I was thoroughly spoiled and had breakfast in bed."

"Good—then as soon as I've changed out of these clothes we'll drive in to Corrie and see about doing some shopping for you. You'll be needing more than those bits and pieces of Kirstie's." He took a hasty glance at his wristwatch and nodded. "We're a wee bit late in starting, so we'll have lunch in Corrie. Will that suit you?" he asked, as if it had just occurred to him to consult her, and Melodie nodded vaguely.

He seemed to have everything so cut and dried that it struck her once more how out of character he was for the man she had been told about before she left Australia. Her friends had described him as rather shy and quiet and, while the latter might be true, she could find nothing shy about this rather forceful character.

"You're not a bit like Catriona described you!"

She had spoken impulsively and without stopping to think what she was saying, and she saw the slight stiffness that pulled back his shoulders suddenly, and the lowering of heavy-lashed eyelids so that the look in his eyes was hidden from her.

"What in the name of heaven has the way I look to do with what I was talking to you about?" he asked. His voice was as low and quiet as ever, but it hinted at coldness, and Melodie's lower lip was drawn anxiously between her teeth before she replied.

"I'm sorry, Neil, I just—spoke what was in my mind, that's all."

"Were you not listening to what I was saying, then?"

"Yes, of course I was!" His steady questioning look suggested she had better explain, and she hurried on, wondering if it would do any good to try. "I was just thinking that you were described to me as being quiet and—" She hesitated in case he should think shy was in some way a derogatory term, but with that steady grey gaze on her it was impossible to hesitate for very long. "I was led to understand that you were rather shy," she finished a little breathlessly.

In the brief glance she gave him she thought she saw his eyes narrow slightly. "Were you now?"

"But I didn't mean that—"

"Shy?" He went on, as if she had not spoken, and

there was a suggestion of mockery in his voice that made her uneasy. "Is that what they told you?" A short and not altogether humourless laugh made her glance up again quickly. "Were you expecting some kind of overgrown schoolboy, Melodie?"

It was a most discomfiting conversation and Melodie wished fervently that she had never made that impulsive remark about his character. "No, of course I wasn't! Just someone—different, that's all."

"No doubt!" The grey eyes held her unrelentingly and she found herself unable to resist looking up at him again. "Well, maybe I was—shy, as you say, when Catriona saw me last, but I'm not the same man she knew. A man can change a great deal in eight years, Melodie, and I'm no different from any other in that respect. I'm thirty-four years old now and a lot of things have happened to change me since Catriona's time here." A hint of a smile just tipped one corner of his mouth and she found herself wanting to reach up and touch her fingertip to it. "Maybe I grew up."

"I know, Neil; I know what you mean."

Her voice was soft, light and barely audible, but she thought she understood what he meant and she wanted to let him know she did. Neil, however, was shaking his head and that ghost of a smile was still on his mouth.

"You know?" From his voice and the way he looked it was obvious that he doubted it, and she felt a warm flush of colour in her cheeks. "How old are you, Melodie?"

The question took her by surprise, but it seemed somehow to suggest that he saw her as little older than Kirstie McKenzie and she resented that more fiercely than she would have believed possible. Her blue eyes sparkling indignantly, she looked up at him. "I don't see that my age has anything to do with anything!"

If only she did not always react so emotionally to him. Even the timbre of his voice affected her, as he stood with his hands still clasped behind him looking down at her, and that hint of mockery in his smile was infinitely disturbing no matter how hard she tried to ignore it.

"I just can't help wondering how it is that a wee bit of a thing like you can always be claiming to understand me so well," he told her. "You've made the same claim before, though you've never explained it, have you, Melodie?"

It was the same discomfiting situation she had found herself in once before with him, and she shifted uneasily in the big armchair. "It's just that— I feel I *do* understand, Neil, that's all."

"Or you've been told something that you think explains the man I am?" Neil suggested quietly.

She got to her feet suddenly, because she no longer felt able to cope while she occupied that big chair and had Neil hovering over her, alarmingly like a bird of prey. Her hands were at her sides but rolled tightly so that she appeared taut and uneasy as she faced him.

"I wish you weren't always so suspicious of me,"

she complained, her voice not quite steady. "Please, Neil!"

"Please, Neil!" He echoed her words, mockingly it seemed, but with something in his voice that made her shiver suddenly. Then he put a hand beneath her chin and looked down at her mouth for a moment or two before shaking his head slowly, as if something he sought an answer to was beyond him. "Och, you've a very appealing way with you, Melodie Carne, and I suspect you're better at getting your own way than most."

"I—I wasn't trying to get my own way."

"No?"

Her heart was thudding hard and she felt as if her legs were about to give way under her, they trembled so much. The touch of his strong fingers on her soft skin was like a caress and she would have given much to have his mouth once more on hers, kissing her the way he had when they stood on the river bank with the storm venting its fury around them.

In fact she felt the need for his kiss with such intensity that it startled her, and she did her best to quell the disturbing and unfamiliar sensations he aroused in her. But he didn't kiss her—instead he let her go, slowly, his fingers sliding across her jaw almost reluctantly, and she felt strangely bereft when he stepped back a pace and stood looking down at her.

"I believe I was once in love with Catriona." The quiet statement took her by surprise, and he must have seen the look in her eyes that questioned his apparent uncertainty, for he shook his head again slowly and there was a wry smile at the corners of his mouth. "I cannot even be sure of it after this long, but whatever the truth was or is, Melodie, I'm not still nursing a broken heart, if that's what someone's suggested—you've no need to feel sorry for me."

"Sorry for you?" It had not even occurred to her that she felt sorry for him, even though she supposed it was true to some extent. "But, Neil, I didn't—"

"Was it not pity that prompted those soulful-eyed looks and the assurances that you—understood me?" he asked, and it was impossible to tell from his voice how he took to the idea. "Did John Stirling suggest that a broken romance was the reason I chose to live in what he considers a white elephant of a house and give my whole time and attention to Ben Ross?"

Melodie tried to shake her head and deny it, but it was more or less what John had said, and it was difficult to deny it with that steady gaze on her. "Not— not really," she said in a small husky voice.

Once more a hand slid beneath her chin and raised her face to him, the grey eyes studying her for a second or two before he spoke. "You're not a very good liar, Melodie, are you?" Briefly his mouth brushed against hers; then he let her go once again and walked over to pick up a well worn briar pipe from an ashtray on the mantel, turning as he began to fill it with tobacco from a jar. "We'd best away and get that shopping done," he said with stunning matter-of-factness. "I've heard shopping for women's clothes can be a long job."

"Neil, I can't!"

Her voice was unsteady and she felt alarmingly lightheaded, as if everything was happening too fast for her to cope, yet still some part of her brain was functioning with sufficient clarity to remind her that she had no cheque book and no means of obtaining another at least until Monday morning. But Neil was looking at her narrowly, as if he suspected delaying tactics.

"I haven't any money and I haven't a cheque book since last night," she reminded him. "I doubt if I'd be given credit in shops where they don't know me."

"You think I haven't thought of that?" he asked, and there was a hint of exasperation in his voice that made her look down at her feet hastily.

"I didn't know," she confessed.

"Keeping an eye on your well-being includes seeing that you're not destitute when your things are lost through no fault of your own," he told her, "as well as seeing that you've a roof over your head and food to eat."

"Neil, you're not responsible for me to that extent!"

"Oh, indeed I am," Neil declared firmly. "I'll not have it said that I fell short in any way—not that I would whether I'd critics to say I did or not." The grey eyes warmed with a smile as he rammed tobacco firmly into the pipe. "I take my role seriously, you know."

"Neil, will you please stop acting as if I'm five years old! I—I appreciate all you're doing for me

and I'm very grateful, but I wish you wouldn't talk as
if you're really responsible for my well-being."

He said nothing for a second or two while he held
a lighted match to the pipe and puffed it into life,
then he looked down at her, his eyes narrowed behind the screen of blue smoke, and she felt herself
shiver with some inexplicable sense of excitement.

"Would you rather I let John Stirling take care of
you?" he asked. "He could take you to buy clothes
and mebbe find room for you in the croft with his
aunt and uncle—and himself, of course."

"You know I didn't mean anything like that." She
felt incredibly small and rather helpless as she stood
there in Kirstie McKenzie's Sunday best, and she
was quite sure that if someone *had* to look after her
she wanted it to be Neil. "I'm—I'm grateful for you
doing what you are for me, and if you could let me
have something to buy clothes, just until Monday
when the bank's open again." Something else occurred to her then too. "If I could have that little
cottage across the yard for the rest of my stay, perhaps," she ventured. "I noticed it's empty."

"Not for long," Neil told her blandly. "I've a new
man starting next week and he and his wife will be
moving into the groom's cottage in a day or two.
We've plenty of room in the house here for you."

"But—"

The grey eyes held hers steadily and there was a
gleam of something in their depths that brought a
flush of colour to her cheeks as he regarded her
through the screen of smoke from the pipe. "Jessie

will chaperone you," he said, "if that's what troubles you."

"It isn't!"

The retort was swift and instinctive, and Melodie felt her heart begin a hard and rapid pounding in her breast when she thought of spending the next month under the same roof with him. Almost as if he found the situation very much to his liking, his mouth curved in to one of those rare and transfiguring smiles that drew fine lines at the corners of his eyes and made them warm and glowing.

"Then for the love of heaven, woman, will you stop raising difficulties! Come away into Corrie with me and let's find you something more flattering than that skirt that's too long for you!"

CHAPTER SEVEN

BEING a house guest at Ben Ross, Melodie realised, would make it difficult for John to visit her as often as he was in the habit of doing and he was probably wondering how best to contact her, since Jessie McKay's assurances that she was unhurt after the cottage fire. It was with the idea of letting him know exactly what had happened that she decided to try and see him the following morning.

He still rode the Ben Ross horses so the stable was the most likely place to see him, even on a Sunday morning, though not too early, she thought. It had simply not occurred to her to get up as early on Sunday morning as she did in the week, and when there was no sign of Neil at the breakfast table she assumed he was taking a well earned-rest.

A remark to that effect, however, brought a sharp response from Jessie McKay. Mr McDowell had already breakfasted and had now retired to the library to read a newspaper, she was informed. He was always early for Sunday morning breakfast because he knew that Jessie only waited to serve him before getting herself ready to walk down to the kirk in Glen Ross.

It was very obliging of him, Melodie thought, although he might simply be one of those men who were completely helpless when it came to getting himself a meal and the arrangement suited him. But Melodie was by now quite accustomed to getting her own meals and said so.

"Oh, but you needn't have bothered about me," she told Jessie when she brought her in a pot of fresh tea. "I can always get my own breakfast if you're in a hurry, Mrs McKay."

Jessie frowned indignantly, her brown eyes gleaming. "Indeed you cannot, Miss Carne!" she said firmly. "For one thing I'll not have strangers in my kitchen, and for another Mr McDowell would not tolerate the idea of his house guest cooking her own breakfast, and rightly so too!"

"Oh, but I'm not really a house guest," Melodie denied, and wondered just what exactly she was. "I'm a sort of refugee, I suppose you could say."

Jessie, however, was not convinced and she looked as fiercely discouraging as ever with her hands folded at her ample waist. "If Mr McDowell says you're to be a house guest, Miss Carne, then that's how you'll be treated, and your meals will be cooked and served to you, as is fitting." Despite her disapproval, it seemed to Melodie that she was prepared to make allowances, and the idea of Jessie's austere character allowing her to relent at all was surprising. "You've mebbe not been told that we serve breakfast early on Sunday so that I've time to walk down to the kirk," she said.

"No, I didn't know or I'd have made the effort."

"Ah well, no matter." She cast an expert and critical eye over the well provided breakfast table and nodded. "You'll have all you need now, I think, Miss Carne, so I'll away and get maself ready."

"Yes, of course, Mrs McKay, thank you."

The austere features relaxed a little more as she nodded, and Jessie turned in the doorway before she went out. "Mr McDowell's in the library," she reminded her, and Melodie nodded.

"Yes—thank you."

"Aye, well." Another brief nod and Jessie was gone, leaving a curiously pregnant silence behind her.

It seemed ridiculous to even suggest it, and yet somehow Melodie could not rid herself of the impression that in her own rather pedantic way Jessie McKay was trying her hand at matchmaking, and when she considered it it was something of a compliment if it should be true. Her employer was in his middle thirties and he must have had other opportunities to take a wife, but she wondered if perhaps Jessie McKay looked upon a comparatively young woman as less of a threat to her position of authority in the household.

Left on her own in the snug little breakfast-room Melodie mused on the prospect for some time while she ate her meal, then realised suddenly what she was doing. Shaking herself impatiently, she put the whole thing firmly out of her mind, for whatever Jessie McKay might have in mind, it was pretty certain that Neil, once her two months' stay was over, would take no further interest in her, and she preferred not to even think about her own feelings on the subject at the moment.

For all her reluctance to dwell on any suggestion of a relationship between her and Neil, she felt that yesterday's shopping expedition had gone rather well. Neil had proved far more communicative than she expected, and she had spent rather more money than she intended because he was persuasive when she hesitated.

In fact the deep pink dress that she was wearing had been bought, she frankly admitted, because Neil had made some passing comment on it in a shop window, but it suited her very well, and she would probably have chosen it anyway. Its colour made a stunning background for her black hair and blue eyes, and flattered her light tan, and she knew she looked pretty in it, which was good for her ego.

On her way to look for John she made a turn towards the back door of the house when she left the breakfast-room, then hesitated as she came out into the hall and looked across at the library door. She changed direction almost without realising she was doing it, and felt a light fluttering beat to her heart as she crossed the quiet hall.

The library door was ajar and she pushed it a little further open before putting her head around the edge. Neil was not relaxed in an armchair, as she expected, but on his feet with his back to her, busy packing tobacco from the jar on the mantel into the same old briar pipe he had smoked yesterday, and she watched him for a moment with a curiously unfamiliar sense of intimacy.

She had half expected to see him in riding clothes, but apparently the daily round of the estate was waived on Sundays, for he was wearing light grey slacks and a navy shirt that showed up the fairness of his hair. He was tall and bronzed, and sometimes with his blond colouring he looked almost Scandinavian so that she had more than once been tempted to ask him about his ancestry. Only the possibility of a curt reponse had deterred her, though it was still in her mind to do so one day.

"Good morning, Neil."

The swiftness with which he turned seemed to suggest that he had not heard her approach, and for a moment his eyes registered such surprise that she wondered if he had forgotten her presence in the house. "Good morning, Melodie." The pink dress was noted and approved, and she felt another quick flutter in the region of her heart. "I hope you didn't mind my not waiting breakfast for you."

"Not at all." She laughed, rather breathlessly, she was dismayed to notice, and walked over to join him, her mission to find John momentarily forgotten. "If I'm too lazy to get up in the morning, I don't expect others to wait for me."

The pipe was clamped firmly between strong teeth and he reached for matches from the mantel to light it with. "I forgot to say that we usually have early breakfast on Sundays." Briefly the grey eyes flicked to her face again before resuming interest in lighting the pipe. "Did Jessie say?"

"Jessie *did* say," she admitted, pulling a wry face. "I was firmly reprimanded for sleeping through half the Sabbath!"

"*Were* you indeed?"

His voice and the way his head came up told her that she had misjudged his tolerance with regard to Jessie McKay, and she hastened to amend the impression she had given. "Oh, I don't mean literally of course," she denied, "but I was very late and she was waiting to get ready for church. If I'd known I'd have come down earlier."

"You may do as you please, you have my word on it!"

Gratified at being indulged, Melodie shook her head, smiling ruefully. "You don't know me," she told him, "or you wouldn't make such a rash statement! All I hope is that you won't live to regret taking me in, once you've found out how hard I am to put up with."

A screen of smoke half concealed his features, but the grey eyes watched her steadily, disconcerting as always. One arm lay along the high old-fashioned mantel, and a foot rested on the brass and iron fender. He looked completely at ease and the effect his relaxed appearance had on her own mood was too reassuring to be questioned at the moment.

"Just as long as you don't get setting fire to Ben Ross as well, I'll not regret anything," he told her quietly, and the charge, however lightly made, startled her.

She looked at him wide-eyed for a moment. "I hope you're joking, Neil," she said, and her voice was huskily uncertain. "You *are* joking, aren't you?"

It was a moment or two before he answered and the concealing haze of tobacco smoke that drifted up before his face made it impossible for her to see his eyes clearly, and guess whether or not he was in earnest. Then he took the pipe from his mouth and inspected its bowl rather than look at her while he answered.

"I'd not joke about the burning of a cottage," he assured her, "but it's not known what caused the fire yet—I expect to hear tomorrow."

"Can they tell?"

Her rising indignation was overriden for the moment by curiosity, and Neil was nodding his head. "Mostly they can these days."

"Then I have nothing to worry about!"

For a second the grey eyes became clear behind the smoke screen, and she noticed that they were serious, though not as much as she expected from his tone. "You didn't leave the cooker burning or anything of that, then?" he asked, and she shook her head firmly.

"And neither do I smoke!" she declared, giving the smoking pipe a meaningful look, "Nor does John!"

"Then it was evidently an electrical fault or something of the sort," he guessed, and looked at her curiously when she frowned. "Does that strike a note, Melodie?"

"Yes, it does." She remembered the flickering light that had annoyed her in the kitchen just before she went to bed. "The light in the kitchen was flickering on and off, it had done it before and I thought it was something to do with the pylons—I'm not very technically minded," she added when she saw him frown.

"Did you not think to say something to me about it?"

"No, I just thought—"

"You were very foolish not to mention it to *some*body," he told her, and sounded very much as if he was scolding, so that Melodie looked at him with a dark look of warning in her blue eyes.

"You're blaming me, aren't you?" she accused, but shook her head without giving him time to answer. "Well, I'm sorry about the cottage, but I refuse to accept that it was my fault that it burned down! You must think I'm a complete idiot to take chances like that—it could have been me that was burnt to a crisp, as well you know!"

"Melodie." His quiet voice belied the gleam in his eyes. "I *know*—remember?"

She stared at him for a moment blank-eyed, her anger dying into the stunned realisation that she had forgotten for the moment he had been in as much or more danger than she had herself, and she shook her head slowly, the tip of her tongue briefly moistening dry lips.

"I—I'm sorry, Neil, I didn't think. You know better than anyone how close it was for me. If it hadn't been for you I'd never have got out of there alive."

There was a glimmer of warmth in his eyes again as he regarded her steadily, and for so long that she wished she could look away instead of gazing at him as if she was mesmerised. "A kiss would never have woken the sleeping beauty *I* found," he told her in his softly accented voice. "I'd to shake you like a rag doll, and even that didn't wake you properly."

She could so easily recall the strength of his arms as he swept her from her bed and thrust her forcibly through the bedroom window out into the night air and safety, that she shivered, a warm glow in her cheeks at the memory of how she had fought him. How she could have forgotten, however briefly, was beyond her.

"I remember," she said, barely above a whisper. "You must have had my guardian angel at your elbow that night."

"It's still hard to believe," Neil said. "I thank God I was out that night, for we'd never have seen the fire from the house until it was too late."

It was a new aspect that Melodie had not thought of before, and she looked at him curiously for a second, her interest plain in her eyes. "I—I didn't know how you came to be there," she said. "I didn't even think about how, only that you were there."

"I saw the flames from the Glen Ross road as I came up from the village," he told her, "and I put my foot down hard. At first I thought it was Ben Ross, you see."

"And you heaved a sigh of relief when you saw it wasn't!" Melodie suggested without stopping to think.

Neil eyed her narrowly for a second, then shook his head slowly. "If I thought you meant that seriously," he told her, "I'd make you sorry you said it—but I think I know you well enough by now, Melodie, to know you sometimes speak without stopping to think."

"I'm sorry, Neil."

"Aye," Neil said softly, "I know you are."

He continued to regard her with the same disturbing steadiness and she dared not look at him again. There was a strangely exciting atmosphere in the big book-lined room that tingled along her spine and brought a flush of colour to her cheeks, and she had completely forgotten about John for the moment. Another swirl of blue smoke curled like a halo about Neil's fair head for a second or two, and when it cleared he seemed to snatch himself back from a moment of daydreaming.

Easing himself away from the tall mantel, he swept a slow and deliberate gaze over her slim shape in the rose pink dress. "Were you going out?" he asked.

His tone suggested that he had hoped she was staying, and Melodie made no pretence of being other than ready to be persuaded. Her conscience urged her to remember John, but if Neil asked her to she would see John some other time.

"I was thinking about it," she admitted, and he nodded.

"You'll be wanting to see John Stirling, of course," he guessed, "to tell him what happened.

He'll be anxious if he hasn't seen you since the fire."
He smiled faintly. "You'd best reassure him."

He was doing no more than voice the self-same
reasons that had made her decide to see John that
morning, but somehow hearing him encourage the
idea struck her as a bitter disappointment when she
had anticipated his trying to persuade her to keep
him company. And, illogical as it was, she resented
her own reaction, so that she shook herself impatiently.

"That's what I had in mind," she told him, and
Neil inclined his head behind his screen of blue
smoke.

"I think I heard him a few moments since—you'll
mebbe find him still in the stable if you hurry."

As if he could not wait to be left in peace again to
read his paper and smoke a pipe, Melodie thought.
There seemed nothing else to say, so she turned
without another word and walked across the room
aware that Neil's grey eyes were following her to the
door, and she had her hand already on the handle
when he called to her.

"Tomorrow," he suggested, "I could maybe drive
you into Corrie to buy paints and whatever it is you
need to start work again."

Melodie half-turned, her hand on the door's edge,
looking at him over her shoulder. "You're in a hurry
to put me back to work?" she asked, and the grey
eyes held hers steadily, suggesting all sorts of reasons for keeping her busy. Like the fact that she saw
less of John when she was working—but that she
swiftly dismissed as unlikely.

"I'm thinking about my painting of Glen Ross," he said. "It was lost with the rest of your things, was it not?"

"Oh yes, of course."

"The sooner you've more paint and canvas, the sooner you can begin another," he told her, but some perverse imp in her make-up made Melodie stick out her chin as she looked across at him standing with relaxed confidence in front of the huge fireplace.

"But you'll be busy, Neil, and I couldn't take up your time. John's on holiday and he won't mind in the least taking me in to Corrie for paints if I ask him." She hastily avoided looking at him as she pulled the door to behind her. "Thanks all the same, Neil."

She hurried across the hall and hated herself for having been so childishly perverse. If only he had not been so ready to send her out to find John when she had thought he was going to ask for her company himself it would not even have occurred to her to react as she had. Shrugging in vague helplessness, she made her way to the rear of the house in search of John—nothing ever happened the way she meant it to with Neil.

JOHN HAD WILLINGLY ABANDONED HIS PLANS to ride when Melodie found him in the stable as she expected, and instead he unsaddled his horse again and joined her for a walk. With his arm about her shoul-

ders and hugging her close she was aware of something a little more intimate in his manner than she
had noticed before, and yet she felt strangely helpless to do anything about it.

It was a lovely bright morning and they walked as
far as the hillside that sloped steeply down to where
tiny Loch Lairdross lay like a blue gem in the rusty
green hollow of the glen, reflecting the morning sun
like a mirror, clear blue and hazed with mist.

It was Melodie who suggested that they sat there
for a while on the springy softness of turf and heather. The view was magnificent and she felt she would
never grow tired of it—the panorama of mountains
and glens enchanted her and she so easily became
lost in the spell of it that she gave only half her attention to John when he spoke.

"What happens now?" he asked, and Melodie
turned and looked at him rather vaguely for a moment. "Where are you staying since you were burnt
out on Friday night—in the groom's cottage in the
yard?"

She thought he knew very well she was not using
the groom's cottage, for it was very obviously unfur-
nished, but he simply did not like the idea of the alternative. "Neil has a new man coming into the
cottage," she told him, confident that he knew it already, "it isn't available, John. Neil took me up to
Ben Ross on Friday night and I've been there ever
since."

From the way his mouth tightened it was clear just
how much he disliked the arrangement, and Melodie

looked again down at the loch rather than at him. "Damn it!" He swore softly and, although she was in part prepared for it, his vehemence startled her and she turned hastily, her eyes questioning.

"I'm very comfortable," she said, "and Mrs McKay is being very amiable on the whole."

"I can imagine!"

His reaction irritated her without her being quite sure why. She had very little choice in the matter of staying where she was and his determined disapproval seemed to serve no useful purpose except to annoy her. "They've been very good to me, John; I don't know what I'd have done without their help, and especially without Neil getting me out of the cottage as he did. I hadn't even a stitch of clothing except the nightdress I was wearing."

John raised a brow and looked at the rose pink cotton dress she was wearing. "Oh, hadn't you?"

"Not a thing!" She spoke sharply because he seemed bent on making things appear suspect as far as her rescue was concerned, and he had no cause to behave the way he was. "I had to stay in bed on Saturday morning—yesterday, until Neil could borrow something for me from a girl who lives on the estate."

Swiftly and briefly John's eyes scanned up and down her shape and he laughed shortly. "Kirstie McKenzie?" he guessed, and Melodie frowned at him curiously.

"How did you guess that?"

"Easy." He shrugged carelessly. "She's the only

female on the estate who could provide you with something to fit."

"You know her too, then?"

"Sure, though not as well as McDowell does!" His words and his voice were obviously meant to convey something that Melodie knew was not true, although similar ideas has passed through her own mind until she learned of Kirstie McKenzie's youth. "He made a beeline for her place when you wanted something to wear, didn't he?"

Melodie frowned, following the implication all too easily, and disliking it. If John knew the girl as he claimed, then he must know how young she was, and the implication he was making concerning Neil was unworthy of him.

"For the reason you said," Melodie insisted firmly. "Jessie McKay told him that she was about my size and Neil went over to see her!" She tilted back her head and looked at him with a hint of defiance in her expression. "And if you know Kirstie McKenzie as you claim to, John, you must know she's only sixteen. I'm quite sure Neil isn't the kind of man to have—that sort of relationship with a girl twenty years his junior. A—a schoolgirl!"

"You must be twelve or thirteen years his junior," John retorted, stung by her criticism, "and it doesn't stop him looking at you the way he does!"

Once before when he had made that same charge, she had not even bothered to deny it, now she did so with less conviction than she hoped. "He doesn't look at me in any special way—you're imagining things, John!"

John's frown did not lessen, but he took her hands in his and turned her round to face him as she sat curled up on the cool turf. His brown eyes were uncharacteristically hard and angry and so was his voice, so that she wondered what jumble of emotions disturbed him as he held her tightly.

"Melodie, can't you move out of there? Do you have to stay in that damned great barn of a place?"

It would never do to admit that she did not want to move out of Ben Ross; she did not yet dare admit it to herself, and she sought some way of answering him so that John would not guess how she really felt about it. Suddenly restless, she scrambled to her feet and John was beside her in a moment, walking beside her as she started down the slope towards the glen. Her hands were swinging, and he caught the one nearest to him and held it tightly in his.

"I don't see how I can move out," she told him, choosing her words carefully, "unless I go away altogether. There are no hotels nearer than Corrie."

"I wasn't thinking about a hotel."

His meaning was clear, of course, Neil had mentioned the idea when she spoke of alternative arrangements herself, but there simply was not room in his uncle's tiny cottage for another visitor. Nor had she the desire to live in such cramped quarters when the vastness of Ben Ross was available to her.

"There's nowhere else for me to go," she told John. "And it seems stupid not to take advantage of Neil's offer."

"I'm more concerned with his taking advantage of

you!" John retorted sharply. "Aunt Marie could find room for you, I'm sure."

"I'm sure she couldn't," Melodie declared firmly. "The croft is far too small, John, and there's barely enough room for the three of you as it is."

"Besides which you like the idea of living at Ben Ross," John suggested with unmistakable meaning. "O.K., Melodie, I get the point!"

"I don't think you do." She eased her hand from his and walked faster, getting a short distance ahead of him until he realised and hastened to catch up. "My choice is limited, John. Either I stay on at Ben Ross or I have to go right away, and I'm not ready to give up the rest of my stay simply because you have some bee in your bonnet about Neil McDowell!"

Melodie had seen that hint of sulkiness before, after Neil had brought her back from their ride on the back of his horse, and she saw it now in the set of his mouth and the dark, glowering look in his eyes. "You're darned right I don't like you being there," he agreed. Bending suddenly, he tugged a sprig of heather from its root and twirled it between restless fingers. "I'm not sure I trust McDowell the way I used to, he's—different from what I thought he was at one time."

"Different?" Her puzzlement was genuine and she looked at him curiously, but John was nodding as if he was quite convinced. "How different, John?"

He glanced sideways at her without turning his head. "I didn't have him figured for a Casanova, now I'm not so sure."

Her own responses to Neil were still too fresh in her mind to allow her to deny the term as adamantly as she might once have done, but she shook her head for all that because she had only her own experience to guide her opinion. "I don't think you have any call to say Neil is a—a Casanova," she denied, and John laughed shortly.

"Oh, I grant you he's quiet," he allowed, "but still waters run deep, and there's that affair that Uncle Jamie mentioned. Maybe that guy is deeper than I figured!"

It startled her to be reminded of Neil's self-admitted love for Catriona Holland, but she could not bring herself to say anything of it to John, so she said nothing. According to Neil he was not now even sure if he had loved his then employer, and Melodie preferred to think he had not—though she hesitated to admit as much even to herself.

"I wish you were anywhere but under his roof," John declared, still far too angry. "I don't trust him!"

"It doesn't really matter whether or not *you* trust him, does it, John?" It was a gentle reminder, but she knew it had had its effect when she saw his face darken and he brought them to a halt, turning her to face him.

His hands pressed hard into her shoulders and his eyes scanned her face for a moment before he spoke. "Maybe not," he admitted after a few seconds of silence, but the admission was made reluctantly. "I kind of hoped I had the right to object to you moving in with him, but I guess I'm getting ahead of things. The fact is you're getting to mean a whole lot too much to me for me to simply sit back and accept the idea of McDowell taking you under his wing—I can't just say nothing, Melodie."

It shouldn't have been so unexpected, she told herself, but lately Neil had occupied her thoughts to such an extent that she had given less thought to John than she probably should have done. It was incredibly hard to know what to say to him, for she was not insensitive to the compliment he paid her, but she simply did not know what to do next.

"Melodie!" His hands gripped her shoulders firmly and she could not have turned away even had she had the inclination to. His head was bent and his voice pitched lower than it usually was, slightly unsteady too and oddly touching. "You know I love you, don't you?"

Melodie did not move for the moment, but stood with her head bowed, looking at the open neck of his shirt and noting absently that he looked far more schoolboyish than she had noticed before. Her heart was beating with a faster beat than usual, aroused by the kind of excitement such a situation was bound to kindle, and she wished she had anticipated this moment before she came with him.

"I—I'm flattered, John, I really am."

His brown eyes sought hard to make her look at him, but she kept her lashes lowered and preferred not to be influenced by them. "I told you I was likely to fall in love with you, didn't I?" he reminded her. "I'm quite serious about it, Melodie."

"Oh, John, I know you are!" She looked up at last, and found the brown eyes even harder to meet than she anticipated. "I—I wish I could say—I mean, I can't say that I feel the same way, John. I wish I could!"

"*I* wish you could!"

He looked so earnest that it was impossible not to be touched, but she wished he hadn't spoken as he had, for it made it so much more difficult for her to decide to stay as she had planned. If John was as much in earnest as he said, then it was going to make matters worse that she was no longer able to see him as often as he was used to.

It was instinct that made her turn her head suddenly and look back the way they had come, and her heart thudded urgently at the sight of a tall familiar figure on the black horse, his fair head as unmistakable as the way he rode.

Sensing her distraction, John turned as well and she saw the swift frown that drew his brows when he recognised Neil. "Arrogant devil he is!" he declared in a hard flat voice. "I never realised it so much before."

"You liked him before." The words were out before she stopped to think, and John was looking at her almost as if he suspected criticism.

"I guess I did," he admitted, once more watching Neil on the notorious Black Knight riding off down towards the river. Then he looked down at Melodie again and his eyes scanned her face in silence for a moment. "Now I guess I'm jealous of him because

he has you under his roof for the next month," he
told her. "I can't pretend to like it, Melodie." He
took her hands in his and after a second or two
raised them to his lips and kissed her fingers. "I want
to marry you," he said, his voice barely above a
whisper, "and McDowell or no, I shall ask you a
hundred times if necessary as long as I think there's
the faintest chance that you'll say you will."

"John—"

He silenced her with a light kiss on her mouth, and
smiled down at her ruefully. "At least give me the
chance to live in hope," he said. "Will you do that
for me, Melodie?"

If only she had not known that Neil was there
somewhere on the hill that sloped down behind
them, still within hailing distance if she should call to
him, she could have given her whole mind to John,
and she looked at him with wide and slightly dazed
eyes while he pleaded with her.

"Melodie?" He kissed her again and this time with
more fervour so that she was momentarily swept
along with his mood and responded without quite realising she was doing so. "Well, at least you haven't
sent me away," he said with a curiously nervous little
laugh. "That gives me a little encouragement!"

CHAPTER EIGHT

THE warmth of the sun on her face when she woke made Melodie smile even before she opened her eyes, and she stretched her arms above her head lazily, revelling in the comfort of the big old-fashioned bed for a moment before she woke herself properly. It seemed hardly credible that it was little more than a week since the cottage had burned down and she had moved into Ben Ross.

The big bedroom already seemed comfortingly familiar and it was certainly a great deal more luxurious than the one she had in the cottage. Its dark-panelled walls gleamed richly in the morning sunlight and the high windows allowed in lots more light than the tiny dormer windows of the cottage had. Jessie McKay had replaced the original heavy red curtains with fresh, lighter ones, though whether on her own initiative or at Neil's instigation Melodie couldn't be sure, but they gave the room a more cheerful look.

A glance at the bedside clock showed that it was quite early, and yet she felt the need to be up and doing. Outside, in the ivy that covered most of the face of the old house, sparrows were cheeping persistently, and from further away above the glen, she could hear the plaintive cries of curlews and lapwings on the morning flight for food.

Suddenly active, she got out of bed and walked over to the window, looking out across the country-side at the scene that never failed to enchant her, especially seen as now from the lofty dominance of Ben Ross. Perhaps she would ride this morning; the view from her window encouraged the idea, and maybe, if she was in time, she could go at least part way with Neil when he went on his daily round.

Having made up her mind, it was the thought of his possibly setting off before she was ready that sent her hurrying through the process of bathing and dressing, and she was so much earlier than her usual time that she caught Jessie McKay unprepared when she peeped round the kitchen door before going to join Neil in the breakfast-room.

"Och, you'll be in a rare hurry this morning," the housekeeper declared with far less rancour than she would have shown little more than a week before, in the same situation. "You bide with Mr McDowell in the breakfast-room, Miss Carne, and I'll have your breakfast for you in just a wee while."

Melodie glanced across the kitchen at the seldom used serving hatch and lowered her voice slightly. "I'm hoping to go out when Mr McDowell does," she confided, "so don't make it too big a meal, will you, Mrs McKay?"

"He'd not like you going without your breakfast," Jessie stated firmly. "He'll wait if you tell him you're going with him."

Still unsure whether or not he would, Melodie gave a light shrug and disappeared. Next door in the breakfast-room Neil showed much the same reaction to her early appearance. He looked pointedly at his wristwatch before he even answered her greeting, and his grey eyes showed laughter as he looked across the table at her.

"Could you not sleep?" he asked, and Melodie pursed her lips in reproach.

"I slept perfectly, as always," she told him. "I just felt like getting up early this morning—you don't mind if I join you, do you, Neil?"

"Not at all, as long as you don't mind me getting on with my own breakfast while you wait for yours." He noted the blue jeans and a cotton shirt she wore and raised a brow. "You look ready for action," he suggested. "Are you anxious to get started?"

He was finishing his meal already, she noted, and hoped that Jessie wasn't going to be too long with her breakfast or she couldn't reasonably expect him to wait for her. "I felt like riding this morning, so I'm giving the painting a miss, for an hour or two anyway."

She had been hoping to hear him say she was welcome to join him and she was disappointed when he said nothing at all about it, but merely looked surprised at her reason for being early. "You're usually very diligent about working during the week," he observed. "Is my painting giving you some trouble—is it maybe not going as well as you hoped?"

"Oh no, on the contrary, it isn't going badly at all, I've got on better than I expected. I just felt—" She shrugged vaguely, watching Jessie as she came in with her breakfast. "I just felt like riding instead this morning, that's all."

Jessie McKay set the meal in front of her and briefly the sharp brown eyes held her gaze, questioning her reticence and wondering at it probably. "Since you're in a hurry to be away," she told her, "I did you only one piece of bacon with your egg, though a good meal in the morning is necessary, to my mind."

"Yes, Mrs McKay, thank you."

"Will you not have more?"

"No, thank you, there's plenty here."

The shrewd brown eyes flicked briefly in the direction of her employer and Jessie folded her hands over her stomach in that now familiar gesture of disapproval. "Aye, well," she allowed, "you'll know your own mind best, I dare say."

Neil seemed to find the byplay mildly amusing and he looked at Melodie in obvious curiosity as he sipped his tea. "Are you not eating properly, Melodie?"

He asked the question of her, but he looked at Jessie for the answer and Jessie was nothing loth to provide a reason for her lack of appetite. Melodie, however, preferred to make her own request and she frowned up at Jessie discouragingly.

"I'm having a breakfast and that's all that matters, isn't it? I just don't want—I mean, I happen to be in something of a hurry this morning, that's all, there's really nothing to make an issue about."

He looked again at Jessie, but the housekeeper shrugged her plump shoulders and reached for his empty plate. "I'll not make an issue, Miss Carne," she assured her, and Melodie found it hard to believe the glimpse of a smile that briefly softened the austere features. "You'll be capable of doing things for yourself, I'll warrant!"

Neil watched the housekeeper leave the room, then looked at Melodie and half smiled. "I do believe Jessie approves of you," he told her. Giving her no time to say anything, he put down his empty cup and looked at his watch. "I hope you won't mind having your breakfast on your own after all—it's time I started out." Getting up from the table, he stood for a moment with his hands resting on the back of his chair while he looked across at her. "I'm glad you're going to give Rusty an outing, he can do with the exercise. You've not ridden much since you've been here, Melodie."

"Not very much," she admitted. "I just don't seem to have got around to it very often, but I thought—"

"Aye well, if the spirit takes you this morning both you and the horse will benefit, I dare say."

"Neil!" He had started to move off, but he turned back when she called after him and fixed her with that steady and disconcerting gaze that she never seemed able to cope with very successfully. "I wondered if I might come with you this morning." She sounded vaguely breathless because her heart was thudding anxiously in case he said no. "Just for part of the way," she added hastily because he had not answered, and blue eyes between thick lashes had never looked so appealing. "I wouldn't hinder you, would I?"

It was several seconds before he said anything, and he continued to look down at her from across the table. She had almost convinced herself that he was going to say he couldn't wait for her to finish her breakfast, when he nodded and smiled. It was one of those rare smiles that lit up his whole face and gleamed warmly in his eyes, and her senses responded to it instinctively.

"You probably will hinder me," he said frankly, "but please come just the same if you've a mind to." She felt lighthearted suddenly and made as if to leave the table and join him, but he waved her back to her neglected meal. "Eat your breakfast first, there's no need to go without your food."

"Are you sure you don't mind waiting for me?"

He was still smiling, his lean face crinkled with amusement at her anxiety. "I'm sure—you finish your breakfast while I go and saddle the horses."

It was less than ten minutes, in fact, before she went hurrying out through the back door of the house and across the cobbled yard to the stable. It was quite incredible how excited she could get simply at the prospect of riding with Neil again, and almost instinctively she glanced up at the sky.

It was clear and blue and there was no chance of

them being caught in a storm as they had been the last time they rode out together. The sun was warm, but there was a light breeze that would probably become cooler as they got further out into more open country, but Melodie anticipated the ride with no less pleasure whatever the weather.

"Ah! There you are." Neil came out of the stable leading the familiar chestnut gelding, and he helped her to mount before going back for his own horse. To Melodie's surprise it wasn't Black Knight he led out but the grey that John had once offered to saddle for her use, and Neil responded to her obvious curiosity with a faint smile. "Black Knight's on the sick list this morning," he said.

"He's been hurt?" She did not like to think of that magnificent creature being hurt, but Neil was shaking his head.

"He has 'flu."

"Oh, but that can be dangerous for horses, can't it?"

"It can be." He noted her quick anxious glance in the direction of the stable as he swung himself up on to the grey, and she thought he appreciated her anxiety. "McKenzie's a good man with horses and you've no need to concern yourself with him, Melodie. Everything that can be done for him is being done. He has medicine that the vet left for him and he's being kept warm, there's not much else we can do for him."

"He's so beautiful!"

Neil's grey eyes were like bright steel in the

tanned leanness of his face, but there was a hint of a smile on his mouth as he quizzed her. "Would you grieve for him less if he wasn't so beautiful?" he asked, and she looked at him reproachfully.

"You know I didn't mean that, Neil!"

He did not reply, but her eyes followed him as he led the way out of the stable yard and on to the soft springiness of turf, and she tried to decide whether or not he was as matter-of-fact about Black Knight's sickness as he seemed to be. Urging Rusty up alongside, she had the opportunity to study his face briefly before he turned to her and smiled, but she thought she saw the depth of his concern for his favourite horse in those few seconds.

"I really am sorry about Black Knight, Neil."

The words were barely out of her mouth before he leaned across and pressed one big brown hand over her two smaller ones. "Aye, I know you are," he said. "And so am I."

He rode close beside her as they went down the hillside, a situation that was more easily achieved on the amenable grey than it would have been on his usual mount, and to Melodie there was a curious kind of satisfaction in their closeness. Neil was relaxed and his mood somehow communicated itself to her.

"You see that slope over there?" His voice brought her out of a pleasant state of dreaminess and she followed the direction of his pointing finger. "Where it looks dark green there, do you see?"

Melodie nodded. "It looks like little trees," she guessed, and he nodded.

"It's a scheme I have for using land that until now has been unproductive," he explained. "They're young conifers—planted on the slopes they'll be profitable timber in years to come."

Melodie gazed across what seemed to be an immense distance at the veritable forest of young trees that clung to the mountainside. The extent of Ben Ross must be even greater than she had realised, and she looked at him curiously.

"You own all that too?"

"I do—and I mean to make it work for me!"

"And those little houses I can see in the distance—are they on the estate too?"

"There are three crofts and all have good tenants—sheep and cattle and a wee bit of cereal, though it isn't very good land for growing much beside animals. The one you can see from here is where Donald Murdoch lives with his wife, the Stirling place you've visited and then over near Glen Bar are the McKenzies. All good tenants."

"And John says there are salmon in the river."

She made the observation when she caught sight of the river in the distance, flowing like molten silver over its rocky bed, reminding her of the last time she had ridden out with Neil. He half turned his head and nodded agreement, and she wondered if he too was remembering that eventful ride.

"That's right," he said. "The river is another good source of income for the estate—we're very lucky it's so well endowed."

"Salmon water is valuable, of course."

' Very much so, and it's been built up over the years to a really profitable asset—the Ras is a wonderful stretch of water, and these days fishing rights are virtually priceless."

"You're a very good businessman!"

The grey eyes looked at her for a moment as if he was unsure whether or not she meant the remark as a criticism. "Is that a virtue or a vice in your opinion, Melodie?"

"Why—a virtue, I suppose." She laughed a little uneasily. "I'm notoriously incapable of even being able to handle a shopping expedition on my own without forgetting half the things I go for, so I can merely stand in awe of someone who is capable of handling an estate this size and making it pay."

From the corner of her eye she could see the strong tanned arm and hand that held the rein nearest to her, and she was conscious suddenly of an aura of power about him, of pride in possession that made her tremble. He felt so strongly about Ben Ross that she wondered if he could ever feel deeply about a woman—she would surely have to be prepared to take second place, no matter who she was.

She almost cried aloud in surprise when once again a large strong hand engulfed her own two and squeezed them gently, and she looked up swiftly with wide eyes, to find herself once more the subject of that steady and disconcerting scrutiny.

"Do you stand in awe of me, then, Melodie? Surely not!"

"I'm—never quite sure." She made the admission

with more frankness than she would normally have done because he had taken her by surprise. Briefly she scanned the lean tanned face, then looked down again at their hands, her own still enfolded in his, a small uncertain laugh shivering from her lips. "I never quite know what to make of you, Neil."

The hand was withdrawn, and she felt curiously bereft without its hard warm pressure. "I'm no great mystery," he said, in that quiet voice she was beginning to find ever more attractive. "Maybe one day you'll realise that, hmm?" Melodie said nothing, but glanced briefly up at him, meeting the warmth in his eyes with a sudden flutter in her heart beat. "In the meantime," Neil went on, "shall we ride down as far as the Ras?"

She nodded, urging Rusty along to match the increased speed of the grey. "The Ras?" she asked, coming up beside him again. "That's a curious name—does it mean something special?"

A faintly sardonic smile touched the firm mouth, but she thought he was nothing loth to explain the curious name to her and the subject was a far less disturbing one than her opinion of him could have proved. "It's another Nordic name," he told her. "There are any number of them around here. It means swift course, and you'll remember how appropriate that is in this case."

She remembered the racing current and the deep grey of the water as it swirled around rocks and boulders in its path, and had to admit it was appropriate. But it was also beginning to dawn on her that there could be a connection between Neil's knowledge of Nordic meanings and her occasional musings on the possibility of his being of the same origin, and she studied him for a second between thick lashes.

His lean strong features could well have belonged to one of the marauding Vikings who for centuries had plagued the Scots, and left their physical impression on the people they invaded along with relics of their culture. His fair hair, thick and silky, fell across half his broad brow, and his grey eyes in the tanned face had the keen, narrowed look of conquest as he rode over his long-coveted land, tall in the saddle and with a hint of ruthlessness in his pride.

The need to know more about him was more imperative than it had ever been, and she felt sure that to know him she had first to know more about his precious land. "Tell me about Ben Ross, Neil."

Neil turned swiftly, his eyes narrowing slightly, as if he found her curiosity suspect. "Are you really interested?" he asked, a slight twist of smile on his mouth. "I warn you it's a subject on which I can wax eloquent, given the encouragement."

"Well, I'm very interested. For instance, why Ben Ross; has it to do with the fact that the Rosses used to own it?"

"It has."

She felt he was going to say more, but when he did not she pressed on. "It's a huge place, isn't it—judging by what I've seen of it."

"It's pretty big," Neil allowed, but his smile left no doubt that it was an understatement. "It stretches from the edge of Glen Ross village in the east, right over as far as Glen Bar to the south, where the plantation is I showed you, and out to the big loch and Ben Midden, west and north."

"Ben Midden?"

She followed his pointing finger as he turned in the saddle. "The mountain over there."

Its distance away surprised her, even though she now knew that in this kind of country distances could be deceptive. "But that looks miles away!"

"About three," Neil agreed with a smile.

"But its name!" She thought she knew what the word meant, and Neil's smile suggested she was right, but it hardly seemed suitable to the stately peak that soared majestically, green and purple against the pale summer sky. "I can't believe I heard you right."

"It means dung heap, to be exact," he told her. "Our Nordic ancestors would appear to have had a taste more for frankness than beauty. The old Scandinavian word was *modding*, and it was probably called that originally."

"Well, it doesn't seem very appropriate for a lovely view like that mountain! But tell me more, Neil—Ben, for instance. Is that Nordic too, or is it Scottish?"

"That's from the Gaelic for mountain peak."

He seemed so close suddenly, as if she had got close to the man behind that dour exterior at last. She heard herself laugh, a light and rather breathless little sound, and she kept Rusty close up beside the ambling grey.

"And are you as much an expert on the Gaelic as you are on the old Nordic names, Neil?"

His eyes, moving slowly over her slightly flushed face, came to rest on her mouth and lingered there for several seconds. They seemed to have the gleam of steel in the tanned face, and Melodie felt a sudden more urgent beat to her heart. She had an almost irresistible desire to reach out and touch him, and she carefully avoided looking at him while he spoke.

"I don't claim to be an expert on either."

"But you seem to know so much about both that you must have taken the trouble to find out. It isn't the kind of thing you learn in school, is it?"

He rode along beside her silently for a moment or two, and she glanced at the lean features in stern profile against the background of hills and blue sky. "My mother gave me an interest in the Nordic names when I was quite small," he said, and Melodie turned swiftly, unable to control the impulsive movement.

In all the time she had known him it was the first time he had made any mention at all of his family, and she could not help feeling that it was of more moment than she could realise at present. Her desire to know more about him was as fervent as ever, but she was afraid of asking too many questions and making him wary of her interest.

He was not looking at her but straight ahead to where the gleaming waters of the Ras tumbled over the rocks with a crescendo of sound like a gathering storm. There was a certain excitement in the sound, as if it could stir up emotions like that last time they had ridden down here, and she wondered what thoughts were going on in Neil's mind as he absently urged his horse on to a slightly faster pace.

"She was Swedish." The quiet, softly accented voice came to her slightly fainter because she had need to come up alongside again, and she put her heels to Rusty and brought him on. "She died when I was ten," Neil went on, almost as if he was unaware of anyone listening, "but I remember how she used to teach me the old names and show me how they were derived."

The urge to reach out and touch him was even stronger, but somehow she resisted it, and she looked up at him with shadowed blue eyes. "You must have missed her terribly," she said. "You and your father."

The way he glanced at her, so swiftly and suddenly, was not the reaction she expected and she held his gaze for a moment, not quite sure what she had said wrong. Then he nodded his head slowly, his face in profile again. "She was beautiful," he said, "everyone missed her—even my father!" He put his heels to the grey suddenly and spoke over his shoulder as the animal surged forward. "Shall we put on a bit of speed, Melodie? I've a lot of ground to cover before lunch time!"

MELODIE GLANCED ONCE MORE at the clock on the mantel and frowned. She had long since finished her own dinner, but she had eaten it alone, and there was still no sign of Neil coming in for his. Jessie would be fretting over it, as she always did when things got out of the comfortable routine she was used to—the wonder was that she now seemed to have accepted Melodie herself as part of the daily routine and the fact could still surprise her when she thought about it.

It was not necessary for him still to be out there in the stable with Black Knight for the animal was much better and recovering fast, but Neil had a soft spot for the mettlesome creature that was his favourite mount, and he had probably not realised how late it was. Melodie looked at the clock again, then across at the door when it opened, somewhat surprised to see Jessie McKay.

"Mr Neil's no in yet, then?"

Melodie shook her head. It was not necessary for Jessie to come and inquire, for she must know that Neil would let her know as soon as he came in for his dinner, so that Melodie suspected some other reason behind the inquiry. She thought she knew what it was and she looked across at the housekeeper and smiled—she seemed so much more easy to read now that she was used to her.

"He's probably forgotten the time. I'd better go and tell him that his dinner's spoiling," she suggested.

Jessie's nod of satisfaction suggested that the offer was exactly what she had had in mind. "It'll come better from you, Miss Carne—you'll not be charged with pestering him as I would if I chivvied him in for a meal."

Getting up from her armchair, Melodie shook her head, pulling a face over the statement. "I wouldn't bank on it—but I'll go and tell him just the same, Mrs McKay."

"I'd be obliged."

"He's sure to be still in the stable."

"Sure to be," Jessie complained. "He dotes on yon black devil, and the beast is well nigh recovered by now too."

"He's very much better," Melodie agreed, taking her jacket from a chair, "but he's rather special, you know, and Neil's bound to worry about him when he's been so poorly."

"Aye well, that's as maybe," Jessie allowed, "but somebody'll need to worry about Mr Neil himself if he disnae eat when he should!"

They walked together across the hall to the rear of the house and it was instinctive for Melodie to glance across, as she so often did, at the huge portrait hanging on the stairs wall. It caught the light where it hung and for a moment the dark hair of the man in the picture was blotted out by a splash of yellow light that slashed across the brow just above the craggy face, and Melodie stopped for a moment and stared, some fleeting familiarity catching her attention before it vanished just as quickly.

Jessie followed her gaze, drawn by her momentary pause. "Yon picture fascinates you, does it not?" she asked, and Melodie shrugged, smiling a little uncertainly.

"For a moment I thought—" She shook her head, the fleeting impression no longer even remembered. "The light can play curious tricks, can't it?"

Whether or not she knew what she meant, Melodie had no way of knowing, but Jessie McKay seemed ready enough to talk about the man, and she had never done that before. No one had mentioned the portrait except her friends in Australia—nearer home it seemed Duncan Ross was not a subject for discussion.

Jessie was glancing back over her shoulders at the painting as she spoke. "He was a braw man for all they say about him," she declared firmly, as if she expected someone to argue with her opinion. "He'd his faults, but he was a fine, braw man."

"You knew him?" She couldn't think why that should surprise her, but somehow it did, and Jessie was nodding her head firmly.

"Mebbe better than most," she said.

From the kitchen doorway it was just possible to see the portrait, though at an angle, and Melodie looked across at it again curiously, unable to disguise or explain her interest in it. "He fascinates me," she confessed, and laughed, unsure of her reasons. "I don't know why—I can't imagine why unless it's because of what I've heard about him. About how he was in love with someone once and she married someone else."

"His cousin." From her tone it might almost have been a personal affront, Melodie thought. "Then they went to live in England and he never did see her again—it broke his heart."

"Poor man!" She glanced again at the portrait, trying to see that strong-featured man as a broken-hearted lover and finding it difficult. "I know that it was Mrs Holland's mother that he loved," she told Jessie. "Catriona told me, that's why he left her Ben Ross when he died, as a kind of gesture, because he loved her mother!"

"And that was the one really wicked thing he did!" Jessie declared vehemently. "She'd no right to the place!"

Still puzzled, Melodie shook her head. "Then who had?" she asked.

It was as if she suddenly recalled herself, Melodie thought, for it was clear from her expression that she intended saying nothing more, that she probably considered she had already said too much. "Ah well, it's all done with now," she said as she turned into the kitchen, and Melodie knew she would not be hearing any more, not for the moment. "I'll mebbe have to cook something else if this dinner is spoiled," Jessie grumbled, and Melodie shrugged resignedly as she turned away.

She had been wise to put on a jacket, for the evening breeze could be very chill, and it was already growing dusk as she made her way across to the stables. The shadow of the house darkened the yard and even the groom's cottage seemed unoccupied for the moment with its new tenants obviously out for the evening, and a sharp east wind stole in off the moors, so that she shivered at a multiple of sensations as she made her way across the cobbles.

Inside it was quite dark except for the one stall where an overhead light burned dimly, and she made her way past the other stalls, her footsteps swishing softly through the straw on the stone floor, to where she could hear Neil's voice, quiet and soothing, talking to Black Knight.

"Neil?"

He turned as she came into the stall where Black Knight stood with a blanket covering him, already feeling well enough to lift his handsome head and glance suspiciously at her from the corner of his fiery eye. Neil was stroking him, his big hands soothingly gentle on the glossy neck, and the animal was going to resent any intrusion into a situation that suited him perfectly, snorting disapproval at her presence.

"I came to warn you that Jessie is about to give notice if you don't come at once and have your dinner." She accompanied the warning with a smile, and noted the wary eye of the stallion on her. "Shall I stay with Black while you go?"

"No, you will not!" Neil declared forcibly. He stepped back from his charge and walked a few paces along towards her, resting one hand on the partition and looking at her with a gleam in his grey eyes. "Neither will Jessie give notice," he added with a crook of smile on his firm mouth. "But I hadn't realised how hungry I was." He glanced at his watch and whistled silently. "Nor did I realise it was so late—no wonder Jessie's having a fit!"

"I had my dinner over an hour ago."

"Then you can come and talk to me while I have

mine." He looked down at her steadily for a second, one brow raised curiously. "Unless you've other plans," he added, and Melodie felt the colour in her cheeks as she shook her head.

"Where would I be going at this hour of the night?"

Neil shrugged. His eyes were steel grey in the tanned and shadowed darkness of his face and his mouth had a slightly sardonic tilt at one corner. "Who knows?" he said. "It's not so late that you can't go out and see a—friend."

"If you mean John, he's gone somewhere with his aunt and uncle this evening, and I know no one else here."

"You know me."

The deep quiet of his voice shivered through her, and she caught her breath at the rapid beat of her heart, her eyes carefully concealed by lowered lashes. "That's true," she agreed, husky-voiced, "but you never ask me out, do you, Neil?"

She was thrillingly aware of his physical presence, but there was also an aura of excitement surrounding them that made her head spin with the sensation it created, and the desire to reach out and touch him was almost irresistible.

"John Stirling's in love with you." His words snatched her back to reality and she blinked at him for a second in confusion, her head shaking slowly. "You're not going to deny it, are you, Melodie?"

It was hard not to deny it out of hand, but she thought he would probably despise her if she did, and she would hate for that to happen. "He says he is."

"Then you'd better believe it, little one!" His eyes held hers for a second, but she could not read anything beyond the faintly ironical smile in them. "Now will you come and talk to me while I eat, or not?"

The temptation to talk to him while he had his belated meal was there, but instinctively she hesitated, patting Black Knight's sleek flanks and not looking at Neil. "Are you sure you don't want me to stay with Black?"

"Quite sure!" He came closer, taking her arm and moving them out of the stall, back from the proximity of the stallion's restless hooves. "He's perfectly all right on his own and I don't trust you two together—Black doesn't like females and you're too impulsive. You wouldn't resist getting too close and he'd probably kick you before I was half way across the yard."

"I don't believe he would." She stepped back and stroked the glossy coat once more, but felt the muscles in the animal's strong flanks twitch in dislike of a strange hand. "I'd love to make friends with him, Neil."

"Melodie!" He gripped her arm firmly and drew her away, coming to a halt in the stable doorway. The grey eyes looked down at her steadily and she felt her cheeks flush with colour as she hastily looked away. "I want you to make me a promise." He slid a hand beneath her chin, lifting her face to him, though she kept her eyes lowered. "Will you?"

"It depends on what it is."

Thick black lashes cast dark shadows on her cheeks, and her mouth had a curious trembling softness when he fixed his gaze on it. His fingers held her tightly, hard as steel on her soft flesh and she tried to do something about the rapid thudding beat of her heart as he looked down at her.

"Don't ever go near Black Knight unless I'm here—promise?" Melodie knew it made sense and she had no intention of doing other than as he said, but she did not answer for a second or two because she was still trying to think clearly and to speak other than in the husky whisper that she felt sure was all she could manage at the moment. The hand around her jaw jerked her face up to him sharply and he leaned closer, his eyes narrowed. "Melodie—are you ready to promise me?"

"Yes! Yes, of course I am!"

He seemed unconvinced for he went on as if she had not spoken, his words warm on her mouth as he bent over her. "It's only in romantic fiction that pretty girls can instinctively tame difficult animals— in real life Black would just as soon kick in your lovely head as look at you!"

"Then I won't give him the opportunity!"

She half expected him to make some bland remark about her being a good girl, and she steeled herself not to mind too much that he treated her as if he was an approving uncle. She was completely unprepared for the firm pressure of his mouth on hers, and her eyes flew wide open in surprise at the first touch of his lips, then were almost immediately hidden again by the long sweep of lashes.

The pounding of her heart was like a drum beat and she felt curiously lightheaded as she placed her hands instinctively to the broadness of his chest, her fingers fanned out over his heart's beat. But before she could respond to the kiss as every nerve in her body urged her to, Neil raised his head and was looking down at her with the gentle warmth of temptation in his eyes, smiling in a way that touched her senses like fire.

"I hope you know how to keep a promise," he said.

She shook her head slowly, her eyes blank with the shock of disappointment and surprise. "Neil—"

He was not giving her his full attention any longer, it seemed, for he walked back into the stall and patted the stallion's neck with a consoling hand. "You're on trust too, ma lad." He glanced back at Melodie and his eyes were warm with laughter. "Just in case this crazy wee creature takes it into her head to come and visit you, try and behave like a gentleman, will you?"

The black tried to turn and watch them go, but he could see no more than Neil's arm being placed around Melodie's shoulders as he led her from the stable and back to the house. The chill wind off the moor whispered across the cobbled yard and made her shiver, and Neil looked down at her and smiled, hugging her more closely as if to shield her from the blow.

Her eyes were like great blue jewels in her small face and made dark as night by the shadows of evening, but he could still make out the slight pout of reproach on her mouth as she glanced up at him, snuggling close in the curve of his arm.

"Don't you trust me?" she asked. "I promised I wouldn't go near Black Knight except if you were there—isn't that good enough?"

The arm about her shoulder tightened still more, and Neil looked at her for a moment in silence, then once more the gleam of white teeth in his tanned face betrayed a smile, and he shook his head. "You're a woman and they're an unreliable breed for the most part—but you're probably no worse than the majority."

"Thank you!"

This time he laughed, a soft deep sound that fluttered across the top of her hair as he bent his head over her. "But prettier than most," he added, and Melodie smiled to herself in the dusk.

CHAPTER NINE

MELODIE was finding it hard to concentrate. The landscape she was working on was nearing completion, but at the back of her mind and impossible to ignore was the knowledge that there was less than two weeks of her scheduled stay left. All too soon she would have to see about finding herself a permanent home, and she had already made up her mind to settle in Scotland. John had warned her that she might find it hard to leave, and his prophecy was proving true.

She paused in what she was doing and gazed across the glen to the soaring majesty of Ben Midden whose elusive magic she was trying to reproduce on her canvas. It was difficult to capture the awesome magnificence of the mountain and at the same time convey that soft, misty look that seemed to change with every minute, but she was quite pleased with what she had achieved so far.

It was warm in the sun and early August had a mellowness that late June had lacked. It added a golden look to everything, but it also gave a slightly more keen edge to the breeze that blew across the sheltered glen below her from the cooler heights of the hills and mountains. It was the first of the changes in character that she had anticipated when she first saw the place and it intrigued and fascinated her with its subtlety.

The sun warmed her face and the breeze wisped her black hair about her neck as she gave her attention again to her work, too intent on her own thoughts to notice anyone approach. The first indication she had that she was no longer alone was when a pair of firm hands curled over her shoulders from behind, and John's voice spoke close to her ear as he bent over her. "Hi, sweetheart!" His lips brushed across her neck in a shiver-inducing caress, and he hugged her for a second before squatting on his heels beside her. "Hey, that's pretty good!"

Melodie turned and smiled, gratified but cautious as always of biased opinions like John's. "It's coming on," she allowed cautiously, "but there's a lot to do to it yet, and I haven't too much time."

"Before you leave here?"

She nodded. Although nothing had yet been said by anyone at Ben Ross about her coming departure she knew it must have occurred to both Neil and Jessie McKay that she would soon be leaving. For her own part, she preferred not to think about it, but it was something that had to be faced sooner or later.

"In less than a fortnight, my two months are up."

"Then what?"

The intensity of his interest drew her gaze, and she looked at him for a second or two with her eyes narrowed curiously. "Why, then I have to find somewhere of my own—somewhere permanent. In fact I ought to be looking already, it probably won't be all that easy to find somewhere."

"Around here?"

She smiled ruefully, pulling a face as she admitted it. "You were right about me not wanting to leave here when the time came; I'm hooked on the Highlands, and I'm going to try and find somewhere not too far from here."

"I see."

Something in his voice made her look round at him again. She sensed something in the hunch of his shoulders that made her vaguely uneasy, and John wasn't looking at her but down at the ground between his feet. Putting down her brush, she absently wiped her hands and looked at him curiously.

"John, is something wrong?"

He took several moments to answer but continued to look down at the ground. Then, as if he had suddenly made up his mind about something, he caught her eye and held it steadily for a second before he spoke. "Melodie, I'm going back to Canada—I'm going home."

"Oh!"

She wasn't sure what she felt about it exactly. She liked John, she liked him very much and she would miss him, but she felt somehow that the fact of his going home wasn't the extent of what he had to say to her. She felt a curious sense of anticipation so intense that she got to her feet suddenly and stretched the cramped muscles in her hand and arm.

Almost at once John was beside her, standing close as she looked down at the glen and the deep, placid stillness of Loch Lairdross. "I'm asking you to come with me, Melodie."

It was not completely unexpected, if she was honest, for John had been asking her at fairly frequent intervals during the past couple of weeks to marry him, as he had said he would, yet somehow she knew that this time it was just a little bit different. It had not been easy to say no at other times, but this time she felt he was even more in earnest, it was like a last appeal, and was that much harder to refuse.

She hesitated, and by hesitating she probably gave him a wrong impression, for he put his hands on her shoulders and turned her to face him, his eyes searching her face anxiously for some sign that she had had second thoughts since the last time he asked her.

"Will you come back with me, Melodie, and marry me in Canada?"

"Oh, John—" She bit her lip and her eyes were wide and anxious when she looked up at him. If only it had not come to this when she was so unprepared for it. "I—can't; I'm truly sorry, but I can't, John."

The brown eyes already showed resignation even before she finished speaking, and he made a grimace with his mouth that was meant to be a smile. "I guess I knew the answer already—I've known it all along. Ever since you were so reluctant to tell me about that ride you took with McDowell!"

"But, John, I—"

He placed a firm finger over her lips to silence her, and he was shaking his head again, that caricature of a smile still in place. "Don't bother to deny it, honey, I know when I'm licked—but I had to try one last time."

"Oh, John, I'm sorry!"

He laughed, but it was a harsh unsteady sound that was completely devoid of humour, and he pulled her close suddenly and kissed her mouth with a swift urgency that suggested it was as much a gesture of defiance, and she hated the change in him. More especially because she felt she had contributed to it, however unwittingly.

"Is it me you feel sorry about, or yourself for loving a lost cause, sweetheart?" The brown eyes scanned her small flushed face with a hint of desperation. "It *is* a lost cause, you know, Melodie. Even if he wasn't still nursing a fancy for his erstwhile boss, he's still far too wrapped up in Ben Ross to give priority to any woman, even one as delectable as you."

It was something that until now Melodie had preferred not to think too much about. She was prepared to admit, though only to herself at the moment, that Neil McDowell had become the most important factor in her life during the past few weeks, but she still shied away from admitting that it was love she felt for him. She did not look directly at John, but hid her eyes with lowered lashes, her gaze fixed on the spot where his throat emerged from the collar of his shirt.

"The question of lost causes or not doesn't arise,

John. I'll be leaving here in a couple of weeks or less, and it's unlikely I'll ever see Neil again."

"And you'll find that quite easy to do, will you?" Melodie looked up quickly, her eyes wide and darkened by a sudden hurt and John was already contrite. "I'm sorry, honey! I shouldn't have made a crack like that, knowing the way it feels to be—" His shoulders shrugged helplessly. "I guess I just wanted to hit back."

Her head was spinning, filled with a chaotic jumble of thoughts and emotions, none of which made much sense to her at the moment. John's remark, inspired by bitterness in his own disappointment, had gone home more deeply than she had been prepared for, but she might as well admit that it would be the hardest thing in the world for her not to see Neil again, if it had to be that way.

If, as John implied, Neil cared too deeply for Ben Ross to care very much about anything or anyone else, then the best solution was for her to go away and never see him again, but it hurt none the less for all that. She clenched her hands tightly at her sides and tried to think lucidly about moving away. It ought to be possible to appear cool and practical about it if she was firm with herself, but somehow she did not think John would be fooled—possibly because his own involved emotions made him able to judge hers more accurately.

"Please—" She swallowed hard, trying to rid her voice of its betraying huskiness. "Please don't apologise, John, you're—you're quite likely to be right about me—I'll probably find it quite easy to just move out of Ben Ross. I'm certainly not going to spend the rest of my life—" She caught her lip between her teeth suddenly, realising how close she was to crying, and dazedly unsure how she came to be in such a state.

"Oh, Melodie, sweetheart!" She was drawn into his arms again and held close with her head resting on his chest while he buried his face in the softness of her hair until it muffled his voice. "I didn't mean to make you cry, honestly, sweetheart—I'm sorry!"

Melodie had her eyes closed, but she felt a tear squeeze between her lashes and raised a hasty hand to brush it away. "I'm *not* crying!" She eased herself away, but her eyes were bright and glistening when she looked up at him. She had not felt this weepy and unhappy when she came out, and she wished she could do something about it now. "I need to be alone for a bit and clear my head—maybe I should go for a long walk before I make a fool of myself!"

"Melodie—"

"No, John, please!"

She was gathering up her things, heedless of how she did it, her hands unsteady and anxious only to have some time alone to think things out. So much seemed to be crowding in on her that she could not think clearly. Until now she had not seen her situation as in any way urgent, but now suddenly it seemed imperative that she made a move away from Ben Ross and from Neil and she had to think it all out carefully and alone.

"When do you go home, John?"

She realised the impression her question had given and saw the look that came into his eyes as she straightened up with her stool tucked under her arm and the rest of her stuff thrust untidily into a bundle.

"I go the day after tomorrow. I'll be busy packing tomorrow, but I thought—"

"Then I'll say goodbye!"

He looked stunned, as if he found it hard to believe that it had finally come to an end, and she felt more touched by his reaction than she expected. "You won't see me tomorrow?"

She shook her head, her eyes dark and shadowed by thick lashes, hiding the turmoil that churned away inside her. "I'd much rather not, John." Her voice too was betrayingly unsteady again and she knew that he wanted to reach out for her. "I—I hate saying goodbye."

"I hate saying goodbye to *you*!"

He had a hand on her arm and his fingers were curled tightly into her flesh. She tried hard to concentrate on his needs and his feelings while all the time her own emotions were hopelessly tangled and made it almost impossible to think of anything else.

"You won't refuse me a goodbye kiss, will you, Melodie?"

She thought how long ago it seemed since she had first seen those brown eyes, gleaming with warmth and friendliness in that pleasantly rugged face. Since he had offered to drive her up to Ben Ross and issued a lighthearted warning about the dourness of

Neil McDowell. It was hard to say goodbye, for she was really fond of John, but not fond enough. She was not in love with him as she was with Neil.

"Of course I won't refuse to kiss you goodbye!"

She said it hastily and a little breathlessly, for it was the first time she had made the admission, even to herself, that she actually loved Neil and it made her feel curiously vulnerable suddenly. She was smiling, a slightly dazed and unsteady smile, as she put down the paraphernalia of paints and canvas once more.

"Goodbye, John, and—thank you for—everything."

He scanned her face swiftly, searchingly, his hands on her arms ready to draw her close. "You won't change your mind and come with me?"

It was a curiously twisted smile she gave him and it did not reach her eyes, then she turned her head and looked down into the glen where the tiny loch lay smooth as a mirror in its setting of hills and mountains. When she laughed suddenly, it had little to do with amusement, and John's arm tightened for a second about her.

"I know it's silly," she said, "but I've the oddest feeling of belonging here."

She raised her face to him and his mouth touched hers lightly. It was a gentle gesture of regret and farewell and it added to her already unhappy mood so that she slid her arms up around his neck and clung to him for a moment, needing his support.

"Maybe you do belong, sweetheart," John said. "I only wish you felt you belonged with me."

IT SEEMED TO MELODIE that a quiet ride on the moors was the ideal thing to help her clear her mind. The ever ready Rusty was available and nothing loth to take an unexpected trip, and it was a lovely day. An initial gallop had rid the gelding of his surplus energy and from then on their pace had been no faster than an easy walk for the most part, but far from its being conducive to thought she found herself relaxing as she so often did when she rode among the now familiar surroundings.

Without intentionally choosing any particular direction she had made for the big loch on the western boundary of the estate, and from there veered north towards the towering slopes of Ben Midden. It was a much greater distance than she had done before, but she was unaware of how quickly time was passing and utterly content to let Rusty amble along at his present easy pace for as long as he liked.

The air was warm, but still fresh enough to cool her cheeks and her forehead, and it was only when she caught sight of a spring, bubbling crystal clear from a rocky outcrop at the foot of Ben Midden, that she realised how thirsty she was. The water sparkled, clear and pure, from a cleft in the rocks some five or six feet up, and ran away over a stony bed to disappear somewhere among the bristling heather, and she felt Rusty's head come up in pleasure at the sight and smell of it as they approached.

Sliding down from the saddle, she climbed over the lower rocks and cupped her hands under the bubbling fount, flinching briefly from its icy coldness over her fingers. The gelding could help himself from the stream lower down, and take a well earned rest at the same time, while she looked around her.

It was so quiet except for the occasional cry of a bird or the odd mysterious small noises that characterised the moorland and she felt at ease as she always did out there. The lower slopes of Ben Midden towered over her, looking much less soft and pretty close to than when seen through a haze of distance and the ever present suggestion of mist. It looked far more rugged and harsh but no less intriguing.

Neil had said something about there being a family of wild cats in the area, and this rocky slope with its multitude of crevices and rock ledges was an ideal environment for them. The temptation to go searching was almost irresistible, but a glance at her wristwatch brought her up short, a silent whistle of surprise pursing her lips.

She scrambled down hastily from the ledge where she stood, all thoughts of wild cats banished in her anxiety to get back without further delay. She was already nearly an hour late for lunch and, though Jessie McKay was remarkably tolerant of her somewhat erratic timekeeping, there was a limit to her tolerance.

It was unbelievable that time should have passed so quickly, and yet when she looked at how far she had come it should not have surprised her. Arriving in the middle of the afternoon for lunch was likely to earn Jessie's disapproval, and Melodie pulled a face when she anticipated the explanations she was going to have to make.

Rusty was still drinking from the stream, dipping his head every so often and enjoying the cool water, and Melodie was never quite sure what happened next. Whether her own movements startled the animal into angry flight, or whether it simply objected to any kind of intrusion into its territory, she would never know, but a spittingly furious cat leapt suddenly from somewhere among the rocks and went hurtling down to the ground in a wild flurry of fur and claws.

Legs stiff and straight, the cat landed close to where Rusty stood waiting, and the sight of it, back arched and every hair of its striped fur bristling in fury, was too much for even the patient gelding. Suddenly confronted by a shrieking creature with venomous yellow eyes, he panicked—he gave a shrill whinny of fear, tossed his head, then took to his heels across the moor before Melodie could make a move to stop him.

Too stunned to move for a second or two, she stared after her mount as he galloped off, tail and mane flying and heading for home as fast as he could go, then she let out a long breath and shrugged in helpless resignation. It would take her at least another hour to walk back to Ben Ross and she was already very late—Jessie was not going to forgive her so easily this time.

She looked around for the wildcat, but it had disappeared. In direct contrast to its noisy appearance, it had vanished as silently as a ghost among the rocks, and she had not even the consolation of see-

ing it for a moment or two. Ben Ross seemed an incredibly long way off but, since there was no chance
of returning any other way, she had no option but to
walk.

Trying to keep track of distance by an occasional
glance at her wristwatch, Melodie thought she had
walked roughly a mile when she caught sight of
someone in the distance and blinked for a moment,
not daring to believe it was possible assistance on the
way.

Her heart was pounding heavily as she stood for a
moment shading her eyes against the sun and
watched the figures coming closer, although still
some distance off. It had to be Neil, she thought,
and half smiled to herself at the thought. He would
have seen Rusty come home without her and come
looking to see what had happened.

The indeterminate figures evolved after a surprisingly few minutes into recognisable shapes and she
could make out Neil's familiar fair head even at a
distance. He was riding Tarquin and leading the run-
away Rusty, and as soon as she was sure who it was
she stood on tiptoe and waved a hand to let him
know she had seen him.

She thought he urged the horses along faster, and
certainly he was with her in a very short time and
both horses were breathing hard as he pulled them
to a halt and slid from the saddle without pause. He
came straight to her, his hands reaching out for hers
before even he uttered a word.

"You're all right?" The grey eyes scanned her face

with a rapid scrutiny that was so intense she felt her cheeks colour furiously. "You're not hurt?"

"I'm perfectly all right, Neil."

She had not realised how soft her voice would sound, how much it would tell him, and she saw the response in the grey eyes at once. His fingers were tight and hard and he pulled her closer, pressing her hands to his chest so that she could feel the thudding beat of his heart which was much too fast for it to be normal.

"When Rusty came back without you, I thought—" He shook his head as if to rid himself of the thoughts that had gone through his mind. "What happened, Melodie?"

"I stopped for a drink at the spring, and—"

"The spring?" His gaze went unhesitatingly to the towering height of Ben Midden. He knew every inch of Ben Ross land—he did not need to question which spring she referred to. "You've been *that* far?"

"I—I didn't realise the time until I looked at my watch while I was drinking from the spring, and then the wildcat—" She looked up at him anxiously, as if she feared he would not believe her story. "I saw a wildcat, I think I must have startled it, and it jumped down from the rocks right beside where Rusty was standing."

It did not really surprise her to see laughter gleaming in the ever-changing grey eyes, and her heart warmed to the glow it gave to his stern face, even though he found her predicament amusing. "So he took off without you and left you stranded," he guessed, and her bottom lip pouted reproachfully.

Even so there was a smile in her eyes when she looked up at him and Neil squeezed her hands, pressing her palms to the warmth of tanned skin beneath his shirt. "You find that funny?" she asked, and he shook his head.

"Not really—I'm just so relieved that you're not hurt I can laugh at any alternative." Again the grey eyes searched her flushed face and settled once more on her mouth. "Does that surprise you, Melodie? That I was worried sick about what I'd find when I came out here to look for you?"

It was a moment before she shook her head. Her senses were reacting to Neil the way they always did, and she felt quite suddenly so lightheaded that she could have laughed for no reason at all—except that she felt so happy.

"I seem to remember that you appointed yourself my guardian, didn't you?"

He said nothing for a moment, but the hands that held her close tightened their hold, and he looked in to her eyes with that steady and infinitely disturbing gaze that she always found so hard to bear. Only at the moment she did not find it hard at all and she met it head on, finding something there that shivered through her like ice and fire.

Then she bent her head suddenly and touched her brow to the spot where his shirt opened. A small pulse at the base of his brown throat throbbed urgently and she raised her head just a little more to press her lips to it with a touch as light as thistle-down.

"Melodie!"

His voice, softer and deeper than she had ever heard it before, sounded close to her ear, and his hands moved to slide around her, drawing her into his arms. Her head rested just below his chin and he held her for a second without moving. It was like a dream to Melodie, something not quite real, and she pressed closer to him, unwilling to break the spell now or ever.

"I came out here because I had—things to think about."

Her voice was muffled, and the words much too prosaic for the present situation, and she closed her eyes in pleasure when his mouth sought a soft spot beside her ear and kissed her lightly, almost teasingly.

"Do you have so much to think about?"

It was a moment before she answered, and she wondered just how much it would take to shatter this dreamlike moment beyond repair. But she loved Neil, she had no doubts at all about that now, and she wanted there to be no secrets between them. Even so she ventured the truth with a wildly beating heart.

"John's going back to Canada, did you know?"

He eased her away from him and looked down into her eyes for a moment before he answered. "Aye, I knew," he said quietly. "Is that what you had to think about so deeply, Melodie?"

His arms were still about her and she thanked heaven that at least that was unchanged. "He asked me to marry him. I said no, of course," she added hastily when she sensed the sudden tautness in the enfolding arms.

Neil slid a hand beneath her chin, lifting her face to him and scanning it closely, as if he searched for something he was not quite sure of. "Of course?" he prompted, and Melodie nodded.

"How could I?" she whispered. "I don't love him, Neil."

"Did he have reason to suppose you did?"

The question was unexpected and she frowned at him curiously for a second before she answered. "No, I've told him each time he asked me that I couldn't marry him."

The grey eyes were deep, unfathomable and they sent a sudden shivering thrill through her whole body as she looked up at him. "And could you marry me?" Neil asked.

"Oh, Neil!"

His arms were tighter, more urgent around her, and the lean hard body had a tautness that bowed her to its unyielding length like a willow to the wind. The grey eyes were closer, dark as grey steel in his tanned face, and his mouth only a breath away from hers so that his breath warmed her lips as he spoke.

"Will you?" His eyes swept swiftly over her face and came to rest once more on her mouth, soft and tremulous with anticipation. "I love you, Melodie, and I've near gone out of my head the past few weeks thinking you were taking John Stirling seriously!"

"Oh, Neil, of course I'll marry you! I was only afraid that you still—"

His mouth, hard and firm on hers, silenced her for a long time, a silence that was broken only by the shifting of the restless horses and the calls of birds among the heather. From her mouth to the softness of her throat and neck, until her head spun with the sheer excitement of him, and she hugged herself close to him, content if they never moved from that spot.

They were riding back to Ben Ross before she thought about how much of a rival the huge acres of the estate were going to prove. John had suggested that any woman who married Neil would have to take second place to his beloved Ben Ross, and she pondered on the possibility of how true it was as they rode into the stable yard.

Neil lifted her down, holding her for a moment and smiling down at her, as if he found it all a little hard to believe, and Melodie stood for a moment in his arms. "I love you." His deep, softly accented voice was like a shiver of sensation through her whole being, and she lifted her face to be kissed.

Her mouth warm and tingling when he released her at last, she looked up at him through the thickness of black lashes, her eyes on his mouth, usually so straight and firm, now half smiling. "As much as you love Ben Ross?" she asked impulsively, and saw the swift frown that drew his brows together for a second only.

The grey eyes were steady, studying her in the way she always found so disturbing. "That's an odd question," he said. "What on earth prompts you to ask such a thing, my love?"

He did not wait for an answer but led the horses into the stable while Melodie followed him, already wishing she had not let her impulsive tongue run away with her yet again. He did not press her to explain but turned and smiled at her in a warm, satisfied way over his shoulder while he unsaddled her horse.

"I'm sorry, Neil."

He paused for a second, looking at her curiously, then draped the saddle over the partition between the stalls and shook his head, "I don't begin to understand you, my darling," he confessed. "I'd best spend the next few months learning what makes you tick." He leaned across suddenly and planted a kiss on her mouth. "It'll not be a hard chore," he whispered.

Walking back across the cobbled yard to the house, he put an arm around her shoulders and tucked her close against him, looking down at her with that same warm, satisfied look as before, and this time it was Melodie who tiptoed and kissed him.

"I love you so much I'm half afraid I'll wake up at any minute and find this never really happened at all."

Neil laughed, his eyes so darkly grey that they were almost black as he looked down at her. "I feel a wee bit like that myself," he confessed.

Recalling something else suddenly, Melodie pulled a face. "I've yet to face Jessie and explain why I'm so late for lunch," she reminded him. "Is she very angry about it, Neil?"

It seemed to Melodie that his booted feet had the sound of authority as he strode across the echoing cobbles, and he did not smile, but his arm tightened almost imperceptibly. He brought them to a halt just outside the back door of the house, and pulled her into his arms, holding her close while he kissed her with such fierceness that she was breathless when he let her go at last.

"Apologise to Jessie by all means, but I'll not have you afraid of my housekeeper! You'll be mistress of Ben Ross very soon now, my darling, and you don't have to be afraid of anybody!"

Melodie looked up at him, her small face serious when she thought of the responsibility her new position would entail. It was far more than anything she had undertaken before and she had her first qualms of doubt. Not that she loved Neil any less, but running that great house would be her responsibility for the most part and she was horribly unsure if she was up to it.

"I only hope I won't prove too much of a disappointment," she ventured, and laughed a little unsteadily. "I'm hopeless as an organiser, as you have reason to know, and when I think of being in charge of somewhere as big as Ben Ross!" She drew a deep long breath and shook her head. "I hope you won't have second thoughts about marrying me!"

He shook his head slowly, kissing her mouth with a lingering gentleness that set her senses reeling with its promise of passion. "I'll not have second thoughts about that," he promised. "No matter how bad an organiser you are, my darling."

He opened the door and as they passed the kitchen on their way through to the main part of the house he put his head round the edge of the kitchen door. "It's all right, Jessie, she's back and quite unhurt!"

"Thank God!" Jessie McKay, straight and solemn as ever, noted the possessive arm about Melodie's shoulders with her shrewd brown eyes, and it seemed to Melodie that the small nod she gave might have expressed satisfaction. "You'll be hungry after all that time on the moor, Miss Carne. Away with you into the dining-room and I'll get you something to eat."

There was nothing to do but do as she said, and Melodie was aware that Neil was laughing as he drew her across the hall with him. Looking up at him, she wrinkled her nose in reproach, and he drew her into his arms suddenly, kissing her lightly just beside her ear.

"What makes you so sure that you'll not be able to manage this house and its staff?" he asked, and Melodie glanced instinctively across at the huge portrait that hung on the wall above the stairway.

Duncan Ross looked down at them with his sharp dark eyes, and she felt as if he could actually see them. Herself standing in the circle of Neil's arms, his fair head bent over her, kissing her neck and the soft skin of her throat. There was something about that portrait that always disturbed her, and yet she could not decide just what it was.

She put her hands either side of Neil's face and gave a moment to studying the strong tanned features that were suddenly almost unbearably dear to her. Then she kissed his mouth and glanced once more at the portrait.

"Maybe because I feel the critical eye of the old master on me," she suggested, only half joking, and Neil followed the direction of her gaze and frowned suddenly.

"Does he bother you, darling?"

Something in his voice, she was not sure exactly what, made her look at him curiously for a moment, then she laughed and shook her head. "Not really," she denied. "It's just that he always seems to be watching me. I suppose—" She hesitated, venturing in to new territory with some misgiving. "I suppose you became quite fond of him, didn't you? Was it he that gave you your—your passion for Ben Ross?"

"In a way," he agreed, and the quiet matter-of-factness of his voice gave her no warning of what was to come. "He was my father."

Melodie stared, first at Neil and then at the man in the portrait, and she remembered suddenly one evening when she had noticed something vaguely odd about the portrait with the light casting a patch of yellow across the head of the subject. The impression had been fleeting, but just for a moment it had looked a little like Neil with his strong dark face and fair hair, only she had not realised it then.

"Your—father? Duncan Ross?"

Neil was not looking at her, but up at the old man in the picture, arrogant and autocratic—qualities that he had passed on to his son in some degree. "He wasn't a man for a home life and a wife and family," he told her, in the same cool voice. "He was a rover, all his life until the last years when he got too old to wander around all over the world, then he sent for me to come and run the estate for him. I was twenty at the time and had no idea I was other than Ramsey McDowell's son—my mother left the old man before I was born."

"Oh, Neil!" Her blue eyes were dark with the depth of emotion she felt for the wrong that had been done him. "And then he left the estate to Catriona—how you must have hated him!"

The grey eyes fixed themselves on her mouth again and a hint of smile showed in their depths. "I think I did at one time," he confessed. "I felt it was mine by right, but now—" He bent his head and his mouth was so infinitely gentle that she clung to it for as long as she could. "Since I met you, my darling, I realised just how much a man can love. I believe he felt about Catriona's mother the way I feel about you, I'm sure of it—he never loved another woman the way he loved her, because it wasn't possible."

"More than he loved your mother?"

Neil took her in his arms again and his mouth was close to hers, warming her lips when he spoke. "He could no more love another woman like he loved that first one than I could love anyone else as I do you, my darling."

Melodie lifted her face to him, her eyes like blue gems in her small face and she kissed him softly with a mouth that was trembling and anxious. "Then I have only Ben Ross as a rival," she ventured and Neil's grey eyes looked deep into hers, dark and challenging.

"I have all I ever wanted from life now," he said. "My father's land and a woman I love even more than the land." He kissed her, a long hard kiss that should have been conviction enough, then looked down at her with his grey eyes warm and gentle. "Does that make you happy, my love?" he asked, and Melodie smiled.

"That's all I wanted to know."

FLORENTINE SPRING

Florentine
Spring
Charlotte Lamb

Two years had passed since Paolo's death and still Nicola lived in a world of grief, steadfastly loyal to a ghost. Since the Farenze family had cut her husband off when they married, Nicola felt no compunction about not telling them of Paolo's namesake, baby Paul.

Domenico Farenze discovered Nicola, quite by chance, in London. Learning of the child's existence, he convinced her to take Paul to Italy for the sake of his aging and repentant grandfather. The change in Nicola's life was drastic.

Her long-standing resentment was almost instantly dispelled, and Nicola learned to love the Farenzes. Unfortunately, that also included Domenico!

CHAPTER ONE

SHE liked to arrive early whenever she was cooking at a new place. Kitchens, like people, varied so enormously. She had to feel her way into the layout of the room, work out a smooth routine, a pattern of movement from oven to worktop and back to the sink. She had always found that half an hour spent in familiarising herself with these details paid off handsomely during the actual cooking.

Today she found herself in a small, cramped room at the end of a narrow corridor. The flat itself seemed spacious and elegant, judging by what she had seen as the hostess whisked her past the several rooms, yet the most important room had been ludicrously ill-designed. Cupboards were tiny and ill-lit. The refrigerator was squashed into a corner and only just held a handful of items. The worktops were at the wrong height, so that she had to stoop in order to see what she was doing.

"Ghastly, isn't it?" The hostess smiled apologetically. She was more or less the same age as Nicola, but exceedingly well dressed. Her sleek dark hair was swathed on top of her head, exposing a slim, tanned throat and shoulders. She had a faintly Latin appearance, despite her obviously English accent, and the black lace mantilla she wore around her shoulders deepened the impression.

Nicola returned the smile soothingly. "I'll manage, don't worry. I've cooked in worse kitchens than this one!"

Mrs Christiansen grimaced. "I didn't think there were any! I'm so grateful to see you—you can't imagine! I only had my baby six weeks ago and I'm still desperately trying to cope with the new situation. My husband has these important dinner parties from time to time. They're part of his job, you know. He's very understanding, but I know he feels I should be able to manage the baby and arrange everything for his party, too."

"Men expect us to wave a magic wand," agreed Nicola, smiling. "I know what they're like!"

"So that is why I rang your agency! Your suggestion for a menu was fantastic, by the way. I adore *boeuf en croute*. Are you sure you can manage it in this kitchen?"

Nicola grinned. "Oh, the *boeuf en croute* is already cooked. I did that in my own oven at home and brought it with me—I shall re-heat it in time to serve it. Don't worry, it will taste fine. I have it wrapped in foil." She began to unpack her basket, hoping that Mrs Christiansen would take the hint and leave her to get on with her tasks.

But the other girl was clearly bored and lonely. She leaned against the door, watching Nicola curiously. "Carl is asleep, and I only have to change. Can I do anything to help?"

Nicola shook her head. "No, thank you, I can manage. We have certain tricks of the trade, you know—corner-cutting! The soup is in this screw-top flask, you see, already prepared. Here is the paté, and here are the fresh sardines. I have to cook the vegetables—all freshly bought, and they will taste delicious, I assure you. Some of them are prepared for cooking, too. It all saves time."

Mrs Christiansen laughed. "You have it worked out to the last item, don't you? I wish I could be as efficient. I'm a hopeless housewife. I can't cook. I panic if the baby sneezes. And I hate ironing."

Nicola hesitated, then glanced at her. "You don't have any help in the flat?"

The other girl flushed. "Yes, I have a daily help. But I would like to be able to do it myself." She paused, biting her lip. "I married straight from school. My husband has been moved three times during our married life—we have lived in Rio, in Milan and here in London. It is much easier to get domestic help abroad than it is here in England."

"So I've heard," said Nicola crisply. She was working while she talked, her slim hands deft and efficient, her clear-skinned face bearing just the faintest flush. The silky dark hair was worn casually tied at the nape of the neck by a ribbon, to keep it out of her way while she worked. "How did you like Italy?"

"Italy?" The other girl laughed involuntarily. "Why, I . . ." She broke off as the door bell pinged. "Oh, sorry—I must answer that!"

Nicola sighed with relief as the door shut behind her. At last she could get on with her work without feeling bound to talk. She worked much better when she could concentrate.

The meal was almost ready for serving when the hostess finally returned to the kitchen. Nicola was standing by the oven, surveying the various pots with a thoughtful eye, doing a last-minute check on everything.

"How is it going?" Mrs Christiansen stood in the doorway, her coral evening dress giving a delightful new colour to her skin. She had an excited sparkle in her dark eyes and a curve to her lips.

"I'm ready when you are," Nicola smiled. She had slipped a frilly white apron over her neat black dress, transforming herself into a waitress.

The other girl sighed. "That's wonderful! My husband will be so pleased! Our last dinner party was a complete fiasco—it started an hour late and was uneatable—the food, I mean!" She looked eagerly at the simmering soup. "I checked the dining-room just now. It looks marvellous. I really do admire your cool efficiency—by the way, what is your name? Please, call me Carla."

"I'm Nicola." She smiled warmly, feeling a sudden liking for the other girl. This eager, pleasant manner was such a change from the way in which she was often treated by the people who hired her services. Some people seemed to think that she was a sort of robot, a machine without feeling or intelligence, who would not have the sensitivity to know when she was being snubbed or insulted. "Shall I serve now, then?"

"Please! I'll go and ask the guests to move through into the dining-room. Good luck!" And Carla vanished with a last cheerful smile.

There were six guests seated in the charming dining-room when Nicola entered, pushing her wheeled trolley before her. The host sat at the furthest end of the table, facing her as she entered. She had a brief impression of fair hair, beard and bronzed face above the usual evening clothes. The others sat, three to a side, male and female alternately. The tall, twisty red candles gave a gentle glow to their faces. The mellow light glinted on silver and glass, chequered the mixed carnations in the centre of the table, making the white ones dark.

The conversation died briefly, then began again, rather too consciously.

Nicola began serving the soup, then went round the table again with sardines to those who had refused soup. No one wanted the paté. She withdrew quietly with her trolley and re-loaded it with the main course, with an alternative of salad on the lower deck. Guests sometimes ruined these parties by being difficult over some dishes and she usually found it useful to have a salad available, with egg mayonnaise or prawns in reserve.

Tonight everyone chose to have the beef, smoking hot and tender in its envelope of pastry. The fresh, well-cooked vegetables were abundant; baby carrots, peas, new potatoes, all served in butter.

While she was serving a young woman with short, light hair she felt herself under observation, and shooting a glance across the table met the eyes of the man opposite.

He, like his host and hostess, had a beautiful deep tan, but he had the advantage of having a sallow skin to begin with, and dark hair which was sleeked down now but which had a springy, ruffled look at the back which, she suspected, was his usual look when he did not remember to brush his hair down firmly. The eyes which met hers were a clear, cool grey. They were assessing her impersonally from beneath well-shaped dark brows. Seeing the instinctive resentment which sprang into her own eyes, the stranger half-smiled, a curiously amused movement of the corners of his mouth.

Nicola glanced quickly away and went on with her task, but she had a vaguely uneasy feeling that she had seen him somewhere before.

When she had finished serving the beef, Carla Christiansen smiled at her. "Thank you, Nicola!"

She smiled back, then, as she was backing her trolley out of the door, once more caught the grey-eyed stranger staring. His expression now was unreadable, but she again felt a flicker of uneasiness as the same sense of familiarity filled her.

Had she met him before? But where? At some other dinner party, perhaps? In the last year she had served at so many. It was impossible to recall all the faces of the guests, although her memory for faces and names was usually excellent.

Why did this one man fill her with a strange foreboding? She was not given to such fanciful feelings, normally.

When she returned with the cold dessert, a choice between a sherry trifle and fresh fruit salad and cream, she felt a pang of further alarm to hear some of the guests speaking in rapid Italian.

Of course, it was nonsense to let that disturb her. London was full of Italians. Sooner or later she had been bound to run into some. There was no reason why any of them should recognise her.

Nevertheless, it was with deep relief that she finally cleared the table and began the washing up. This task, too, she had well organised. Some of it had already been done, in the intervals between courses, by the simple expedient of soaking the dishes in hot water so that they were easy to wash.

She had almost finished when the kitchen door opened. She glanced round, expecting Mrs Christiansen.

It was the grey-eyed stranger.

"Good evening," he said in perfect English. "I hope I'm not intruding, but I wanted to have a word with you before you left."

"I'm sorry," Nicola said stiffly, "I'm very busy. If the meal was not satisfactory..."

He cut her short with a gesture, his eyes narrowing at her tone. "The meal was superb. That is nothing to do with what I have to say. Correct me if I'm wrong, but..."

A face appeared at his elbow and Mrs Christiansen interrupted him, her voice rising in astonishment.

"Domenico? What *are* you doing in the kitchen?" Then she gave an amused smile. "Or am I being indiscreet?"

For a moment, the stranger seemed to hesitate, his face blank. Then he laughed. "I was congratulating your cook on that amazing meal—remembering other meals I have eaten under your roof, my dear Carla!"

Now, as these two spoke to each other, Nicola could hear the faint echo of an Italian accent beneath their perfect English. It sounded most clearly when they spoke each other's names.

"Go back to the others, Nico! I have matters to discuss with Nicola now." Carla shooed him casually, as a mother shoos a child, her face full of affection. He obeyed her, smiling, but turned before closing the door to look sharply at Nicola.

"I don't know how to thank you," Carla said gratefully. "You have made the evening a great success. My husband's business friends were impressed. I have no doubt I shall be bombarded with questions about you! Tell me, do you find this work rewarding? You like cooking?"

"I love it," Nicola smiled.

"But do you work every evening?"

"Most evenings, yes."

"Do you not find that a burden sometimes? Wouldn't you rather work during the day? At a hotel, for instance? Or a good London restaurant?"

"Most really good London restaurants and hotels prefer to engage men. Women, oddly enough, are at a disadvantage at that level of the catering trade. I like to work in private homes, to meet people. And working for the agency I can pick and choose my times of work. I can always ask for a week off without becoming too unpopular. Sometimes I don't work for days, then I work every night for several weeks. The money evens up in that way."

"You are not married, of course?" Carla sighed.

Nicola's face was pale. "No," she said flatly.

Carla misread her tone. "Oh, I'm sorry—am I being too impertinent? To be honest, I took a liking to you on sight, and my guests are more business acquaintances of my husband than friends of mine—apart from Nico, of course," and again her face lit up as she said his name.

Nicola watched her curiously. She seemed strangely attached to the grey-eyed Domenico. Were they related? Or old friends?

Carla moved back to the door. "I shall tell the agency how pleased I am when I pay them. Would it offend you if I gave you a tip?"

"It is very kind of you, but tips have to go into a common pool. Thank you for offering—please add it to your cheque when you pay."

"It seems so impersonal," Carla said wistfully. Impulsively she unclasped a very pretty bracelet from her wrist and offered it to Nicola. "It is only costume jewelry, of course. Please, keep it as a memento. We shall be leaving London quite soon, going back to Italy. It will suit you. The green stones bring out the colour of your eyes."

Nicola was touched. "How very kind! Thank you. I shall treasure it."

She left early, half afraid that Domenico would come back once Carla had rejoined her guests, and hurried home. It was just striking eleven by the hall clock as she let herself into the flat she shared with her sister, Vanessa, and her school-friend, Bess Walsh.

Both of them were in bed. Vanessa was always in

bed by ten-thirty. She was a fashion model, at present much sought after by photographers because her elegantly feline features somehow fitted the modern scene. Vanessa's life was ruled by laws more unalterable than those of the Medes and the Persians. Ruthlessly she forced herself to rise at seven. A leisurely bath was followed by a breakfast of orange juice and black coffee. Then she spent an hour getting dressed. She left for work punctually, worked long, arduous hours, and ate only as much as would preserve the breath of life, without adding an ounce of flesh to her slender body.

Tall, perfectly poised, with blonde hair curled in tight, abundant little ringlets, her blue eyes were fringed by long, false black lashes which deepened the blue to violet in some lights.

Bess was curved and small, with huge brown eyes, rather like the centre of a pansy, and masses of soft, silky-brown hair to match. She was Nicola's oldest friend. They had been at school together from the age of five upwards, and had progressed side by side through high school, and on to the same domestic science college later.

Only after they had both completed their education did they part for a while, but the parting had been brief, although, on Nicola's side, it had been deeply influential. Those six months apart from Bess had been the most eventful of her life. When she met Bess again she felt she was a different person, and she had been grateful for Bess's kindness and sympathy at that time.

Bess was not a sponge, soaking up tears, however,

or a cushion on which to lean. She was sturdy, sensible, full of calm common sense, and immeasurably reassuring when one was unhappy.

She had decided to teach, on qualifying in domestic science, and she found it satisfying to show others how to do the things she did so well, herself.

She had been teaching at a local school for the last three years. Nicola depended on her, for support and help, but recently she had begun to wonder how much longer she would be able to do so. Bess had become increasingly friendly with one of the other teachers, a friendly, quiet man who taught mathematics. They were neither of them demonstrative people, but Nicola suspected that they were growing very close.

Even Vanessa, rarely observant where other people were concerned, had said the other day, "Bess is beginning to smell of orange blossom. We shall have to find a new flatmate."

Flatmates were easy to find, but where would Nicola find another reliable babysitter for Paul?

She tiptoed into the bedroom she shared with him. A faint light shone beside his cot. He lay, curled on his side, a pink hand against his cheek, lips apart, lashes thickly clustered on his curved cheek.

The dark hair, golden skin and fine features were all so poignantly familiar. She stood, looking down at him, sighing. He grew more like his father every day! Sometimes she wondered if she could bear it, and at other times she knew that he was healing scars inflicted by love and loss, gently burying bitter memories beneath fresh ones of joy and delight.

She could never bear to lose him! She turned, on an impulse, and went softly back to the shared sitting-room of the flat. She dialled a number, standing in the dark. It rang for a long time, but at last someone picked up the receiver, and a cross, sleepy voice asked, "Yes, who is this?"

"Drew, it's Nicky."

"Nicky? Good lord, girl, do you know what time it is? You know I go to bed early during the week!"

"I'm sorry, but it was urgent," she said.

"Did something ghastly happen at your booking? Nicky, you weren't molested? I've always been afraid of something like that..."

"No, Drew. It..."

"You burnt the dinner? Did they blow their tops? I'll defend you, my dear. Don't get excited..."

"Drew, will you *listen*?"

He took a long breath, laughed. "Sorry, *mea culpa*! Speak, I am all ears."

"All tongue, you mean!"

"Darling, so beastly!"

"Drew, stop interrupting! Listen, if anyone asks for my name and address you won't give it to them, will you? No matter what they say?"

There was a little silence. She could picture him, his eyes narrowed in intelligent conjecture, his honey-coloured hair ruffled from sleep. Drew was far too shrewd for concealment to be possible.

"Darling," he drawled at last, "you know it's a house rule—Christian names only. No surnames or addresses. I've always stuck rigidly to it, haven't I?"

"Yes, I know," she admitted. "But..."

"This time it's different?" His voice was thought-ful. "How very interesting. Why, exactly? Who's on your trail? Thwarted lover? Jilted old flame?"

"Neither," she said crisply. "I think I'll take a few days off, Drew. Can you cancel any bookings you've taken for me?"

"I'll take a look in the book tomorrow. Call in early in the morning, will you? I'll pay you and confirm that you're free for a while."

Nicola rang off and wearily went into the bath-room to wash and clean her teeth. It was almost mid-night by the time she finally fell into bed.

She dreamt of Paolo, following him endlessly through dark mazes of dreams, where his slim figure seemed always just out of reach, yet tantalisingly close. Once he turned to look back and smile at her, but his features dissolved in a sickeningly elusive fashion, and she found herself staring at the face of the grey-eyed stranger she had met earlier that night. She woke, sobbing in bitter disappointment, to hear Paul calling her.

"Mummy . . . up! Up *now*, Mummy! Want up now . . ."

It was just seven-thirty. She felt heavy-eyed and dull. She lifted Paul from his cot and took him through into the bathroom. Vanessa was just drifting out of it, leaving the room heavily scented and the windows steamy.

Vanessa kissed Paul, gave her sister a vague smile and vanished in the direction of the kitchen, her brief white towelling robe making her look like an elegant boy with long brown legs.

Bess had already prepared Paul's breakfast when Nicola carried him into the kitchen. His orange juice stood on the tray of his chair beside a boiled egg which was keeping warm beneath a vivid yellow egg-cosy in the shape of a felt chicken.

Paul silently set to, being an eager trencherman, and while he was busy with his egg Nicola sat down to nibble a slice of thin toast.

"An egg would do you good," said Bess, eyeing her. "You look wan this morning. Sickening for a cold?"

She shook her head. "Bad night."

"Paul's teeth?"

"No, just my own thoughts," said Nicola.

"What's wrong?" Bess looked worried.

"Nothing, really. I think I need a break. I've done a lot of late work recently. I've asked Drew for some time off."

Bess nodded. "Good idea. Paul should be old enough for the nursery school soon—then you could get a part-time job during the daytime."

When Nicola arrived at the agency office Drew greeted her with a broad grin.

"I've had two inquiries already, ducky—one from a man with a very deep voice. I choked him off, and he didn't protest too much. Soon afterwards I got a call from the woman who hired you last night. She wanted your address so that she could thank you personally, she said, but I refused. She tried to insist, but it did her no good, so she rang off, too. She wanted to book you again, she said, for tonight. I told her you were otherwise engaged for the next week."

"Thank you, Drew. I'm very grateful." Nicola was conscious that she was trembling, and she hoped that her voice was not too betraying.

Drew looked at her closely. "Now, do tell—what is it all about, darling? The feller, I could understand. But why the female?"

"It's too complicated," she said quickly.

He gave her a cheque and a duplicated statement. "These are the jobs you've done. This is your share of the tips . . ." He explained the various details briefly, and she thanked him as she put the cheque away.

The telephone rang just as she was leaving, and Drew took her hand to detain her with a silent gesture.

He spoke in a tone which told her that this was a highly valued client. When he had put the telephone down, he grimaced at her. "Sorry, ducky, that was the Countess of Navestock—she wants you to cook for her tonight—a very important dinner for two. She asked for you by name, so I could hardly refuse. She always praises you to the skies."

"For two? But she always has her own maid for small meals. It's only for the big formal occasions that she calls us in, usually!"

"Her maid is off sick, apparently. Food poisoning, no doubt." Drew laughed. "Nicky dear, I'm sorry. I can't afford to offend her, though, especially as she always mentions us to her friends. I've had a dozen clients, at least, through her dropping our name. That sort of word of mouth advertising is worth gold."

She sighed. "I suppose so. All right, Drew, I'll do it. What menu, did she say?"

"She leaves it to you. Buy it and bring it with you. Expense no object."

"Something really special?"

"I gathered so! Enjoy yourself for once—cook your favourite recipes."

Nicola found the idea vaguely appealing. It would certainly make a change to cook a small meal really superbly.

She pushed Paul in his pushchair down to her favourite shops and bought various ingredients. Then she rang Bess at the school to ask if she would be able to babysit again that night. She had a rota of sitters for when Bess and Vanessa were both out, but it would need time to organise it.

Bess was free, and curious about the Countess. "Is she entertaining a lover, perhaps?"

"She's seventy years old," Nicola laughed.

"So what? There's no age limit, is there? It's time you found yourself another man, Nicky. You're stiffening at the mental joints."

Nicola did not answer. Pain stabbed suddenly, making her dumb with anguish.

"Oh, Nicky, I'm sorry," Bess said impulsively. "I should have held my tongue, but I can't help feeling that you must put the past behind you one day, and the longer you put it off the harder it will be for you."

"It's probably the correct attitude," Nicola said angrily. "I've no doubt I'm a psychological mess! But it's one thing to talk about it, another thing to do it."

"Nicky, he's dead! He'll never come back!" Bess spoke gruffly, conscious of the bitterness she must be causing.

"I know he's dead!" Nicola's voice broke. "I never forget it for an instant."

"But you don't believe it—not believe it in an accepting way, Nicky. You're hanging on to him all the time, aren't you? You won't let him go."

"Bess, you don't understand . . ." Nicola swallowed hard, then said more calmly, "I must go now. See you later."

Paul was asleep when she left the flat that evening. She found her way to the Countess's adorable little Chelsea house, which was only a stone's throw from their own flat, and rang the door bell.

When the door opened her heart missed a beat and turned over. The man who had opened the door was the grey-eyed stranger, Domenico.

Instinctively, without thinking, Nicola turned for flight. His hand shot out and caught her wrist. His fingers were long, cool and very strong.

"It isn't any good," he said gently. "I recognised you at once. I saw a photograph of you once. I was certain you were that girl with long dark hair and a face lit by a million candles . . ." He had dropped into Italian, fluent and easy, knowing that she would comprehend him.

She tried to pretend, shaking her head. "I'm sorry . . . what did you say?"

But she knew it was hopeless, and so did he, his smile faintly sardonic.

"You and I are related, you see." He shrugged.

"Paolo was my cousin! A second cousin only, but I knew him from birth upwards. He told me many things about you, Nicola. He was very much in love with you."

Hot, blinding tears sprang to her eyes. She pulled at her hand to free it from his grip. "Let me go! I want no part of your family. The Farenze family ignored my existence while Paolo was alive. They sent no one to his funeral. I only want to forget them now." She kicked his ankle hard and fled, taking advantage of his momentary surprise. There was an alley running behind the houses and she ducked into it, hiding in the shadow of a crooked, ill-grown lime tree beside the crumbling wall. His footsteps came hastily towards the alley, paused as he glanced along it, then went hurriedly past up the road.

CHAPTER TWO

WHEN the sound of Domenico's footsteps had died away, Nicola walked slowly out of the alley, tears spilling down her cheeks. A cat in one of the hidden gardens gave a long, ear-splitting scream which made her jump. A car drove past, its headlights piercing the darkness, making her momentarily blind.

She jumped and gave a terrified gasp as a figure stepped out of the shadows and seized her arm firmly.

"You're going to have to speak to me sooner or later, Nicola. Why not get it over with?"

She sighed slowly, in resignation, and said icily, "Very well, as you're so persistent, but I would prefer it if you would call me Miss Mayfield."

"Why do you call yourself by your maiden name? Are you ashamed of Paolo's name?"

"I want nothing to do with his family—I prefer to forget that he was a Farenze." She wanted to sound dignified, yet was uneasily afraid that she merely sounded ungracious.

"And so you have cut your husband out of your memory?" The deep voice was stern.

"Hardly that. I loved Paolo. His name was irrelevant to that love."

"A man is what his past has made him, and the Farenze family made Paolo," said Domenico quietly.

"He cut himself free from them," she cried indignantly. "After he had come here to England, he felt finally emancipated from the shackles of your family history. For most of his life the family attempted to bind him. Only by escaping from Italy altogether could he find himself."

"Is that what he told you?" asked Domenico thoughtfully, guiding her back to the Countess's house.

"Yes, Paolo told me the whole truth. We were very close." Her voice quivered and she lifted her chin defiantly.

Domenico closed the front door and turned to face her in the soft light of the chandelier which hung above them. His grey eyes were speculative. "I sometimes think it is a tragic error that the English do not go into strict mourning for the dead. This stiff upper lip of yours is not always a good idea. You are clearly still trapped in the web of grief. You speak of Paolo as though he were transparent as glass."

"To me he was!"

He shook his head. "No. He was an Italian, subtle and delicate, yet strong as the thread of the silkworm. Paolo certainly spoke the truth to you—the truth you wished to hear. But what of all the other truths, those truths you did not wish to hear? Are they not equally true?"

She looked at him without comprehension. "What are you talking about? Do you deny that your family wished to own Paolo, to force him to do their bidding? That after he had broken away, met me and we were married, they refused to write to him in acknowledgment of his news? That they never wrote to him again?"

Gravely he shrugged his broad shoulders, in a silent, Italianate gesture. After he had hesitated for a moment, he said, "These are one picture of the facts. Yes, it is true that the family wished Paolo to obey. His father is an old man—he was fifty when Paolo was born. It is hard for the old to understand, to communicate with the young. Paolo was the younger of two sons. The elder was to inherit most of the estate. It is stupid to divide and thus to weaken. Paolo, his father desired, should marry one of his cousins, a wealthy heiress. Thus he, too, would be provided for, would be safe. But Paolo refused— worse, he left home. His father was angry, was heartbroken."

"Heartbroken? Do you expect me to believe that? After what happened?"

"Please, wait. Judge when you know more. There is much you do not understand. Paolo wrote to say he had married. Whom, the family eagerly demanded, had he chosen—this Paolo who had refused a wealthy heiress? Can you imagine their feelings when they heard that he had chosen . . . a cook? A servant?"

"Of all the snobbish . . .!" Nicola choked with bitter humiliation. "So that's why? I wasn't good enough for the Farenze family?"

"Paolo did not explain that that was why they were so angry?"

"He only said that they'd wanted him to marry for money, not love," she said, her eyes flashing. "Paolo told me the truth, as I said. He only left out the most wounding part of the truth. He didn't want me to know they had rejected me personally."

He had been speaking in Italian. Now he reverted to English, and spoke more rapidly. "His father might have forgiven him in time had he not been taken ill, himself, soon after your marriage. The shock caused a stroke. He did recover, slowly, but when your telegram arrived informing the family of Paolo's death, his father was still desperately ill. It was thought better to keep the news from him for the time being, but I was under the impression that someone wrote to you with the family sympathy. Surely wreaths were sent?"

"Nothing," she said coldly. "Paolo went to his grave with no mourners but myself and my family."

"I do not understand that," he said, frowning. "There must have been a mistake. I was certain . . ." He broke off, shrugging. "Well, that must wait. There are other things to discuss. Paolo was not the only loss for his father. Three months ago Paolo's brother, Cesare, died of a tropical disease, while he was in Africa on a sales mission."

"I'm sorry," she said stiffly. "He was married, wasn't he? Did he have children?"

"No, there were no children. His wife died in childbirth a year ago. The child died, too. She was a delicate little creature, poor Luciana."

"So the Farenze estate passes to . . . who?" Nicola was pale and suddenly alarmed. Did he know, had he found out, about Paul? She had never considered the legal question before, knowing that Paolo had had nothing to leave his son. But now, with the Farenze estate possibly his inheritance, what should she do?

She wanted nothing to do with Paolo's family. She had deliberately omitted to inform them of Paul's birth. She had wanted no part of the Farenze family, and she had suspected that, if they knew she expected a child, they might attempt to interfere, even, perhaps, to try to make some legal claim for the child.

Now her doubts remained, but her fears were deeper. Paul was English, was hers. His father's family should have no part of him.

Domenico was speaking casually. "There is no direct heir now. No doubt Lorenzo will decide when he makes his will—so far he has refused to make one."

"But until he does? Who would succeed?"

"I fancy I am the nearest male heir," Domenico shrugged.

She looked at him curiously. He appeared indifferent, but was he? From a few things which Paolo had said, she imagined that the Farenze fortune was enormous.

He looked down at her, his grey eyes smiling. "Now, we have cleared away some of the tangled wood of the past, haven't we? Perhaps now you will consider my request."

"Oh, you wanted me to cook dinner for you and the Countess?" She was deliberately obtuse, her tone bland. "Where is the Countess, by the way?"

"She was kind enough to act for me in this little plot," he said with a grin. "As you long ago suspected! And what I have to ask you is nothing to do with dinner . . . I want you to fly back to Italy with me this week, to see Paolo's father."

"Never!" Her voice shook with burning indignation. "No, never!"

He looked down at her sternly, his brows drawn together in a reproachful frown. "He is an old man, soon to die. He has lost both his sons, and, whatever you may think of him, they were beloved sons. Why will you not grant him one small act of charity?"

"What charity did he and his family show me?" Nicola winced as she thought of Paul. She could lose him if she allowed the powerful Farenze clan to discover his existence. She must not permit them to suspect that there was a child. She turned on her heel. "No, I'm sorry, it's impossible. Goodnight."

He did not pursue her. She glanced back as she turned the corner, but there was no sign of him. But she was glad when she was back in the safety of the flat, despite the difficulty of fencing with Bess, who was bursting with questions at this sudden early return.

She rang Drew next day and told him that she had not cooked for the Countess after all. "It was not required," she added calmly.

"Aha!" Drew was instantly alert. "So the Countess was in the plot, eh? I am positively dying of curiosity, you know, my sweet. Won't you tell? It isn't the Mafia, is it?"

"Something along those lines," she said flippantly.

"No! Really?" Drew was half fascinated, half incredulous.

"I'm kidding," she said, and switched the subject for a few moments, before ringing off.

Each morning she awoke with a feeling of nervous anticipation. She hardly dared to go outside the front door in case she bumped into Domenico Farenze. But day succeeded day, and she saw no sign of him, and gradually her fears were lulled.

He had said that he was flying back to Italy soon. Surely, she thought, as she did the shopping a week later, he must have left England by now. She could relax again. He would have been in touch somehow if he had not accepted her word as final. He had had the look and manner of a man who acts decisively. Since he had not contacted her again she might assume that he had dismissed her from his memory.

The Farenze family, after all, had never shown any interest in Paolo's wife before. It was doubtful if they felt any now. Domenico Farenze had, presumably, acted on a sudden whim when he invited her to visit the Farenze home in Italy. He could not have been serious in believing that old Lorenzo Farenze could have any real desire to see his dead son's widow.

Well, he must be forgotten now, Nicola told herself, smiling down at Paul as she pushed him along, singing to himself in a tuneless voice.

The sunshine was fragile, falling like the petals of a yellow rose on the rooftops and chimneys of London. Every now and then a passing cloud eclipsed the sun and the streets grew dull again. Then the cloud moved, and the faint gleams of gold re-awoke on the shop windows, the chrome of cars, the gently fluttering leaves of the plane trees.

As she turned to cross the road her heart was seized and twisted with fear. A tall, dark man was standing on the other side, staring across at her. Her vision was clouded briefly. Then her heart resumed its normal rhythm and she saw clearly. It was a total stranger.

The experience left its mark, however. She saw that, from now on, she would never be free of fear. Even if Domenico Farenze had returned to Italy by now, he might appear in London at any time. What if he visited the flat? Discovered the existence of her son?

She looked down at Paul's dark head in a passion of grief. They must never know about him. She knew enough about the family to know that they would attempt to gain possession of the boy—their money could buy them lawyers who would use every trick in the legal book on their behalf.

She wondered if she should visit a solicitor. She did not know enough about the law to know her rights. Could they do anything? Surely a mother, a widow, was safe enough. An English court would never allow a child to be taken away from its English mother—and, for all that his father had been Italian, Paul was English, for he had been born here, and registered as the child of a British subject.

All the same, she could not vanquish the fears which possessed her.

She had very little money, and the Farenzes were

wealthy. They had weapons which could be dangerous.

I must vanish again, she told herself. I'll leave London, take Paul into the country. She had sometimes looked at advertisements for a housekeeper which stated that one child would be accepted. She could find a job like that, take Paul with her.

What about Vanessa? She bit her lip. She was very fond of her sister. But if Vanessa, if anyone, knew where she had gone, it would be dangerous. Reluctantly, at the very back of her mind, she was aware that she suspected Vanessa of being slightly unreliable. Her sister was capable of spite, of occasional acts of dishonesty—not in the crude sense of stealing, but in the personal sense of breaking her word or deliberately performing some mean act. Vanessa, if she was bribed in some subtle way, might possibly tell the Farenzes about Paul. Nicola had several times been hurt in the past when her sister did such things. She could not afford to trust Vanessa this time. Once Vanessa knew about the Farenze fortune which awaited Paul, she might be tempted.

She bought several magazines and took them back to the flat. She cooked Paul's lunch and fed him. Then, while he played on the floor with his dog on wheels, Spotty, she sat down with a cup of coffee and studied the advertisements for housekeepers.

Several seemed interesting. She ringed two of them in red and began a hunt for writing paper. Paul had got tired of Spotty and began to bang on his old saucepan with a wooden spoon, chanting loudly.

Someone rang the door bell. Nicola glanced at her

watch. The baker? She found her purse and went to the door, Paul toddling at her heels with his saucepan precariously waving around his head.

She opened the door and then went white, her fingers clutching at the handle so that the metal burnt against her skin.

Domenico Farenze stared past her at the child, then his brows jerked together in a straight, black line.

Paul tugged at her skirt. "Up, Mummy . . . up?"

Automatically she bent to pick him up, her arms clutching him convulsively.

He wriggled. "Too tight . . ." Imperiously, his small face a faint echo of the frown which Domenico Farenze wore, he smacked her softly, rebuking her.

Domenico reached out towards him, lifted him firmly from her arms, ignoring Nicola's cry of bitter protest.

He held him away a little, studying him. The boy stared back in unconscious mimicry.

They were oddly alike. She saw the resemblance even as she resented it. No wonder Domenico had seemed familiar when she first saw him . . . he was the positive image of her own son, although Paul was so small and young. The softness of Paul's baby face would one day toughen into this strong, powerful mask.

"Paolo's eyes, his nose and jaw . . ." Domenico spoke softly, but anger burnt in every syllable.

She was silent. Their eyes met. He was, she saw, as pale as herself . . . but his pallor was the result of rage.

One of the women who lived on the floor above came past, staring curiously at them. Domenico, catching her sideways look, waited until she had gone, then said, "Must we discuss this out here? Am I not to be admitted? You can have no further reason for keeping me away from your home."

Nicola stepped back to permit him to enter the flat. He carried Paul into the sitting-room and sat down on a chair, with the child on his lap.

It was galling that the child so obviously found him fascinating. Galling—and astonishing. In the past Paul had been known to scream at the very sight of a strange man. Many of Vanessa's escorts had fled, shaking, after an encounter with Paul, and Vanessa had often complained bitterly about Paul's hostility towards her boyfriends.

Domenico Farenze, however, apparently found favour in the child's sight. Paul was busy inspecting every inch of this interesting newcomer; peering into his ears, lifting his collar to inspect his tie, fingering the gold watch on his tanned wrist and gently touching the dark hairs on the back of Domenico's hands.

Domenico allowed the child to inspect him while he spoke, in a calm voice calculated not to alarm the boy, to Nicola.

"How old is he?"

"He's two," she admitted.

The dark brows lifted. "He was born after Paolo's death, I gather?"

She nodded.

"You did not see fit to tell his family that you were expecting a child?" The tone was withering.

"If any of his family had been sufficiently interested to come over to his funeral they would have seen for themselves. Paul was born a month later."

"Paul?" The voice softened on the name, and the boy raised his head to give an abstracted smile, returning at once to his scrutiny of the watch.

Domenico looked at her sharply. "You had no right to keep his birth a secret from his father's family!"

"They ignored me, why should I think they would be interested in my child?" Nicola stressed the possessive "my", looking at him with bitter eyes.

"You knew that we would be interested," Domenico said calmly.

She laughed angrily. "Only because he was a useful tool in your ambitions for the Farenze family! Do you think I wanted my child to get involved with all that stupid plotting, to be used by his grandfather as a pawn in some money game?"

"Ah!" Domenico shook his head. "You resent the money?"

"I resent the way in which it's allowed to dominate your lives. I don't want that for my son."

"You have no choice," Domenico said softly.

Fear held her silent for a few seconds, then she swallowed and said hurriedly, "Paul will never have anything to do with the Farenzes. I shall make certain of that. He is English, he was born in this country. He is my son—I'm his only legal guardian. There is nothing the Farenze family can do about that."

Domenico shrugged. "We shall see. We will get

the best lawyers. Paul, after all, is the son of an Italian, and now the heir to a great fortune. I think his grandfather will fight for him. I know Lorenzo. Once he knows of Paul's existence he will want to have him brought to the Villa, to have him brought up as an Italian."

"He is English," she insisted.

The grey eyes held hers. Did she imagine it, or was there a glint of pity in them? "Would Paolo, his father, have said so?"

The question was like a blow to the heart. She stared at him, wide-eyed and white-faced. He stared back in silence, watching her closely.

When she had first met Paolo one of the things which had drawn her to him had been his Italian gaiety, the charm and warmth which shone out of his face. He had been eager for a family, ecstatic when he knew she was going to have a child. She recalled, now, with a pang, how often Paolo had said that when the child had been born they would take it to Italy.

"*Cara*, we will take it to the Villa, to see the old Farenzes in the rain; the bronze statues of his ancestors, all green with age, as if they wept green tears down their long Roman noses."

Teasingly, she had said, "Him? What if the child is a girl?"

Paolo had laughed, wickedly. "Then I shall beat you and we shall try again, and that will be fun, too." But she had known from his smile that whether girl or boy, the child would be wanted. Paolo adored babies. He was so unlike Englishmen.

Where an Englishman ignored a pram in the street, Paolo would eagerly inspect the inhabitant, admiring it noisily, delighting and astonishing the mother.

The sound of a key in the latch made her jump. Paul looked up and shouted, "Tanty Van . . . Tanty Van!"

Vanessa, cross and weary after a long stint in the salons, paused in the door and hurriedly rearranged her face as she saw the stranger with her sister.

Domenico rose, a smile curling his mouth, and half bowed, waiting to be introduced.

"My sister, Vanessa Mayfield. Vanessa, this is Domenico Farenze."

Vanessa looked startled, then curious. She smiled at him, holding out a languid hand. "Related to Paolo, I gather? My sister is never very specific."

He took her hand and raised it to his lips, kissing it lightly with a faint gesture of amusement. "I am a second cousin—no closer than that, I'm afraid. Your family seems to produce beautiful girls, Miss Mayfield. Are there any more of you?"

"No, we are the only two samples," said Vanessa with amused pleasure. "But please, call me Vanessa."

"Tanty Van . . ." Paul murmured, tugging at Domenico's trouser leg in an attempt to re-establish ownership of this fascinating new friend.

Domenico grinned and picked him up, thus missing the flicker of irritation on Vanessa's beautiful face at Paul's nickname for her. She detested being called Van, and even Paul's age could not give him licence to use the loathed abbreviation.

When Domenico straightened, with Paul in his arms, Vanessa was all smiles again.

"Oh, Nicky love, I wonder if there's any salad in the fridge? I'm starving, but I'm so exhausted after work..." She gave her sister a sweet, trailing smile.

Nicola nodded, resigned, and vanished to prepare a light meal. She made a fresh pot of coffee at the same time. When she returned to the sitting-room, it was to find Vanessa leaning back against the cushions of the sofa with her blonde curls spilled like sunshine on the green silk.

Paul was seated at the little coffee table, building brick palaces with Domenico Farenze.

"Where will you eat the salad?" Nicola asked her sister.

"Oh, I'm too tired to move. I'll have it on a tray here, thank you, Nicky." Vanessa tilted her head to smile, looking even more like a Botticelli angel, her delicate features and pale complexion enhancing her fragility.

"Would you like some coffee, Mr. Farenze?" Nicola made her voice cool yet not hostile. She had been thinking hard in the kitchen, and she was beginning, for the first time, to have some slight doubts about her decision to bring Paul up ignorant of his Italian inheritance.

Domenico's remark about Paolo's love for his home country had gone to her heart. She had forgotten many things, obsessed with her resentment of his family.

Domenico glanced up at her. The sun struck in across the room, picking out coppery lights in the fine dark hair. Her eyes were pure, cat green as she looked back at him, slanting and bright with dislike.

He smiled mockingly. "Thank you. I would indeed like some coffee. Your coffee is excellent."

Nicola could not find fault with the words. It was the tone which pricked at her. She knew, obscurely, that he was making fun of her in some devious way of his own.

When she returned with the coffee she found Vanessa listening to him intently, picking at her salad in a desultory fashion. She had eaten the lettuce and tomato, but was leaving most of the pink ham. Vanessa had little appetite for meat or fish. She was practically a vegetarian.

Nicola poured the coffee and took them each a cup. When she had seated herself on a small pink brocade chair, Domenico glanced at Vanessa. "I have been telling your sister the background to my visit," he said softly.

Nicola tensed. "Oh?" She looked at her sister.

Vanessa did not quite meet her eyes. "You haven't been strictly honest with us, have you Nicky?"

The accusation took Nicola's breath away. After a pause, she asked indignantly, "What are you talking about?"

"You never told us that Paul was the heir to the Farenze estate! You allowed us to believe that Paolo left you penniless. We've been so sorry for Paul, poor fatherless little boy—and all the time you knew very well that the Farenzes would jump at the chance to help you. Why have you let Paul live in this little box of a flat when he could have had a wonderful home in Italy?"

"I've always paid my way," Nicola said in a quietly angry voice. "I've never borrowed money from either you or Bess, have I?"

"We've babysat for you hundreds of times, though! Without payment!" Vanessa hurriedly added, "Not that the money is really relevant, but our whole attitude to you was based on a lie. You told us nothing about Paolo's background, did you? You were always secretive, Nicky."

"Paolo was my husband. What else should I have told you?"

"Were you ashamed of his Italian connections?" Domenico bit the words out.

"They were ashamed of me," she retorted. "You seem to forget that! Paolo told them about our marriage, but they ignored me. I told them about his death, and they ignored me. Why on earth should I have tried again? I know when to give up."

"You were hurt," said Vanessa, jumping up to kiss her. "Your feelings were wounded . . . but now Domenico has come to make amends, to give Paul everything he needs . . . a home, toys, good school. A future to be proud of!"

Nicola pushed her coldly away. "This is none of your business, Vanessa. Paul is my son. If his relations want to see him they'll have to come to England to do so."

"How can you be so hard, so unjust?" Vanessa looked round at Domenico appealingly. "I suppose it's because she has had to toughen up to face the world, to make a living for herself and Paul. She had no other choice after Paolo's death."

"She has a choice now," Domenico said softly. "I want her to come to Florence, to the villa up in the hills of Tuscany, looking down over the vineyards and olives to the bright roofs of the greatest city of Italy. The Farenzes have lived there for hundreds of years. Paul is the last direct descendant of the old merchant princes of our house, and he must grow up in the ancestral home. His father's soul would desire it."

Vanessa breathed a long sigh. "Oh, Nicky, how can you hold out against that? You couldn't be so hardhearted!"

Nicola gave her a glance of pure irritation. Domenico intercepted that look and grinned, his eyes gleaming with deep amusement.

Paul looked up, curious at the sudden silence. Domenico knelt down beside him and smiled at the boy.

"Paul, would you like to come and pick ripe peaches from your own tree in a big garden? Would you like to splash in a fountain, throw pebbles from the top of a high, high tower down into a stream?"

Paul's eyes grew round. "Yes, now!" He lifted his arms to Domenico. "Go now!"

Domenico kissed him on the tip of his nose. "Not now, Paul, but very soon."

He looked round at Nicola, his grey eyes challenging. She stared back at him without answering, feeling the conflicting tug of different emotions—a desire to stay here, in the known security of England, and see Paul grow up here, and the new feeling, smothered and yet growing, that Paolo would have wished his son to grow up in Italy.

Almost pleadingly, she said, at last, "I only want to do what's best for Paul."

"I will book the seats for the first possible flight," Domenico said. He glanced at Vanessa. "I'm sure your sister will cope with any details which you have to leave unsolved."

CHAPTER THREE

When he had gone Vanessa gave Nicola a long, curious stare. "Are you out of your skull, darling? Turning down that sort of money? I wouldn't mind if you had any sort of future to offer Paul, but you're as poor as a church mouse and always will be! Why, even when you marry into a wealthy family you go out of your way to offend them."

"Paolo was brought up with all this wonderful background you've been telling me about," said Nicola. "He ran away from it!"

"Did he?" Vanessa laughed and shook her head. "He carried it around with him, Nicky. You know that—if you'll only be honest for one minute!"

Nicola stood still, staring at her. "What does that mean?"

Vanessa shrugged, the pale gold curls fluttering against her lifted hand as she began to brush her hair. "Paolo had the sort of manner money always gives you—arrogance..."

"He was not arrogant!" Nicola flared.

"Oh, it was courteous and gallant, but it was still arrogance. Domenico has the same manner." Vanessa shot her sister a long, thoughtful look. "You noticed that, didn't you?"

Nicola flushed. "Paolo was nothing like Domenico!"

"Domenico is more reserved, rather more impressive—he has an air of authority, although he disguises it with courtesy. Perhaps all Italians are like that—the iron hand in the velvet glove?"

Nicola laughed. She remembered Paolo, watching her with an appealing face when he had been out all day at the races after swearing never to gamble again. Vanessa just did not know what she was talking about.

"Don't judge by appearances," she said, a little forlornly. There had been other incidents in her brief married life which made her doubly wary now. She had told herself then, as she told herself now, that it had been the pernicious influence of his wealthy background which had so fatally weakened Paolo's character, and had killed him in the end.

Paul was never to be tempted in that way. He was to have a steady, sober British upbringing. Even a small child can learn to obey, to be polite, to be cheerful when he has to go to bed, instead of screaming to have his own way. Regular hours and quiet, gentle firmness were essential.

Nicola mentioned some of these points to Drew next day, when she called in to ask his advice, and he laughed helplessly.

"The British nanny to the rescue, eh? Character-building, if not empire-building? Nicky, you're a scream!"

"It isn't funny! I want Paul to be happy, and money seems to have the opposite effect."

"Rather depends on the quantity and who's dishing it out, surely?" Drew was as near to serious as he

ever achieved, his face wry. "I mean, obviously we
all need some money. We must eat. What you need,
Nicky, is a solicitor."

"What for?" She was puzzled.

"Advice, darling, advice!"

"I've told you—I don't want any money from the
Farenzes. I shall allow Paul to visit them for a short
time, then I'll bring him home again."

"Nicky, if you're wise, you'll call in a solicitor,
find out the legal position. If there are any doubts as
to the guardianship of the child, have them ironed
out before you go to Italy. Better to be safe than sorry."

"How can there be any doubts? He was born
here."

"Of an Italian father!"

"But his father is dead, and I'm his guardian
now."

"By English law, yes, but I'd check Italian law if I
were you. You don't want to run into any little local
difficulties, do you?"

She stared at him in alarm. "I suppose not. Yes,
I'll do that, Drew!"

She visited a solicitor immediately, and he listened
with interest to her story.

"Well, of course, there is little doubt as far as English law is concerned, and probably none in Italy,
either, but there may be some legal document concerning the inheritance which covers the possibility..."

"Would it be binding on me, though?"

"If your husband signed it, bequeathing his rights

in his heirs to some executor; for instance his father—then this might be a danger to you."

"What would it mean?" She was pale and alarmed.

The man shrugged. "I couldn't say, since I don't even know if such a document exists. It would be likely, in the case of a large estate, that some such document was drawn up, to protect the estate in the event of the control over the heir passing out of family hands."

"As it has?" She had a sudden premonition that this was more than just a vague possibility. Domenico had been so insistent, so sure of himself. "Can I be protected against it?"

"While you're on English soil, of course. Your custody of the child would be of paramount importance since you are his mother. No court would agree to separating you for a purely financial motive?"

"But if he was taken to Italy?"

"Without your consent? We could undoubtedly fight the case in the Italian courts."

"If I took him there myself? Once we were there, could he be taken away from me?"

"I'm sure not, but I could make certain of that, if you wish. I will ask for sight of any documents relating to the guardianship of the child before you agree to go to Italy."

"Would you do that?" She gave him Domenico's telephone number at his hotel in London. He rang at once and made an appointment to see Domenico.

Domenico came to visit Paul again next morning.

He gave Nicola a sharp look as she admitted him to the flat. "I've just seen your solicitor. A trusting little creature, aren't you?"

She flushed. "I don't trust you, or your family."

His lip curled scornfully. "And, despite all your brave talk, there is the question of the Farenze fortune to be investigated!"

Her eyes flashed. "I meant what I said—the money means nothing to me! I wouldn't touch a penny of Farenze money. I can earn everything I need. I'm a good cook." She eyed him with biting contempt. "I may not be socially acceptable to the Farenzes, but a good cook can always earn a living, especially these days, when good cooks are hard to find. There are twice as many jobs as there are applicants. I can live handsomely on what I earn."

"A long speech," Domenico drawled. "Methinks the lady doth protest too much!"

Paul looked from one to the other of them in dismay. He did not like raised voices and angry expressions. Like most children, he was sensitive to the atmosphere around him, and now he plucked at Nicola's skirt. "Mummy . . . Mummy!"

She looked down, saw his worried frown, and bent to pick him up in her arms. Forcing a bright smile, she said, "I'll make some coffee for our visitor, shall I, Paul? And cold milk for you?"

"Uncle . . ." Paul broke into relieved smiles, holding out his hand to Domenico. "Uncle, carry me!"

Domenico took him, raised him to his shoulders and let him ride there, crowing with delight and holding tightly to the thick dark hair.

As Nicola made the coffee, watching the two of them, she thought that it would have been like this if Paolo had lived. He would have been a doting, indulgent father.

Domenico caught her passing frown of pain, and misunderstood. Giving Paul his saucepan and spoon to play with in a corner, he said sharply, "Too bad you don't like to see me with the boy—you will have to get used to it. I intend to see a great deal of him from now on! I am the nearest thing he has got to an uncle."

"I wasn't even thinking about you," she cried. "I was thinking about . . ." Her voice broke and she turned away.

He caught her shoulders and spun her to face him, his fingers biting into her flesh. She stood, head bowed, tears burning in her eyes but unshed.

One hand roughly forced her chin up so that he could see her face clearly.

"Did you take a vow of perpetual widowhood?" His tone was cruelly mocking. Nicola stared at him in dislike.

"I don't expect you to understand!"

"Try me! I am not so lacking in perception!"

"Paolo was his father—a father who never saw him!" The tears fell, now, as the words expressed what she had only felt before. The salt stung her eyes, her skin, her lips. She felt a rending anguish, then a strange, drowning relief.

His hand came up again, a handkerchief firmly wiped her face, as if she was a child. She felt weak, her instinct was suddenly to lean upon him, cling to him. Her breath came raggedly. She could hear her heart beating faster.

Slowly, quiveringly, she glanced up at him through her lashes, and found his grey eyes fixed on her face. Cold anger hardened his face. He was frowning, his lips tight.

"I will not be a substitute for Paolo," he said icily.

She gasped. Her hand swung up, hit his cheek before he had had notice of her intention. His fingers caught her wrist, dug viciously, pulled her hand down against her side.

"You forget the child," he murmured between clenched teeth. "And next time you feel the need for a man, pick someone else." His eyes glinted angrily at her. "Someone who is too blind to realize that you are only looking for a pale imitation of what you had with your husband. No man of any spirit would marry a girl so obviously obsessed with a dead man, or permit himself to be used as a stand-in for another man."

"You . . . you . . ." Nicola stammered helplessly in her fury, the bitter depth of her humiliation. The fact that part of what he said was too painfully true made her anger with him worse. For a few weak moments she had almost abandoned her sense of reality, almost allowed herself to pretend that this dark stranger who looked so like Paolo was, truly, her dead husband. It had been a ridiculous piece of folly. She could not, now, even understand what had made her behave in such a degrading fashion.

She made the coffee in silence, poured him a cup and vanished into her own room, leaving him to play with Paul alone. In her room, she looked at herself in the mirror, saw the hair loose around her pale face, the tearstains on cheek and eyelid, the faint pink around her eyes.

She groaned. How could she have behaved like that? It was despicable.

She would never be able to forget it, never be able to forgive Domenico for having been quick enough to comprehend the emotions passing through her. He had been too clever, too perceptive.

He is dangerous, she thought angrily. How can I bear to see him, feeling that he reads my thoughts so easily?

She sank on to the bed, covering her face. It was humiliating to feel oneself so transparent.

Vanessa, surprisingly, arrived back home early, explaining that she had a slight headache and the salon was so stuffy. "I needed some air . . ."

"Did Madame Annette mind your leaving early?" Nicola was disturbed. Vanessa had been back early three times this week.

Domenico, stretched out on the sofa, his long legs crossed in front of him, stared mockingly at Vanessa as, a little pink-cheeked, she shook her head.

"I'll fix you a salad for lunch," Nicola said.

"Why don't I take you out somewhere?" Domenico asked lightly.

Nicola stood still, looking from one to the other. Vanessa gave a charming little start of surprise, laughed, bit her little finger as she pretended to consider the suggestion.

"That's very sweet of you—I eat so little!" She

fluttered her lashes at him, her Botticelli face full of gentle sweetness.

"I'll eat enough for both of us," he promised, a trifle dryly.

She giggled. "Well, thank you, then, Domenico! I'd love to have lunch with you."

Nicola walked abruptly into the kitchen. It suddenly occurred to her that this was just what Vanessa had been angling for—it was why she had come home early so often since Domenico started coming to the flat to see Paul.

Why didn't I realise before that Vanessa was interested in him? I'm a fool.

Was he interested in Vanessa, though? He was not a man one could read easily. That cool manner of his disguised far too much.

She began to prepare a salad for her own lunch. Paul had eaten his, and was taking his afternoon nap. He ate his lunch early. A sound behind her made her turn her head. Domenico lounged against the door.

He returned her cold glance. "To revert to our earlier discussion for a moment, I have put your solicitor in touch with our solicitor in London. They will sort this out between them. I have agreed that there be some sort of agreement that Paul is in your custody, and that Lorenzo and myself will not seek guardianship in any way during your lifetime. They'll draw up some document for us both to sign."

"And Lorenzo Farenze?"

"He will sign, too, of course."

"Have you been in touch with him yet? Does he know..."

"About Paul? Yes, I have spoken to him on the telephone. He was . . ." His voice broke off suddenly. He shrugged, lifting his shoulders in an alien gesture. After a moment he went on crisply, "Lorenzo had thought himself without descent—his sons dead without issue. Suddenly to hear that he had a grandson . . ."

She saw that he was striving to keep all emotion from his face and voice. Was he a man who distrusted emotion? Even feared it, perhaps?

"I hope he understands that Paul is not to stay in Italy for ever? I have not promised any more than that he may visit his grandfather. That is all."

He gave her a look as inflexible as steel, his mouth parted in a dry, sardonic smile. "We will cross these bridges when we come to them. Let the old man be happy for a while. My main fear was that, in giving him such news out of the blue, I might bring on a heart attack."

"Joy never kills anyone," she said flatly.

"You are a stranger to joy," he retorted, his glance mocking and scornful. "Hiding in the shadows of life, turning your face from the sun—how would you know anything about joy? If you were not a mother, you would doubtless have taken the veil." He moved closer, staring down at her. "Is there blood in your veins, you chilly little creature, or are you frozen for ever inside the green ice of those eyes of yours?"

The click of Vanessa's heels along the corridor made her jump back from him. She had been half hypnotised by the soft Italian voice—he had lapsed

into Italian while he spoke, and she suddenly realised that he used Italian whenever he was talking intimately. Was that because it was the language of his
heart, the tongue he heard inside his head even
when he spoke English? She herself spoke Italian
fluently. She had learnt it at school. It was her
knowledge of Italian which had brought her into
Paolo's life.

Paolo had been staying at the hotel in which she
was working during her last vacation at college. She
had taken a temporary summer job while waiting for
the results of her final examinations. Finding that
she spoke Italian quite well, the proprietor had used
her as an interpreter in cases of emergency.

One day Paolo had had a bowl of hot soup spilled
over his new suit in the dining-room. He had exploded into fountains of excitable Italian.

Baffled and horrified, the head waiter sent for Nicola from the kitchen. Prettily, dimpling and soothing, she had talked Paolo out of his rage. Faced with
a pretty young girl who spoke his language, he was
not difficult to calm.

She had dinner with him on her night off that
week. She walked with him in the mornings. He
wrote her ardent little notes. Their courtship had
been sudden, feverish and swept everything else out
of their heads.

Paolo cabled home that he was marrying her.
They waited for an answer, but all that came was a
brief, icy note telling him never to bring her back to
Florence. The family would never forgive him.

"My father does not even write himself," Paolo
said bitterly. "This is not his writing!"

"Perhaps we should wait," Nicola had murmured unhappily. "I don't want to come between you and your family, dearest."

Paolo had seized her in his arms. "You are all my family, now. My darling…"

That afternoon she was persuaded to give up her job. Paolo bought a special licence and they were married so soon that she barely had time to consider exactly what she was doing. They were both of age. There was no reason why they should wait, Paolo urged her. Blind with love, she followed him.

SHE SAT, staring out of the window, sunk in reverie, quite forgetting Domenico.

Vanessa joined him, slipped a hand into his elbow and looked up at him in surprise as he made no movement.

He was watching Nicola with eyes so cold that Vanessa looked almost alarmed. His lean dark face was as rigid as carved wood. The taut mouth and jaw, the clenched teeth, all spoke of icily controlled rage.

Vanessa was puzzled. What was wrong? She coughed, and he started. She saw a shutter slip down over the grey eyes. He turned slowly, gathering his wits, and gave her a smile.

"You look quite charming, my dear girl. A breath of spring—a true Primavera!"

She lifted bewildered blue eyes. "A true what?"

"You do not know the Botticelli painting? It is a painting of the essence of rebirth, of springtime; girls dancing in a wood, the Graces, nymphs in fragile gossamer dresses—and in the foreground, a girl like you, slender and graceful, with flowers strewn on her gown and in her golden hair! You must have seen it somewhere. It is one of the most famous paintings in the world." His voice had been warm with mellifluous Italian enthusiasm as he spoke, but Vanessa carefully noticed that his eyes watched her sister over her head.

Was he interested in Nicola? she pondered coolly. But if he was, why did he look so coldly at her? Had they just had a row? Yes, she decided, that was it. There had been an atmosphere you could cut with a knife whenever she had seen them together. They just did not hit it off.

Good thing, she decided thoughtfully. Nicky was not quite in her own class, perhaps, but she had a certain something. Vanessa wasn't quite sure exactly what it was that her sister did have—she only knew that it could be pretty potent at times. She had lost boys to Nicky in the past—and without Nicky apparently lifting a finger to achieve it.

This time it's different, she thought, as she and Domenico left. This man is different. I'm no longer as young as I would like to be—in my profession one is past it at twenty-five. I only have a few good years left in this business.

"What exactly do you do for a living?" She smiled up at him as she asked the question, softening the curtness of the words.

"I work in the business, of course," he said in some surprise.

"What business?" She frowned.

"Why, surely Paolo must have talked about it?"

Vanessa shrugged. "He talked about Italy, but never about your family."

Domenico's face tightened. "I see."

"Don't look so hurt," she said softly. "I think Paolo knew that Nicky hated to hear him talk about his home. She felt guilty because he had given it up for her."

"You think so?" He looked sharply at her.

"I'm sure of it. I know Nicky." She laughed softly. "I've known her all my life, after all. She was totally wrapped up in Paolo—the sun shone out of him for her. When he was killed she was like a walking ghost for months. If it hadn't been for little Paul I think she would have died herself. Only the fact that she had him to look after pulled Nicky through that time."

"But Paolo died two years ago—more than two years ago! It will soon be three years!"

Vanessa sighed. "Yes—she's amazingly faithful, isn't she? I don't think I could be quite as single-minded as Nicky."

"You believe she still loves Paolo?" His voice was curt.

"She's never even looked at another man since."

He nodded slowly. "She is walled up with the dead—as I had thought myself! I am sorry to hear you confirm my suspicions."

She shot him a wary look. "Sorry?"

His eyes widened. "But yes . . ." His voice grew suddenly very Italian. "It is not healthy for a girl so young to think only of a man who has been dead for two years."

VANESSA SAT CROSS-LEGGED on the carpet in the sitting-room that night, brushing her hair, her blue eyes fixed on her sister. Bess was sewing a neat little jacket for Paul, on the other side of the room. She made a great many clothes for him. She enjoyed designing clothes for children.

"Do you know much about the Farenze family, Nicky?" Vanessa asked.

"Very little," Nicky replied indifferently.

"They're stinking rich," said Vanessa.

Nicky looked at her without speaking.

Vanessa flushed a little. "Well, why didn't you tell us about that? What else haven't you told us? You never mentioned that they were wine exporters, did you? That Dom is here on business, selling wine to this country? That that was what Paolo was doing over here in the first place before he threw up his job with the family to take that terrible job as an interpreter?"

"You have been busy, haven't you?" Nicky was angry. "You must have had fun extracting all that information."

"Why did Paolo give up his job? Because he resented the way they treated him and the way they ignored your marriage?" Vanessa smiled unpleasantly. "Or was there another reason?"

Nicky looked at her sister with resentful irritation. "Why must you keep talking about this? Change the subject."

"Paolo couldn't, of course, have embezzled company funds to finance his gambling?"

Nicky froze, her eyes widening. "What? Is that

what Domenico Farenze told you?" Her voice was high and tense.

Bess put down her sewing and looked at her anxiously.

"Vanessa, stop this! You're upsetting Nicky. Don't listen to that nonsense, Nicky. Vanessa is only trying to get at you."

"I'm only trying to clear away a few of the veils she's hung around her statue of Paolo on his pedestal," Vanessa said tartly. "I think it's time Nicky admitted the truth to herself. Paolo was no angel. He gambled, he lied—and he killed himself when he drove that sports car of his the wrong way down the motorway. Come to that, he damn near killed a few other people at the same time. If that other car hadn't managed to avoid him there would have been other graves in the cemetery now."

Bess sprang to her feet as Nicky ran out of the room. "My God, Vanessa, I sometimes think you hate your sister! Why did you have to drag all that out just now?"

"I'm a little tired of Saint Paolo and his good works. Nicky has the chance of the good life if only she'll snap out of this. She could be one of the richest women in Italy—live in a fabulous medieval villa and wear the Farenze emeralds." Vanessa's blue eyes had a starry, rapt look and her voice was breathless. "Why the hell did Nicky have to be such a fool!"

Bess looked at her contemptuously. "You really mean, why didn't I get the chance of all that? You would jump at it, wouldn't you, Van?"

"Don't call me that! And why shouldn't I want the good things of life? Dom told me tonight that, as the widow of Paolo Farenze, Nicky is entitled to wear a necklace of emeralds as big as postage stamps, square-cut and set with diamonds." Vanessa bit her thumbs helplessly. "And Nicky couldn't care less!" Her voice wailed in despair. "She couldn't care less!"

"So, in order to persuade her to accept what the Farenzes have to offer, you set about destroying her memory of her husband? How low can you sink?" Bess looked at her with disgust.

Vanessa hardly heard her. "Nicky has got to change her attitude. She must realise that it's ridiculous to blame the Farenzes. Paolo was as much to blame as them. She mustn't alienate them. She must forget Paolo."

"You aren't thinking of going to Italy, too, are you?" Bess asked in sudden dismay.

Vanessa looked at her defiantly. "Why not? Nicky will need moral support."

"Moral support!" Bess snorted. "You're joking, of course!"

"Make fun of me as much as you like," Vanessa said with a toss of the light golden curls. "But Dom has already said that I shall be very welcome at the Villa Farenze. I'm Nicola's only surviving relative, after all. It's a good idea for me to meet her new family. They'll be able to see just what sort of background she comes from—and they can forget all that stupid nonsense about her being a cook."

"She is a cook, though," said Bess in mock innocence. "And a damned good one, too."

Vanessa threw her an irritated glance. "She's a Cordon Bleu cook, yes, but it's only a sort of hobby."

"Come off it, Van," Bess teased. "They aren't going to swallow that—and Nicky will never allow you to tell lies about her. Her pride would choke her."

"Nicky's pride makes me sick," Vanessa snapped. "She ought to have some sort of brain surgery. She's a certifiable lunatic! In her place..."

"We all know what you would do in her place," Bess murmured sardonically. "Grab everything that was going and run for the nearest exit!"

"I'm not that mercenary," Vanessa said crossly. "I just feel that Nicky should accept what's hers by right."

"And you're going with her to make sure she does accept it, even if you have to twist her arm to make certain?"

Vanessa's lovely face set in grim determination. Had any of her admirers seen her in that mood they would have been taken aback to see the tenacity and strength beneath her delicately feminine features.

"I'm going to Italy with her, and nothing is going to stand in my way," she murmured, half to herself.

CHAPTER FOUR

PAUL was sick in the car as they drove from the airport to the villa at Florence. The flight had upset him a little, but the long drive had a far worse effect, and by the time they had reached the green Tuscan hills he was whimpering and a pale yellow colour.

"Keep him away from me!" Vanessa shrieked as he was sick, drawing her elegant white skirt away from his vicinity.

To Nicky's surprise, Domenico was gentle and efficient in that emergency. He handled Paul calmly, cleaned up the car seat and was philosophical about the ruin of his own trousers.

When Nicky tried to apologise, he said dismissively, "Forget it! He couldn't help it."

"You must have your suit cleaned and send me the bill," she said ruefully.

The grey eyes narrowed. "I said forget it!" The tone was like a slap in the face.

She flushed and fell silent. They had been met at the airport by a uniformed chauffeur. His formal courtesy made her feel like an impostor, in her simple yellow linen travelling suit, as she followed him to the car with Paul in her arms. Domenico had sat in the back with Paul, and Vanessa had pleaded to sit there too, claiming that she always felt nervous at driving in the front seat. Nicola had given her an amused smile, seeing through this rather blatant attempt at dividing them.

Her own mind was far too occupied with what was to come, the first meeting with Lorenzo and the rest of the Farenze clan.

She tried to recall all that Paolo had said about them, but he had really said too little, and what he had told her had been so scrappy.

His mother, of course, had died years ago, but his father had not married again. He had married so late in life, and was a man who found personal relationships hard, as far as she could guess from what little she knew about him. Lorenzo was an old man now, weakened by illness, yet still no doubt as awe-inspiring as he had sounded when Paolo spoke of him.

Vanessa was asking Domenico questions along the same line. "Who else will we meet besides your uncle?"

"My own mother," he said. "My father is dead. My mother lives at the Villa. Then there is my cousin Bianca—she lives there, too?"

"Does the whole family live at the Villa?" Vanessa laughed in a brittle fashion, her eyes narrowed. "What does Bianca do?"

"She helps to run the house, and does secretarial work for Lorenzo. She is a remote cousin, actually. Her parents live in Rio de Janeiro, but she gave up travelling with them to come back to Italy and work for Lorenzo."

"She's an only child?"

He shook his head, his face hardening. "She has a brother."

Vanessa watched him curiously. "You make that sound ominous!"

"Leo is an idle layabout," he said tersely.

Vanessa laughed. "Don't tell me he lives at the Villa, too?"

"Lorenzo is foolish enough to permit him to live in the old watch-tower. Leo pretends to paint there."

"Pretends?" Vanessa asked, raising an eyebrow.

"He is no more an artist than I am," snapped Domenico.

Dreamily, Nicola murmured, "Portrait of a Happy Family!"

Domenico leaned back against the leather upholstery, his gaze on the back of her shining dark head. She glanced into the driving mirror above her, and their eyes met. His were narrowed to steely points of light, hers wide, innocent, with hidden contempt in their green depths.

"No doubt you will prefer Leo's version of himself," he drawled. "He sees himself as the second Michelangelo. But be careful, Nicola, he demands tribute from the worshippers at his shrine. Beautiful girls flock to kneel at his feet in homage, and Leo expects them to be unstinting in their admiration."

Vanessa laughed. "He'll be disappointed where Nicky is concerned—she isn't susceptible."

"No?" Again the grey eyes sought Nicola's in the mirror. "I wonder. Even grief must have an end."

Nicola turned her head aside, her lids flicking down over her green eyes, and stared at the distant prospect of dusty roads, tapering cypress and green olive groves. It was like the backcloth to some old Italian painting, brought to life by magic, lacking only the Madonna and Child for the foreground. Instead of a stable and a star, she saw the gleam of chromium and bright paint, the tourists in the coach in front, drinking from cans and eating crisps.

Then they turned up a steep hill, between crumbling old walls, climbing steadily along a deserted, narrow lane. The snarl of the traffic was left far behind. They were the only vehicle in sight until they came upon a cart, pulled by a weary donkey, plodding along in front of them. The driver, in blue shirt and jeans, grinned and waved as he pulled aside into a convenient opening.

A little further up the wall again opened and a wide gateway showed before them. Snarling lions sat, crouched on their hind legs, paws upraised above carved stone shields, upon the gate posts.

"The Farenze lion," Domenico said to Paul with a quick smile, gesturing to them.

Paul's blank look brought a look of reproach for Nicola. "You have not told him about the Farenze lion?" asked Domenico in a deep, stern voice.

She shrugged. "Told him what?"

"Paolo never mentioned it?"

She thought back. "I'm not sure . . ." There had really been so little time—they had had so many other things to talk about. She gave Domenico a defiant look. "Paolo and I had better things to do than discuss his family history all day."

His black brows jerked together. A cruel, biting

look spat from the grey eyes, and the firm mouth thinned.

He looked down at Paul. "The first Farenze was a rich merchant many hundreds of years ago. He travelled to the Far East. The king of that country gave him a lion cub as a present, and when he came back to Italy the cub came too. It followed him everywhere, like a pet dog. When it grew large, it stayed faithful and loving to him. It protected him when he went hunting, and when an enemy attempted to kill him, the lion sprang at his assailant and drove him away. For years the lion went everywhere with him. Then one day he went to a banquet alone, and his enemies served him poisoned wine. He ran from the banquet, dying. The lion sat outside, waiting for him. The Farenze fell at his lion's feet, and the beast sat there, growling, refusing to let anyone come near."

Paul was breathless, wide-eyed. "Then what happened?" he gasped in excitement.

"His master's little daughter was persuaded to come and lead the beast into its cage so that the Farenze could be buried. They held a splendid funeral procession. Everyone suspected that the Farenze had been poisoned, but they could not prove it, nor did they know who had done it, for he had several enemies. During the funeral procession the widow of the dead man insisted that the lion follow the coffin, led by a golden chain held by the little daughter. Suddenly the lion sprang at one of the mourners and killed him with one blow. Dying, the man cried out his guilt—he had poisoned the Farenze!"

Paul's mouth was a perfect circle of astonishment and total belief. "How did the lion know?"

Domenico shrugged. "Who can say? He may have suspected him by coincidence, or he may have smelt the guilt on him. Or the Farenze may have whispered his murderer's name as he died."

"What happened to the lion?"

"He was kept, an honoured guest, in his cage until he died, and, as you see, he was adopted as the emblem of our house. The lion of Farenze is famous throughout the world. It can be seen on shields throughout the Villa."

Paul stared up at the gates. "He looks fierce and brave."

Domenico touched the boy's dark head with one gentle hand. "You are going to meet another such in a moment…"

Paul's eyes grew wider. "A lion?"

Domenico shook his head. "Your grandfather. As the head of the family, he bears the title Lion of Farenze—it has always been so for centuries. It used to have some meaning in the world. We are poorer now, and have no power, but the title remains as a reminder of what the family expects from him who is the head of it—courage, gallantry, fidelity."

Paul looked half bewildered, his soft baby features taut with anticipation.

"He's too young to understand you," Nicola said sharply. "I won't have him loaded down with ancient history at his age—all these empty, forgotten legends are meaningless now. This is the twentieth century, not the Middle Ages."

Domenico's arrogant features tightened. For a second he looked more medieval than the house towards which they sped. His cruel, frightening glare made her draw back. "I want him soaked in his family history," he said in tones of soft menace. "Saturated in it! He will one day inherit this, after all. The earlier he learns about the past from which he springs, the more likely it is that he will understand himself. We are all rooted in our past. We draw nourishment from it, as flowers do, and turn our faces to the sun like them, to find the strength to reproduce that past in the future."

"What," Vanessa demanded, "are you talking about? What sun?"

His grey eyes were suddenly wickedly amused. "The sun of love, of passion—what else?"

She laughed. "Oh, now we're on a subject I can understand."

The car was moving at a smooth pace along a gravelled drive between high, clipped hedges. Through gaps in the hedges now and then they caught a glimpse of a formal Italian garden, the garden of which Paolo had often spoken to her.

Box hedges, cypresses green and elegant, paths which were slippery with moss and a few scattered weeds, rain-greened statues of muscled gods and lightly draped goddesses who were, she knew, in reality statues of past members of the family; there they all were, as Paolo had described.

The garden was a cool, shadowy place, a little sad, as though it would have liked to blaze with colour under the hot Italian sun. The few flowers trailed elegantly from fine stone urns, or were massed together in painted wooden troughs along walls.

Beyond them, white and walled in from the sun, stood the Villa. Built in the sixteenth century, around a central courtyard, it turned away from the dazzling light and heat, providing a cool place for the languors of the day. The walls had few windows. Most of the rooms looked out on the courtyard.

More of the naked gods stood along the parapet above them, most of them defaced by time and weather. A hand, a leg, even a head would have vanished over the years. Birds used them as perching posts. They were spotted with moss and even a few brave plants which had taken root in cracks in the marble.

Nicky saw, from Vanessa's face, that her sister was deeply disappointed. She had been expecting a magnificent palazzo, no doubt, and found only a large country villa, in beautiful grounds, but so old that now it was crumbling away minute by minute. Time had cracked the stone, crumbled the masonry, sown the seeds of destruction everywhere.

Yet the old house had still a sort of splendour. Mellow, dignified, it looked on the face of time and was not disturbed. It was dying slowly, inch by inch, and in its decay it was perhaps even more beautiful than in its heyday.

As she gazed up at it, her eyes dreamy with appreciation, she felt Domenico's piercing look, and looked round to meet it.

He was staring at her, speculative, questioning, almost hopeful. Involuntarily, she smiled.

"It's lovely," she said softly.

His expression lightened. The grey eyes smiled back.

"Oh, yes," Vanessa cried instantly, not to be out-done. "I'm bowled over! Fantastic! It's so . . . " She sought for the right word and failed to find it. Weakly, she finished, "So . . . old . . . "

Nicky's eyes danced. Domenico, watching her rather than Vanessa, grinned. "Yes," he said solemnly to Vanessa, "it is old, isn't it?"

The car shot through an archway into the central courtyard. The dazzling whiteness of the scene outside gave way to cool shadows. They climbed out of the car and turned as someone came out from under a wooden terrace-roof.

Plump, black-eyed and black-haired, the woman was dressed in the same sombre hue. Her sallow skin had never known the touch of cosmetics, Nicky instinctively guessed. Her hair was drawn back from her round face in a tight, neat bun, scraped away out of sight so that her face looked oddly naked. She was middle-aged, soft-stepping, her black eyes hostile as she looked at the two girls.

"Angelina," said Domenico, moving to kiss her cheek. "How are you, *cara mia*?"

She accepted his kiss, her face softening. Over his shoulder her eyes alighted on Paul, riding on Nicky's shoulder, his small head drooping wearily.

She pushed Domenico aside and came to Nicola. "Give me the boy," she said in a hoarse, harsh voice.

Nicola's hands tightened on her son. She frowned. The stab of the black eyes was full of cold hostility, but she smiled coolly at the other woman. "Thank you, but I think I'd better keep him with me for the moment. He's not used to strangers."

"Let Angelina take him," said Domenico. "You are tired. There is no need to be alarmed. She was Paolo's nurse—she knows very well how to look after children."

Nicky looked quickly at the sallow face. Angelina stared back, unsmiling, and attempted to take Paul from her again.

"No!" Nicola said sharply. "He's in a strange country, among strange people. That's enough for him to cope with at present. He needs the security of my presence for a little while until he's used to being here." She looked at Angelina again, and spoke in Italian. "If you will show me the room you have prepared for us, I will take him up there myself."

Angelina looked surprised. "She speaks our tongue," she said to Domenico.

He nodded. "Show her the room for the boy, Angelina. They are both of them exhausted."

Suddenly the quiet courtyard erupted with sound as a door banged and an old man came out, the stick on which he leaned clicking along the cobbles. Heavy and bowed, with a great noble head framed in silvery hair, he stared at Nicola and the child for a moment, his black eyes shining in the lined map of his face.

In husky Italian, he said, "The boy..."

Domenico turned, with outstretched hands, to take Paul from his mother, but Nicola shook her head firmly. She walked slowly across the courtyard and stood in front of the old man, looking at him calmly.

"Paul," she said gently, "this is your grandfather."

The little boy raised his weary head and his eyes, shaded by drooping lashes, looked curiously at the newcomer.

Lorenzo Farenze stared back at him, taking in the dark hair and eyes, the fine features and straight, Italian nose.

"Are you the Lion of Farenze?" Paul asked eagerly.

Lorenzo shifted his glance to Nicola and a faint smile touched the corners of his mouth. "So? He has heard the family legends already. That is good." He smiled at Paul, nodding his leonine head. "*Si*, Paolo, I am the Lion of Farenze—but one day, little one, you will be the Lion. Would you like that?"

Paul considered the novel idea. He was pleased. "Yes," he said thoughtfully, "I would like to be the Lion of Farenze. I'll bite people."

Lorenzo threw back his head and laughed loudly. Nicola gave Domenico a bitter look.

"It seems my son has inherited a fatal family characteristic," she said.

Looking down at her with mocking amusement, he said softly, "Ah, but we are faithful, and where we love we are tenacious. That you should appreciate!"

"Give me the boy," Lorenzo demanded, cutting into this talk. "I will take him to his room."

"He always sleeps in my room," Nicola said quickly.

Lorenzo lifted indifferent shoulders. "That is as it should be—he will need care in the night, yes? But that was in England. Here in Italy there is Angelina, who has nursed his father, and is aching to watch over the little one."

Nicola politely insisted, "It's very kind of her, but I prefer to keep him with me."

Lorenzo turned a cold, arbitrary countenance towards her. "That is no longer suitable. You are the widow of my son. Here, there are servants to do these tasks."

"No one but myself will do anything for Paul unless I wish it," she said quietly.

The black eyes spat at her, demanding capitulation. Without flinching she stared back, her mouth set in a straight line.

Lorenzo gave a growl. "What is this, Domenico? She is stubborn as a mule! In a pretty girl this is not expected..."

Domenico laughed. "She is English, remember. The breed is stubborn and independent. It is maddening, but there is nothing to be done for the moment but accept it."

"Have you no pretty coaxing wiles, child?" Lorenzo shook his head. "That is how a woman gets her own way—by pleading and pleasing, not with this defiant pigheadedness."

Vanessa laughed, drawing the attention to herself. "I'm afraid you won't get coaxing from Nicky. She has always despised that approach."

Lorenzo looked at her in amused interest. "But...what a beauty! Who is this?"

"Nicola's sister, Vanessa," Domenico told him, and introduced them.

Lorenzo bowed over Vanessa's hand in a courtly gesture. "*Bella signorina*," he murmured. He looked from her to her sister. "You are not alike, you two? You have the head of a Botticelli madonna, while your sister has a head of black silk, with lights of fire..."

Vanessa laughed softly. "How very apt! You are clever, *signore*. You read characters at sight."

"Is there fire in your sister?" Domenico asked, his grey eyes flicking over Nicky. "I thought it was all ice behind those green eyes."

Vanessa frowned. "Nicky has only ever been impulsive once—when she met Paolo."

"Ah, she was on fire for our Paolo!" Lorenzo seemed amused by this.

Domenico's mouth thinned. Sardonically, he said, "What a riddle she is—this girl with lights of fire on her head and ice in her eyes!"

Vanessa wound her hand through his arm. "Nicky is waiting to take Paul to bed. Poor pet, she's tired." The tone was gentle, but Vanessa was irritated.

They moved inside the house, and found themselves in a lofty marble-floored hall, from which a staircase wound upwards into shadowy regions. A girl stood waiting for them, her hands folded before her in a classical attitude of patience which was belied by the angry set of her red mouth.

"Ah, Bianca *cara*, come and meet Paolo's wife and son!"

Lorenzo's voice was warm, but uneasy, as though he half expected the reaction he indeed got.

"Am I to curtsey to the new lady of this house?" The voice snapped like a curving whip and the black eyes bit at Nicola across the hall.

Lorenzo grew scarlet with rage. "What is this? How dare you speak like this in front of strangers!"

"Oh," the girl mocked, "they are strangers, are they? But strangers who must be placated, be made much of . . . almost worshipped . . . for they bring you a new heir for your fortune, don't they?" She curtsied deeply, her lips bitterly smiling. "Welcome to the Villa Farenze, *signora*. Before you came we were secure in our little company. Suddenly all is changed—the despised servant girl who stole our Paolo has magically provided us with a new heir, a wonderful boy to carry on our family name! So all the hate is forgotten overnight. The servant girl is to be transformed into a lady . . . flattered, cherished, spoilt."

"Bianca, stop this!" Domenico strode forward to seize her shoulders, but she avoided him. Her black eyes were full of unshed tears as she glared at Nicola. Bianca was slender, golden-skinned like a peach, with smooth black hair and an exquisite little face. But now she looked like an avenging angel as she flung her insults.

"I am wicked, am I not? I speak the truth—and that is always wrong in this house!"

"You speak nonsense," he retorted.

"Are you, too, won over to her? Do you forget the grief that marriage caused us all? Poor Barbara . . . rejected by Paolo when it had been understood for so long that she was to be his wife?

Think of her shame and grief—my best, my dearest friend, who should have been part of this family!"

Nicola looked at Lorenzo. Quietly she said, "This is no scene for Paul to witness. I would like to go to my room."

Angelina nodded and beckoned. Nicola followed her, ignoring Bianca's raging weeping. She glanced down once as she turned the bend in the stair and saw Domenico with his arms around the other girl, stroking the black hair gently, his mouth an inch above her bowed head.

Angelina looked down, too, and smiled. "Ah, that one will be tamed soon, when Domenico marries her and teaches her the purpose of these passionate urges she feels..."

"They are going to be married?" Nicky felt a chill run over her skin as they climbed into the upper floors. The stone walls must be damp, she told herself. Why else should she begin to tremble with an aching coldness?

CHAPTER FIVE

THE room which had been made ready for Paul was enormous. His cot, clearly bought specially for him, was painted white and embossed with colourful drawings of animals. The bedclothes were all exquisite—the quilt white hand-sewn with gay flowers, the sheets a delicate lavender. Beside it stood a toy cupboard. Shelves above it held pretty picture books, a clown puppet and some games. An adult bed took up the other half of the room.

"I shall sleep there," Nicola indicated politely.

Angelina looked mutinous. "It is not as the order was given," she mumbled.

"I am Paul's mother—I shall sleep in his room, as I have always done until now. It would be a mistake to change too many things at once. When he is used to this place I may move out of the room, but for the moment it is wisest to make him feel as secure as possible."

Angelina listened with a doubtful air. She shrugged. "As you wish, *signora*." There was a grudging respect in the tones, however, and Nicola could see that the other woman's attitude to her had altered since their first clash downstairs. The discovery that she could speak Italian had made Angelina rather more inclined to like her, Nicola suspected. It made her less of a foreign intruder, presumably.

Paul sagged weakly on to the bed, his head lolling. Nicola began to undress him, and Angelina gestured to the wash basin on the far side of the room. Paul wriggled as his mother washed his face and hands. His yawns were wider now and he could hardly keep his eyes open.

Nicola tumbled him gently into his cot. In his pyjamas, his dark hair slightly damp and curly on his forehead, his eyelids lowered over the bright black eyes, he looked more of a baby than ever.

Angelina knelt beside the cot and gazed at him through the bars, her face engrossed. Tenderness lit the sallow skin, gave lustre to the eyes.

"He is his father's child! So beautiful! An angel!"

Nicola smiled, amused and touched. "He looks angelic now, yes," she agreed wryly. "But you'll have a hard job keeping up with him once he's wide awake."

Angelina laughed eagerly. "*Signora*," she said, in a husky voice, "you will permit that I look after him? You will not keep him all to yourself?"

Nicola was both ashamed and moved. "I shall be very grateful for your help, Angelina," she said quickly. She had not wanted to hurt the other woman.

"His father was like my own child," Angelina explained humbly. "I was happy to tend him, to hold him in my arms. It will be a joy to do so with this little one, a joy I had not believed possible." She looked up at Nicola, her lips trembling. "I hated you, *signora*—see, I admit it freely. I believed you wicked for stealing our Paolo from us. But that is past. You bring me another Paolo, so I am in your debt now. You will forgive me for the hatred?"

"Of course," Nicola assured her gravely. "I do understand, you know. I see how you must have felt."

Angelina's gratitude made her face softer, more youthful. She looked once more at Paul. He was fast asleep, his thumb in his mouth, his cheeks flushed.

"He sleeps, the small one. Will you permit that I show you the room we made ready? We could move the cot into that room tomorrow."

"This room will suit me very well," Nicola assured her. "Tell me, who else lives here, besides Bianca and Signor Lorenzo?"

"There is Domenico," said Angelina. "He lives here, too—and his mother, of course."

"Signora Farenze was not there when we arrived?"

"She rarely leaves her room until the evening. She is very delicate."

"I understood she was in charge of the household?"

Angelina nodded. "But of course—she gives the orders. Bianca is too young."

"When will I meet Signora Farenze?"

Angelina shrugged. "She asked that you be brought to see her as soon as you had rested after your journey. If I turn down the covers on this bed will you rest?" She moved to the window and let down the blind. A cool shadow made the room peaceful. Nicola looked longingly at the bed.

"It would be pleasant," she admitted.

Angelina gestured to her to sit on the bed. Kneeling, she removed her shoes. "I will call you an hour before dinner. You may then bathe and change—tonight the Signor Lorenzo changes for dinner in your honour. But now—sleep if you can."

To Nicola's astonishment she slid into a light sleep immediately on closing her eyes. Her weary body relaxed. The coolness of the room brought rest and refreshment. She awoke at six when Paul began to stir, his long sleep leaving him hungry and curious about this new home.

"I want my tea," he demanded as she smiled at him. "Why are you in bed, Mummy? Is it morning?"

"It's evening," she said, laughing. "You slept for a long time. Stay there and I'll see what I can find."

She went to the door and peered out. A narrow corridor wound on either side of the room. She vaguely recalled having come from the left, and moved towards it to look for the staircase.

A door opened. Domenico came out and stood still, staring at her, his brows arched in amusement. "Barefoot?"

She flushed, looking down at her toes in surprise. She had forgotten to put her shoes on when Paul called her.

"I was looking for Angelina. Paul is hungry."

He opened the door behind him once more and gestured. "Kill two birds with one stone—come in and meet my mother and ring Angelina at the same time."

"Ring her?" Sleep had apparently made her stupid because she did not seem to understand him quickly enough.

"There is a house telephone system. There is a phone in your room. You merely dial the kitchen and speak to Angelina. A house this size needs some sort of communication. We couldn't shout, could we?"

She flushed again, thinking that he was a supercilious beast. How should she have known about this telephone system? She had not been told about it. There was no need for him to drawl with such mockery.

The room into which he ushered her was luxurious without being over-ornate. The ceiling, high and covered with stucco cherubs, was somewhat muted by the delicacy of the curtains and carpet—a gentle pastel green. The bedclothes matched, and on the green pillows lay a frail, lined face, the eyes almost astonishingly alive as they smiled across the room at Nicola.

"Welcome to the Villa Farenze, my dear," said a soft Italian voice.

Nicola smiled back. Domenico's mother had fine silver hair, brushed loose about her face; eyes of the same colour as her son, and a mouth of great tenderness and spirit.

She did not look Italian, Nicola thought vaguely. "What a lovely room you have," she murmured politely.

Signora Farenze laughed softly. "Yes. I like to have a great deal of green around me. It reminds me of England."

"England?" Nicola's voice rose in surprise.

The old lady looked at her son in inquiry. "But you have not told her? Why not, Nico?"

He looked sardonically at Nicola. "She was so violently anti-Italian that I thought it might sound like an apology if I told her I was half English myself."

Nicola threw him a cold glance, then turned back to his mother. "You're English?"

"I was born there," smiled the Signora. "But my family lived here in Italy for so long that I am really more than half Italian myself. Italian is my tongue, although of course I speak English, and I do love to be in England in the spring." She sighed, her eyes seeking a print of a Constable landscape which hung opposite her bed. "I shall never go there again now. I must live on my memories."

"Which part of England did you come from?" asked Nicola.

"Norfolk was where my relatives lived. That was where I stayed when I went to England for a holiday each year—always in the spring. So green and new. Everything seemed freshly born each morning." Her eyes rose to seek the blue Italian sky outside her window. Dusk was softly veiling it now, a melancholy, romantic deepening of the colour. Nicola saw that Signora Farenze in fact had blue eyes, a pale blue which was several shades brighter than the grey eyes she had handed on to her son.

Looking back at her again, the Signora laughed. "But I chose Italy, and it is Italy which holds my happiest memories of life. I would not be happy anywhere else. Divided loyalties are always the most painful."

Nicola nodded. "Yes, I think you're right." She thought of her son and winced. A terrible choice awaited both of them.

Signora Farenze noted her expression and sighed sympathetically. "Yes, you too know the pain of choice!"

Domenico had moved closer. Nicola could feel him just behind her shoulder. "She married an Italian," he said harshly. "When she did so she made her choice. A wife must belong to the land of her husband—the Bible tells us so."

His mother frowned and looked surprised. "Nico! You speak with unkindness to Nicola." She smiled at the girl. "You permit me to call you that? You will call me Aunt Francesca?"

"Thank you. I would like to."

Domenico moved to the bedside table and picked up the telephone. He spoke crisply, in Italian, then replaced the receiver. "Angelina will bring Paul some tea at once. She asked what he would like—I told her to bring a boiled egg and some bread and butter. That will suit, I imagine?"

"Perfectly," she said stiffly.

"When shall I have the happiness of seeing him?" Aunt Francesca asked eagerly.

"Shall I bring him to see you now? He is awake."

"Would you do that for me? That would make me so glad."

Nicola hurried back to the room she shared with Paul. He was sitting up in his cot staring at the toys on the shelves. "Are they for me?" He spoke in a hushed voice. "Or is there another boy here?"

"I think they're for you," she told him.

"Can I play with them now, Mummy?"

"Later, dear. I want you to come and meet a new

auntie—you must call her Aunt Francesca. She's very old, so you'll be good, won't you, Paul?"

"Yes, Mummy," he promised. "Mummy, are there lots of people in this family?"

"I think there are quite a few people," she agreed.

He sighed. "Are they all old, every single one? No children at all?"

She laughed. "We'll have to ask Aunt Francesca about that, dear. Come along and see her." She lifted him up and carried him along the corridor to the other room.

Domenico was seated beside the bed. He looked sardonically at her bare feet and she wished angrily that he would stop teasing. She wished, too, that she had remembered to put on her shoes. She was so used to running about barefoot in the flat in London that she found it hard to remember that here things were not quite so informal.

Signora Farenze was charmed by Paul, and made him sit on the bed beside her and talk to her. He asked her about other children, and she said sadly that there were very few in the family, but that there were distant cousins who had children of his age and older.

"We must invite them here to play with you," she promised.

Angelina came in a moment later and took Paul back to his own room for his tea. Nicola softly slipped away, too, and found that Angelina had already run a bath for her. Fluffy white towels hung on the towel rail. Jars and bottles of deliciously scented things stood on a glass shelf high above the wash basin. The water was delicately fragrant and Nicola slid into it with gratitude, feeling her tired muscles relax.

When she returned to her room she found Paul back in his cot. Angelina was singing to him in liquid Italian, her dark face intent. He was yawning as Nicola kissed him goodnight. Long before she had finished dressing he was fast asleep once more.

They dined at eight, she had discovered from Aunt Francesca. Domenico took her down to a cool, shuttered salon on the courtyard side of the house. The floor was of ancient blue-white marble, veined and polished by many feet. Candles flared, smoking a little, in the breeze which blew in from the courtyard through open glass doors. The curtains hanging beside them moved swishingly, blowing back into the room.

The scent of geraniums, heady and drowsy, wafted across the room. She could see them, massed in a stone trough outside, their vivid scarlet and salmon pink making a bold splash of colour against the growing darkness.

Somewhere, not too far away, someone played a guitar. The notes plucked gently at the silence. The tune was unfamiliar, but Nicola found it nostalgic and insidious, a haunting melody full of love and yearning.

She ate veal in a rich wine sauce, and pasta, and drank wine made from grapes grown in the family vineyards.

Vanessa talked, laughed, gestured. A golden halo seemed to glitter around her Botticelli head, as she smiled intimately at Domenico. He was attentive, bending towards her to smile, murmuring, raising his glass in a silent toast.

Bianca sat opposite them, glowering. She picked at her food, pushing it around on her plate as a child might do, her lower lip caught between her small, white teeth. Oddly, for all her hostility and rudeness, Nicola was suddenly reminded of a child—a naughty, hurt, defiant child.

Lorenzo Farenze sat at the head of the table, his leonine head lowered as though he were about to charge. He wore a black dinner jacket, plain white evening shirt, and black tie.

Vanessa had spent a long time in choosing the perfect evening dress for her first dinner at the Villa. She had rejected several before finally deciding on a classical gown of champagne silk, uncluttered and elegant, which left her throat and shoulders bare and emphasised her delicately feline look.

Nicola had only packed two dresses suitable for evening wear. She had chosen a flower-printed chiffon for tonight. It was pale green and had the shadows of yellow flowers drifting over its folds. She had allowed Vanessa to comb her hair up into a french roll, but had decided when she saw herself in the mirror that it gave her rather a severe appearance.

Domenico passed her the fruit bowl, his grey eyes assessing her with a cool flick of the lids. "I prefer your hair down," he said calmly. "It does not suit you like that—you look like a schoolteacher."

"Oh?" She chose something from the bowl without even seeing what she held.

Bianca said maliciously, "We expected you to look like a street-walker!"

"Bianca!" Lorenzo's voice struck her like a whip. "Have you lost all manners? How dare you speak so to a guest!"

"I am not a hypocrite, that is all!" she spat back, tossing her black head defiantly.

"You behave like a gutter urchin," he said menacingly. "I will not tolerate it in my house. You mend your manners or you go."

"You would turn me out for her?" Bianca was aghast and white.

"You offend a guest at my table," he said sternly. "You must be punished for it."

"Where would I go?" Her eyes were like wet black stones as she stared at him.

"Your brother has room enough in his house. Either you watch your tongue or you go to Leo."

"What's all this about me?" The voice drawled from the doorway into the courtyard and all eyes turned towards it.

The man who stood there was curly-headed, dark and broad, with a handsome face full of wicked amusement. He held a guitar in one hand, the brightly coloured strap hanging. His silk shirt was orange, his tight pants black. He looked for all the world like a Spanish flamenco dancer, thought Nicky with relish. She glanced at Domenico and found him watching her closely.

The grey eyes were narrowed, the face grim. She looked away from him, suppressing a smile. She remembered his warnings about Leo's attitude to women. Certainly, she thought, Leo was obviously very attractive to the opposite sex. His stance as he lounged against the wall told her that. He expected to arouse their interest.

"Come in, Leo," said Lorenzo in a resigned voice.

"Why wasn't I invited to this distinguished gathering, or need I ask?" Leo strolled into the room. "You've finished your meal, I see. Am I too humble to join you for coffee?"

"I did not invite you because I wanted to keep the party small for this first evening," Lorenzo said sharply.

Leo's bright, impudent gaze skimmed their faces. He grinned at his sister, swiftly inspected Vanessa and then Nicola.

"Paolo wrote to us that Nicola had hair like black silk," he said flippantly. "So I suppose I may guess which is the mother of our little Principino!"

She gave him a long, thoughtful look as he stared at her. "Yes, I'm Nicola."

The insolent eyes surveyed every visible inch of her, at leisure and with some appreciation. "Paolo had good taste," he commented at last.

Domenico's hand stiffened where it lay on the table. Nicola, looking away from Leo's gaze, saw the long fingers curl into a fist, the knuckles show white.

"Sit down, Leo," Domenico said icily.

Leo drew up a chair and sat down between his mother and sister. He grinned at Domenico. "Do I feel a rapier at my ribs? I wonder why."

"Nico probably feels as I do, that you need a lesson in good manners," snapped Vanessa.

Nicola blinked in astonishment. She had never heard her sister speak so sharply to an attractive man before. It was incomprehensible. Had Vanessa taken an instant dislike to Leo? Or was it merely that she was siding with Domenico against the newcomer? A newcomer, of course, who had apparently been unimpressed by Vanessa's golden beauty, a fact which, in itself, was enough to make her detest him.

Leo was looking at Vanessa now, though, his eyebrows raised in mute astonishment and wry mockery. Vanessa flushed under his gaze. Leo laughed softly as she looked away.

"Are you going to teach me manners, *signorina*?" His drawl was charged with taunting amusement. "Nico, introduce us!"

"Vanessa knows who you are, Leo," snapped Domenico. "She is Nicola's sister, Vanessa Mayfield."

"A charming name," Leo murmured. "Two such beautiful girls! Yet so unalike! Yours was a lucky family. Are there more of you in England?"

"No," Nicola told him, since it was plain that Vanessa would not speak. "We are the only two left."

"And are you both to live here at the Villa?"

Lorenzo exerted himself once more. "Leo, you will drink your coffee and be silent. I have told you what I think of your manners before. You will lead your wild life in your tower—here I expect at least lip service to my ideals."

"Dear Uncle Lorenzo," he murmured, tongue in cheek.

Bianca stirred uneasily, her dark eyes seeking those of her brother. Nicola saw that she appealed to him to placate Lorenzo Farenze, and that Leo first shrugged, then smiled reassurance. Clearly, despite his flippancy, Leo had affection for one member at least of this household.

"You paint, I understand?" she asked politely, in an effort to lead the conversation into safer topics.

"In a fashion," Leo nodded, his expression changing.

"Do not permit him to lure either of you into his tower on a pretence of painting you," Domenico said sharply. "His paintings are unrecognisable as people. They have no limbs or features—they are mere wraiths of shapes, splodges of pale paint."

"My cousin the art critic," Leo drawled.

"I am not ignorant of art," Domenico said. "You are a typical dilettante, Leo. Art, for you, is an excuse for idleness."

Leo's eyes narrowed. "I bow to your superior knowledge, cousin." The sarcasm was charged with hostility.

"Idleness which affords you time for your real occupation," Domenico went on bitingly.

"And what is that?" Leo asked, his lip curling with hauteur.

"Flirtation, amusing yourself by playing with the emotions of silly young girls!" Domenico stared at him with icy implacability. "You are a menace, Leo. You turn their heads and break their hearts, and it is left to us to placate their families and smooth down furious fathers."

Leo leaned back, fiddling with the spoon in his saucer, his dark eyes narrow and half veiled by drooped lids. "You make me sound like Don Juan, cousin. I hope that the two newcomers in our midst realise that this tirade from Nico is a warning specifically delivered for their benefit?" He let his lids rise. His eyes trailed over Vanessa, rested on Nicola. "Do you feel yourself in danger from my charm, *signora*? If so—heed Nico and beware!"

She smiled, slightly embarrassed. "I doubt if I am in any danger, but thank you for the warning."

Leo's eyes widened and were fixed on hers for a second or two. His smile deepened and became more genuine. The deliberate impudence left his face. He rose, bent across the table, lifted her hand and kissed her fingers with dramatic gallantry.

"Nicola," he murmured. "An enchanting name..."

She laughed. "I think you're a fraud," she said lightly.

He looked at her in inquiry. "Is that kind?"

"You like playing games," she nodded quizzically. "And you are always surprised to find that other people don't understand your rules!"

He laughed out loud. "Beautiful and clever—a combination not often met with in this drab world! I salute the memory of Paolo—he found a perfect jewel. Nicola, you and I shall be friends, yes?"

She let his eyes hold hers, saw sincerity beneath the flaunted impudence, and felt a curious liking and sympathy for him. "Yes," she said quietly, "we shall be friends, I think."

Domenico's chair scraped across the marble floor. "Shall we remove to the courtyard for an hour, Lorenzo?" His voice was icy with restraint.

CHAPTER SIX

WHEN Nicola woke up next morning she was at first bewildered to find herself in a strange room, but a few seconds later she was sitting bolt up, smiling at Paul, who had climbed out of his cot and wandered across to sit on her chest with a thump expressive of affection and hunger.

"Want breakfast," he mumbled, choking her with a hug around her neck.

She kissed his nose. "You shall have it, my pet. Let Mummy get up and she'll help you dress."

The door opened and Angelina glided into the room, bearing a tray, her sallow face wreathed in smiles. Paul recognised her vaguely and gave her a congratulatory beam, seeing the food she carried. Someone who anticipated his wants in this fashion must be encouraged.

Delighted, Angelina laid the tray down. "*Buon giorno*, Paolo!"

Paul scrambled down from the bed and toddled over to her. "My breakfast?"

He scanned the contents of the tray. Fruit juice, boiled eggs, coffee and hot rolls. "Pop and squeak," he said crossly.

Angelina was bewildered. "What does he say?" she appealed to Nicola, who laughed.

"He wants the cereal he has at home. Paul, for today just eat an egg."

"Negg," he agreed amiably. He looked around, waiting for the usual ritual to commence. "Bib?"

Angelina hurried to produce one from the drawers in which she had bestowed their clothes last night. Paul patiently waited while she tied the bib around him.

"Negg," he murmured, picking up his spoon. Angelina split and buttered a roll for him, and he looked at it in consternation. "Soldiers?"

Angelina was aghast. "Soldiers? How is that?"

His mother interpreted once more. "He likes to have sliced bread and butter cut into fingers, thin pieces. He calls them soldiers." She patted Paul's rosy cheek. "The roll is delicious, darling. Don't be so conservative."

He frowned, then accepted the roll. Silence fell, a contented silence, during which Paul ate and the two women watched him with fascination.

"I look after him for you, *signora*," Angelina offered eagerly. "You are to go for a ride in the car with the Signor."

"The old Signor—or Domenico?" Nicola hesitated.

"The old Signor—Signor Lorenzo himself."

Paul looked up, interested, spoon in hand. "The lion, my grandfather," he said thickly through his mouthful of food.

"Don't speak with your mouth full, my darling," Nicola said absently, but with a smile. "Do you know where we're going, Angelina?" she went on.

"To visit the vineyards this morning, and then to drive down into Florence," said Angelina.

Nicola said thoughtfully, "That should be very interesting. Are you sure Paul won't be too much trouble?"

Angelina's laughter was convincing. "It will make me very happy to look after him! Will he stay with me, do you think? He will not be shy with Angelina?"

"He is used to being left with babysitters," said Nicola. "Once he gets to know you, and to feel at home here in the Villa, he'll be quite happy. Paul is a well-adjusted little boy."

"He is an angel," the other woman nodded vigorously.

Paul had finished his breakfast. He drained his cup of milky coffee and set it down with a bang, wiping his mouth on his bib.

Angelina bore him off to the bathroom while Nicola looked through her wardrobe for suitable clothes. She chose a white linen dress and a broad-brimmed hat. They were simple enough for everyday wear, yet elegant enough for a visit to Florence.

When she had seen Paul dressed she departed for the bathroom herself. When she descended, dressed and ready for the morning, she found Paul playing on a small tricycle in the courtyard while Angelina watched him, a basket of vegetables in her lap which she was busily preparing for lunch. Her plump hands moved deftly while she kept her dark eyes on Paul.

Nicola watched them both for a moment before she stepped out to speak to them. Paul greeted her enthusiastically, waving one small hand as he cycled.

"Mummy, see me—I've got a bike!"

"It belonged to one of my cousin's children," Angelina explained with a smile. "He is too big for it now."

"Paul is in heaven, isn't he?" Nicola watched her son with pleasure. It was wonderful to see him so happy. "Thank you very much, Angelina. I'm grateful. Paul has always wanted to be able to ride about freely. Life in a London flat can be restricting for a small child."

"I am glad you are honest enough to admit so much!" The voice behind her made her start and turn, her cheeks pink.

Domenico eyed her quizzically. "I did not think you would ever admit that it might be good for Paul to live here!"

"Having money and freedom may be pleasant, but they are not always the wisest choice for one's children," she said quietly.

He stared at Paul, circling cheerfully, making a hooting noise as he turned. "The child looks happy. What is wrong with that, my puritan?"

"Nothing," she said flatly. Angelina looked from one to the other of them blankly, puzzled by the very obvious tension which stretched between them.

"Lorenzo wants to take you to the vineyards today. Then he has booked a table for lunch at his favourite restaurant in Florence—it's small and dark and serves the best food in Italy."

She looked at Paul. "Angelina mentioned it earlier. She's going to watch Paul for me."

"And you agreed?" His tone mocked her. "Wonders will never cease!"

"You have totally the wrong impression of my attitude to Paul," she said crossly. "I wanted to be around until he got used to the new surroundings, but now he's beginning to feel at home here I see no reason why I shouldn't leave him in capable hands for a while."

"How did you manage while you were at work? Did your sister look after him?"

"Sometimes," she admitted. "Our other flatmate was very kind, too. I managed somehow."

He looked at her through narrowed eyes. "Yes, you are very capable, aren't you?"

The word made her sound unfeminine and dull. She turned her head away to hide her chagrin. A loose strand of shining hair fell along the line of her cheek and she idly tucked it back behind her ear until she could get to a mirror to rearrange her hair style in its smooth chignon.

Vanessa erupted into the courtyard, slender and angelic in a modern imitation of peasant costume—a white broderie anglaise blouse with puff sleeves threaded with pale blue ribbon, full swirling skirt of crisp floral cotton tied at the waist with a wide sash of blue satin. She looked like a little girl, her gold curls bouncing, her eyes bright and interested.

Nicola felt a little shiver of alarm, though, as she met Vanessa's vivid blue stare, and saw the thinly veiled rage which her sister permitted to show briefly. Vanessa was angry, yes. But why?

"How long have you two been down?" Vanessa spoke lightly, but Nicola was suddenly enlightened. Vanessa suspected her of having stolen a march by getting up early. The pursuit of Domenico was serious enough for Vanessa to resent any lost moment of time with him.

She moved back into the house, leaving Vanessa with him, and found Lorenzo drinking black coffee in a sunny morning room, every inch of which was crammed with plants, leaving only a couple of wicker chairs and a wicker table free.

Lorenzo smiled at her. This morning he looked fragile and worn. The excitement of the day before had clearly left him tired. His skin seemed more yellow than ever, his eyes embedded in folded wrinkles. Despite this, his expression was one of deep happiness, and Nicola felt that Paul's arrival had given him a joy he had imagined lost to him for ever.

"You know my plans for today? You approve them, *mia cara*?" He spoke to her with a voice so gentle, so deep and mild. She looked back, with astonishment, at her image of him—the image his son, her husband, had created in her mind. The two pictures did not coincide at any point. This kind and serious man was not the domineering, autocratic father Paolo had described. Had she misunderstood, or had Paolo seen another side of him?

"I am looking forward to seeing the vineyards," she agreed. "Are you sure it will not tire you?"

He shook his head. "I shall enjoy showing them to you. Nicola, we have much to say to each other. Domenico will drive us. If your sister sits with him in the front of the car, you can sit beside me in the back and listen to what I have to tell you. Will you do this?"

"Of course, Signor Lorenzo."

He took her hand between both of his and gazed at her gravely. "Can you not call me Pappa?"

She hesitated, flushing, and he sighed.

"Well, we will not hurry. *Festina lente* . . ." He looked up, a trifle quizzically at her face. "Do you understand that?"

She shook her head, smiling.

"It means make haste slowly—it is Latin, an old Latin tag which we use. Old age brings an appreciation of time which the young would not understand, *cara*. The hours speed by. We long to slow them down, to cling to their tails and make them pass like snails instead of racehorses."

"Paul will help you with that," she said gently. "Children do seem to make time pass more slowly."

He stood up, courtly and gallant in his immaculate linen and exquisitely cut suit. "Children and beautiful women," he agreed, taking her hand.

A sleek limousine took them to the vineyards. As Signor Farenze wished, Nicola sat in the back with him while Domenico drove with Vanessa beside him. The windows were wound right down so that a stream of fresh, sweet air flowed around them. They passed olive groves, pastures full of cypress and goats grazing on rough, rocky hillocks and the endless vineyards, green with the new life at the moment.

"How sweet the air is here," Nicola sighed, breathing deeply. "It seems to be fragrant."

"Fragrant? Yes, yes, the air of the hills is sweet as honey, as strong as wine." Signor Farenze sounded vague, though he spoke clearly and intelligibly enough. His eyes were fixed on her face, a frown on his lined forehead.

She looked back, waiting for him to go on with whatever it was he had wanted to say to her. After a moment of silence, he said softly, "*Cara*, I know how you have felt about me. I have been a blind, foolish old man, and it would have been mere justice if you had denied me my grandson. When I heard of the marriage, I was so angry that I had a stroke. They told you?"

"Domenico told me, yes."

"And you no doubt thought it was the hand of God!"

"Oh, no," she said, shocked.

He shrugged his shoulders, lifting his hands in a Latin gesture of wry acceptance. "But yes, I believe it was, in a way. I was brought to see that I did not own my son, that nothing in life is for ever. We all have our possessions on a short lease from God. Our own bodies, our own minds, are only a loan from the eternal. I learnt late, and in a hard fashion—but I think I learnt well. When Domenico telephoned to tell me that I had a grandson living I was quite out of my head with joy. Angelina feared for my life, I think."

Nicola touched his hand. "I am glad you weathered it!"

He laughed. "Once the shock passed I was so eager to see the boy that I would have turned away death's angel from my door with my own hands! For this, *cara*, this is my chance of redemption—this boy is sent to me for a reason."

She looked at him uneasily. What did he mean? Surely Domenico had told him that she did not mean to stay here in Italy for ever?

He saw her expression. The dark eyes stayed on her face, trying to read her thoughts. "You will not take him away from me now? I am not long for this world. I shall not have much time with him."

"I . . ." Nicola's voice failed her. She saw Domenico's head turn slightly, knew that he had been listening intently to what the old man said, that he, too, was waiting for her to answer.

Vanessa spoke before she had had a chance to gather her thoughts, to phrase her reply gently.

"Of course we will stay, *signore*. Where else should Paul be but with his grandfather, in his father's old home? Paolo spoke about the Villa so often! He loved it so much. He would have wanted his son to grow up here."

Lorenzo leaned back against the cushions with a long, hard sigh. Domenico looked at Nicola, in the driving mirror, and she saw the tautness of his tanned features. He knew very well that Vanessa did not speak for her. Lorenzo might be fooled, but Domenico was not.

"You forgive me, *cara*?" The whisper made her start, and she turned to smile at him.

"Yes, I forgive you."

"We made a bad start, you and I. Now we shall begin again, for Paolo's sake."

She nodded. "Yes, for his sake."

"I wish I had known of his death earlier. It grieves me that there was no one from his family at his funeral. They did not tell me because I was so ill, but they should have done. Death cancels all debts.''

"Someone wrote to me," Nicola said slowly. "Who was that?"

He looked thoughtful. "Was it your mother, Domenico?"

Domenico shook his head. "No, nor was it myself. I do not know who wrote. What did the letter say?"

Nicola did not answer for a moment. "It doesn't matter," she said at last. "I forget exactly..."

Domenico eyed her curiously in the mirror. "You mentioned this before. I must find out who wrote. Who was in the house? Bianca?"

Lorenzo looked astonished. "Bianca would not have written on my behalf, surely."

"She might have written on her own behalf," Domenico said with a flat intonation.

Lorenzo clicked his tongue. "So? This letter was . . . not a kind one?" He looked at Nicola anxiously.

"Not very kind," she said grudgingly, wishing she had never asked. "It doesn't matter. The past is past."

"I must ask Bianca about this," Lorenzo said sternly.

"Please! I thought we had agreed that we should have a general amnesty about the whole past? Isn't Bianca to be given the same chance?"

Lorenzo smiled reluctantly. "You are generous, *cara*."

Vanessa turned to look at Nicola, her eyebrows arched in irritation. "Oh, she's very generous," she said sweetly, but her eyes darted angrily at her sister. "I hope you aren't making a mistake about Bianca, though, Nicky. I'm very much afraid she detests you."

Lorenzo frowned. "That is not good news. How dare that chit set herself up against me?" The autocrat was not buried, it seemed, merely dormant.

The car swung, at that moment, into a narrow drive, and the subject was abandoned, to Nicola's relief. They had arrived at the Farenze vineyards.

Lorenzo insisted on showing them round himself, although Domenico offered his services. Leaning heavily on a stick, his leonine head defiantly raised to sniff the air, the old man walked beside Nicola between the vines. When they reached the house once more he was exhausted, pale and breathing heavily, and Domenico eyed him angrily.

"You have overdone it, Lorenzo!"

"Is she to see the vineyard with anyone but me?" The deep voice was stiff with pride. "It was my duty, my honour. She is the mother of the next Lion. I shall not see the child reach his majority—and Nicola must watch over his inheritance during the years between. I wanted her to know as much as possible."

Domenico was tight-lipped, narrow-eyed. "You did not trust me in this, Lorenzo?"

The old man looked at him with compunction. "I do not want to offend you, Domenico! It was not a matter of trust. It was the desire of my heart..."

"You will put a woman in charge here?" Domenico asked him coolly. "How could that be?"

"She is my grandson's mother! Who has a better right? Who has more of an interest in seeing the business thrive?"

"But a woman, Lorenzo?" Domenico's voice was hard. "How could she make decisions, plan ahead, manage the staff?"

"I am not talking of the everyday running of affairs," the old man said with an irritable gesture. "That will still stay in your hands, of course, Domenico."

"Then what did you mean?" Domenico's face was cold. Nicola opened her mouth to protest that she wanted no part in the business, but Vanessa gripped her arm tightly, her nails digging into her sister's flesh, and surprise held her silent. She looked at Vanessa. The blue eyes were bright, and fixed on the two men. What was Vanessa up to? Nicola thought.

Lorenzo was speaking again, his voice arrogantly offhand. "You will be responsible to Nicola, of course. You will answer to her for what you do."

Domenico's features were suddenly rigid. Nicola saw his grey eyes freeze over, his mouth tighten into a thin, angry line.

"You expect me to be answerable to a woman? A woman ignorant of the special problems of this business? A foreigner who knows nothing of Italy, of labour problems, of export and import?" The words stung like ice-tipped darts, and Nicola flushed bitterly.

"What makes you think I want any of this?" Despite her sister's attempt again to silence her, she burst out into stammered anger. "You've both been talking about me as if I was invisible! Why didn't you ask me? I would have made this ludicrous argument unnecessary, since I have no intention of accepting these plans for my future. What my son does when he is of age is another matter. I shall not stay here to run the Farenze business, or interfere with the rest of the family in their running of it."

Lorenzo looked with bitter anguish at Domenico. "See what you have done! You will drive her away from Farenze! Or is that your desire, Domenico Farenze?"

Domenico seized Nicola by the elbow and propelled her away from the rest of the party, pushing her lagging feet along by sheer brute force, half carrying her. He stopped when they had reached a silent corner of the green vineyard. His hand dropped from her elbow. Resentfully, she rubbed the red mark he had left on her flesh.

"Must you always behave like a caveman?" she demanded.

He stared, then laughed, yet still angrily, his grey eyes sparkling. "You think me too impulsive? That is odd. I would have said the same of you."

"What must the others think? We can't just rush off like this!"

He thrust his hands into the depths of his pockets in a most uncharacteristic gesture and rocked to and fro on his heels. "I had things to say to you which would not bear an audience."

"Oh?" She was alarmed and uneasy.

"You will not hurt Lorenzo, Nicola—do you hear?" His voice was abrupt, intimate. "He is not long for this world."

The finality made her blink up at him. "Are you certain of that, Domenico?"

"His doctor assures me of it," he said sombrely. He turned and stared at the green vines. She watched him, thinking how magnificently he dominated his surroundings, his dark head arrogantly tilted, the straight nose and powerful jawline giving him a strength which the commanding grey eyes emphasised.

Quietly, she said, "You began the argument, though. I do not want him to leave me control of the Farenze estate. I would prefer it to remain in your hands."

He shrugged. "Lorenzo would not have been hurt by that, my dear girl. He understands a male reluctance to work under a woman. The discussion would have been resolved amicably."

"How?" she asked in disbelief.

"By a compromise, of course." His grey eyes taunted her. "Something of which you are totally ignorant. You flew off in a tantrum without waiting to see how we would resolve the problem."

Nicola ignored his teasing. "What compromise?"

"I imagine Lorenzo would have agreed to a joint trusteeship, with both you and me working in harmony." His mouth curled mockingly. "Harmony of a sort!"

She turned away to pluck a green leaf, her cheeks flushed. "Oh! I see!"

"Would that be acceptable to you, too?"

She hesitated. "It would mean that I must stay here in Italy, of course."

"Of course," he said.

She felt a strange reluctance to give a definite answer. "I don't know..."

"Think about it," he advised her. "I will speak to Lorenzo. We will leave the situation for the present. Time will resolve it, no doubt."

They walked slowly back through the green valleys of vines. A gentle shadow lay over them. The sun had climbed high overhead and the distant hills shimmered with a blue haze which was fast vanishing in the noontide heat.

Domenico paused to look down at her. Forced to stop, too, she flushed slightly as she met his grey gaze.

"What was it like to be in love with Paolo?" There was a cynical twist to his lips as he asked the question.

Astonished, she stammered, "What a strange thing to ask!"

"Is it? But it must have been a strange affair, Paolo and a shy young English girl! You are nothing like the girl of whom he wrote to me—I had a certain picture of you, dark hair and bright green eyes, dazzlingly lovely!" He spoke in an odd tone, half lazily, half angrily.

"You still resent me," she said on a sigh.

"I? Why should I resent you?" He looked searchingly at her.

"Don't you? Everyone else did, and I think both you and Bianca still do!"

"You are wrong," he said flatly. "You cannot understand my feelings. And I think you are attempting to evade my question. When you think about

Paolo what do you feel?" There was an urgency about the question which puzzled her.

She shrugged. "Strangely enough I think I have a hazier idea of him now than I did in England. Coming to Italy has changed me somehow." She frowned. "I think it has shaken the kaleidoscope, altered the pattern. Paolo seems a different person against this background."

"How different?" he asked her sharply.

"The things he told me about his family . . ." She broke off, feeling a disloyalty to her dead husband in this discussion. "No!" She turned away. "Let's drop the matter, shall we?"

Lorenzo looked at her hopefully when she joined him again. "Has Domenico soothed you, *mia cara*?"

Domenico grinned lazily at him. "I think the ruffled feathers are smoothed down again, Lorenzo! All women need to be stroked."

Nicola glared at him, chin up. "How unwise of you to expose your tactics to me, Domenico! I will anticipate your moves in future."

Lorenzo chuckled delightedly. "Ah, I envy you, Nico—to be young, to enjoy the battle of the sexes! And with such a lovely creature as Nicola . . ."

Vanessa, listening with narrowed eyes, looked at her sister in a frozen silence. Nicola, meeting that look, was alarmed. Vanessa was quite capable of mischief if she felt herself threatened and she had already made her interest in Domenico only too clear.

CHAPTER SEVEN

THEIR first visit to Florence was so exciting that Nicola still had the dreams in her eyes when they arrived back at the Villa. Leo, lounging in the courtyard with his inevitable guitar, greeted her with a smile of curiosity.

"You look like a girl in a trance!"

"I feel like one. I've just been to Florence."

"Ah!" His eyes shone with deep pleasure. "Florence is one of the seven wonders of the world. A city of giants."

"Giants?" She was bewildered briefly.

"Artistic giants," he explained. "All of the great Renaissance artists came here—the city is crammed with beauty, choked with it. What impressed you most?"

"The Medici tombs," she said, with a shiver. "The atmosphere in there—a brooding power, ice cold and menacing! I've never felt anything like it!"

Leo grimaced. "Is that what you will take back to England with you as your chief memory of Florence? The menace of the Medici chapels? What about Michelangelo's David? The Perseus? What about...."

"What about allowing Nicola to take a peaceful siesta?" Vanessa's drawl was insulting and Leo shot her a furious look.

"Does art bore you, my beautiful?" His dark eyes flicked her contemptuously. "Never mind—we can't have brains and beauty, can we?"

"Am I supposed to feel insulted?" Vanessa purred at him. "Sorry, but I don't! Most artists are just spongers who use their art as an excuse for getting out of doing any work. Nice work if you can get it— but don't expect to be admired for it as well."

Leo strummed negligently, his handsome face an insolent mask. Over the music he murmured, "How is the fishing coming along?"

Vanessa was taken off guard. "Fishing?" She looked at him in puzzled inquiry.

"You are trailing the hook for Nico, aren't you?" Leo watched her from the shelter of the broad-brimmed hat he wore, his lips curled in a mocking smile.

She flushed scarlet and glared at him, then turned on her heel and vanished into the house.

His smile became a grimace. His fingers swept the strings with an angry flourish. "That sister of yours is a feline!"

"Vanessa is rather spoilt," Nicola agreed. "She's used to a lot of admiration."

"What does she do for a living?"

"She's a model."

"Successful?"

She nodded. "Very."

He grimaced again. "I see! And despises anyone who's not a financial success? She has an ambitious look when she forgets to smile—a woman's face in repose tells one a great deal. Vanessa's features are potentially exquisite. Her thoughts twist them into grotesque mimicry of beauty."

"Oh, Leo!" Nicola protested. "Vanessa is nothing like that!"

"I'm an expert on faces," he said flatly. "An artist has to be! I spend my time reading them so that I can put them on canvas. I'm sure I'm right about your sister."

"You may have grasped a faint part of the truth," she said slowly. "Vanessa is ambitious, I agree, but the rest is mere caricature."

He shrugged. "Now you have a gentle little face. I'd like to paint you, Nicola. Would you let me?"

She grinned at him. "After what Domenico said about your ulterior motive?"

"Oh, Nico was pulling your leg!"

"Was he? I rather suspect you're the Don Juan he described."

Leo laughed, her eyes dancing. "I adore your English sense of humour, *cara*."

"Don't change the subject," she smiled, tongue in cheek. "Is this a genuine invitation, or are you trying to lure me into your spider's web?"

"Bring Paul and I'll paint you as a Madonna with Child," he offered solemnly. "Lorenzo will be highly delighted and pay me a fat fee and I shall be able to feel a delicious sense of virtue in the process."

"Paul will be a very effective chaperone," she agreed. "He's as sharp-eyed as a wagon-load of monkeys."

Leo pretended to groan. "Why did I say it? Why?"

LEO'S STUDIO was situated at the top of an old watch-tower which stood on the summit of the hill, over-looking both the Villa and the road down into the valley.

"In the sixteenth century a watch-tower was necessary. One's enemies were quite capable of mounting a sudden attack. The Farenzes were no more popular than the Medici, although of course we never quite climbed to their heights of power. During the Middle Ages the struggle for eminence somehow left us out on a limb—we didn't have the Medici tenacity, although we had their ambition."

Nicola watched Leo's face curiously. He had an intent light in his dark eyes as he talked about his family. "You're proud of being a Farenze?"

He grimaced. "Proud? Can one be proud of belonging to a race of cut-throats and bandits? Like any other family we used dirty methods to make our money. Money has that quality—have you noticed? It makes your hands dirty."

"But all the same you do feel the romance of it," she insisted with an understanding smile.

He laughed, a little self-deprecatingly. "You see too much, *mia cara*."

"You all use that phrase," she said thoughtfully. "*Mia cara* . . . it sounds so much better in Italian. 'My dear' in English sounds rather patronising."

"English is a language which tends to sound pompous," he said lightly.

"Oh, no," she protested. "The language of Shakespeare and Milton?"

"And of Queen Victoria and Gladstone, too," he teased, winking at her.

Nicola was forced to laugh. "Well—" she conceded, with a little gesture of acceptance. Her neck ached already, she wanted to scratch somewhere around her shoulder blade and her head felt so heavy that she was half afraid it would fall off at any moment. Sitting for one's portrait was by no means an enjoyable experience, she decided somewhat ruefully.

Leo paused, eyeing her. "Tired?"

"Exhausted," she admitted.

"Like a short break?"

"It would be heavenly!"

He grinned and laid his brush down on the tall stool behind him. "Right, then. Come and have some coffee."

Stretching, her muscles almost squeaking after their enforced inactivity, she gave a groan of delight. "Coffee? What a delightful thought. Shall I make it?"

He shook his head, unscrewing a flask he produced from a covered basket lying among the litter which lay everywhere in the studio.

"I made it before you got here." He poured her some steaming black coffee into a china mug, added a little milk from a bottle which stood in a corner. Nicola accepted the mug gratefully, inhaling the delicious fragrance as if it were the odour of nectar.

"Can I see what you've done so far?" she asked.

Leo sharply shook his head. "No! I prefer the sitter to wait until I've finished. Once you've seen the picture you change your attitude. I don't just paint your body, you know—I'm trying to get your essential spirit on to the canvas. I've known a sitter be so incensed by what I'd painted that he put up the shutters for the other sittings, and I could not see anything of what he was thinking or feeling. The only emotion I could get was this great black cloud of rage between us."

"So you painted that?" Her tongue-in-cheek question made him grin at her, flipping a long index finger against her cheek.

"You can be quite wickedly perceptive in your way, Nicola! Yes, I painted that."

Her lashes lifted suddenly and she looked at him shrewdly. "Was that Nico?"

Leo's brows rose into an arc of astonished amusement. "Yes, it was!" He spoke in English, but with that delightfully grave Italian intonation. "How did you guess that, I wonder?"

"From his attitude to you. I wonder what it was you saw that made him so angry?"

Leo shrugged. "*Mia cara*, I do not even know myself. When I paint I am not consciously interpreting what I see—I merely paint intuitively. Whatever it was that angered Nico was something I had seen with my eyes but not comprehended with my brain. He saw it, and felt . . ." he lifted his hands, grimacing, "what shall I say? Naked?"

Nicola was thoughtful as she returned to the house later. Looking back, she saw Leo at his studio window, at the top of the old tower, wearing a black shirt splashed with many colours, daubed when he wiped his brush against his chest. He raised a hand in mimed greeting. For a second she saw him as a wizard in a fairy story, at the tower window, conjuring up storms. Leo had something of that dangerous quality. Things happened around him. Whether by chance, or the accident of his nature, or because some deep native mischief in him made him enjoy causing trouble, Leo created situations which were potentially stormy.

What had he seen in Domenico's face?

Domenico had objected strongly when Leo first broached the idea of painting Nicola and Paul as a Madonna and Child. His face dark with rage, he said the idea was ludicrous.

"Leo couldn't paint such a subject without being blasphemous," he told Lorenzo.

The old man was studying Leo soberly. "You think you can do this, Leo? You think it will be good?"

Leo was serious for once. "I have a feeling, Lorenzo." He held out his hands, their long tips steady. "Here . . . I feel certain it is what I must do."

Domenico laughed harshly. "Dramatic nonsense! You should have been an actor, Leo. You missed your vocation."

"Nico!" Lorenzo looked at him in surprised reproach. "Nico, Leo has talent. If he will take this seriously, it could be a picture worth hanging on our walls."

"Of course," Domenico said stiffly, "if it pleases you, Lorenzo, there is no more to be said. You must do as you wish. My own opinion is that Leo is up to one of his tricks."

Nicola decided, at that point, to intervene, in the hope of bringing some sort of peace.

"Whether the picture is good or not, it will be fun," she said lightly, smiling at Lorenzo. "Paul and I will enjoy it enormously. I've never had my portrait painted before. It will be a new experience."

Domenico's lip curled at the edges in a faint sneer. "Oh, it will be that, no doubt," he said sardonically.

Later, finding him alone in the courtyard before dinner, she had tentatively broached the subject once more, only to find him still bitterly opposed.

"I can't see that it will do any harm," she had said in mild bewilderment.

His glance was cool and sharp. "Your marriage seems to have left you strangely innocent."

She had flushed. "What has my marriage to do with this painting?"

"It is not your image only that Leo has designs on," he had said cuttingly.

"Oh!" She had been silent for a moment. "Well, of course, I know his reputation. But I am a grown woman, you know. I've been responsible for myself for years—I know how to cope with most techniques. Men have tried all sorts of tactics in the past—from the sad, little-boy-lost approach to the sweep-you-off-your-feet-before-you-have-time-to-realise-what's-happening approach. I've seen them all, at one time or another, and I know all the answering moves." Her green eyes glowed up at him, wide with laughter. "Leo will have to be pretty expert to take me in, I promise you."

"Oh, he will?" Domenico sounded odd, staring down at her with narrowed eyes. Before she had guessed his intention he had seized her wrists, pulling her close to him, so that she overbalanced and fell against him, her hands wriggling in his grip.

"Don't be ridiculous, let me go!" she cried angrily.

He bent his head and sought her mouth, and twist and struggle though she did, he found and held it briefly, his lips hard and hot against hers.

She felt a sweet, drowning happiness. Then she was free, her lids still flickering with startled surprise. Domenico stood back from her, his hands pushed down into his pockets.

"You were saying?"

She glared at him, angry that she had been so aroused by his meaningless kiss. How dared he behave like that?

"Yes," she said scathingly, "brute force is the one technique which is hard to counter, but then I don't see Leo as the brute type. Unlike you, he's more likely to use persuasion than force."

She was glad to see dark colour rising into his face. At least she had managed to sting him!

WHEN SHE REACHED THE VILLA, after her walk back from Leo's tower, she found Lorenzo and Paul in the garden together, bouncing a ball. Lorenzo's great age and Paul's youth made them both a little uncertain of their strength and occasionally unsteady on their feet. They were ideally suited as playmates, and Nicola was deeply moved by the sheer quiet happiness she saw in the old man's lined face. He was enjoying a sort of Indian summer in the companionship of his beloved grandson.

She waved to them, and they waved back cheerfully. "I'm going to change for lunch," she said. She wore one of Vanessa's dresses for her sittings, since it was just the shade of blue which Leo had wanted her to wear, and had a full, yet simple, cut which was very suitable for the subject.

In the cool, marble hall she found Domenico talking to one of the other servants and Angelina. Domenico dismissed them with a nod, and turned to look at her in a level, measuring way which made her chin rise in defiance immediately.

"How are the sittings going?"

The question sounded innocuous enough, but she knew that it was calculated to provoke her. "Very well," she answered in the same cool style.

His glance flicked her from head to foot. "That dress does not exactly make you look like a virgin mother."

She shrugged. "It's the right colour. That's all Leo wanted."

"All?" The tone was sardonic.

She lifted innocent green eyes to his face. "Yes," she said softly, then turned to go upstairs.

His hand caught her elbow and she looked round. His face was oddly uncertain, the eyes half hooded by his lids. "Nicola," he said huskily.

Her heart seemed to stop, then go on beating much faster, leaving her oddly trembling and pale. "Yes?" she managed to ask in a faint whisper.

The click of a heel on the marble floor broke the brief spell and his hand dropped from her elbow. Blindly, on impulse, she fled up the stairs without another word. As she turned the bend on to the first landing she caught a glimpse of Bianca, golden and vibrant, staring across the hall. Domenico had vanished.

Nicola changed with fumbling fingers. The bell which summoned the household to lunch was rung violently while she was just doing up her last button.

She gave herself a fleeting glance in the mirror and ran to the door. It opened as she reached it and Violetta, the cook, smiled shyly at her from the corridor. She was a cheerful, plump woman of fifty, with white-tipped dark wings of hair curved across the top of her head and capable, dimpled brown hands.

"*Signora*," she began breathlessly, "tomorrow is my brother's feast day, and I wondered if you would permit me to make a cold lunch before I go so that I may take the whole day?"

"Of course," Nicola agreed warmly. She had taken over some of the household arrangements from Signora Farenze, at her own suggestion, and had for several days been giving the cook her orders. Aunt Francesca had insisted that Nicola was far better able to choose a menu, and order the food, having been trained for the task. Glad to be of help, Nicola had attempted to be tactful with the cook, who, after all, had been cooking at the Villa for a long time. Nicola suddenly had an idea which pleased her.

"Cook, it would be a better plan if you did not have to do any work on your brother's feast day—then you could leave here tonight and be at home for the whole day. I will do all the cooking tomorrow."

Violetta's eyes grew round with astonishment and reproof. "You, *signora*? That is not suitable."

"Why not? I'm a cook! I am not an expert on Italian food, but I think I could make an eatable meal for the family just for once."

Violetta was struggling for expression, her lips trembling. "You will do my job, *signora*?"

Nicola suddenly realised that Violetta feared to lose her position at the Villa. She laughed and patted the other woman's hand in reassurance. "Oh, I couldn't do your job for more than one day, Violetta!" She spread her hands wide in emphasis. "Your job is quite safe, don't worry."

Violetta sighed with relief. "Then thank you, *signora*. I shall be grateful to go tonight. I see so little of my family, and this will be a great family gathering. You are very kind."

She turned to go, curtseying. A moment later Nicola, having given a last look around her room to make sure she had not left anything, followed her, in time to hear a peculiar confusion of sounds out of which she managed to fish first a wild cry in Italian, then a thud, followed by a number of bumps and bangs mixed somehow with the sound of a bouncing ball.

She ran to the stairs. Violetta was just landing at the bottom, her skirts flying, her arms waving in desperate search of some hold.

By the time Nicola had reached her, the rest of the household were there, too. Violetta was white with pain. Domenico, gently examining her where she sat on the marble floor, said with a grim look that she had broken her arm.

"Broken her arm? Oh, poor Violetta!" Nicola knelt beside her. "We must get a doctor at once."

"Hospital," Domenico said crisply. "I'll take her in my car. She'll have to have the arm put in plaster."

"But the pain . . ." Violetta was groaning piteously.

"Driving might be excruciatingly painful," Nicola told her. "I suppose the doctor couldn't come and give her an injection to stop the pain before we drive her to hospital?"

Domenico went to the telephone, speaking calmly, then came back. "The doctor is out on a case. We have no alternative but to take her into Florence at once."

"Cushions," Nicky said urgently. "We need cushions to support the arm." She flew off to find some.

When she returned with an armful of fat cushions, she found Domenico holding a glass of brandy to Violetta's pallid lips. The servant was drinking it meekly.

"Oh, good idea," Nicola congratulated him. "That should be a help."

She went out to arrange the cushions in Domenico's car. Vanessa, Bianca and Lorenzo stood, helplessly, watching the scene. Vanessa detested any form of illness or pain. She was quite pale herself, merely from watching Violetta's agony.

"Let her rest here for a moment before we try to move her," said Domenico when Nicola returned to the hall. "The brandy will need time to work. I gave her a pretty powerful dose." He spoke in English so that Violetta should not understand him. "She'll be out like a light if she isn't used to it."

Indeed, Violetta was looking a little better already, her colour returning slightly and the strained agony of her features much less pronounced.

"How the hell did it happen?" Domenico looked up the stairs. "What made her fall?"

"It must have been this," said Bianca, surprisingly, pointing to Paul's red ball, which lay in a corner of the hall. "I saw it roll away from the stairs as I ran out. She must have fallen over it." She gave Nicola a sullen look. "I've told Paul how dangerous it is to leave his ball lying about where people can fall over it, but he does need to be watched to make sure he does these things. If his mother isn't ever with him, how can he learn?"

"I heard the ball bouncing as Violetta fell," Nicola admitted unhappily. "I'm so sorry if it was Paul's fault. I'll speak to him about it and get him to see how serious it is."

Lorenzo's voice struck in harshly. He did not look at Bianca. "It could not have been Paul who put the ball on the stairs. He and I came in together and I saw Angelina take him upstairs. I myself placed the ball on the table over there."

"Paul must have come down again to fetch it," Bianca said in a shrill voice, looking suddenly pale.

Lorenzo turned his head slowly and looked at her, his eyes stony.

"Angelina would never permit the child to go up or come down the stairs without her. It is impossible."

Bianca drew a ragged breath. "No, well, it is . . . perhaps it was not the ball, then. Violetta may have just slipped . . ."

Violetta raised her head weakly. "It was the ball." She looked at Lorenzo. "It was in the shadows . . . I could not see it there."

"There was only Nicola upstairs?" Lorenzo sounded heavy and regretful.

Nicola looked at him in astonishment. "I didn't leave the ball on the stairs! Why on earth should I?"

Lorenzo inclined his head. "Indeed, *mia cara*. Why on earth should anyone deliberately leave a ball on the stairs for someone to trip over?"

CHAPTER EIGHT

THEY drove Violetta into Florence as soon as she was sufficiently tranquillised by the brandy. Even so, Nicola had to sit with her in the back of the car, gently soothing her, as she lay back, surrounded by cushions but wincing every time Domenico went over a bump in the road.

The roads down into Florence from the hills were old and not too well attended to—for all Domenico's care it was inevitable that Violetta should suffer a little.

The were all grateful and relieved when she could finally be handed over to a doctor at the hospital. She was not too badly injured, apart from her broken arm, and when she insisted on being sent to her own home from the hospital in time for her brother's feast day, Domenico left instructions at a local taxi office that she should be picked up and driven home whenever the hospital were able to discharge her.

During the drive back to the Villa Nicola was silent in her seat. It seemed so far-fetched to imagine that someone had left a ball on the stairs deliberately, in order to cause an accident, but as Lorenzo had said, what alternative was there? The ball could not have bounced up the stairs into the darkest part. Someone had put it there. Who?

She already knew the answer, of course. Bianca. The other girl had betrayed herself in every look, every word.

Why had she done it? Nicola shivered, imagining what might have resulted from such an accident. They had been lucky. Violetta had only broken her arm, but it might have been her neck.

Lorenzo had said no more after his cryptic few remarks about the possibilities. He had turned and stalked back into the dining-room. Vanessa, wide-eyed and curious, had given her sister a long, inquiring look, then followed the old man. What had happened to Bianca? Nicola could not remember. She had been too stunned to notice. Her mind had been too busy trying to take in just what had happened, and all the implications of it.

Domenico drew the car suddenly in to the side of the road. She blinked up at him.

"Why are you stopping?"

"We both need a drink," he said curtly.

Then she realised that they had parked near an inn. Stiffly, she climbed out of the car and followed him into the shadowy interior. The proprietor came out, wiping his hands on a white apron, and smiled at them. "*Buon giorno!* What can I get you?"

Domenico spoke to him in Italian, smiling. The man nodded and vanished, returning with a bottle and two glasses.

They sat down at a table near the open door. Pine trees cast a deep shadow over the dusty white road. A pigeon somewhere whirred softly. They were the only customers. The siesta heat kept everyone indoors. The proprietor, with a smile, sank down into a chair and dozed lightly.

Domenico drank the red wine with a stern expression on his face. Sipping hers slowly, Nicola wondered if he was angry with her, and why. Was it possible that he did believe she had left the ball on the stairs?

"We shall have to find someone else to cook," he said abruptly. "I'll get Angelina to choose someone."

"Why not me?" she asked.

He looked at her in astonishment. "You?"

She smiled. "I am a cook, remember? I would enjoy doing the cooking for a while. I can brush up my Italian recipes."

"It's ridiculous," he said curtly. "Out of the question."

Her spine stiffened. "Why?"

"You're a member of the family, not a servant," he snapped.

"I am a cook; professionally," she snapped back. "You don't think Lorenzo would object, do you? He didn't mind Leo painting my portrait. Why should he mind *me* cooking his dinner?"

"That was different."

"I don't see how."

"Then you must be blind," he said coldly.

"Explain it to me, then. Enlighten me." She used a tone every bit as sarcastic as his own.

"Lorenzo's pride would be hurt—it's as simple as that. You are the mother of his grandson. If people got to hear that you'd worked in his kitchen as a cook, he would be ashamed."

"But that's ridiculous!"

He shrugged. "Possibly!"

"It's downright archaic," she said angrily.

He gave her a cool look. "That is your opinion. You are not a proud old man who is desperately clinging on to the last shreds of family glory."

"We'll see," she said in a tone of calm determination. "I'll speak to Lorenzo myself. I think I can make him see sense."

Domenico laughed. "You are almost as myopic as Lorenzo is, aren't you?"

Nicola was baffled. "What? I don't understand you."

"No," he murmured under his breath. "You're right—you don't."

LORENZO WAS AT FIRST ASTOUNDED, then horrified, then, as she coaxed and pleaded, mildly hurt.

"But, *mia cara*, it is not right that you should work as a servant in my house when you are its rightful mistress."

Cunningly, she smiled down at him. "If I am rightful mistress then I may do as I choose, Lorenzo. It would make me happy to cook for you and Paul. I love cooking." She gestured. "It's hard to explain, but it satisfies something deep inside me."

The leonine old head nodded sagely. "You are a woman. It is your nature to like to cherish and feed your family. Ah, *cara*, I understand now." With equal cunning, he peered up at her. "But when will you call me Pappa, daughter?"

"When I am cooking for you in my own kitchen, Pappa," she said, laughing at him.

He threw back his head and roared with delight. "You are all female—how I regret the years I lost by my blind folly in rejecting you at first!"

Her dark hair shone as she bent her head to kiss his withered cheek. "Never regret, Pappa. Let us just enjoy what we have now."

He looked at her with deep pleasure, admiring the gentle curve of her mouth and cheek, the bloom of her tanned skin, the whiteness of her neck, and her smiling green eyes.

"*Mia cara*, you must marry again. It is wicked to waste such loveliness on a child and an old man. You were formed for love."

Nicola blushed and laughed. "Time enough for that! I'm not past my first youth yet, I hope."

"You will not make the mistake of loving Leo?" He looked at her anxiously. "Leo is gay and charming, but he is not serious enough for you, *mia cara*."

"Leo is my friend," she said gently. "No more than that, I promise you. I like him, that's all."

Lorenzo sighed deeply. "Good, that is reassuring. I have worried about it. Domenico spoke to me, warning me about allowing Leo to see so much of you..."

"Oh, he did, did he?" Her tone was indignant. The green eyes spat fire.

Lorenzo looked at her casually, then with narrowed eyes. His mouth curved. "So..." He relaxed with a smile. "So..."

His tone alerted her, and she stared at him, suddenly wary. What did he mean by that expression? she wondered. But her probing glance could not read his thoughts. The wrinkled features smiled amiably, but hid their secrets.

THERE WAS GENERAL SURPRISE and consternation when the rest of the household discovered that Lorenzo had agreed that Nicola might take over the cooking until Violetta was better.

Vanessa was outspoken in her disgust. "Are you mad, sweetie? I thought the idea was to make the old man forget that you were ever a cook. He'll despise you for offering to work in the kitchen—he'll think it's where you really belong. And others will think so, too—and say it out loud."

Nicola laughed. "Bianca?"

"Who else?" Vanessa's voice was thin with anger. "She makes me so mad I could scream! She looks straight through me half the time, as if I was invisible, and when she does notice me it's just to be really unpleasant. Snobbish, spiteful little cat! I'd hate to give her an excuse for sneering at us."

"Why take any notice of her?" Nicola asked quietly. "She's very young, and rather silly. I think she feels rather uncertain of herself underneath all that arrogance."

"You have to be kidding!" Vanessa laughed in a hard way.

Nicola shook her head. "I'm serious, Van."

"Don't call me that! You know I hate it."

"I'm sorry. I'll try to remember, but childhood habits die hard, and I always did call you Van when we were little, didn't I? Don't you remember?"

"Of course I remember," her sister snapped. "I've

always tried to stop you using that ridiculous childhood nickname, but you were as stubborn then as you are now."

"I don't mean to be stubborn," Nicola sighed. "It is just that I do love cooking, and I feel useless when I'm not doing something."

"You've got time to spare for Paul now," Vanessa pointed out. "That isn't being useless, is it?"

"Paul has Angelina waiting on him hand and foot. I see more of him than I used to do, but Angelina does all the work. I just play with him."

"I give up," groaned Vanessa. "You sound as though work was sacred!"

Nicola laughed. "In a way that is what I think," she admitted with amusement. "We're like machines. If we aren't in regular use we rust and decay."

"I'm not getting rusty," said Vanessa, looking down at her own long brown legs with satisfaction. "I'm having the time of my life here. I sunbathe, read magazines, relax—it's the best holiday I've ever had. The only time you ever sit down for more than two minutes is when you're sitting to Leo." She shot Nicola a cool, blue-eyed look. "He isn't going to be pleased if you're in the kitchen all day. How can he paint you then?"

"He'll have to paint you instead," Nicola said lightly. "After all, ever since we got here we've heard how very paintable you are, Vanessa."

Vanessa flushed angrily and gave her a fierce glare. "Sit for Leo? I'd rather do the cooking!"

Leo's mocking voice came from the door. "My God, a fate worse than death!"

Vanessa spun, suddenly pink to her very hair. Her blue eyes stabbed at him across the room. "Eavesdroppers hear no good of themselves—didn't you know?"

"Another cliché, *mia cara*. What a very limited little mind you have!"

Nicola was puzzled by the cruelty in his voice. Did Leo really detest her sister that much? She looked at Vanessa unhappily. Was it her imagination, or had her sister winced at Leo's words?

Vanessa gave a bright, hard little smile. "Not too limited to see your little game, Michelangelo! Nicola will be very rich when Lorenzo dies, won't she?"

Leo's eyes narrowed to dark, mocking slits. "I think you have misunderstood the situation, my dear." His English was formal and oddly grave. "Everything is for Paul. Nicola will merely be a trustee. Dear Domenico, also, I believe."

"But any man who married her would hold a whip over Domenico's head," Vanessa purred.

Leo pretended surprise. "Why, so he would!"

"And you would love to do that, wouldn't you?" Vanessa added with a long, smiling glance.

He bowed sardonically. "How well you read my mind! Almost one would think we thought alike."

There was a silence, then she turned on her heel and left the room, banging the door behind her.

"Must you tease her like that, Leo?" Nicola was disturbed by the scene she had just witnessed. "Vanessa doesn't have much of a sense of humour, I'm afraid. She may seem very lighthearted, but she takes life seriously."

"Seriously?" Leo laughed. "Please, *mia cara*, do not make me laugh so much. It hurts."

"I don't think you understand Vanessa. She wants a great deal from life."

"Money? Clothes? Parties? I had noticed." His voice was coolly sardonic, and there was a bitter twist to his lips. "She is not hard to understand, *cara*."

"Have you ever asked yourself why she wants those things so badly?" Nicola was sober. "Because when she was young she was rather hurt by the first man she ever loved. He was callous and selfish. After that Vanessa was determined to succeed, to be secure. She's never talked to me about it, but I watched the change in her. She was always gay and fond of fun, but she hardened after she'd broken with this man. Now she thinks money solves everything."

Leo watched her face thoughtfully, frowning. "You have much fondness for her?"

"She's my sister. She puzzles me at times, but I suppose I have a basic feeling of concern for her."

He grinned. "In other words, you are fond of her, but she often slaps you away when you try to show it?"

She sighed. "I'm afraid that's more or less the case, yes. Vanessa isn't very demonstrative."

Leo nodded. After a moment he asked. "What is all this about you taking over in the kitchen? You aren't serious?"

"I certainly am!"

"But what about my portrait of you? How can I finish it if you are forever cooking?"

"I shall fit an hour or so into the morning routine," she said easily. "I shall need a day or two to get used to the kitchen, but after that I've no doubt I shall find time to spare for you."

He grimaced. "You make me sound like the dentist! I have worked hard on this portrait. It is important to me."

"More important than food?"

He grinned. "You forget, I cook my own meals. I've a modern kitchen in the tower."

"What do you cook?" She was curious. "I can't imagine you as a culinary genius."

"I am superb," he said modestly. "I can do an excellent spaghetti. My salads are crisp and delicious. I make a superb tomato and beef sauce."

She laughed. "I'm very impressed. What else?"

"Else? What more is necessary?" He looked offended. "Salad and spaghetti—the basic stuffs of life. I live like a king."

"Mmmm . . ." She eyed him reprovingly. "I had noticed! Tell me, Leo, do you sell your paintings?"

His dark eyes danced. "Suspicious female! Yes, I do, quite frequently."

"Do they sell well?"

"Are you investigating my income for the revenue people, or is this a personal interest?"

She flushed. "I'm sorry, it was rude of me. I was just interested."

"Why?" He was suddenly serious.

"Why?" She shrugged. "Just vulgar curiosity, I suppose, and a certain concern for you. It would be painful to paint pictures one couldn't sell. I'm glad you sell them."

He watched her, head on one side. "Nicola," he murmured uneasily "you aren't getting... well, how can I put it? Interested in me?"

She laughed at his wary expression. "Poor Leo, did you suddenly feel the breath of pursuit on your neck? No, I'm not in full chase. You can relax. My concern was as sisterly as my feeling towards Vanessa."

He gave her an amused grin. "Well, I'm not certain that that is a complimentary remark, but I think I'll take it as being meant for one. And seriously, Nicola—I'm glad you and I can be just good friends. I would hate to hurt you, but I have never seen you in any more intimate light."

"Nor I you, Leo," she said cheerfully. "So we can both forget it, can't we?"

He bent his head and kissed her lightly on the mouth. As he raised his head again he smiled down at her. "Sweet, sweet Nicky, I am so glad you came to the Villa."

As they moved apart Nicola caught sight of Bianca in the courtyard watching them with an intent, unreadable expression. The other girl flushed as Nicola's eyes met hers, then, turning on her heel, she hurried away.

That evening they had a simple dinner of soup and a mixed fish salad; anchovy, prawn, shrimps, with cold rice moulded into a ring filled with a smooth white sauce flavoured with mushroom and onions.

The next morning Nicola started work in earnest, poring over cookery books for an hour before she decided on the various meals she would make in the next few days. She always liked to plan ahead so that she could use any left-overs for a meal on the following day. Minestrone was a particularly useful way of using meat or vegetables left from the previous day.

By the third morning she felt that she could afford to leave the kitchen for an hour or two in the morning so as to sit for Leo. Her first two days as cook had been highly successful. She had served veal escalopes and canelloni, veal in a white sauce wrapped in pancakes and a filling bowl of perfectly cooked spaghetti with a sauce made from tomatoes, mushrooms, beef and herbs. Each meal had gone well. She felt that she had proved herself and could now relax.

In a way, she thought, as she walked across the green lawns to the old tower, the spaghetti had been the most demanding dish to cook. The sheer simplicity of it made it essential that it be exactly right. No Italian would miss a mistake in the cooking of spaghetti. She might disguise a slip in her veal or canelloni—but not in spaghetti.

It pleased her that Lorenzo had said, "And now shall we have some English cooking, *mia cara*? Some soggy pudding and underdone beef?" His mellow laughter had delighted her, despite the insult to her national dish.

"If you would like to try some English dishes," she had said, tongue in cheek, "you certainly shall! I shall be delighted to cook them for you, Pappa!"

The whole table had reacted to that deliberate use of the name. Bianca had stiffened and cast her a dark-eyed look. Domenico's head had come up, the grey eyes narrowed. Leo, invited especially for that meal, had grinned and winked, while Vanessa had given her a smile of approval. Even Signora Farenze, frail as a tiny bird in her chair, had seemed surprised.

Lorenzo had been enchanted, not least by the way everyone else reacted. He was not yet past the pleasure of making people stare in astonishment or reproof, and it amused him to see that the growing affection between himself and Nicola had a profound effect upon the rest of the family.

He said to her, later, when they were alone, "I like to make them jump! It proves to me, as well as to them, that I can still make my mark on life. When I was a young man I had a fine time with the girls. Then I discovered the joys of business, the power politics of the financial world. I am past them now, money and girls both. I sometimes wake up in the night and pinch myself just to make sure I am not dead. But you and Paul have given me a new lease of life, *mia cara*. I can feel the sap in my veins again."

"Don't overdo it," she said with a scolding note. "You were running about with Paul for too long yesterday."

"Running?" He laughed loud and long at that. "Did I run, *cara*? You astonish me!"

"Promise me not to tire yourself," she pleaded. "I know you're enjoying yourself, but slow down a little. You'll enjoy life even longer if you do."

"Domenico has spoken to you! He is more of an old woman than his mother!" Lorenzo was sulky, like a little boy whose new toy was being snatched away.

"We love you," she said gently. "That's all!"

The leonine head lifted proudly. "So? Is that true, *cara*?" And at her smiling nod, he shrugged. "Then how can I have the coldness to resist? I will be more careful, for your sake, Nicola, if not for my own!"

LEO SAW HER APPROACHING across the grass and waved to her from his tower window, leaning down to smile and call a greeting.

"How nice, Nicola," he said as she came into the studio, a little breathless from the stairs. "I am so glad you could come this morning."

She flopped into the chair he had placed for her on the raised dais. In the finished portrait she was to hold Paul on her lap, but for the moment they were using a doll as a model since Paul was not easy to keep still for any long period, and was merely a noisy distraction to Leo.

Leo arranged the pose once more, coolly adjusting her arms and the tilt of her head to suit himself. "Lean back a little . . . yes . . ." He stood back and studied her dispassionately, looking more like a surgeon than an artist.

The thought made her grin, and he looked quizzically at her. She told him her thought in a light tone.

"You looked as if you were deciding which arm to cut off rather than how best to pose me!"

"Surgeons and artists have a similar education in one way," Leo said gravely. "They need a good idea of anatomy, and they must take into account the patient's state of mind as well as his body."

"And they often make enemies after the event," she added in a half-serious voice.

Leo nodded, smiling. "That is certainly true of artists—I'm not sure about surgeons, but I imagine people often resent them. We both of us see too much of the truth about people. The human mind detests being seen so clearly."

Nicola was silent, staring at the blue sky which was all that she could see from the window. They were way above the level of the trees in this room. To see the ground one had to stand at the window and look down, and she suddenly wondered if that was not dangerous—looking down on the rest of the world created a false sense of superiority in people. Perhaps that explained the arrogance of the medieval men who had built this place!

A voice broke in upon the absorbed silence in which Leo liked to work. He groaned and laid down his brush.

"Bianca!"

Nicola looked round with an embarrassed feeling of uneasiness. She always felt that Bianca disliked her, and being in her presence was not a pleasant experience. The other girl seemed to stare with such hostility! Nicola knew perfectly well that she had no need to feel guilty. She and Paolo had loved each other. Yet Bianca's cold stare always made her feel that she had in some way hurt her by marrying Paolo. Bianca was a girl whose loyalties were simple and tenacious. She loved Barbara, the girl who should have married Paolo, and she would not forgive Nicola for having hurt the other girl, even unknowingly.

Bianca came into the room and stopped dead at the sight of Nicola

There was a cold silence, then Leo grimaced. "Well, little sister? What do you want?"

Turning from her antagonistic contemplation of Nicola, the other girl tossed her head. "To speak with you—alone!"

Leo threw her an angry look. "Very well, you ill-mannered little shrew! Nicola, *cara*, you will excuse me? And excuse, too, my bad little sister who should be beaten for her insolence if my father were not so many miles away in South America?"

Bianca snapped, "Do not dare to apologise for me, Leo! And to her..."

"I would apologise to the devil if you treated him as you treat Nicola," he said sternly. "You are a fool, Bianca, and an ill-bred one, too."

Bianca flounced from the room without answering, and with a sigh Leo followed her, telling Nicola to seize the chance of relaxing for a few moments.

She got up, stretched herself and began to wander around the room, inspecting the various half-finished or finished paintings. They were either very modernistic or in a purely representational style— either wild explosions of colour and shape, or portraits of perfectly recognisable people. Obviously Domenico had been a trifle harsh when he dismissed Leo's portraits as unrepresentational. Or had Leo deliberately teased him into this belief? She knew Leo well enough by now to know that he was capable of such behaviour. Leo rather resented Domenico's special status at the villa. They were both cousins, equally closely related to Lorenzo, and Leo felt that Domenico had an unfair advantage in that he had gone into the wine business while Leo had become an artist. This had made Domenico decidedly the favourite of Lorenzo, and a power at court.

On a desk near the window stood a box of sharp pencils and a loosely tied portfolio. Nicola idly picked at the knot and it fell apart, the papers fluttering out. She managed to shuffle them back into their pile, and then her busy fingers were stilled as she realised, with astonished wonder, that she was gazing at some superb pencil drawings of Vanessa.

Leo had used the finest pencils, the most delicate lines, never explicit, always implying tentatively. Vanessa's hair seemed to flow, like coiled snakes or eddying water, around a face of exquisite purity.

Only a closer inspection revealed other facets of the drawings. The eyes were perfectly shaped—yet held fathoms of meaning within their depths. Cold knowledge, snake-like, secret. The mouth was parted on a gentle sigh, yet hinted at cruelty and greed in the sweet, fine curves.

Leo had deliberately invested the pictures with a burning intensity. Innocence and purity formed the shell within which he sketched selfishness and corruption. Vanessa looked like a fallen angel.

Transfixed, enraged and astonished, Nicola stared at one after another of the drawings. When had he drawn them? Why had he drawn them? Only a bitter hostility could explain away the way in which he had invested Vanessa with such terrible qualities.

A step on the stairs made her turn, a drawing in her hand. Leo stopped dead in the doorway, staring.

"How could you?" She was too angry to speak

clearly, her voice stammered out words. "So unkind . . . untrue . . . if she ever saw them she would be so hurt!"

Leo walked across the room in silence. He took the portfolio from her, deftly pushed the drawings into place and tied the knot tightly.

"No one need ever have seen them if you had not pried, like Pandora," he said curtly.

She acknowledged the justice of that. "I'm sorry if I overstepped the line. I didn't know you would mind. You've let me see other drawings, other paintings."

"I would not have left these out if I had known you were coming this morning," he said, putting the portfolio into a wall cupboard and carefully locking the door.

"But, Leo, why have you done them?" Bewilderment made her ask him.

"Can we change the subject?" His voice was sharp. "Leave me some private corners of my life!"

Nicola flushed at the snub and returned to the dais, but the spell of their earlier session was broken. Leo painted for a while, but he seemed uncertain, and at last he flung down his brush with a black look.

"Oh, clear off!" He spoke in terse English. "The day is ruined. I can't paint today."

CHAPTER NINE

NICOLA was soaking leaves of lasagne verde when Vanessa sauntered into the kitchen, her slender body sheathed in elegant black pants and a fragile white chiffon blouse which looked as if it had been spun by spiders.

"You look gorgeous," Nicola said appreciatively.

Vanessa shrugged, for once indifferent to a compliment. "Nicky, I think I'll go home tomorrow."

Nicola dropped two leaves of the pasta together and muttered irritably as she tried to separate them before they became irretrievably welded. When she had achieved this, she looked round at her sister incredulously. "Are you serious?"

Vanessa flushed and avoided her gaze. "Quite serious."

"But why? Is something wrong? Someone upset you?" Then, quickly, "Bianca?"

Vanessa laughed. "Bianca? You must be kidding! She couldn't affect me by one jot or tittle."

"Then why? I thought you were enjoying yourself."

Her sister fiddled vaguely with a bowl of eggs, following their shape with one finger. "I suppose I'm homesick."

Unconvinced, Nicola said softly, "What is it,

Van? I can see you're really unhappy. What's wrong?"

"I . . . I don't know." Vanessa twisted a strand of curly golden hair and began to bite it, like a schoolgirl. Nicola could remember when her sister used to do this during their childhood, and the sight made her feel protective and alarmed. Surely something must have gone seriously wrong for Vanessa to lose her poise.

Had Vanessa, by some ghastly chance, seen Leo's drawings of her?

When had Leo done those drawings, anyway? By stealth? Or from memory? She had never seen him openly drawing Vanessa. The two of them had been sharply antagonistic ever since the first day.

"If you told me I might be able to help," she said gently. Her sister looked at her, almost hopelessly, her blue eyes round and misty. If Leo had ever seen her looking like that, Nicky thought, he would not have drawn those savage portraits of her. We never really know very much about each other. Even close friends can be shocked and surprised to discover some new, unsuspected facet. She knew that Vanessa had never understood anything about her own marriage. Into these areas of one's life one forbids entry even to a sister, and each person sees a different angle of the whole personality.

Vanessa groaned faintly. "Oh, Nicky! I think . . . I think I'm in love." She said it in tones of horror and revulsion, as if she predicted her own death. For a second Nicky was merely amused. She laughed aloud at the comic expression on her sister's face as she said the words of doom. Then, seeing that Vanessa was hurt by her laughter, she sobered quickly.

Vanessa had turned away in offence. Nicola caught her arm.

"I'm sorry, I shouldn't have laughed. But you looked so funny as you said it!"

"It may be funny to you, but I'm not laughing." Vanessa sounded stiff in her indignation.

"I can see that," Nicola agreed gently. "It's Domenico, of course?"

Vanessa's blue eyes opened wide. "Domenico? No!" She looked startled.

"No? But . . ." Nicola's voice trailed away as Vanessa looked at her dumbly. "Oh, no!" she whispered. A spear of understanding shot through her and she winced. "Not . . . Leo?"

Vanessa silently nodded, biting her lip.

"Leo!" Nicola understood everything now. Of course, Vanessa must be wrenched with pain, knowing that Leo detested her and that her feelings for him were totally unrequited. Vanessa's only other brush with love had been so disastrous, so painful, that fate might have been kinder this time. How tragically ironic that Vanessa, the cool and self-reliant, should fall in love with a man like Leo who despised her.

"I see now why you want to go away," Nicola nodded. "I'll speak to Lorenzo. What shall we say? That you have to get back to work?"

"Why not? Any excuse will do. Lorenzo will be indifferent—He only wants you and Paul. He won't

even notice I've gone—no one will. Least of all
L . . ." Vanessa broke off, grimacing, tears not far
away.

"How long have you . . ." Nicola began, then
stopped, realising that this was a question she should
not ask. Even sisters have no right to pry into the secrets of love.

"The first time I saw him," Vanessa said grimly.
'He made me so angry, but at the same time he
made everyone else look pale and dull. I tried to fall
for Domenico. He's quite dishy himself, and he'll be
a fantastic husband—but I just couldn't see him.
Leo seemed to dominate everything I looked at. It
got so bad that I couldn't even sleep. I know he detests me—he shows it plainly enough—but it makes
no difference. I feel sick every time I set eyes on
him."

Nicola put her arms around her, forgetting the lasagne verde. Food was of no importance. If the
lunch was ruined she would make a salad. One could
always ring the changes with a mixture of strange ingredients.

She stroked the blonde curls and Vanessa, for
once indifferent to the ruin of her careful make-up,
put her head on her sister's shoulder and wept until
her mascara had run into little spiky lines down her
wet cheeks.

"MUST SHE GO AT ONCE?" Lorenzo was surprised.
"But I had planned a little surprise for you both—a
party!" He beamed at Nicola, his wrinkles seeming
to double as his smile grew.

She was as surprised as he could have wished. "A party?"

"And you shall not do the cooking, *mia cara*. You have cooked for us so beautifully, but now we shall demand that you permit someone else to do it until Violetta returns. Violetta has a cousin—Anna. She is a widow, a very good cook and cheerful, and she wants to come to us." He shook his brown index finger at her. "She needs the money, *cara*. You do not!"

In the face of such an argument, Nicola had no reply. She smiled apologetically. "That had never occurred to me. I'm sorry. Yes, of course Anna must come."

Lorenzo was delighted. "You have impressed us with your skill, *mia cara*. Such sauces!" He bunched his fingers, kissed them with an air. "And even your soup was always a new experience . . . the rich bisque you served yesterday—I was greedy and I suffered for it in the night. I am of an age when greed can be cruel."

"When will Anna come?" she asked after a few moments.

"She came to see me this morning, to beg for the chance to show what she can do—she knew, of course, that you were cooking, and she said that she would work with you, but I told her that you had only been doing the work until we had decided who to employ in Violetta's place."

"Cunning Pappa!" said Nicola with amusement.

"She would resent you otherwise," he said with a wink. "I disarmed her hidden resentment, I hope."

He shot her a long look. "Do you find others who feel like this? Bianca, for instance? Does she behave better now? I spoke to her after the incident of the ball on the stairs. She could have killed someone. I was very stern with her, and I hope I have made her repentant."

Bianca's hatred might have been pushed underground, thought Nicola, but it was not completely invisible. It showed through at odd moments. Her eyes were always revealing.

"She was very fond of her friend Barbara?" she asked Lorenzo with some curiosity.

"Bianca? Oh, do not believe all she tells you, dear child. It is true that Bianca was fond of Barbara, but there is more to it than that. Bianca was half in love with Paolo herself, I think. She was at an impressionable age. These young girls can feel so deeply! She felt, when he wrote of his marriage to you, that he had slapped her face! Consider, *mia cara*! If Paolo were to disobey me and marry a poor girl, one who worked as a cook—why had he not looked at Bianca, whom he knew very well adored him?" Lorenzo shook his leonine head in pity. "Poor Bianca! She burned with hatred and with love—and that is why she acts as she does."

"I did suspect it," Nicola said slowly. "Barbara married someone else?"

"Not yet, but she is to do so quite soon, I believe."

"I heard a rumour that Bianca was to marry Domenico," she said casually, and waited with painfully held breath for his reply.

Lorenzo shrugged. "Bianca has transferred her emotions to Domenico, it is true. I have thought that they might make a match, but I have ceased to interfere in the affairs of others since you came, *cara*. I made so terrible a mistake over you. Who am I to say who shall marry whom? It would be mere folly."

"And . . . Domenico?" Her voice was husky. Lorenzo glanced at her from beneath lowered lids and smiled, a little cunningly.

"You must ask him yourself, *cara*. Ask him if he is in love."

LORENZO HAD DRAWN UP A LIST of the guests who were to come to the party he was giving in honour of Nicola herself. He gave it to her, later, and asked her to order some printed invitations from a stationer in Florence who would print the actual names while she waited.

Domenico offered to drive her into the city when he went himself after lunch. His working hours were flexible since he had his office actually in the Villa itself. The clerical staff of the business pursued their duties in an office in Florence, and Domenico commuted between the Villa and Florence. Lorenzo still descended on the firm from time to time, and several other male members of the family worked for the firm, too, but Nicola had not yet met them.

She was to do so when they came to the party, for a large number of the names on the list, she saw, were members of the Farenze family.

It was, she discovered from Domenico on their drive down into Florence, a widespread family, not all of them people with money. The family instinct is such, in Italy, that there was close contact between them, of whatever social class.

"After all, blood is . . ."

"Thicker than water," she finished for him, with a nod.

He shot her a look. "We are proud of our past, but we are also proud of our future. We may no longer command the same influence, but Lorenzo still feels a deep affection for everyone of his blood. The children, particularly. He adores children."

"So I've noticed," she smiled.

"Paul is special," he agreed. "Paul is his own grandson. Lorenzo loves all children, but those of his family mean more."

"I shall feel as if I'm on display," Nicola said ruefully. "They will all come, I suppose?"

"All of them," he agreed wryly. "They will flock from the far corners of the earth to see what manner of creature has produced the next Lion of Farenze. Their eyes will strip you to your very bones."

"Farenze eyes have that capacity," she nodded drily. "I've noticed that, too."

His grey eyes slid sideways to survey her. "Is that aimed at me?"

"Or Leo," she added.

"Leo . . . Ah, yes, Leo. How is his portrait proceeding? Have you seen it?" His expression had taken on a new cast, a cold sarcasm.

"He will not allow that."

"How surprising!" The dry tone irritated her.

"But from the other portraits I've seen I have no

doubt it will be remarkable. Leo has considerable talent, I think."

He flipped a quizzical eyebrow. "You sound defiant. I wonder why?"

"I know you don't agree," she said crossly.

"You know nothing about me." The voice hardened, grew strangely alien and offhand.

Nicola was silent for a moment, wondering why he was angry.

Domenico drove on, staring ahead. After a while he asked suddenly, "Are you in love with Leo?"

She was shaken and looked at him in alarm, her pulses hammering, her skin white with shock. The green eyes widened and filled with unconscious pain.

It was only then, faced with that question, that her brain knew what her heart had known for so long. She was not in love with Leo. No. She was in love with Domenico himself, a love which now, being acknowledged at last, flooded her whole being with a stinging emotion, compounded of joy and hurt.

She had left his question unanswered too long, and Domenico's face tightened. "I see," he said coldly. "I suspected as much."

"No," she stammered, hot and trembling, desperate to convince him that he was mistaken. "No, of course I'm not in love with Leo. I can't think why you should get that impression."

"You need not pretend with me," he said coolly. "I know you too well now, Nicola. You went first white, then red, and such violence can only indicate deep emotions. I'm sorry for you. Leo is not the man for you—he'll make you miserable. I warned you at the start, but you wouldn't listen and I knew then that is was useless. You're obstinate and wilful." His voice dropped the words like icy pebbles into the stream of her mind, and Nicola listened, wincing. How he disliked and despised her!

What was the point of arguing with him? He would believe what he wanted to believe, and it was better for him to believe she loved Leo than to suspect she loved himself.

They were approaching the city now. The cars tore round them, hooting, their drivers leaning out to shout and swear at each other, horns blaring permanently. Italian drivers have a sort of death wish; they drive in perpetual competition, cutting each other out, scraping wheels and bumpers. It is less like a drive along a road than a chariot race updated, with all the violence kept intact.

Only yesterday Lorenzo had shown her a medieval map of Florence hanging on the wall of his library. The blue sky arched overhead, the white bridges, the little huddle of houses fenced in by the old city wall. Ahead of her she saw the modern city, in some ways still faintly reminiscent. The wall still ran here and there, but the city had sprawled out from the walls into the green countryside. There were the landmarks she had come to know and recognise with warmth—the Campanile, the Duomo, the church spires. She felt strangely familiar in this place, as if she had always known it. It was smaller than London, more compact and with a definite centre which all felt with the heart. The Uffizi; the Loggia dei Lanzi, and those beautiful statues which seemed less like the product of man's hands than the genius of nature herself; here one felt the heart of the city beating.

Domenico parked the car and offered to show Nicola the office of the printer, but she refused, politely, wishing to be alone. She wanted to explore further the new world which had opened—to know the limits of her love. What of that old love, her brief marriage with Paolo? How did her love for Domenico measure up to that?

She walked without haste through the narrow, medieval streets, past open doors in which sat old men, women sewing, children playing with gaudy plastic toys. Above her were crumbling walls, windowsills gay with geraniums in boxes and pots, cats perched on high, giddy roofs. The pavements were cracked and sloping. A stall sold early fruit. The vendor shouted in pidgin English as she passed, spotting her nationality in a way which amused her.

It pleased her to find her way, without help, through the maze of little streets. She felt that she was really getting to know the city.

The printer was delighted to accept the order, and talked to her as he complied with it, shouting above the rattle and clump of his machinery.

When she left his shop, the invitations safely in her bag, she walked around aimlessly for a while, enjoying the sunshine and the busy life of the city. It was fun to go into a shop and buy some biscuits, speaking Italian so well that the shopkeeper could not quite be certain that she was a foreigner. She beamed at him as she left, enjoying his doubt. She bought chocolate for Paul, a pair of fine leather slippers for Lorenzo at a street stall, for Italian leather goods are both cheap and superb.

When she had realised that it was growing more difficult to get about through the increasing crowds, she made her way wack to Domenico's office. He had said he would be there at five o'clock. She found that she was late. He was pacing up and down beside his car looking both annoyed and worried.

He turned on her angrily as she joined him. "Where the devil have you been? I have been out of my mind. Alone, in a strange city—anything could have happened to you! Why didn't you telephone when you knew you would be late? And what in hell's name have you been doing to be so late?"

Nicola waited until he ran out of breath before replying to this tirade.

"I'm sorry, but I was just exploring. I wanted to see as much of the old city as I could."

He glared at her, teeth tightly clamped together, then after a moment he jerked open the door of his car. "Get in!"

Nicola obeyed meekly. He shot away from the car park as if he were in a race to the moon. She peeped sideways and found him staring at the road ahead, his jaw clenched. There was more to his anger than her late arrival, she decided. Had something happened?

"I should have rung you," she offered gently. "I really am sorry, Domenico."

He glanced at her. "Oh, forget it," he said brusquely, the grey eyes cool.

But after a moment or two he began to talk, quite cheerfully, about the old part of Florence, lamenting various changes, and predicting further decay unless some money was spent by the Florentines.

"Italy is going through a bad patch at present. We are falling behind in the industrial race because of inflation and soaring costs..."

"I know the story," she groaned. "You forget, Britain has had the same problems. I sympathise. Inflation is poison."

They talked about national problems for a while, until the city was left far behind, and the car began the steep climb into the green Tuscan hills.

"Do you now intend to stay in Italy?" He asked the question abruptly.

She hesitated. "I didn't mean to when I first came, but now that I've got to know Lorenzo I feel somewhat different about the whole thing."

He nodded. "Now you know Lorenzo . . ." The tone was dry. "It has nothing to do with Leo, of course."

She was surprised that he had brought Leo up again, but she took the chance to deny his belief that she loved Leo.

He listened to her stammered denials impassively. "You are a little too vehement," he only said, when she had finished.

"If I want to stay now, it's for Lorenzo and Paul," she said. "Lorenzo loves Paul. I was afraid that he would try to treat Paul the way he treated his father, but that hasn't happened."

"He is very old now, and too aware of the short

time he has left," Domenico agreed. "He wants only to enjoy Paul's company."

"That's what I think," she agreed gently. "It's wonderful to see them both together. I'm glad I brought Paul, now. He would have missed so much. He has no father to remember, but at least now he will have his grandfather. It will enrich his life."

He sighed deeply. "You are wiser than you were, Nicola."

"Yes," she said, "I think I am."

"And Paolo? Has being here, at the Villa, brought to life his memory for you? Or has Leo pushed him out of your heart at last?"

"At first I thought a great deal about Paolo—naturally," she agreed. "But lately I think he has become even more of a memory to me. At last I have laid to rest the ghost of an old bitterness. My resentment towards the Farenze family had kept grief alive, but that's over now."

Domenico was silent for a while. "I can understand that," he said slowly. "It is wise of you to put your grief behind you. I am sure you know enough about men to know that any man who married you would feel some jealousy towards your dead husband. After all, you loved him enough to marry him. That would lie between you and anyone else."

Nicola shivered. "Only if he felt I didn't love him even more, surely."

His voice was harsh. "But could you? How could he believe you loved him more, and how could he bear it if he suspected you loved him less than a dead man?"

"I loved Paolo as a girl loves," she said passionately.

"And how is that? Tell me?" His voice was cold, merciless, probing her thoughts regardless of how much pain he caused. For a second she almost hated him.

"How could you understand? You're not a girl. I was romantic, eager for love, swept off my feet by a glamorous foreigner. Paolo and I scarcely knew each other. We married in a whirlwind and then he died shortly afterwards."

"And in between?" Domenico's voice pierced and wounded. Nicola looked at him angrily, on the point of tears, her eyes wide and wet.

"In between . . . what do you want me to say? That I discovered that my husband was a hot-headed gambler, that he loved to drive cars too fast and to flirt with every pretty girl he met, that he spent money as if it was water . . ." The words spilled out hotly, flooding out of her in aching gasps. "How do you think I felt when he was killed? Torn between a ghastly sort of relief and a terrible anguish of guilt and remembered love? I was in hell for months!"

They had entered the Farenze gates. The lions snarled down, paws upraised as though to strike her. She was sobbing wildly, her whole body shaking with grief and the complete breakdown of her long silence about Paolo.

Domenico braked. The car shot to a smooth halt beneath the trees. He turned in his seat, his hands reaching out for her.

"*Cara*," he whispered huskily, "I am sorry. So this is how it really was . . ."

She pushed him back, trembling violently. "Please . . . I can't bear it . . . I must go."

Before he could stop her she had opened the door of the car, slipped out and begun to run away, into the cool depths of the formal garden. He, too, climbed out of the car, as if to follow her, then paused and stood, one hand on the warm bonnet, staring after her.

She passed out of sight behind a hedge. The grey eyes gazed blankly over the statues, the gravel paths, the ferny banks beneath the trees. Then Domenico climbed back into his car and drove on to the house, his lean face a cool mask.

CHAPTER TEN

LORENZO himself had promised to speak to Vanessa about staying on for a few more days in order to be at the Villa for the party given in her sister's honour.

Nicola went straight to her sister's room, when she had washed and changed after her weeping, and found Vanessa sitting on the bed contemplating a long evening dress of a heavenly blue shade, full-sleeved and low-necked, with great sweeping skirts which swished and murmured most satisfactorily with every movement.

"I gather," Nicola said with amusement, "that Lorenzo persuaded you to change your mind?"

"Mmmm...Nicky, what do you think? This dress or the white one? This is gorgeous, but the white one does something for me."

"I should wear this one," Nicola said firmly. "It's more romantic."

"Do you think so?" Vanessa studied it, head to one side. "I want to look positively stunning, Nicky. I want to make him sit up and take notice. I want to knock him for six. Do you think this is the right dress for all that?"

"Wear it and see," came the answer.

"Oh, but I have just this one last chance. I can't afford a gamble—it must come off." Vanessa's voice had a strange, dry desperation which wrung Nicola's heart. Her lovely sister had been tumbled off her pedestal with a vengeance!

"You won't have much competition," she pointed out gently, but Vanessa merely sighed.

"You'll be there. Do you think I don't know he prefers you?"

Flushing, Nicola said, "You're wrong, Van. Really—it may sound corny, but we're just good friends. There's never been anything more than that."

Vanessa fixed her wide blue eyes on her. "I can't believe it. He's spent such a lot of time with you— painting you hour after hour, alone with him in that ridiculous tower place..."

"Leo means nothing to me, or I to him."

Something about the certainty in Nicola's voice managed to get through. Vanessa looked at her sharply, probingly, and apparently believed her.

"Well, that's one family problem the less," she said with rueful amusement.

Nicola was suddenly touched. "You suspected that Leo and I were... well, romantically entwined? Yet you didn't reproach me at all? You were very unselfish, Vanessa."

"If he loved you what point was there in saying anything? Only after I realised you weren't in love with him, even though I still thought he liked you, only then could I bear to let you know how I felt."

"How did you guess I didn't love him?" Nicola asked curiously.

Vanessa hesitated. "I... don't quite know how..."

She looked shyly at her sister. "I saw you looking at Domenico—I'm sorry, I wasn't being vulgarly curious. It just dawned on me."

Nicola laughed. "We're a couple of lunatics, aren't we? Falling for men who ignore us! Perhaps we'd better both go home."

That evening, after dinner, she and Lorenzo sat and wrote out the invitation envelopes and slid the stiff, silver-edged cards into them, firmly stamping them and putting them into a neat pile.

Leo strolled over to watch them. "Am I invited to this extravaganza?"

"Of course. Only behave yourself." Lorenzo gave him a long, stern look.

Bianca, sitting to one side with pale, angry features averted from them, stiffened even further as she heard these words, and Nicola felt an icy little chill as the black eyes darted sidelong in bitter hostility.

She had ceased to make little overtures to the other girl. Bianca merely rejected her coldly, contempt in every line of her face. She saw Nicola's wish to be friendly as a sign of weakness, and despised her. Bianca's Italian blood was productive of great pride and hauteur. She would rather have died than try to win over an enemy; jealousy and envy had corroded her mind. When Domenico came back into the room, having been to speak to someone on the telephone, Bianca tried to draw him to her with an eager smile. He gave her a brief, faint smile in return, but came to sit beside Lorenzo to speak to him.

They discussed some business matter for a moment or two, then Domenico glanced, at length, at Nicola. During dinner he had avoided her. He had been almost silent, withdrawn, but now the grey eyes alighted on her face, stripping her emotions mercilessly.

She shrank from them, involuntarily, lowering her own eyes in self defence. Domenico's hard mouth compressed further. The grey eyes narrowed to mere flinty slits.

Leo, glancing from one to the other, was engrossed in amused speculation.

"I'm tired," she said hastily, jumping up. "Lorenzo, will you excuse me if I go up to bed now? I think I did too much walking in Florence today. I was on my feet all afternoon in the sunshine, and it's given me a slight headache."

The old man frowned. "I am sorry to hear that, *mia cara*. Have you some tablets to take? Shall we find you something? A cachet?"

"I have some tablets, thank you," she said, smiling gratefully down at him.

Leo unexpectedly stood up, his carriage easy and lazy, and to her total astonishment kissed her lightly on her mouth. The black eyes danced as he grinned down at her astonished face.

"Goodnight, my dear Nicola," he murmured softly. "Sleep well."

The silence in the room was profound. She could feel the eyes of everyone there fixed upon her. Lorenzo was startled, quizzical, a little annoyed with Leo. Domenico was grim, watchful. And Vanessa...she dared not even look at her sister.

Stumbling to the door, Nicola felt dizzy and sick with the combined effect of her afternoon in the sun, and the shock of Leo's kiss. Leo, naturally, had been mischievous. The kiss had been a tease. But for whom?

She made her way to her bedroom and opened the door. While she was doing the cooking, Angelina had removed Paul to her room so that he should not disturb his mother when she was tired in the early morning. The room lay silent and empty in front of her. Nicola moved wearily towards the bed and switched on the lamp beside it.

Then she screamed. On the coverlet of her bed lay Paul's teddy bear. He had been disembowelled—his stuffing lay scattered on the bed. His head had been wrenched off and lay at the foot of the bed, the glass eyes staring sadly up at the ceiling.

Running footsteps sounded on the marble floors somewhere and Domenico burst into the room. "Are you all right?" He raced across to her, caught her, his arm around her back, and looked at her searchingly. "Why did you scream?"

Nicola was shaking, sickened not so much by the sight of the teddy bear as by the hatred behind the senseless act of destruction.

His eyes rose, saw the bed, narrowed as he took it all in. "My faith!" he breathed savagely. "Who did this?" Then his glance moved to the dressing-table. She saw his face tighten yet further, and she, too, turned to look.

Across the mirror, written in scarlet lipstick, was the one word *Morte* ... Death!

She could not stop the trembling of her body. Slumping down on the edge of the bed, she whispered, "Please, call Vanessa . . . I can't sleep here tonight..."

"No, no, of course." He hesitated. "Will you be all right if I leave you?" But at that moment Vanessa and Leo came into the room together.

"What was it? A rat?" Leo's tone was amused for a moment, but he suddenly saw the remains of the teddy bear, and the writing on the mirror, and his smile faded. "My God!"

The hostility between him and Domenico was evident as the other man let go of Nicola and turned to face Leo. "I suppose we do not need to look far to find the perpetrator of this disgusting piece of work?"

Leo met his glare unsmilingly. "Bianca? The girl is sick, I think. If she did this..."

"If?" Domenico's voice was harsh. "Can you doubt it? Who else would have done such a thing?"

Leo's face lengthened. "What am I to do with her? She must be so unhappy to do such things. I am at a loss." He looked at Nicola. "*Cara*, I am sorry— what can I say to you? I am ashamed that my sister does these things."

"Why don't you send her back to your parents in South America?" suggested Vanessa quietly. "They are the right people to deal with the problem."

Leo looked at her with dawning excitement. "But of course—why didn't I think of it? That is what I shall do. She needs love and care and security."

"You can't send her back," Domenico said curtly.

Nicola looked at him in pain. He meant that he would look after Bianca, of course, that she must stay here at the Villa.

Nicola closed her eyes. She was so tired. If only they would all be quiet, let her sleep. She could almost sleep where she sat . . . yet not quite, for how could she bear this room now, with its echo of bitter hatred? The room was filled with dark memories, haunted by Bianca's unhappiness and desire to wound. The girl had come in here stealthily, taken a child's toy and destroyed it, deliberately and savagely. There was something terrifying in the destruction she had wreaked upon such an object. Nicola could not quite banish an unbidden thought—that, with a little more time, Bianca's sickness might bring her to worse deeds. Paul himself, helpless child though he was, might conceivably have been her final target.

She shuddered as the idea took hold in her mind. Paul! Her little baby. In such hideous danger!

An icy coldness seized her limbs. Bianca's mind was poisoned, she reminded herself. In a way what she had done had been a cry for help—wasn't that what the medical jargon usually said? There was much to be said for it, she told herself wearily. She had seen from the start that Bianca was unhappy. No healthy, normal mind had committed these acts.

Aloud she said, "I'm sorry for her. Very sorry . . ." She opened her eyes. The room was spinning round, in a strange fashion. Faces revolved, too— Vanessa's frowning, Leo, white and disturbed. And Domenico . . . She looked at him in drowning regret, then Vanessa bent and said, "Come on, honey. You can share my pad tonight." Nicola began to cry then, at the kindness in her sister's voice.

She slept deeply that night, but it was a sleep disturbed by dreams. She found herself in the Villa garden, running down the alleys between the clipped green hedges, facing a vista of blind walls which always seemed to recede before her. She could smell the scent of rain on the leaves, hear birds calling sweetly somewhere not too far off. But the silence of the garden held her as immovably as a shimmering spider's web holds a fly. Her brain was thudding with terror, her pulses beat dizzyingly. She knew she had to go on running, running. But why?

Then she saw Paul, standing on the top of one of the blind walls. He called, holding out his arms. She tried to answer, but her throat was parched and dumb.

Then Bianca came along the wall towards him, lips stretched in a soundless, terrifying smile. Nicola knew Bianca would push him, knew he would fall and be killed.

She screamed, then, again and again, and suddenly found herself on the wall in Paul's place. He had vanished. Bianca laughed and pushed her, hard, and she began to fall, slowly, her skirts spreading out like a parachute. Down and down she fell, with that strange, echoing slow motion which dreams often show us. Panic and fear made her stomach rise, and she closed her eyes against the relentless pull of gravity.

She opened them again, on a daylit bedroom, with the scent of coffee fragrant in her nostrils, and

Vanessa seated, cross-legged, on the end of the bed, smiling at her.

"Welcome back to the land of the living. You slept like a log."

"What time is it?" Nicola turned her head to look at the bedside table. The little jade glass clock showed the time as ten-fifteen. She was aghast. "That late?" She moved hurriedly, to get out of bed, but Vanessa laid a compelling hand on her arm.

"Hang on a minute! You're to stay in bed until lunchtime!"

"Who said so?"

"Would you believe, Lorenzo?" Vanessa laughed. "He was very upset about last night."

"They didn't tell him about the bear? They shouldn't have done so! It might have alarmed him and brought on another stroke!"

"He can't be wrapped in cotton wool for the rest of his life," Vanessa said. "Anyway, Domenico didn't give him any details, just said Bianca had broken something of yours and upset you. Lorenzo was up in arms at once."

"Domenico wants her to stay here," said Nicola flatly. "You heard what he said last night. He'll find a way to protect her."

"He's taking her to South America," Vanessa said lightly.

Nicola sat up. "He *what*?" She stared at her sister, wide-eyed and incredulous. "Domenico is going all the way to South America with Bianca?"

Vanessa shrugged. "Apparently he has business contacts with a firm over there and he decided to kill two birds with one stone—take Bianca home and do some business at the same time."

"When are they going?"

Vanessa began to pour them both a cup of coffee, and pushed one cup over to Nicola's side of the tray. "They've gone," she said succinctly.

"What, already?" Nicola's hand shook slightly as she picked up her cup.

"Domenico doesn't hang about, does he?" Vanessa offered her a roll. "Once he's made a decision—wham!" She whistled softly. "He really is quite something—but marriage with him would be like living with a steamroller. Butter? Cherry jam?"

Nicola automatically took butter, dipped a spoon in the luscious thick black cherry jam and spread it on her roll. "So Domenico won't be here for the party?"

"I doubt it!" Vanessa shot her a curious glance. "Is it serious with you, Nicky? I mean, are you trying to fight it off? I've had symptoms of love before now, but I've treated them like the onset of a cold, and dosed myself against them."

Nicola laughed huskily. "What do you take? I may need the advice."

"I make myself notice all his bad points. I mentally make fun of him and laugh myself out of it." Vanessa was half serious.

"Did you do that with Leo?" asked Nicola.

Vanessa sighed. "Frequently. It didn't work for once, so I just gave up the unequal struggle."

"Was that painful?"

Vanessa gave her a grin. "Honey, it was a relief!"

"A relief?" Nicola was amused. She sipped her coffee and felt the warmth spreading through her chilled body, untangling the conflicts of the long night.

Vanessa ran her fingers through her blonde curls. "It is a strain, fighting off love. One gets tired of the struggle. I think maybe I was ready to meet Leo—success is wearing, and I knew I couldn't stay at the top of the modelling tree for much longer. I'm not a young girl any more. I've had a fantastic career, but even that's lost its original excitement."

"Bored with your career, Van?" Nicola smiled away the sting of her mockery. "I can't believe it!"

"Maybe I'm not as tough and opportunistic as I thought I was," said Vanessa. "When I came out here with you it was to further my chances of snatching Domenico—you knew that. I would have sold you down the river then, Nicky. I wanted to grab him while I had the chance. Then one look at Leo and my world went topsy-turvy." She grimaced. "And, in a crazy sort of way, I was thrilled. It was twice as exciting as my success as a model. I felt dizzy and elated at one and the same time. So I let go all my old ideas and just..." she spread her hands in an expressive gesture, "just fell all the way down."

Nicola touched her hand gently. "I wish he would feel the same way, Vanessa. Maybe if you stayed..."

Vanessa shook her head. "I'll stay until the party, then I'm going. I'm not sorry I ever met him, Nicky—I'm glad, even if he never looks at me. It was worth it."

"I'll miss you," said Nicola. "It was fun sharing a flat with you and Bess."

"You'll stay here at the Villa, of course," her sister replied casually. "I'm glad you've seen sense over that. Paul's happy here, much happier than he was in that cramped little flat in London. He has so many people around him; Angelina, Lorenzo, the Italian kids that come to play with him twice a week. He has room and sunshine—what more could he want?"

Nicola sighed. "I shall be homesick now and then. And there's the problem of Domenico."

"Domenico?"

"It will be unbearable, living here in the same house, knowing he is indifferent to me."

Vanessa nodded sympathetically. "Maybe it will be all for the best if he marries Bianca and stays over in South America!"

Nicola was silent, her body shocked into immobility. Then, in a dry voice, she asked, "Is that what you think he'll do? Did he actually say so?"

Shrugging, Vanessa said, "No, he didn't actually say so, but it looks pretty obvious, doesn't it, Nicky? Why else would he go all that way just for her? Why would he protect her as he has? He must be serious about her, and, let's face it, Bianca may be a little screwy, but she's a ravishingly lovely girl. Just the dark-eyed beauty for an Italian like Domenico."

Nicola walked stiffly over to her wardrobe and began to search for something to wear. Her fingers moved through the clothes, but her mind was abstracted. Vanessa was right, of course—Domenico must be in love with Bianca. Perhaps he would never come back to the Villa Farenze, and she might never see him again. It would, in a way, be the kindest thing, for her own sake, this sudden, unexpected parting, and although it hurt now she would recover quicker, as one does from one swift, sure cut from the knife of a surgeon. She told herself so, calmly and soberly, but it made no difference. It hurt intolerably just the same.

CHAPTER ELEVEN

WITH Domenico out of the way, and Nicola released from the self-imposed duties in the kitchen, Leo insisted that she spend most of the daylight hours in his studio posing for him. He was in a hurry to finish his portrait of her so that he could present it to Lorenzo at the party. She brought Paul with her several times so that Leo could draw him, but Paul would not sit still long enough for any detailed pose to be possible. He wriggled and shouted to get down, and was very interested in the paints and filthy pieces of paint-daubed cloth which Leo left strewn around the room.

"He's like an eel," Leo said discontentedly, watching the little boy squeezing an empty tube and crowing with delight as a tiny squirm of white paint oozed out. "Put that down, you imp of hell! You'll get dirty and then Angelina will nag me until my ears drop off."

Paul laughed and toddled off to peer over the windowsill at the earth far below. Catching him hurriedly around his small waist, Nicola looked down too, her head circling dizzily for a moment. Green and leafy, the world seemed to revolve far below. She saw Vanessa strolling along an alley in the garden, her full skirt blowing back from her slender legs. Leo joined them and Nicola, glancing up, caught an odd expression on his handsome face.

Her suspicions arose, but she quelled them firmly. She was rather too eager to believe that Leo had some hidden interest in Vanessa—she refused to allow herself to be too hopeful.

"Your beautiful sister seems to be at a loose end since Domenico went off to South America," he drawled over her head.

Carefully staring out of the window, she said casually, "Oh, Vanessa wasn't ever really interested in Domenico."

"No?" He sounded doubtful. "She gave a good imitation."

"Vanessa has always had a lot of admirers," Nicola said. "She moves in that sort of world—models attract men like flies, but it doesn't mean anything very much."

"Just routine? A flirtation and then goodbye— *ciao*!" He made a practised gesture, halfway between a shrug and a wave. "I somehow don't think Domenico knew that!"

Slowly, Nicola asked, "You think he was more serious than that?"

"She's very beautiful." Leo's voice was husky. Nicola hazarded another quick glance upwards. He was staring down at Vanessa, his face unguarded briefly. Nicola drew in her breath in surprise and embarrassment at what she saw in that dark face now. Leo looked down hastily, met her eyes and dark angry colour rose in his cheeks. The black eyes flashed.

"I'm sorry, Leo," she stammered. "I . . . didn't

know . . . you gave me no inkling that you felt like . . ." Her voice died away as she realised the sheer absurdity of trying to apologise. What could she say? She had seen something he had tried to keep hidden—once more, as when she had seen his portfolio of sketches of Vanessa and misinterpreted them as hatred. They had been the product of angry emotion, but it had been love, not hate, that dictated them.

Once she would have blithely seen this as a happy ending. Vanessa was in love with Leo. Now, it seemed, Leo loved her, too. Nicola sighed. Maturity brought new problems. Her own marriage to Paolo had taught her that love is not always enough. She had loved Paolo, but her memories of him were tainted by her realisation that he was not, in fact, the man she had believed him to be when she married him. Side by side with her love an angry dislike had grown—a dislike of what he did rather than of Paolo himself. She had not ceased to love, but she had ceased to be happy with him.

Leo, she saw, disliked some of Vanessa's characteristics. Unlike herself, Leo had seen these faults from the start. He was attracted to Vanessa, yet saw her clearly. Could any marriage prosper with such a foundation? Could Vanessa be happy with a man who brought to their relationship the clear-eyed perception which Leo had shown in those sketches of her?

Leo passed one hand over his face. "You should have taken up art," he said hoarsely. "You have extra-sensory perception, I think—or X-ray eyes! I hope you'll forget it, now, though. No heart-to-heart chats with big sister?" His eyes flashed to her face, held her own gaze soberly. "Promise? This is an official secret!"

She hesitated. He did not, of course, know how Vanessa felt. But would he change his mind, even if he did? She did not know him well enough. He had read Vanessa as an ambitious, hard-headed woman capable of callous and cruel determination in the pursuit of her ends—the sketches had made that brutally plain. If Leo knew that Vanessa loved him, would he alter his opinion of her?

Leo shook her, frowning. "Did you hear me? Promise not to say a word to your sister."

"I promise," she said reluctantly, then dived to intercept Paul, who had crawled into an interesting tunnel made by some paintings leaning against a wall. She pulled him out, hoisted him into her arms and said goodbye to Leo.

"We must go to lunch."

He nodded. "I think I've got as much as I need. He is the world's worst model. I'll concentrate on the background now. I've only got one more day to finish off."

"Do you want me to come over again?" she asked.

He shook his head. "No, I don't think so, thank you. Your face is finished."

"Can I see?" She had not yet set eyes on the picture and was longing to see it.

"No," he said firmly. "You can wait, like everyone else. You'll see it in good time."

Signora Farenze was in the courtyard when Paul
and Nicola came back into the house. A shaft of sunlight fell short of her chair, leaving her in shadow.
She wore her usual black dress and was reading a
newspaper, her spectacles on the end of her nose.
She peered over them and smiled.

"Paul! How are you today?"

"Hungry," he said, bouncing over to her. "I could
eat a horse!"

"So hungry? How terrible! Fortunate that here
comes Angelina to rescue you from this starvation..."

Angelina came soft-footed and seized him, shrieking with delight. She smiled at Nicola and bade her
good-day with an affection which, on that first day of
their arrival, Nicola could not have predicted. How
much all their attitudes had changed, she thought,
watching as her son was carried off, chattering excit-
edly while Angelina listened in amused fascination.

Signora Farenze looked up at her shrewdly. "You
are thoughtful today, *mia cara*?"

"The party has made me excited, I suppose," said
Nicola, a little evasively.

The old blue eyes narrowed. "The party? And
Leo's portrait of you, eh?"

Blankly, Nicola said, "The portrait? Oh, that...
yes, I suppose that, too."

Watching her carefully, Signora Farenze said, "I
hope you were not too angry with little Bianca? She
has had a disturbed childhood—so often away from
her parents during her early years, and never really
feeling she belonged anywhere, even here at the Villa. I do not think her actions were truly personal."

"I think she loved Paolo," Nicola said firmly. "That is how I read the situation. She was in love with him, and hated me for marrying him. But how can we ever really understand the motives of other people? Even when they tell us why they did things, it may not be the real truth. People often quite unconsciously rationalise their motives even to themselves."

Signora Farenze inclined her head slowly in assent. "You are right. Bianca's motives were probably more complex than we know. But you do not feel that what she did could influence your feelings for her brother?"

Nicola flushed. "For Leo? No. Why should it? I like Leo. He's far more serious than he appears on the surface, and I'm sorry for him in some ways. Bianca and he were never very close, I gather."

"No, they did not live together in childhood. Leo was sent to boarding-school and then to art college. He has only really known Bianca well since she came to live in the watch-tower. She came to the Villa, too, with the idea of living there with him, but Lorenzo insisted that she lived in the house, here. It was more suitable."

"Lorenzo has been good to them," Nicola commented.

Signora Farenze shrugged. "They are of the family!" She studied Nicola closely. "I will be frank with you, *mia cara*. Are you in love with Leo?"

Nicola shook her head. "No."

There was a little silence, then the old woman sighed gently. "I am glad—so glad, *cara*."

Nicola laughed. "Why?"

Signora Farenze smiled. "He is not the right man for you."

ON THE EVENING OF THE PARTY, Nicola got dressed carefully and went down to inspect the salons which had been prepared for the guests.

A cold buffet had been laid out on the damask-draped tables in the dining room. Silverware, glass and immaculate white napkins added the finishing touches to a beautifully laid meal. The piles of plates at each end of the tables, the elegantly arranged flowers, had all been seen to earlier. Bowls of salad, cut slices of bread and piles of freshly baked rolls stood along the back of the table.

Arrayed in front of these were salmon and egg mousses, caviar, cold rice with prawns and vegetables, paper-thin slices of Parma ham with melon, cold legs of chicken, cheese and pickles, and many other party dishes.

Nicola wiped a finger over a glass to check the cleanliness, nodded in satisfaction and wiped the glass again with a napkin. She put one last touch to a flower arrangement, then stood back. She could find no fault with it.

"Where is the champagne?" Lorenzo came up behind her and made her jump.

"In the kitchen, being kept at the right temperature." She looked at him inquiringly. "Well? Are you pleased?"

He looked round the room. "Sure. It looks fine." He spoke in English, jokingly, then with a grin of relief reverted to his own tongue. "You look very beautiful, *mia cara*. I shall be very proud of you to-night."

"She looks like a firebird," said Leo, coming in from the courtyard through the open window.

Eagerly, the old wrinkled face turned to him. "The portrait? Where is it?"

"It isn't quite finished, you know," Leo said warningly. "It isn't framed, and I have a lot of last touches to make."

"But I can see it? You promised we could put it on show tonight to the guests." Lorenzo looked disappointed.

Leo shrugged. "Just as you like. I brought it over—but if anybody lays a finger on it I won't be responsible. The paint isn't quite dry yet. It takes days to dry off properly."

"Let me see it," Lorenzo implored.

Leo went back into the courtyard and came back at once, wheeling an easel on a small metal frame supported by two wheels, rather like the base of a shopping bag on wheels. He rested this in one corner and delicately whisked off the cover.

The others walked forward slowly. The portrait had a formal background—for a moment Nicola could not quite decide what it was, but then she suddenly realised that it was the garden of the Villa; the alleys and hedges, the green cypress and box trees, the fountain in the centre, spraying silver droplets of liquid around the mossy paths. In the foreground she sat, Paul on her lap, her face faintly darkened by the shadow of a cypress. She was smiling at the child, a gentle, mysterious smile which made her face unfamiliar to her. She felt quite peculiar as she stared at this representation of herself. It looked like her, yet not like her.

Paul, however, was distinctly himself. His fine-featured face, delicate and golden-skinned, was alive with laughter and mischief. He was leaping up to kiss her, his plump hand on her throat. The dark hair, dark eyes and Roman nose were all there, softened in babyhood, yet oddly reminiscent of the features of the old man who stood in front of the painting lost in silence.

Leo was pale. He shifted nervously, watching them like a hawk. "Well?" His voice was hoarse.

Lorenzo slowly turned to look at him. Without one word he opened his arms wide and Leo instinctively moved into the embrace. Lorenzo kissed him on both cheeks, patting his shoulders. There were tears in his dark eyes.

Nicola watched sympathetically, close to tears herself. Leo, freed from his uncle's embrace, turned to look at her, and she smiled at him.

"You've taken my breath away, Leo," she said. "The painting is so beautiful!"

Leo's mercurial spirits soared. He seized her, kissed her warmly on the lips, his hands holding her shoulders lightly. Vanessa, walking into the room at that exact moment, stood stock still and stared with wide-stretched eyes in a pale face.

Leo looked up as he released Nicola and saw her. On the new flood of his delight, he grinned wickedly. "Tonight is a festival of love," he said lightly. "No one escapes without paying a forfeit." He reached out to take Vanessa's arm, pulled her close and bent to kiss her.

Angrily, she pulled away, her free hand pushing at his chest. Leo was aroused. His dark face reddened, then he dragged her forcibly into his arms and kissed her hard, his bent head showing a red stain of rage where the black hair ended.

Lorenzo looked shocked, then amused. Silently he tiptoed out, winking at Nicola as she followed him.

Vanessa, taken off guard, melted into Leo's arms, her own hands curving up to stroke the curly hair. There was a long silence in the salon, then Leo abruptly pushed her away from him, looked down at her with narrowed eyes and strode out of the room.

Vanessa remained, her hand at her lips, trembling.

THE GUESTS WERE MET at the entrance to the main salon by Lorenzo, erect and smiling in his black dinner jacket, with Nicola at his side in a long dress of white chiffon, tied at the waist by a sash of purple, and with a matching purple edging to the layered sleeves, which fell in widening cascades to her wrist. Her hair was looped through a golden ring and fell in a sleek curve to her shoulders.

A small cluster of musicians played a mixture of popular music and popular classics in the courtyard. The door into the garden was left wide open so that those guests who chose to stroll there, in the light of some coloured fairy lights strung from trees and bushes, could enjoy the distant lilt of the music.

Nicola began to have a sense of complete unreality after a time. She shook hands with Farenze after Farenze; Antonio, Pietro, Vicenzo—the names clicked in her head while the faces came and went, dark, smiling, curious faces which all bore a strange resemblance one to the other. They complimented her on her son, admired the portrait, which Lorenzo had had placed prominently nearby, stared and visibly noted Lorenzo's affection for her.

Vanessa stood nearby, with Leo and Signora Farenze, distinctly the second string of the welcoming party. Leo was very distinguished in black evening clothes, pale and oddly withdrawn on such a gay occasion. Now and then he and Vanessa exchanged glances. Their eyes met and rapidly drew away again. Vanessa was trembling slightly, her blue eyes very bright and fever-lit. She had not spoken to him since their kiss. It lay between them, though, as a crater marks the site of an explosion, and they each guardedly walked around it.

When most of the guests had arrived, Lorenzo and Nicola began to circulate, talking at more leisure to those whom Lorenzo was particularly eager for her to meet.

She smiled and answered polite questions with polite answers, and wondered with sombre resignation where Domenico was now—in what tropical heat did he sit, with Bianca, sipping wine and watching the distant stars of the South American sky? Half of her nature seemed dead. She had to keep up appearances, for Lorenzo's sake, but it cost her a great deal to smile and pretend gaiety.

Once or twice she glanced around to watch her sister, looking fragile and romantic in her drifting blue dress, the centre of an admiring crowd. Leo was somewhere on the periphery, watching Vanessa too, with his dark eyes narrowed.

Nicola wondered if, after all, there was hope for them. If they truly loved each other they might overcome all the barriers that nationality and personality could erect between them. Like a bulldozer love can smash all obstacles, she thought sadly.

A plump dark matron in vivid red silk, still carrying the traces of a once remarkable beauty, spoke to her, and she turned back to listen, smiling courteously. Lorenzo, under cover of his hand, winked at her, and her eyes flicked back an amused gratitude for his kindness and understanding.

Half an hour later Lorenzo held up his hand for silence, standing on a chair so that all the guests could see him. "A cold buffet is laid out in the dining-room, and I hope you will all enjoy the food, but first, my friends and members of the Farenze family—I have a small ceremony to perform!" He slid a hand inside his dinner jacket, brought out a flat case.

"There is a tradition in the family—you will all have heard about it. The bride of the eldest son wears the Farenze emeralds." He looked down at Nicola's suddenly astonished face and smiled. "Well," he went on, "Nicola is my son's widow and she has never formally taken possession of what is hers by right. She knows, as you all must know, that I did not welcome her marriage. I want you all to hear me tell her now that I bitterly regret that stupidity. She is more that I deserved—she is the most enchanting bride any Farenze has ever brought into our family, and I am honoured and proud to give her these emeralds." He bent and handed her the case with a flourish.

She automatically took it, stared at it, then stammered something incoherent.

Lorenzo laughed. "You see how modest she is, my English daughter-in-law? She says she does not want them, the emeralds which the Farenzes have treasured for centuries! Men have died for them, yet Nicola does not want them!"

The guests laughed politely, but there were curious, hungry gleams in the eyes of some of them as they stared at the flat blue case.

Lorenzo took it back from her, eyeing her bent head with some tenderness. But Nicola was too embarrassed by the public interest in all this to do anything but stare at the floor.

Fumblingly, the old man opened the case and took out the necklace. It hung from his two hands, flashing like green flames as it moved through the air. He bent and slid it around her throat, and she jumped as the cold stones came to rest against her warm skin. The other guests gave a long sigh of pleasure, staring at the beautiful things, but Nicola felt unbearably trapped.

She looked up, desperately, then her heart gave a leap of joy and pain, for there, at the salon door, stood Domenico.

His grey eyes met hers with cool evaluation, and

unknowingly she sent him a silent plea for help. He came towards her, through the crowd, and Lorenzo beamed down at him.

"Domenico!" Pleasure and affection lit the wrinkled old face. "You are back! How is Bianca now?"

"She is safely with her parents," Domenico said quietly. "But now, Lorenzo, you have monopolised Nicola long enough. I think I may claim the pleasure of taking her in to supper."

Lorenzo's shrewd eyes slid from one to the other, then a cunning smile crept over his face. "Of course, of course," he said enthusiastically.

Domenico crooked his arm and bowed. Shyly, Nicola slid her hand through his arm. The crowd parted, and curious, knowing eyes followed their progress into the courtyard.

The shadows swallowed them. The musicians, playing with hot, perspiring faces, watched them walk through the garden gate into the starry night.

Nicola's legs trembled beneath her as she walked. She swallowed. What did this return mean? Was Domenico, then, not intending to marry Bianca after all? Or had it merely been postponed while she recovered her health?

She glanced up at him. His profile was cool and unreadable as ever.

Huskily she said, "I wasn't expecting you back tonight. You were not in South America long."

"I was longer that I could have wished," he said. "It seemed an eternity."

She wondered what that meant. A strange, hesitant sort of happiness was beginning to spread through her veins. She was afraid to believe what she saw in his eyes.

"My mother tells me she is certain you do not love Leo," he said abruptly, and this very roughness was excitingly hopeful, for Domenico was not usually so lacking in poise.

"I told you that myself," she said softly.

He stood still, turning towards her. The warm dark sky spread overhead. There was a gentle sound of cicadas, and the breeze stirred in the cypresses.

Nicola looked up into Domenico's dark face with wide, incredulous eyes. Could she be mad, or was that a growing hunger she saw in his face?

His hands gripped her elbows. Thickly, he murmured, "You know I have been jealous of Leo, jealous of Paolo, of every man who ever looked at you? I think I loved you even before I met you, from the first time I saw that photograph of you which Paolo sent me so long ago . . ." He released her and took out his wallet, brought out of it a small snapshot, a little crumpled and yellowing. Nicola stared in disbelief, then laughed.

Her own face, years younger in time and experience, looked up at her.

"You kept it?"

He grimaced wryly. "All these years! Yes. I even cut Paolo off—after I had met you in England. Because I knew then, *mia cara, mia carissima . . .*"

She was still incredulous. "You were very unkind to me then, Domenico."

"I was sick with hunger," he said thickly. "Nicola, could you ever . . ." His voice faded, but his eyes spoke for him.

She laughed, on a caught breath. "Nico!"

Then she was in his arms and sky, stars, warm breathing garden vanished in a whirl of sparks more fiery and more dramatic than the Farenze emeralds. She clung, kissing him back with all the love and hunger of long starvation, and he held her so that she thought her bones must crack under the impact.

When at last she raised her head the world spun in a dizzying circle, but she merely laughed, and framed his lean face in the cup of her two hands.

"I love you, Domenico Farenze, more than I loved Paolo, more than I thought possible for any woman to love any man. If that will not satisfy you, I'm sorry—it's the best I can do today," and she laughed up at him. "Tomorrow I hope I'll do better!"